ATTORNEY KATE MARSTON HAS LANDED A HIGH PROFILE CASE THAT COULD EITHER MAKE OR BREAK HER CAREER.

Her client is a controversial judge who has been charged with murder. Her investigation leads her into the shadowy and dangerous world of organized crime, hard-ball politics, and big-time college football. It also leads her to an alternative suspect -- her father. Will she be able to avoid this ethical minefield and give her client zealous representation? Or will her duty to her client be compromised by family loyalty?

Early Praise for Fast Break

"FAST BREAK is a gripping tale of social and political intrigue, set against the sweltering milieu of Florida's Panhandle. The shocking twists in this legal thriller come fast and furious." A great read!—*Joseph Souza, author of The Neighbor.*

"Lewis combines crisp writing, honest dialogue, nuanced and layered plotting, and intriguing and complex characters to maximum advantage in this compelling tale of courtroom intrigue and murder. With a startling ending which seems inevitable, and yet also surprising, *Fast Break* is a five-star winner from an author at the top of his game."—*Claire Matturro, author of Skinny-Dipping and The Smuggler's Daughter.*

"A well-executed fast break is not only a work of art and a thing of beauty; it is wonderfully symbolic of a life in motion, fast, furious, but hopefully, under control. It requires a combination of finely tuned spatial skills, depth perception, speed, balance, and instinct; a mind's eye that lets you see even that which is not in your line of sight.

And I loved to be in the middle of it."

FAST BREAK

Terry Lewis

Moonshine Cove Publishing, LLC
Abbeville, South Carolina U.S.A.
First Moonshine Cove Edition May
2022

ISBN: 9781952439315

Library of Congress LCCN: 2022907947

For Jim and Geri

About the Author

Terry Lewis was a trial judge in Tallahassee from 1989 to 2019, where he presided over a variety of criminal and civil cases. He is now a private attorney specializing in arbitration and mediation. His professional awards include Judge of the  Year, Florida Law Related Education Association – 1993 and 2013, Judge Harvey Ford Leadership Award - 1996, and Trial Judge of the Year, American Board of Trial Advocates, Tallahassee Chapter - 2000.

Shortly after Terry became a judge, he began writing fiction, and several of his novels have been published. His legal thrillers, set in Tallahassee, explore that ambiguous gray area that resides in the conflict between law and morality.

Terry is a past board member of the Mystery Writers of America, Florida Chapter, and was co-chair for Sleuthfest '07, a crime writer's conference. He was also on the advisory board for the Florida Book Awards. He lives in Tallahassee with his wife, Fran, and their Border Collie mix, Pepper. Terry likes to relax with a good game of tennis or basketball, a good book, or film.

https://terrylewisbooks.com

Acknowledgment

I am indebted to Dr. Chris Van Sickle, Dr. John Mahoney and Professor Charles Ehrhardt for their help in my research. My wife and daughter, Fran and Angie, were early and helpful readers, as were a number of others, including Michael Whitehead, Liz Jamison, Charlie Wilkinson, Pat Murphy, Harriet McDonald and Diane Carlisle. I appreciate their valuable comments. As always, thanks to my agent, Evan Marshall, for his guidance, courtesy, and professionalism.

FAST BREAK

Chapter One

The phone call that would change everything, that would lead me to question the principles and the people I held dear, was only minutes away.

But I didn't know that, of course. I was sitting in Courtroom 3A, waiting my turn as Judge John Rowe plowed through a rather large motion docket. Rowe, who had spent most of his career on the criminal court bench, conducted court the way he played football for the University of Florida in the late sixties—focused, determined and efficient.

Still, I was beginning to check my wrist watch and wonder if I would get out in time to pick up my daughter, Maggie, before her after-school program closed, or whether I should try to make other arrangements. Thankfully, my motion to suppress was called up just after four o'clock.

Jim Barr was the prosecutor on the case, a tall, thin man of about forty, with short cropped hair and large, black framed glasses, all of which combined to give him the look of a businessman, circa 1961. He was a likeable guy and a competent attorney, but, like many of his colleagues, burdened with an extremely large case load that of necessity required a bit of triage. Some cases, the more minor ones, simply could not command the same level of attention as the more serious ones—something I hoped would be in play this afternoon.

Barr called only one witness, the arresting officer, and he went through his direct exam quickly. When he finished, he nodded with satisfaction at the officer on the stand, turned to me and said, "Your witness, Ms. Marston."

Ken Gautier, or Kenny G, as he was known in defense attorney circles, had carved out a career by making drug busts from traffic stops. He was smart, coolly professional, and unwavering in his commitment to say or do anything to make a case. And most of the time, it stuck. But not this time, I hoped.

Kenny G had stopped my client for a traffic infraction, the old stand-by broken tag light violation, searched the car after "detecting the strong odor of marijuana" and turned up a small amount of cocaine and a good deal of marijuana, plus an assortment of drug paraphernalia.

Gautier, being his usual snarky self, fell for my misdirection on cross, which was to suggest that he was lying about the tag light being out. He indignantly denied that the tag light violation was just a pretext to justify the stop and search.

I stared at him, my incredulity clear. "But you do admit that you have a history with Mr. Allen, don't you?"

"What do you mean, a history?"

"What I mean is that you've arrested him two times for drug offenses. In one, the charges were dismissed, and in the other, a jury found him not guilty. That really bothered you, didn't it?"

Gautier burned silently for several seconds, then regained his composure and said, "I have participated in previous arrests of Mr. Allen. That is true. But that has nothing to do with why I stopped him that night."

I let the stink of Gautier's lie hang in the air for a few moments, stealing a glance at Rowe to gauge his reaction, but the judge was stoned-faced. I felt confident that Rowe would do the right thing, but I didn't want this to hinge upon him having to weigh the credibility of my client versus that of a police officer. Fortunately, I didn't think I'd need to. I would use Gautier's own words to anchor my legal challenge to the search.

My argument to Rowe was simple.

"All that the traffic code requires, Judge, is that a tag be illuminated so as to render it clearly legible from a distance of 50 feet to the rear. If

Officer Gautier ran the vehicle tag number before he made the stop, as he testified, then the tag had to have been clearly visible for a distance of 50 feet. Accordingly, there was no infraction, and no legal basis for the stop. I handed the judge two cases on point.

The room was silent for about a minute as both the judge and prosecutor quickly read the cases. Rowe looked over at the prosecutor when he had finished. "Mr. Barr?"

"It would have been nice if Ms. Marston had provided these cases before the hearing, Your Honor, but as it is, I'd request some time to research the issue and provide the court with any additional authority I find."

Rowe shook his head and cut him off with a wave of his hand. "The time to do your research, Mr. Barr, is before the hearing, not after. I'm granting the motion." With that he closed the file and handed it back to the clerk. Hearing over.

Barr took it in stride. He nodded when I said I would prepare a proposed order, then he put away his file and pulled another out, ready for his next case. I steered my vaguely relieved but confused client toward the bailiff, whispering explanations to him. On my way out of the courtroom, I couldn't help giving Kenny G a small smile and nod of the head. And to his credit, he nodded and smiled back at me.

I was halfway down the hall, feeling pretty good about myself and in control of things, when that call came in on my cell. The calling number looked vaguely familiar but I couldn't immediately place it.

"Hello."

"Hi, Katie. It's Renny Goodwin. How's it going?"

Several possibilities raced through my mind as to why Judge Warren "Renny" Goodwin was calling me, and on my cell phone. Goodwin sat on the criminal bench, so perhaps he was calling to tell me he had appointed me to a case, but that was unlikely. That was usually done by written order, the lawyers chosen on a rotating basis to represent a defendant when the Public Defender had a conflict. I had been on this conflict list for several months now and had yet to be personally notified by a judge of an appointment.

He and I were not close, but he and my parents were good friends. Maybe it had something to do with them, a surprise party maybe, or a question about a potential gift. I held the phone up and looked at it as if might somehow give me an answer. It didn't.

"Katie, you there?"

I put the phone back to my ear. "Yeah, sorry judge, I'm fine. How are you?"

"I'm doing okay."

After a few seconds of silence, I asked, "What's up?"

"Can we meet tomorrow morning, maybe for coffee or something, somewhere away from the courthouse?"

I knew then, for certain, that this had nothing to do with an appointment to a case, or with my parents. I repeated my initial question. "What's up?"

After another long pause, he said, "I think I may need to consult with a criminal lawyer."

Chapter Two

The Black Dog Café was a coffee shop located in one of the small buildings clustered on the north side of Lake Ella. I pulled into the unpaved parking area, wedged my Yukon in between a Chevy pickup and a large pine tree. I did a quick check in my rear-view mirror, pulled a few errant strands of hair back away from my face and re-did the band that held the pony tail in place.

I took the steps up to the entrance two at a time. Inside, the rich, deep smells of roasting coffee beans and fresh baked pastry wrapped me in their warm, welcoming embrace. There were about five or six customers in the small room, about the same number out on the deck-- where a thin layer of frost still covered the rails, and large heaters kept the cold at bay. Goodwin sat by himself, coffee in his hand, newspaper in front of him. I gave the young guy behind the counter my order and headed out onto the deck. The judge looked up as I crossed the threshold. He put down his coffee, stood and walked the few steps to meet me half way.

Judge Warren Goodwin was in his mid-fifties, handsome, with a full head of curly brown hair that looked as though it never had been, and never needed to be, combed. At a distance, he could pass for ten years younger, though as he got closer, I noted the creeping gray in his hair, the bags around his eyes, and the loose skin around his shirt collar.

Renny, as my parents called him, had made a pretty good living as a civil rights lawyer, and had been active in politics, though he never ran for public office himself. He preferred to work the back rooms, behind the scenes where, he said, the real power was. He had, in fact, been instrumental in getting my father appointed to the bench. The more cynical might attribute ulterior motives in this, but I think Renny truly did, and does, like and admire my father very much.

It was the main reason I had agreed to meet with him. That, and curiosity. The man was smart, articulate and charming, with that intangible magnet which, for lack of a better word, might be called charisma. But I had personally experienced his less charming side, and was immune.

After my first semester at college, at one of my parents' Christmas parties, a drunken Renny Goodwin had groped me. He grabbed my ass with both of his hands and pulled me toward him. I could feel his hardness against me, and pushed him away, disgusted, but unable to say anything. He apologized, saying he was trying to hug me and his hands slipped. I just nodded, tried a small joke about cutting him off, then made an excuse to leave him as quickly as I could.

We never spoke of it, nor did I tell my parents. I shook it off, telling myself that he was extremely drunk at the time. But if I am honest, it changed forever my image of the man, and the incident has always been an invisible barrier when we are together.

Now he took my outstretched hand in both of his and gave me a smile, a huge one. "Katie, so good to see you." The steam of his breath held in the air an instant, then disappeared. He pulled out a chair for me. "Can I get you a latte or something?"

"I've already ordered."

He nodded, sat back down in his chair, took a sip of coffee, and as he did, looked around the café and beyond, discreetly but noticeably.

"Looking for someone?"

He smiled, not so huge this time. "I think I may be under surveillance."

"Isn't everybody?"

He frowned. "Probably just being paranoid, but doesn't hurt to be careful."

I nodded, but was thinking it was too cloak and dagger for my taste. I removed my glasses and was wiping the lenses with a napkin when a young man showed up with my coffee, unusual for the self-serve place. After he walked away, I put my glasses back on, copied the judge's conspiratorial mode by leaning toward him, and said, "Okay, Judge, what's this all about?" surprising both of us with my directness.

But he appeared glad that I had prompted him. He looked from side to side, then back to me. "Debra Brown from TPD called me yesterday, just before I called you. Wants to talk to me about the Castillo case."

Elena Castillo was the daughter of a former U. S. senator, sister of the current Florida Speaker of the House, a young, beautiful lawyer with whom I practiced briefly. Several days ago, she was found dead behind the high-rise condo in which she lived.

I looked out onto the lake. The winter sun was beginning to break through the mist that hung just above the surface. I blew across my coffee and took a sip, waiting.

Goodwin said, "I think they might consider me a suspect in her death."

My eyes widened involuntarily, but I lowered them to hide my reaction and blew across my coffee again. "Why would you say that?"

He seemed to consider my question for a long time. "I assume everything I tell you comes under the attorney-client privilege."

"Of course."

Arms resting on the table, he looked me directly in the eye. "Elena and I were seeing each other."

I thought I detected a hint of pride in his voice, which made me want to slap him. "What do you mean, seeing each other?"

"The relationship was intimate."

"You mean sexual?"

"Yes."

"How long?"

"About six months."

I remained silent then, waiting for him to continue. He said he and she worked on a couple of bar committees together. She appeared in his court from time to time. They stayed late after a bar meeting once, having drinks. One thing led to another. He ended it three weeks ago, he said. There was no need for me to know the details, he added.

"Does your wife know?"

He looked off over the deck toward the lake. "No, and I'd like to keep it that way."

I pictured his wife, Marci, a pleasant, attractive woman. She was a friend of the family, too. I thought of their two daughters, Robyn and Meagan, who were not that much younger than Elena Castillo. "If Marci doesn't know, why do you think the police know anything?"

He looked down at his coffee. "I was very careful. We both were. But I can't be sure. There could be something in her condo or at her office, maybe on her computer. Maybe she let something slip to a friend. I don't know." He looked out over the lake again as a couple of joggers, clad in warm-up suits, passed along the sidewalk that circled the lake. "And there was something in Brown's tone of voice, a smugness that said she knows something, or suspects it. She was enjoying herself too much, trying to rattle me a little, I think."

"Did she?"

He shrugged. "Here I am meeting with a criminal lawyer."

"That still begs the question, Judge. Why would they suspect you of her murder? What evidence could they have?"

"To your first question, the answer is, they don't like me. And the answer to your last question is, nothing, unless it is planted or manufactured."

I gave him a doubtful look. "They don't like me? That's all you got? A little paranoid, aren't we?"

He held up his hand. "You know as well as I do, Katie, that I'm not exactly one of law enforcement's favorite judges."

No, you're not. There is a perception in some circles that you have a bias against cops."

"Not true. I only follow the law."

I shrugged, but said nothing.

Goodwin shook his head slowly. "I don't have any friends in the religious-right-winger crowd, either—which is Bill Lipton's political base."

Bill Lipton was the elected State Attorney. "Let's face it. You've been on the wrong side of some pretty controversial cases."

"Depends on your perspective, but yes, I've had to rule on some hot button issues—abortion, school vouchers, and I had the cop killer case, too."

"Not to mention some of the cases you had when you were in private practice--the nude dancing joint, the smut movie house."

"I prefer to call them the dance club and the art theater cases. Classic examples of the repression of free speech."

"Uh huh. Whatever. The point is, I would agree that you might not be real popular with these groups, and I've heard the talk that they are looking for someone to run against you next election. But manufacture evidence? Frame you for murder?"

He shrugged and raised his hands, palms up. "Look, maybe they wouldn't necessarily try to frame me, but they might be a little too eager to believe the worst, to infer more than the evidence will support. If they find anything embarrassing on me, they will milk it politically for all it's worth."

I waited a few moments before responding, the ardor, the passion and paranoia of his words still lingering in the air. Why shouldn't his indiscretion be used against him, I wanted to ask him, but said instead, "What is it you want me to do?"

"Here's my dilemma. Their inquiries may be innocent, just following up with anybody who had regular contact with the victim."

"Fairly standard," I said.

"On the other hand, maybe they suspect we had something going on and want me to confirm it, then use it to embarrass me publicly. Or worse, try to tie me to her death in some way." He hesitated. "Problem is, I don't know which it is. And either way, I don't want my relationship with the recently departed to become public knowledge. I don't want that humiliation for my wife and daughters."

"Not to mention yourself," I said, surprising myself again with my directness.

"Don't be so quick to judge what you don't fully understand, my dear."

"Let's get something straight," I said, setting my coffee down on the table and fixing my eyes on the man. "I'm not your dear. And you don't get to tell me what I think is right and wrong. It's not that difficult to understand. You cheated on your wife with someone half your age. Now you are sorry, not for doing it, but because you might be discovered. Am I missing something here?" He said nothing. "I didn't think so." I waited a few seconds before continuing, surprised at the hostility in my voice, though not sorry about it. "But you didn't come to me for moral advice. So, my question remains, what do you want me to do?"

The judge had leaned back a little, away from the sting of my scolding, his face red, but he maintained his calm. He raised his hands, offering conciliation. "You are quite right, Katie. There is a measure of selfishness in my desire to keep this quiet–and I appreciate your candor in pointing it out to me."

Sure he did.

"What I am asking you to do is help me figure out the best way to go on this. I don't want to make them suspicious, but I don't want to tell them about the relationship if I don't have to." He hesitated, then added, "I need to get some idea of what they know, what they suspect."

The judge sat calmly as I took a sip of coffee, put the cup down on the table and leaned back in my chair.

"My advice is this. Cooperate fully with them. Tell them about the affair. It's my experience that these things come out anyway. Candor is generally your best bet. It will make you look less suspicious to them and if they don't have any evidence to tie you to her murder, if it is murder, they will quickly ignore you in favor of more promising leads. Perhaps they will show some class and keep the information confidential, but even if they don't, it won't be the worst thing that could happen. You'll take a hit politically, but nothing you can't overcome by election time. Regardless, you tell Marci, today, all about it. Don't let her get blindsided."

The judge nodded his head slowly, almost absently, whether in agreement or not, I didn't know.

"On the other hand," I said, "if you feel you have something to hide, whatever that might be, then don't talk to them at all, at least not about your relationship with Elena. If they are suspicious, then so be it. They probably were anyway. But they won't have the corroborating evidence from your own mouth."

He nodded once and rested his chin in his two hands, his elbows propped on the table. "Okay. See what you can find out without going to the police directly and raising suspicions, discretion being a priority. I'm meeting Brown and her partner, Oscar Manning, at three o'clock this afternoon."

I looked at my wrist watch. "I better get on it, then." I pushed myself back from the table.

"And Katie, I fully expect to pay for your services."

"So do I."

He shook his head and smiled. Then, no doubt intending to convey his sincerity, he reached over and placed his hand over mine. "Thanks, Katie. I really appreciate this."

My skin crawled just a little at his touch. I had seen that look before, under circumstances that made me question its genuineness now. I gave him my fake sincere look in return, took my hand out of his and said, "Of course."

Chapter Three

College Avenue, between Adams and Monroe, rests on the crest of one of Tallahassee's highest hills. The tall buildings on either side block the sun and create a wind tunnel of sorts along the street, and as I turned the corner that afternoon, I buttoned up my jacket and pulled up the collar against the chilled wind that rushed at me. I had gotten in a couple of quick pick-up basketball games during lunch and the cold air felt good on my face.

Halfway up the block, I paused in front of the glass French doors, the etched lettering on which read "Law Offices of Morganstein and Stevens." To the side, a small wooden sign read, "Kate Marston— Lawyer." I stepped into the large octagonal lobby, its cathedral ceiling a soaring thirty feet above the oak floors, its walls tastefully decorated with original oil paintings, all of which reflected the influence of partner, Paul Morganstein.

The receptionist smiled at me. "Good afternoon, Ms. Marston."

I preferred she call me Kate but had long ago given up trying to break her of what was, after all, a good habit for a receptionist. "Hi Jennifer. Is Ted in his office?"

"Just a moment," she said, lifting up the phone. "I'll check."

I called Ted within minutes of leaving the Black Dog Café that morning, which now seemed long ago. I needed to stay under the radar if I was to accomplish my client's goal. I needed a buffer, someone to fish around the courthouse, feel out law enforcement and prosecutors, clerks, judicial assistants and others, without it being traced back to me, and Goodwin. Ted Stevens seemed a logical choice for the assignment.

He'd had his share of personal problems, but he was one of the best trial lawyers around, and well liked in the legal community. He also enjoyed a good relationship with the police and prosecutors. Part of that was goodwill from his days as an Assistant State Attorney. Part of it was that he'd represented several law enforcement officers in divorces, buying or selling real estate and other legal matters. He got good results and he gave them discounts.

Ted was about six-two, two twenty-five, with unkempt, dishwater blond hair and a boyish charm that made you want to hug him. Indeed, his fitting nickname was Teddy Bear. I knew that the female clerks, judicial assistants and other court staff would bend over backwards to help him. He had just the right combination of empathy and persistence that seemed to ease the information right out of people.

When I told Ted what I wanted, there was silence on the other end for a few seconds, then, "Who's the client?"

"That will have to remain confidential."

"I see." Another pause, shorter. "What's my time frame?"

I told him.

"Oh, good. I thought it was going to be a rush job."

We arranged to meet at two o'clock, plenty of time for me to get over to Goodwin's office before his appointment with the detectives.

"Hey, Katie."

I turned in the direction of Ted's voice as he came toward me. The limp was still noticeable but barely, and he was walking without the cane. As he came into the light of the lobby and got closer, I also noted that the slight sag on the left side of his face was not as pronounced. He had made remarkable progress in the last several months. Considering that the man had been shot in the head from close distance, he was lucky to be alive.

And luck had definitely played a big part in it, the bullet being a .22 caliber fired at just the right angle so that it did not penetrate as it could have. He liked to say it had confirmed what his mother had always said, that he was very hard-headed. The injury to his brain had caused stroke-like symptoms—partial paralysis on one side, slight difficulty with speech and a short-term memory problem. But he had worked hard at his rehabilitation and was expected to make a full recovery.

"Hi Ted."

He looked back in the direction from which he had come, then turned again to face me. "You mind if Paul sits in?" It wasn't really a question.

"Sure," I said, and followed him down the hallway.

Paul Morganstein's office opened onto a small courtyard, which was where he sat, in a wicker chair, an open file on his lap. He was dressed in a dark, double-breasted suit, buttoned up against the cool air, kerchief just visible in the pocket. His naturally wavy hair was slicked back, and he was sporting a new thin mustache. The theme music from *The Godfather* started playing in my head.

He looked up when Ted and I came through the door, placed the file on the end table next to the chair and motioned us to take the seats on either side of him. The smell of cigar smoke lingered in the air and the evidence of its source lay in the ashtray next to Paul.

"Hello, Katie." He smiled. "You're looking great."

Even though I knew it was bullshit, I couldn't prevent the blush that lit up my cheeks. Paul had a knack for making you feel special, as if he saw only your positive attributes. It was part of what had made him a popular boss for me and others when I worked for him at the Public Defender's Office.

Indeed, I almost came to work with Paul and Ted when I left the firm. They had asked, and it was tempting. I got along well with both of them, as well as their associate, Theo Williams, and thought I would be a good fit here. The timing had not been good, though. Paul and I were on opposite sides in a civil case. I disclosed to him a document my co-counsel had intentionally withheld from a required production, the proverbial smoking gun memo that sealed the case for Paul's client.

My senior partner was livid, and I decided this was not the kind of law I wanted to practice. I left soon thereafter, but I declined Paul and

Ted's offer. It might look like a quid pro quo, I told them. Maybe later.

Besides, this was when I was going through the divorce from Craig and decided that I wanted a more flexible schedule so I could attend to Maggie a little more. Teaching a couple of classes at the law school gave flexibility, but didn't supply sufficient income. Paul then mentioned that perhaps I might start my own practice. They would rent me space at a very reasonable rate, and there was the possibility of referrals. Perhaps, he had said, it might work into something more.

I agreed.

We had no formal association, but Paul and Ted had referred some cases to me and associated me on a few others. I was not making what I had pulled down at my old firm, but it was a decent living, especially considering the reduced hours—and I was my own boss.

"I'm fine, thank you," I said, plopping down in one of the wicker chairs. "And you?"

"Overworked and underpaid."

"No, no," Ted said. "That's my job description."

Paul looked over at his partner, then back at me. "I have to say I was as intrigued as Ted about your assignment. Very mysterious."

I shrugged, but said nothing, and he didn't press it. Both of us then turned our attention to Ted.

The lawyer pulled a small spiral notebook from his back pocket. Looking over at me he said, "I tend to take a lot more detailed notes these days to compensate for the short-term memory loss." He hesitated, glancing quickly in Paul's direction, then back to me. "Not that it's a real problem. It's just a precaution advised by my doctor. Besides...." He gave me a blank look for several seconds, then looked over at Paul. "What were we talking about?"

I stared into his face. "You were talking about how you have a little problem with short-term memory loss."

Ted turned to me, smiling, enjoying the look of alarm that I had not been able to mask. "Gotcha."

I hit him in the arm as both he and Paul chuckled. Then I joined them.

Ted flipped the front cover over, looked down at his notes and began reading. "The State Attorney has not convened the Grand Jury yet, so it's a pretty safe bet that they don't have a clear suspect, at least not a high profile one. Word going around is they are looking at homicide. I don't know the details but I'm told that the forensics at the scene support murder, rather than suicide or accident. Other than that, everybody in law enforcement, whether directly involved in the case or not, is pretty tight lipped. No indication of what evidence they have, no hints as to suspects. They're keeping a lid on this one."

"Likely suspects, from your investigation?"

Ted gave me a small, crooked smile. "I'm good Kate, but not that good. Give me a little more time and maybe, but no, I got no names."

"What about the victim? Anything useful on that angle?"

He gave me a shrug. "Somewhat. Although the cops and other official types were reluctant to talk, there were plenty of lawyers, clerks and folks who work the other side of the street, and at the capitol, who were happy to share stories, rumors and speculations about the recently departed."

"Yes?"

"Some liked her, others did not. Most everyone respected her intelligence and her ability. Some questioned her ethics, suggested that she would do whatever she needed to do to win. Very ambitious."

"Runs in the family," Paul added.

Ted looked at me. "You worked with her for a while, didn't you? At the firm? You probably know as much as anyone I talked to."

"We overlapped, time-wise, at the firm, but we didn't really work on the same cases, nor run in the same social circles, I might add. We both volunteered with Refuge House, represented abused women in domestic violence cases, but we worked separately on those. I didn't really know her that well, but I would agree that she was very smart and very ambitious."

"One interesting story for illustration," Ted said. "I was talking with Linda Benton. You know Linda?"

I nodded. Linda was with a small firm and had a general practice. She was active in the Tallahassee Women Lawyers Association, had been president a couple of years back.

"Anyway, we got to talking out on the terrace there on the second floor of the courthouse, and I turned the conversation around to Castillo. She told me about a deposition a few months ago in a case they were both involved with. Products liability action. Linda was representing the retailer. Elena had the manufacturer. Somebody else, I forget who, was representing the supplier. Anyway, Brent Cooper was the plaintiff's lawyer. You know him?"

"Thinks he's God's gift to women?"

"That's the one. Anyway, he made the mistake of getting a little too familiar with Elena during the deposition, apparently put his hand where it shouldn't have been. She reamed him a new one in about twenty seconds, called him a little dick with a big ego. He tried to make a joke and said something like how would she know what size he was. Elena reaches under the table, grabs his crotch. Linda said Brent's face turned as white as a baby's bottom and he just stared at her. Everybody did. They couldn't believe it. Elena smiled and said, 'Yep, just as I thought.'"

Paul's body shook as he laughed. "Wish I could have seen that."

"So, the bigger the ego, the smaller the ...?" I left the last word unsaid, looking at the two men.

Paul raised his hands, smiling. "No comment."

"He wishes to plead the fifth," Ted said.

My cheeks flushed as we shared a little nervous laughter. I looked at Ted. "Okay, let's focus. Any boyfriends? Romantic interests? Sexual partners?"

"Well, let's see. The senior partner at the law firm, the President of

25

the Senate, the Governor's general counsel, to name a few of her rumored paramours. All gossip, of course, but I get the feeling that Ms. Castillo was, how shall I say it?"

"A free spirit?" Paul said.

"I was searching for another word, rhymes with nut. But like I say, she had a reputation of doing whatever she needed to do to get what she wanted. Let's just say in this regard that her feminine wiles were not tools she left in the box."

"Feminine wiles?" I gave him a doubtful look. "Did you really just say feminine wiles?"

He shrugged. "Seemed the appropriate, more polite term."

"Anything else?"

"Linda also said something that suggested Elena might have had something going on with a judge."

I tried to keep my face blank. "Really? Which one?"

"Didn't say it directly. Just seemed like she was hinting. She said one time she and Elena were debating what was most important in winning a case. Linda said she thought it was picking a good jury. And Elena said more important than the jury you pick is the judge you screw--and she didn't say screw."

At this he looked at me closely. I pursed my lips but didn't say anything.

"Probably nothing, just a joke, but it got me thinking." Again, he looked at me, as if searching for a tell on a poker player. "Made me wonder if maybe your client might be Renny Goodwin."

Chapter Four

The wind was still whipping along the street as I exited the building, but this time I left my jacket open, enjoying the blast of cold on my face. It had gotten very warm suddenly in there, and not as a result of the temperature.

Ted's words had stung me with their simple and uncanny accuracy. I did my best to keep my face neutral as he studied me closely, looking for a sign that he had guessed correctly. Afraid that my voice might betray the implicit lie, but more afraid of the implication if I didn't respond immediately, I said, "Interesting. How do you figure that?"

"I notice you didn't deny it."

"Nice try, counselor, but I will neither confirm nor deny."

"He smiled, looked first at Paul, then at me. "Okay, you have a client who wants you to make inquiries, discreetly, concerning the investigation into the death of Elena Castillo. Now, it could be someone in the family, perhaps the father, who doesn't quite trust the local police to do an adequate job, or keep him informed. Maybe he wants to make sure nothing is overlooked, or that some embarrassing things about his daughter are kept confidential. At the very least, perhaps they can be minimized, or spun."

Ted studied his hands which were folded in front of him on the table. "Doesn't mean that I think that's the situation. I don't. More likely the person is local, a male in a position of authority, someone for whom disclosure of his relationship with the deceased would be embarrassing. Given the information on our victim, I'm thinking the relationship was probably sexual in nature, and the guy is married. Hence his insistence that you not divulge his identity to anyone, including me."

He looked down again at his hands. "Another clue is that the person came to you. Why you? You're teaching a couple of law classes. Your practice is more part time than full time right now, and you haven't been here long enough to even be listed in the phone directory. So, it makes sense that the person is someone who knows you personally, or knows someone close to you. As far as I know, you don't have a connection with the family of the victim. Could be the guy in the governor's office, or in the senate president's office, but again, those guys are not in your circle either, to my knowledge. Could be your former senior partner, but somehow, given the rather unpleasant circumstances surrounding your departure from the firm, I don't think he would be coming to you for help."

I frowned. "Okay," I said, my voice neutral, "what else?"

"Then I thought about what Elena supposedly said to her friend about the relative importance of judges and jurors, and I thought, maybe it's a judge--a judge who doesn't want his private romantic liaisons to become public. And who would fit the bill? By nature and predisposition, Goodwin would be a good choice. He is a notorious flirt, with an ego as big as a house. Castillo appeared before him on occasion in criminal court, and they were on some bar committee together, I think."

"Bench Bar Liaison Committee," Paul confirmed.

"Yeah, and I remember seeing them chatting it up at Bar meetings. Didn't think much of it then, but . . ." He let his sentence drop off with the silent implication. "And then there's the connection to you. Goodwin is close to your dad. And he was the judge before whom you practiced the last couple of years you were with the Public Defender." He studied me again, grinning. "Yeah, makes a lot of sense to me."

His smugness was annoying, but his reasoning impeccable. All I could do was smile slightly and say in a monotone, "I can neither confirm nor deny," but I felt my poker face disintegrating and wanted to get out of there before it betrayed me. The two lawyers could be trusted with the truth, but that wasn't the point. I had been instructed not to divulge the client's identity. With a look at my wrist watch, I thanked Ted, quickly said my goodbyes to him and Paul, and left to meet with my still, if barely, undisclosed client.

Goodwin's judicial assistant, Naomi Watkins, was talking on the phone as I entered the office. She put her hand over the speaker. "Hey, Katie. Go right on in," she said, motioning with her head toward the judge's inner office. As I walked past, I wondered just how much the assistant knew of her boss's personal business. She had been with him since before he came onto the bench and was by nature both nosy and observant—and very loyal. If subpoenaed, would she tell what she knew? Would she have a convenient lapse of memory? How far would her loyalty extend?

The judge was sitting at his desk, which was located at the end of a long rectangular conference table. He motioned for me to close the door, which I did, and took a seat up next to his desk. There were a couple of stacks of files, papers, magazines and newspapers on the corner, but otherwise the desk and conference table were free of clutter.

"You want some coffee?" he asked as he looked in the direction of the coffee pot behind him on the credenza."

"No thanks." As my host poured his own cup, I took in anew the flavor of the office, which bespoke of its occupant, orderly, but not overly so. On the entire length of the east wall was a built-in floor-to-ceiling bookcase surrounding a double window in the middle. The shelves contained the multi-volume set collection of all reported Florida appellate decisions as well as numerous legal treatises and other reference books. There were also some works of fiction—mostly legal thrillers and mysteries by Grisham, Turow, Lewis and others.

The other three walls contained a variety of photos, plaques and framed certificates: Legal Aid Foundation President, ACLU president, Neighborhood Justice Center, Guardian Ad Litem. There were photos of Goodwin with two former governors, a former president, and other political figures. The family photos, which were plentiful, seemed a mockery, the smiling, seemingly happy faces looking down on the office's occupant. Centered on each remaining wall were three Salvador Dali prints: The Persistence of Memory, Rose Meditative, and Burning Giraffes in Brown. How appropriate, I thought, given the surrealistic circumstances of my presence here.

The judge appeared calm and relaxed as he took a sip of coffee and then set it down. "So, Counselor, what have you to report?"

His mock formality seemed a poor attempt at humor, but I shrugged it off and summarized the results of my rather quick and incomplete investigation --or rather, Ted's. As he listened, Goodwin folded his hands under his chin and rested his elbows on the desk, as if he were considering the legal argument of an attorney in a case before him.

"Did my name come up at all?"

"Only what Ted said."

"And you didn't tell him I was the client?"

I shook my head.

He nodded once, slowly. "Good."

It would be a mistake, I reiterated, to assume the detectives had only the same information we had obtained. "It's still my advice that you tell them the truth, the whole, embarrassing truth. The other option is to not answer any questions concerning your relationship with Elena. Just tell them it's none of their business. No explanations, no partial answers, no hints. Nothing. But above all else, whatever you say, don't lie to them."

"Makes sense," he said, though his tone seemed non-committal.

I looked at my watch. "Well, I better take off. Best I'm not here when the detectives show up. Don't want to give them any additional reason to be suspicious."

He seemed to be considering this suggestion when Naomi buzzed him on the phone intercom. He pressed the speaker mode button.

"Yes?"

"Judge, Detectives Brown and Manning are here."

Goodwin looked at me as he spoke into the phone, "Send them on back."

Detective Debra Brown came in first, followed by her partner, Oscar Manning. I knew both from my days at the Public Defender's Office. Oscar was the older of the two, probably in his late forties or early fifties. He was short, a bit overweight, and wore his gray hair in a crew cut that reminded me of the old television show, *Dragnet.* Just the facts, Ma'am. Debra was about ten years younger, three inches taller, and had a lean, muscular build. Her brown, curly hair was shoulder length, and layered. Both were experienced homicide detectives. They stopped just inside the doorway, respectful, waiting for the judge to invite them closer, which he did.

"You both know Ms. Marston, don't you?" Goodwin said.

They assured him they did, as they looked in my direction. Oscar was the first to speak. "Hello, Katie. Nice to see you. It's been a while." Debra grunted something under her breath, nodding to me.

"Oscar, Debra," I said.

There was a long silence, finally broken by Goodwin. "Ms. Marston is advising me on a civil matter. We weren't quite done, but I thought your investigation should take priority."

There was some more silence, uncomfortable silence, as the two detectives exchanged glances.

I said, "Would you like me to step outside?"

"Nonsense," the judge said. "No need to inconvenience you, Katie." He turned to the detectives. "Any reason Ms. Marston can't sit in?"

The two detectives gave a collective shrug. If they were to insist that I not be present it would be an admission that their visit was not as innocent as they perhaps wanted to imply. Oscar was again the one to speak. "Okay with us if it's okay with you, Judge."

Goodwin, who had been standing, took to his chair once more and motioned for us to be seated as well. He smiled at the detectives. "Now, how can I help you?"

Oscar laid his file folder on the table in front of him. "Just routine stuff, really. We're checking with people who knew Ms. Castillo."

"So, was it definitely a homicide?"

This time it was Debra who answered, while looking at me rather than Goodwin. "We're treating the death as a possible homicide. We have to. But we also haven't ruled out accident or suicide." She looked back to Goodwin. "You did know the deceased, didn't you, Judge?"

"Yes."

"When was the last time you saw her or spoke to her?" It was an innocent enough question, in and of itself, but it was potentially damning, depending on what they knew.

"I don't really remember. Maybe it was in court week before last. I think she may have had a case, a plea or something."

"How about outside of court?"

Goodwin looked up toward the ceiling as if looking for the answer there. When he looked back at Brown, he said, "I don't really remember. Maybe at the last Bar meeting, which was the first Tuesday of the month."

"Did she seemed depressed, anxious, agitated?" Oscar this time.

"No, not that I recall. She seemed pretty normal."

Oscar looked over at me, as if for confirmation. I said nothing and kept my expression neutral. He turned his attention back to Goodwin. "And that's the last time you had any contact with her?"

The detective's tone was pleasant, as if just verifying something everyone knew and accepted, but I sensed something more. Perhaps the judge did too. "Not that I remember." It was an answer that might be doubted, might be made to seem incredulous in the face of compelling evidence that there had been an encounter, but to say you don't recall something is not the same as denying it—and everyone in the room knew it.

Debra Brown looked closely at the judge. "What exactly was the nature of your relationship with the deceased, Judge Goodwin?"

"What do you mean?"

"I mean, was it strictly professional or was there something . . . more?

Okay, I was thinking, good cop, bad cop time. "That's it," I said, before anyone else could speak. I turned to Goodwin. "Sorry, I know I'm just an observer here, but my defense attorney antennae come up with these types of questions in a homicide investigation. I would advise you not to answer that question."

I then turned my attention to the detectives. "He, of course, has nothing to hide, but it's the principle of the thing. It's none of your business what his relationship was with Elena, unless you consider him a suspect in her death. And if that's the case, you should be reading him his Miranda warnings before asking any more questions."

Brown's partner raised his hand up, smiled. "Whoa, now. Nobody said he was a suspect."

I noted the careful choice of words—conciliatory, disarming, but not a straight out denial either. "Besides," he said, "since the judge is not in custody, Miranda does not apply."

Of course it didn't. I was bluffing. But the response when I brought it up told me a lot—and none of it good.

Oscar looked over at Debra and frowned. "And please excuse my partner, Judge. She's not the most tactful person in the world." He turned back to Goodwin. "We don't mean to pry, and quite frankly, it really is none of our business—the nature of your relationship with Ms. Castillo."

He hesitated, letting the hurt feelings heal just a bit before saying, "But of course, everything we can find out about the victim and her relationships might be very helpful. I assure you we would be discreet."

Silence filled the room as the two detectives looked at Goodwin expectantly. He in turn, looked down at his folded hands. Finally, he looked back up at them and said, "The very nature of your question implies some misconduct on my part and that is, quite frankly, insulting. It does not deserve the dignity of a response." Oscar started to protest, but the judge waved him off. "That being said, I can assure you that my relationship with Ms. Castillo was strictly professional."

I willed my face to remain impassive, but inside, my stomach cramped. Why, oh, why did clients insist on lying to the police? Especially when it was not necessary. Especially when the client was a lawyer and judge, familiar with the ways of such things. Especially when I had specifically warned against it. It never ceased to amaze me how otherwise intelligent people could be so stupid. Sensing the continued danger for Mr. Big Mouth, I broke in. "Okay, I hope that clears that up." I rose from my seat, hoping to indicate the end of the interview.

Debra and Oscar, however, were not quite through. The two of them smiled at each other ever so slightly. The look on Brown's face was close to a sneer. "No romantic involvement?"

"Are you deaf?" I said, my voice rising just a bit with anger and concern. "He just said it was strictly professional."

Goodwin raised his hand, though, and to my unbelieving ears, said, "No, that's okay Kate. I have nothing to hide." He turned to Brown, hesitated a moment, then said, "We worked together on committees. She appeared before me in court. I tried to be a friend and mentor to her, but that was all. Quite frankly, Ms. Castillo could be rather provocative in her speech, and hinted to me on more than one occasion that she found me attractive, that sort of thing, but I took it as harmless flirting. I never encouraged her, and nothing ever came of it."

The arrogant, egotistical bastard. Not only did he think he could lie with impunity, he had come up with one that made him look like a chick magnet. If you're going to lie, Judge, try to come up with something at least plausible.

"Uh huh," Brown said. It was obvious that nobody in the room believed him. "Ever been to her condo?"

I wanted to interrupt but felt powerless to do so, and some part of me felt it only fair that Goodwin lie in the bed he had made, so to speak. Let him extricate himself.

"Yes, when she had an open house upon moving in a few months ago."

"Any other times?"

"Not that I can recall." No hesitation.

"Any reason there might be e-mail messages from you on her computer?"

Goodwin's eye twitched, faint but noticeable. I wondered if the detectives saw it. "Only relative to our committee work together, or other legal business, probably in response to something she sent me."

The detectives exchanged one more glance, then both stood. Oscar said, "Thank you Judge Goodwin. Again, I apologize for the personal nature of the questions, and we appreciate your candor. If we have additional questions . . ."

"Sure," the judge said, "feel free to call any time."

"I'll walk you out," I said, as the detectives headed for the door. Out in the hallway, I grabbed Oscar on his arm, gently pulled him close, and whispered, "I know the judge is not a favorite of law enforcement, Oscar. Still, no need to embarrass the man with this." It was a statement, an observation, but there was a question in there as well.

Oscar punched the call button for the elevator then turned back to face me. His smile had a melancholy aura about it, a silent protest to the brutal world in which he operated, but to which he refused to surrender. He placed his hand gently on mine. "Katie, a little advice, girl. Get your fee up front, and make sure it's a big one."

Chapter Five

The familiar burning in the lungs grew stronger, more insistent, and my calf muscles tightened with every step, but my mind was focused, my breathing rhythmic. I was aware of the dogs barking in the distance, the melodic, seemingly orchestrated chirping of birds, and the exotic smell of decay and rebirth. But all exterior noise was muted, senses suppressed, supplanted by a heightened awareness of the internal, a melding of mind and body.

This last leg of the run, mostly uphill, was always the hardest. And, as always, I embraced it. I embraced it with a masochistic obsession typical of long-distance runners and other addictive personalities, an urgent, elusive search for that Nirvana that dances just beyond the body's physical limits.

My mom likes to say that ladies don't sweat, they glow. I smiled at the thought now, my T-shirt clinging to me, the sweat rolling off in large drops as my legs churned up the street. My Aunt Mary Beth, who is also my doctor, says perspiration is a good thing, the sign of an efficient body at work. I kind of like this notion better. The fact is, I sweat like a guy, even in the dead of a Tallahassee winter, and it can be pretty gross at times. But it's also strangely comforting, an exorcism of all sorts of poisons, physical and mental.

A few lights were on in the houses I passed, my neighbors along Hillcrest Avenue preparing to greet the day. As I got closer to my house, I slowed to a walk, breathing hard. I headed up the driveway, picking up the newspaper along the way. Passing through the garage, I noticed the boxes out of the corner of my eye. I stopped and stared at them for a long moment, confronting the jumble of feelings that, unlike the boxes, could not be tightly sealed and stacked away in a corner.

Craig was supposed to have gotten them out weeks ago. It was silly, really. The boxes didn't take up much room, and certainly there were more important concerns. Don't sweat the small stuff, right? But sometimes, it was the small stuff that pulled the emotions to the surface, shoved them right in your face.

I opened the door to the laundry room and stepped inside. Bandit, the feline mistress of the manor, so named for the black rings around her white face, looked up at me expectantly. She was sitting on her haunches, next to her dish, above which a small sign read, *The Queen Eats Here.* The cat started pacing, meowing at me and rubbing up against the washer, then the sides of the doorway leading into the kitchen. When I didn't stop to feed her, the meows got louder, more insistent.

"Can you wait just a minute, Your Highness?" I asked, uselessly, then made my way into the kitchen, put the newspaper on the counter and retrieved a can of cat food from the refrigerator. Bandit walked ahead of me toward her dish, fluffing her tail and looking back at me from time to time, as if to make sure I was coming. When I emptied the contents of the can, she rushed over to it, stopped, sniffed at it for a moment, then looked up at me as if to say, "You mean this is it? I got all excited, almost undignified, for this old, cold stuff?"

I stood there a couple of seconds, giving the queen a look back that said, "You don't like it, don't eat it. But you're not getting anything else." Then I turned and walked back to the kitchen. When I glanced back, I saw Bandit eating her food. Once again, effective communication resulting in peace, harmony and understanding.

The clock on the microwave read 6:27 a.m. as I eased down the hallway to my daughter's room. As I stood in the doorway, my heart swelled. Maggie was tall for a ten-year- old, with long arms and legs–just like her parents. She lay diagonally across the bed, no covers, one leg dangling off the side. I walked over to the bed, bent and kissed her softly on the forehead.

"Time to get up, sport."

My daughter grunted and turned over on her side, pulling the covers over her. When she didn't move again after a few seconds, I used my mock stern voice. "Okay, Maggie. I'm going to take a shower. When I get out, you better be up and dressed."

The child stretched her legs and arms, twisted her torso to look at me. "I will." I gave her a skeptical look. "I'm awake. I'm getting up. Just give me a minute."

"Don't go back to sleep."

"I won't."

In my bedroom I loosened the band that had held my hair in a pony tail, removed my clothes quickly and headed toward the shower, stealing a furtive glance at the image of my naked body in the wall mirror as I passed. Instinctively, I pulled back my sloped shoulders and walked the last few paces with exaggerated erectness, the voice of my mother playing in my head, telling me to stand up straight.

I was also reminded of one of Craig's jokes, about a man who goes to buy a bra as a gift for his wife but doesn't know her size. The sales lady, trying to be helpful, asks discreetly if his wife's breasts are the size of grapefruits. No, the man says, smaller. How about oranges? she asks. No, smaller, he says. The sales lady frowns a moment, then says, eggs, perhaps? The man brightens up and says, yeah, eggs. Fried.

"Jerk," I said aloud, turning on the water in the shower, testing it with my hand, then stepping in. I stayed in a little longer than usual, letting the warm, soothing spray of the shower wash away the negative thoughts and memories. By the time Maggie and I started out from the house, my equilibrium was back.

We walked the block and a half to Kate Sullivan Elementary. I reminded her that her dad would be picking her up that afternoon, then hugged her, and watched as she walked away, turning once to wave to me just before she disappeared inside the building. Soon, this little ritual would be an embarrassment for my ten-year-old, to be avoided at all costs, so I savored it while it lasted. I turned then and walked the short distance back to the house, got in my Yukon and headed toward the law school.

The local newspaper ran a front-page article this morning under the headline, "Grand Jury Investigates Castillo Death." The article itself provided nothing really new about the case, and there was no mention of any connection to Goodwin, but that gave me little comfort. Maybe Oscar Manning had just been pulling my chain, but I didn't think so, and his parting shot was on my mind as I navigated the traffic on Tennessee Street.

I went back into Goodwin's office to tell him what Oscar had said, and chastised him for not following my advice. He was, however, unrepentant and unconcerned. "They were bluffing, Katie. They don't have anything." He hesitated, then added, "That's not to say they won't come after me. They probably will. This is all about unseating me next election. Whether they can get a grand jury to indict me or not, they'll let it leak out to the press that I'm a suspect, or a person of interest, and it won't matter what happens after that. The damage will have been done."

A melancholy tone had crept into his voice as he made these predictions, but now he gave me a huge smile and slapped his hand down on the desk. "But as they say, politics is a contact sport." He leaned back in his chair. "Yeah, they'd love to take me down. But I'll be damned if I'm going to help them by admitting to an affair that they will be unable to prove."

I was tempted to observe that, if they did try to make a case against him, and they could prove the affair, he would have done much to help them by lying about a fact important to the investigation. I sensed that he already knew that, though. He had no doubt calculated the odds, weighed his options, and made a choice. A bad one from my perspective, but his to make. I couldn't worry about it now.

As I turned onto Bronough Street, I did my best to push aside thoughts of Goodwin's rather inexplicable case of foot-in-mouth disease, and just enjoy my new Norah Jones CD the rest of the way. I made the turn onto Jefferson Street a little before eight, my destination just in view.

Unlike the full-time faculty, I didn't have a reserved parking space in the school's lot, and usually opted for the large lot at the civic center. This day, however, the gods were smiling down, and a metered space on the street, right in front, magically appeared as I approached the school. I quickly braked, drawing the ire and horn blast of the driver behind me, then whipped my Yukon into the spot.

Well, 'whipped' is not a completely accurate description, as it took several back and forths to maneuver the SUV into the space, all of which infuriated the driver behind me even more. I'm not sure what he was saying to me as he stepped on the gas and flew by me as soon as he had enough room, but I'm pretty sure it wasn't, "Have a nice day."

I didn't much like driving the gas guzzling Yukon, but when we were dividing up the property in the divorce, it was either that or the even bigger Suburban. I would have been just as happy, even more so, during our marriage, to drive a more modest sedan, or even a small SUV, but Craig insisted he got the best deals on the larger, top of the line models, and that he had a certain image to maintain as the owner of an automobile dealership. Besides, he said, they were safer.

Couldn't argue with that latter point, though I also couldn't argue with the suggestion of one of my friends and fellow divorcees that there was an inverse relationship between the size of a man's car and the size of his other prized tool. I had not shared this theory with my husband, which was a matter of some regret. I needed to sell the Yukon and get something a little more reasonable.

I went directly into the main building and picked up the handouts for my class from the copy center. Then, with a little time to kill, I stopped by the office of Professor Charles Everhart.

The professor had been with the College of Law almost from the beginning, except for a brief stint as a judge on the First District Court of Appeal. It was a position which lost its appeal rather quickly, as Everhart liked to put it, clearly enjoying the pun, and from which he resigned after only one term. He missed his students, he said, not to mention any other normal social interaction.

Though his time on the bench had been relatively short and many years in the past, some people still addressed him with the title of the office, something that both puzzled and slightly annoyed him, though he never said precisely why.

He had taught a variety of subjects over the years, but mostly Torts and Evidence. His treatise on the latter subject was a must-read and reference book for just about every lawyer and judge in the state. He was also the one person most responsible for securing my current teaching position with the school. I considered him a mentor and friend.

The door to his office was open. He was sitting, leaning back in the large executive chair, his feet propped up on the desk and a book in his lap. He looked up when I knocked on the door frame and motioned me to come in. "Hello, Katie," he said, smiling, removing his feet from the desk and sitting up in his chair. "What a pleasant surprise." He looked at me over his reading glasses, motioning with his chin for me to have a seat. "How was your holiday?"

I plopped down in the chair opposite him. "It was nice. Got to spend some quiet time with my daughter. All my siblings were in town for Christmas. A little hectic, but a good time. How about you?"

The professor ran his hand through his hair, which was completely white now, but still full. "Judy and I hibernated up at our place in North Carolina. Lots of snow, lots of log fires and hot chocolate, pleasure reading. Judy did some painting. I watched a lot of bowl games. It was great. Hard to come back."

I frowned. "You can't fool me. You took work with you, I'm sure."

"No, I promise." He raised his hand up. When I frowned again, he said, "Well, just a little work on the revision of my book, but really, I took it pretty easy the whole time." He waited a beat, then smiled at me, the skin wrinkling along the sides of his eyes. "How's your class going this semester?"

"Okay, I guess. You should ask the students."

"You had a good time teaching last semester, though, didn't you?"

"Oh yeah, I enjoyed it. But it was a lot of work. I'm always a little anxious too, standing up there like I know what I'm doing. All those students typing away on their laptops like my words are from the sacred tablets or something. Lots of pressure."

"Well, it gets easier each time you do it. After a while, you get to where you can do it in your sleep. In fact, I think I may have done just that a couple of times, back in my old partying years." He grinned at me. "Anyway, I've heard a lot of good things from the students, so you must be doing something right. I think they really respond to your more clinical approach, the way you bring the real world into the classroom."

I shrugged, a little embarrassed and pleased at the same time.

"They get enough of the straight lecture crap," he continued, "from stuffy old professors who couldn't find the courthouse with a map."

"Present company excluded, of course."

He peered at me over his reading glasses. "Of course."

After a few seconds of silence, he changed the subject. "Did you hear about Elena Castillo?"

"Yeah, that was awful. Do they know anything more about how she died?"

"I didn't see anything in the paper today--other than the investigation is on-going and a grand jury was being convened. You hear anything?"

"Not really." I felt a little guilty, playing dumb and pumping him for information without divulging my purpose, but I couldn't ignore a possible source. "Do you think it was suicide?"

"I have no idea. She was a former student, but I didn't really know her that well."

"Was she a good student?" I asked.

"Not as good as you, of course."

"Of course."

"But better than most." He looked out the small window onto the east lawn of the school. "She was a very focused person, knew what she wanted and went after it with a single-mindedness that was a little unusual in such a young person."

I nodded slowly, reminded then that Elena had seemed to me older than her years.

The professor folded his hands in front of him. "Do you think there might be some connection to the NCAA thing?"

The NCAA thing was an investigation into accusations of gambling by FSU's starting quarterback, Richard "Ricky" Hobbs. The junior had not expected to be playing the position at the beginning of the season as he was third string, behind Brice Mason and his back-up, Adrian Brewster. But Brewster had abruptly left the team before the first snap of the first game. After a disappointing 0-2 start, and a tragic, career-ending injury to Mason, hopes of another national championship were dashed. Hobbs was given the nod as the new signal caller, but no one gave him much of a chance at a winning season. After all, he had some mighty big shoes to fill.

The youngster had answered the skeptics by breaking all kinds of records on the way to a nine and two record and a top five ranking at the end of the regular season. And he was exciting to watch, scrambling in the backfield, going for the risky, breath-taking play more often than was prudent, yet somehow managing to come out on top. He had people asking, Brice who?

The rumors that he had placed bets on games, though never one involving FSU, surfaced with a couple of games left in the regular season. The school announced an investigation into organized gambling on campus, never referring to Hobbs by name. Then, two weeks before FSU was set to play Texas A&M in the Orange Bowl, Hobbs was charged by the State Attorney's Office with gambling and, in a separate incident with grand theft for accepting unauthorized discounts from a female fan working the cash register at Macy's. The school announced that Hobbs was being suspended from the team pending an investigation and would not play in the bowl game. FSU ended up losing the game.

"Well," I said, "Elena Castillo was representing him, supposedly pro bono. And I've heard that her family is behind the proposed constitutional amendment to allow casino gambling. You think there's some truth to the rumors?"

Everhart had, for many years, been the faculty representative to the Atlantic Coast Conference, to which FSU belonged, and an unofficial consultant on all matters relating to the NCAA. His thoughts on the subject would carry considerable weight. He seemed determined, however, to keep them to himself. "I have no idea," he said. "Just wondering."

"Hmm," I said, my tone hinting at my skepticism, but I didn't push it. "Who do you think will be representing Hobbs now?"

He pursed his lips, then said, "Perhaps Jeb, for show, paired with someone else to do the heavy lifting."

The 'Jeb' to which he referred was not the former governor, but John Edward Bradford, senior partner of my former law firm. "That sounds about right," I said, which seemed to close out the subject.

Soon, we were engaged in an earnest discussion of FSU sports, expanding into ACC teams, then other collegiate teams. Neither of us really cared too much for the professional level but we shared a love of collegiate athletics. Mostly, we focused on FSU's basketball teams, both of which had started out well this season, though neither had yet to be tested by any major opponents.

I was about to say something about the glass being half full, when I noticed a couple of students had lined up in the hallway, no doubt waiting to see the professor. One of the things that endeared Everhart to the students was his willingness to share his time and advice. Taking another look at the students, I saw myself several years before in what seemed another life.

"Well, I better get to my class," I said, standing.

"Thanks for stopping by, Katie. Good to see you."

With one more wistful look at the students I passed, I headed toward the stairs.

Chapter Six

I was driving Maggie to her basketball game, lost in thought, when I had a vague sense that my daughter had just said something. I gave her a quick, sideways glance.

"What?"

Looking straight ahead, she tucked an errant strand of hair underneath her head band and said, "I need money for the field trip Friday—to the Challenger Space Center." When I didn't respond, Maggie turned in her seat to face me and added, "It's twenty-five dollars."

"I know how much it is. I thought your father was going to give you the money for that."

She shrugged. "He said he didn't have it, and that I should get it from you."

I stopped at a traffic light, stared at Maggie, not trusting myself to speak. My daughter apparently took my silence for agreement, or at least an opening to relay the rest of the message. "He also said he couldn't afford the new basketball shoes. He said you should pay for them with the child support money he gives you."

The light changed and I surged forward. "He said that?" I did my best to keep the incredulity, the sarcasm from my voice.

Maggie, looking straight ahead, nodded once. "Uh huh." Her tone of voice and manner suggested she was just stating a fact that was beyond dispute—a blind acceptance of what her father had told her. "And he has to live in that apartment instead of a house." She hesitated, then added, "He doesn't have any food hardly in his refrigerator, Mom. We have to go out to eat a lot when I'm with him."

I turned off Ingleside, into the parking area for the Lafayette Park

Recreation Center, found a space close to the gym and pulled in. I felt my face begin to redden. The Marital Settlement Agreement spelled out that we were to split, fifty-fifty, all costs related to Maggie's sports and extracurricular activities. If one person paid, they were to send a copy of the receipt and the other was to reimburse half within thirty days. I was already up on Craig close to four hundred dollars. In our last conversation, he agreed to pay for the next four hundred in expenses instead of reimbursing me. Now this. Typical.

Twenty-five dollars for a field trip was no big deal, and even four hundred, though it was not insignificant, was not going to break me. But by God, he agreed to pay it, and he should pay it. What was worse, he had involved Maggie in it, poor-mouthing to his daughter, and blaming me for it. I also had to admit I was a little upset that Maggie would fall for his line. She was only ten, and desperate for her father's love and approval, but still . . .

I wanted to ask her whether she thought it cost more to eat in or to eat out. And how much did she think that car he drove cost? How much did she think he spent on his girlfriend? Maggie deserved to know the truth, didn't she? Why should I let my ex-husband tell our daughter lies, try to poison her mind against me, and not fight back with the truth?

Good questions, all. But as much as I wanted to ask them, I knew I shouldn't. Very basic parenting principle for divorcing parents-- don't involve your child in disputes with your ex and don't say negative things about him or her to your kid.

It was something they emphasized in the Kid's First class we had to take as part of the divorce process—the one that Craig had to be dragged to. He didn't need parenting lessons after ten years as a father, he said. He obviously had not been listening during class, either. Still, Maggie thought he walked on water. I gave myself a body shiver, trying to shake the anger from it.

"I have to give the money to the teacher tomorrow morning,"

Maggie said. "Maybe you should go ahead and give it to me now, so we don't forget."

Doing my best to hide a frown, I reached over to my purse, pulled out my wallet, found the required amount and gave it to her. Maggie reached over to her backpack, put in the money, then zipped it up. "Got to go," she said opening the door and hopping out. "Coach don't like us to be late." And then she was gone.

"**Doesn't** like us to be late," I corrected, though my daughter was beyond earshot, hurrying to the entrance. Shades of my mother again. Then I muttered, "You're welcome."

* * *

Maggie took the pass on the wing, looked inside quickly, then fired it back out front to Penny Hunt, the point guard. Penny was my next-door neighbor's kid, a short, stocky ten-year-old who was, by far, the best ball handler on the team. She took the ball and dribbled to her right, her blonde ponytail bouncing behind her, then whipped a bounce pass to the other forward, Shanika Thomas. The defense instantly shifted over, looking to prevent the pass inside.

Meanwhile, Maggie had turned and crossed through the lane along the base line. Shanika held the ball aloft, looked toward the middle, then turned and delivered a two-handed pass to Maggie, who was now positioned on the base line about twelve feet from the basket. She turned and squared up to the basket, preparing to shoot.

The low post defender looked confused, and hesitated a little too long before rushing out toward Maggie, who got her shot off well before she could get close. The ball arched nicely toward the basket, and then fell through with a swish. The small group of fans in the bleachers erupted into yelling and cheering, my scratchy voice louder than most. There were calls of "nice shot," and "all right, Panthers," and a couple of chants of "Maggeee, Maggeee." The girls on the bench squealed with delight. Coach Bob Cohen allowed himself a moment of exultation before changing gears and urging the girls to get back quickly on defense. As the opposing team brought the ball across mid court, their coach called time out.

I looked at the time clock on the end wall. Less than thirty seconds were left in the third quarter. The score was 24-18, pretty high for this age group. Although the other team had kept it close the whole game, the Panthers had led since the opening tip off.

The team had done well so far this season, with only one loss in five games. What a difference from just a couple of years in the overall quality of play, and the difference between the newer and the older players. Hardly any of the new kids knew much about the game—Maggie looked like a pro in comparison. Most of them dribbled a little, picked up the ball and ran a few steps, then started dribbling again. Defense was strictly optional. Whether on defense or offense, they just followed the ball around more out of curiosity than any fixed notion of what they were supposed to be doing. It was remarkable how quickly kids learned new things.

As the buzzer sounded, ending the time out, the players broke their huddle on the sidelines. Maggie smiled and waved briefly to me, then searched the stands, for her father, no doubt. I looked at my watch, then at the gym entrance, and fought back the resentment I felt growing. He had better show.

I was sitting with two other "basketball moms." To my immediate right was Barbara Bogan and next to her, Debra Hunt, my next-door neighbor and the mother of Penny. It had been awkward since the divorce. Craig and I and Debra and Jim had often done things together, but Debra's loyalty to me had never been a question, and was one of the things that had kept me balanced and strong during the separation and divorce.

Barbara had a deliciously irreverent sense of humor and an occasionally biting tongue. Like me, she was recently divorced, having completed hers a few months before mine began. She had a "been there, done that" attitude that had been helpful in freeing me from feelings of guilt and low self-esteem. Her daughter, Becky, was not one of the better players on the team, but that never dampened Barbara's enthusiasm.

In the last play of the quarter, the opposing team scored, cutting the lead to four. During the break between quarters, Coach Bob walked down the sideline in front us, spoke briefly with the official in charge of the clock, then walked back to the team, smiling up at us and waving as he went by.

"I wouldn't mind going one-on-one with him," Barbara said, nudging me with her elbow. On the other side of her, Debra smiled briefly.

I shook my head. "Easy, girl. The man is married."

"All of the good ones are." She chuckled and then added, "I don't mean to imply, of course, that all of the ones that are married are good ones." She laughed heartily at this, but it was a sad laugh just the same. "Speaking of which," Barbara said, "where is your ex? I thought he was coming tonight. I'm tired of being the only obnoxious parent."

"Who knows," I said, looking over at the entrance again.

"Asshole," Barbara said, shaking her head. "I will give Ed that, anyway," she said, looking to her right, where her ex-husband sat with another man about twenty yards down the row. "He may have been a lousy husband, but he's a good father. Hell, he spends more time with the kids now than he did when we were married, and, I think we get along better. Go figure." She was silent for a few seconds, then, as if reading my mind, she patted me on the arm and said, "It'll get better."

"Promise?"

"Sure."

There was silence then for several seconds until Debra changed the subject. "I saw you on the five o'clock news today."

"Yeah?"

"It was about the grand jury investigating that Castillo woman's death."

"Elena."

"What?"

"The Castillo woman, her name was Elena. I used to work with her."

"Oh," Debra said. "Anyway, I saw where a judge was a witness. They said you were his lawyer."

I nodded. "Warren Goodwin."

Technically, he had not been a witness. He told me he took my advice and declined to answer questions, asserting his Fifth Amendment privilege against self-incrimination. But, in typical Goodwin fashion, and against my advice, he insisted on explaining why. He told the grand jurors that when he heard what Oscar said to me, about getting my fee, he knew that the decision to charge him had already been made. And since he knew they could have no real evidence against him, he reasonably feared that a case was being manufactured. He would not, he said, bring the rope to his own lynching party.

Barbara, who had been uncharacteristically silent during Debra's questions, jumped in now. So," she said when I didn't elaborate, "what happened?" Both women were staring at me, waiting for my response.

"Have no idea," I lied. Grand jury proceedings are secret. It's just the witness, the prosecutor and the jurors. It's a criminal offense to reveal what goes on in there."

"Hmm. . ." both women said in unison, clearly intrigued. "Boy," Debra said after a few seconds, "that sure would tend to put a damper on the gossip."

We all chuckled at this, and I said, "Yes, I suppose so."

The conversation died then as we focused our attention back on the game. The other team kept it close for a while, but with two and a half minutes left to go in the game, the Panthers pulled away to a comfortable eight-point lead. It was at this point that Craig and Brenda walked through the entrance near the goal to our left.

My ex-husband was a tall, thin man with auburn hair and fair skin, traits of the Waters family that he had passed on to Maggie. He was always well dressed, and was that night, wearing tan slacks, a blue and tan plaid sport shirt, with a navy blazer. He looked particularly handsome, I thought, as I watched him walk toward the stands. And I hated him for it.

"Ah, there's the ex-hubby," Barbara said, nudging me unnecessarily. "And he's brought the cow with him." Barbara had made it clear that she had no use for Craig, or his girlfriend, but I knew she was just being supportive. Brenda was a bit overweight but she was certainly no cow. Voluptuous would be a better description. With her large hips and ample bosom, she was the opposite of me, physically. And I hated my ex for that as well.

Brenda was dressed in black pants, tan blouse, a black and tan suede jacket, and a good amount of gold jewelry, her bleached blonde hair shoulder length and curled under. As I watched the couple walk in front of the bleachers, I could feel the familiar knot in my stomach, smaller now but still there. And the image that was the companion to the knot forced its way into my consciousness.

It was from the dealership's Christmas party, year before last, at the home of Craig's parents. I was looking for an empty bathroom when I saw Craig coming out of the game room. Before I could call out, he walked off in the opposite direction. Then, as I started to go into the hall bathroom, I saw Brenda come out of the same room. The woman hesitated just outside the doorway, styled her hair with her hands quickly, adjusted her skirt, and then walked off in the same direction as Craig.

A lot of wives would have been instantly suspicious, but I didn't think much of it at the time, a product of my naiveté, I suppose. There was, after all, a bathroom there as well. For all I knew, there had been other people in the room, too. But something inside me registered the significance of the scene, the logic of its reality too strong to be denied. So, it got stored away, somewhere in the recesses of my mind. Which is where it stayed until about six months later when Craig told me one evening after dinner, simply, directly, that he wasn't happy in the marriage, hadn't been for a while, that he had fallen in love with someone else, and that he wanted a divorce.

The details of that conversation are still vague in my memory because somewhere along the line I went on autopilot. The weight of his words had been the equivalent of a cement truck crashing on my chest, the hurt, the pain so overwhelming that I wondered why I didn't just melt into a pool of jelly right there on the living room floor.

That image of Brenda Mott adjusting her skirt, standing just outside the game room that evening, came tumbling out of that place in the back of my mind where I had stored it, its significance then clear. And it continues to pop back up every time I see them together. It was more fleeting now, less painful, but I suspected that it would be there a long time, perhaps forever.

They took seats several feet away and a couple of rows higher. I turned and made eye contact with Craig, who nodded, then started coming toward me. Brenda gave me a small wave and smile, which I pretended not to see. Craig sat down next to me.

"Hey, Kate."

I detected the familiar scent of his cologne. "Craig. Glad you could make it," I said, instantly regretting the sarcasm. He didn't seem to notice. Barbara and Debra had made a point to move down a little bit and pretended to be engaged in some intense conversation.

"How's our girl doing?" Craig looked over to where the teams had resumed play.

"What can I say? It's hard to be humble when your kid's the star."

He smiled. "How are you doing?"

I wanted so very much to tell him the truth, to vent about the boxes in the garage, about him not showing up for visitation like he was supposed to, about the child support he hadn't paid, the negative comments to Maggie. But I didn't.

"I'm fine," I said simply.

After an awkward several seconds, Craig excused himself and went back to sit with his girlfriend. When the buzzer sounded at the end of the game, Maggie's team had won by seven points. After they shook hands with the opposing players and had a team huddle, Coach Bob dismissed them and Maggie went charging toward Craig.

"Daddy! I didn't see you come in."

"Yeah. That's 'cause you were too busy scoring." Craig gave his daughter a big hug. "I saw enough to know that." Just as I came up, he said to Maggie, "Hey, listen, you want to come spend the night with me tonight? We'll go get a pizza or something. What do you say?"

Maggie looked over at me. "Oh, Mama, can I?"

Damn him! He doesn't show up when he's supposed to. Then, when the mood strikes him, he wants to disrupt her whole schedule. "You still have homework to do, honey, and you don't have your pajamas, or your clothes for school tomorrow."

Maggie's face showed disappointment, then resignation. She knew I was right, which was more than could be said for her father.

"No problem," he said. "We can swing by the house and get your stuff." He turned to me. "Don't worry. I'll make sure she does her homework and gets to bed at a reasonable time."

Maggie looked at me again, hopeful. I realized that I could win the battle but the cost would be high.

"All right. Bed time is nine-thirty, now." I turned to Craig. "And you'll take her to school tomorrow?"

"Sure."

I gave my daughter a hug. "Okay, sport. I'll see you after school tomorrow."

I lingered at the gym a few minutes, talking with Barbara and Debra, then took my time driving home, so Maggie and Craig would be gone by the time I arrived. The idea of a pizza had sounded good, and I considered getting one to go from Little Italy's, but it was late and I didn't want to have to wait for it. Thirty minutes later, I had fixed myself a turkey sandwich, grabbed a bag of chips and a Diet Coke, and was sitting in front of the television watching a re-run of CSI. Bandit was in my lap, enjoying the rub on her ears and head, purring contentedly.

When the phone rang, the startled cat jumped up, knocking the can of Coke over. I cursed and reached over to set it upright, minimizing the spill, spreading out my napkin to absorb the liquid. The phone rang a second time and I picked it up. "Hello?"

"Kate, this is Marci Goodwin."

Chapter Seven

The Goodwins lived in Los Robles, a small enclave in Midtown which contained an eclectic mix of houses, from spreading Mediterranean estates crowded onto acre lots to small English cottages on a quarter acre. I drove past the stucco, Spanish archway and eased slowly down Cristobel Drive, to where it looked like a block party was in progress. Well, no, not anything as festive as a party. More like a neighborhood fire drill, where folks leave their houses and stand around waiting for the fire department to give them the okay to go back inside.

The night air was cold and crisp, and the moon full, its light creating a kaleidoscope of color and patterns as it filtered through the spreading branches of the live oak trees that dotted the landscape. People were standing around in clothes not suited for the cold, as if they hadn't thought they would be outside long and now were too interested to go back in for a sweater or coat, or too embarrassed to come back out if they did.

Three patrol units and two other unmarked cop cars were parked on and about the Goodwin property. Close by was a panel van with "Eyewitness News" painted on the side, just above the trademark eye of CBS. This was not a good sign. Someone had alerted the news media.

I parked as close as I could and walked quickly up to the Tudor style house. In my peripheral vision I could see the cameraman and reporter for Channel 6 look my way. I averted my face and hoped they had not recognized me. When I approached closer, one of the uniformed officers, placed to maintain a perimeter, came out to head me off. The stiff leather equipment belt squeaked as he walked.

"Sorry, Ma'am, you'll have to stay back."

"I'm Kate Marston, attorney for the Goodwins. I'd like to see my clients."

"I'm sorry, Ma'am, but no exceptions. You'll have to wait until they're through in there."

"Listen, Officer," I hesitated, reading his name on the badge, "Jackson, I know you have your orders, but the Goodwins have the right to have their attorney present while their house is searched. If you ignore my request, not only will I file a formal complaint, you may jeopardize whatever evidence or statements might be obtained during the execution of the search warrant."

It was a bluff, but it got the officer scratching his chin, considering his options and the possible consequences. He tilted his head slightly and put his hand up to the microphone clipped to the flap on his shirt. "This is Jackson out front. I have a white female who identifies herself as Kate Marston. Says she's the lawyer for the Goodwin family. Should I allow her back?"

Even from where I was standing, I heard Oscar Manning on the other end of the radio, first emitting an expletive and then, after a brief hesitation, telling him to let me back. "That's affirmative," the officer said. Then he stepped back and to the side a bit. "You can go on back, Ma'am, through the front door. Another officer will greet you there."

Just inside the door, the other officer tipped his head slightly as I came in and pointed, wordlessly toward the living room. Marci Goodwin was seated on the couch, looking pale and small. Her honey blond hair was pulled back in a tight bun. She rose when I came into the room, met me half way across the floor and gave me a small hug, as if greeting a guest at a party. I could smell the citrus scented shampoo in her hair. She was dressed in a pair of black slacks and sweater. Her eyes were red, puffy, the make-up a little smeared. "Katie, thank you for coming."

"Of course," I said. "Where's Renny?"

"They took him away." When I didn't say anything in response, she added. "He said I should call you. What is this all about?"

Marci Goodwin had sounded upset, alarmed, but under control on the phone when she told me the police were at their house. I didn't know whether it meant her husband had confided in her, as I had urged, so that she was prepared for this possibility, or whether it just meant she had an inner strength on which she drew in a crisis. I suspected it was the latter. "What did he tell you?"

"He said it was all quote, bullshit, end quote, that it was a witch hunt by his political enemies, and that I should call you."

Obviously, the good judge had not told his wife a thing. "Do you have a copy of the search warrant?"

She reached over to the end table next to the couch and retrieved a document. I took it and began to read.

The first page was the warrant itself, a description of the Goodwin house, how to locate it and the scope of the search, that is, what sorts of things the officers were supposed to be looking for, including clothes, fibers, CDs and DVDs, e-mail and other documents stored on personal computers relating to or addressed to the victim, that sort of thing. The effect was to allow a search of just about anything.

The most important part, the affidavit of probable cause, the recitation of facts upon which the judge had relied in issuing the search warrant, was not attached. This was not unexpected. The detectives were not required to give a copy of the probable cause affidavit to the person who was subject to the search, only the warrant itself. Oh well, a girl could hope, couldn't she? "Is this all they gave you?"

She nodded, and I turned toward the officer, introduced myself, and told him I would like to speak to Oscar Manning or Debra Brown. The man gave me a frown, but momentarily he spoke into the radio on his shoulder, then told me that Detective Manning would speak to me shortly. In less than a minute, Oscar appeared in the entry to the living room. He wore a dress shirt, sleeves rolled up on his forearms, and a tie, which was loosened around the collar.

"Counselor, good to see you, even under such unfortunate

circumstances." The man looked tired, a little tense, and despite the circumstances, I thought his words sincere.

"Likewise," I said. Then I glanced back at Marci Goodwin, seated on the couch, and motioned for Manning to move with me into the dining room. The detective acquiesced. "Oscar, I need to be present during the search, as a representative of the Goodwins, to observe the scope and verify what is or is not seized."

"Not gonna happen," he said, shaking his head. "You are here as a courtesy only." His face and his tone registered a finality that did not invite challenge.

And I decided not to. After an awkward silence, I asked, "Can I at least have a copy of the probable cause affidavit?" The detective frowned and began shaking his head, but then seemed to have second thoughts. It was only a matter of time before I could get a copy, at the latest the next morning from the clerk's office. "As a courtesy?"

Oscar reached into his back pocket and pulled out a folded document. He hesitated, holding it up. "What the hell," he said, then handed it to me. "Read 'em and weep." Then he turned and left me standing there.

I scanned it quickly, searching for the key facts: The location of the body suggested a straight drop; granular residue from the balcony on the front, back and the side of the victim's clothing; blunt trauma to the back of her head, which the Medical Examiner concluded occurred before the fall; the carpet appeared to have been recently vacuumed, yet there was no bag in the vacuum cleaner; surfaces wiped down; no sign of forced entry; the only items that seemed to be missing were the victim's laptop, some CDs and DVDs, and a flash drive device the victim typically kept on her key chain. All of this pointed toward murder rather than suicide or accident. What came next was the evidence that supposedly pointed toward Goodwin as the murderer.

The key card records showed that he left the courthouse at 10:35 p.m. on the night of the murder. One of the condo residents saw him outside the victim's unit around 10:45 p.m. Although many of the surfaces had been wiped clean, a fingerprint lifted from the sliding glass door to the balcony was a match to Goodwin. Phone records showed calls between them that night, at 10:15 and 10:30 p.m. as well as in the preceding weeks.

Forensic examination of Goodwin's work computer revealed e-mails between the two, the tone of which, according to the affiant, suggested some kind of romantic involvement. Examples were given over a period of several weeks:

C: Enjoyed the "fun" raising activity last night. Needless to say, you passed the audition. I didn't realize you were a man of so many talents.

G: Good cause, and you are the talented one! And the real fun "riser."

C: I need to see you.

G: In camera inspection?

C: That's right.

G: Call my back-line number when you come over. I'll let you in.

C: I need to see you.

G: Can't break free tonight.

C: Boo hoo.

G: I'll make it up to you.

C: Yes, you will.

On the evening the victim died was this:

G: You want me to come over?

C: No.

The affidavit also noted that all these e-mails had been deleted on Goodwin's computer, and the trash folder emptied, in an apparent attempt to conceal the communications, and that there were likely many more that could not be retrieved. It was stated that Goodwin's alibi was uncorroborated, and finally, that he told detectives he had neither seen nor talked to the victim for two weeks before her death, and had denied any relationship with the victim other than professional.

Fairly damning, but it could have been worse. Much worse. I was already thinking of alternative interpretations for the e-mails and phone calls. Eyewitness identification, contrary to popular belief, was notoriously unreliable. I wondered if the building had surveillance cameras, or other records that would show who came and left the building that night.

I took a few moments to absorb what I had read, composed myself, then walked back into the living room where Marci Goodwin remained seated on the couch, demure, ankles crossed, as if she had been having tea and conversation with a friend. She stood when I entered the room. "Can someone please explain what's going on?" she asked. "I should call the children, but I don't know what to tell them. What should I tell them, Katie?"

I hung my head. I couldn't repeat what my client had told me, but she deserved the truth from somewhere, and soon. I handed her the probable cause affidavit and looked away as the woman read it. When she had finished, she handed it back to me. "Thank you," she said simply, then sat back down on the couch.

I sat down next to her and grabbed Marci on both shoulders, willing her to look at me. "I know this is a nightmare for you, and it will likely get worse before it gets better. Please know that I will do everything I can to help, as I know Mom and Dad will. I don't wish to sound too cold or uncaring, but right now, I have to focus on the legal end of this. It will be up to you and Renny to deal with the rest, on your own terms."

She nodded, perhaps getting a hint of the underlying message.

"And yes, you should call the kids. Tell them their dad has been arrested and charged with murder. They will find out soon enough. See if they can get here by tomorrow morning. I'm going to need a united front at First Appearance in order to gain his release on bail. Family support will be crucial."

Again, the woman nodded, but I had the feeling she was a thousand miles away. I said her husband would be tied up in booking for a while, but that, if she liked, she could follow me out to the jail to see him. I would stay with her, though, until the officers left. The offer of emotional support seemed to please Marci. I explained what was likely to happen, procedurally, gauging her reaction. Marci talked about not seeing it coming, showing her controlled rage at the humiliation her husband had brought her. But she was of my parents' generation and culture. By the time we headed off for the jail, she was wearing her stand-by-your-man face.

Chapter Eight

Marci Goodwin, her daughter, Robyn, and I met my father early the next morning at the employees' entrance to the courthouse on Calhoun Street. Meagan, the couple's other child, was in route from Athens, Georgia, and would not arrive until sometime later that day.

Normally, in Leon County, First Appearance hearings were conducted by video, with the defendants at the jail, and everyone else, judge, lawyers, court staff and victims, at the courthouse. It made sense from both a cost and security perspective. The State Attorney, Bill Lipton, had arranged, however, an exception on this day for a special defendant. I felt certain it was so the prosecutor could take advantage of the publicity, make sure the press got photos of the judge, symbol of power, dressed in jail house blues, shuffling into court with handcuffs and leg irons.

Lipton was a pretty decent guy, but when he put his blinders on and rode his high horse of puritanical morality, he saw no shades of gray, nor was he distracted by self-doubt. He would have no concern for any embarrassment caused to the judge or his family, which was obvious from the way the arrest and search had been handled.

Dad gave us all hugs, lingering with Marci. He held on to her shoulders with both hands, arms stretched out, looking at her and asked, "You doing all right?" in a tone that suggested he knew she wasn't, much as you would at the funeral of a loved one.

And, in a way, it was like a death in the family. No matter what happened relative to the criminal charges against him, Judge Warren Goodwin's life and that of his family would never be the same. Whether it would be reborn, and in what form, remained to be seen, but the somewhat idyllic life they had led could never be recovered.

Marci Goodwin nodded. Her eyes were red and reflected a deep weariness, but she was composed, dignified, and very pretty. Her honey-blond hair, which had been up in a tight bun last night, was loose now, shoulder length, making her look both younger and softer. My defense lawyer's mind was assessing her impact on a jury. She would be a sympathetic figure, displaying the grace and composure of an innocent who must suffer a very public embarrassment caused by the sins of her husband. Her visible support of him would be viewed as sincere, which it was, born of love and loyalty. Her mere presence would speak eloquently to the jury of her faith in the basic goodness of her husband.

Robyn, who was a few years younger than me, had inherited her mother's honey blonde hair and good looks, but not the grace under fire. She looked tense and very uncomfortable, as if she was ready to lose it at any time. Marci Goodwin put her arm around her daughter's shoulder and said to my dad, "Thank you for arranging to have us avoid the public entrance. I know we can't escape the glare forever but every little bit helps, especially now."

"Of course," he said. "Here, follow me." Then he turned and walked toward the employee elevator. We all got in and rode in silence to the third floor, down the deserted hallway to his office. The welcoming aroma of freshly brewed coffee greeted us and we all accepted a cup before taking seats around his large conference table. I took the coffee eagerly. It was my fourth cup in the last two hours. It had been a long night and I was operating on only about three hours of sleep, making up the difference with caffeine.

I had called my parents right after leaving the Goodwin's house last night.

"Hello?" My mother's voice had an anxious tone about it, as if expecting bad news. It increased when she learned it was me on the other end.

"What's wrong, Mary Katherine? Are you alright? Is it Margaret

Anne? Have you been in an accident?"

"Whoa, Mom. I'm fine. Maggie's fine. She's with Craig tonight. No, this has to do with Renny Goodwin. Could you ask Dad to pick up the extension so both of you can hear?" When my dad got on, I gave them an abbreviated version of the events.

Strangely enough, neither seemed shocked by the news. My father asked, "Will you be representing Renny, then, in this matter?" His tone of voice registered something more than neutrality, but I wasn't sure what.

"I don't know. It appears he will probably want me to, but I haven't committed to it. I wanted to talk with you first."

My mother said, "I think it's a bad idea, honey. This is a sordid mess and nothing good can come of it. I love Renny to death. You know that. But it was irresponsible of him to involve you in this. This town is crawling with lawyers. Did he have to pick the daughter of his best friend?" She said this, it seemed, more to my dad than to me, but as it was a rhetorical question, neither of us answered. "Besides," she continued, "you said you wanted to have a more flexible schedule, to have more time with Margaret Anne. You can't do everything, you know. Something will have to give. Will it be your daughter who suffers?"

"Now Martha Anne, don't be sending her on a guilt trip," my father said.

"Why stop now," I said. "It's worked so well lo these many years."

"I'm sorry, Mary Katherine. I don't mean it that way. I just want you to make a considered decision."

"Have you made a list of the pros and cons?" This was my dad's standard advice when faced with a major decision. Indeed, I had always found it to be a useful exercise and now I articulated for them the list I had already composed in my head.

"He is a long-time friend of the family who has asked for my help."

There was no comment from my parents on this observation.

Loyalty to friends was a highly valued character trait in the Marston family, so this was a given.

"A high-profile case means a lot of exposure," I said. "If I handle myself well, I get a boost in standing in the legal community, which would help attract clients in the future. Judge Goodwin is a somewhat controversial figure, but he has a sizable base of loyal supporters who would certainly view his defender in a favorable light. Even his detractors appreciate that he would want a good lawyer. Also, on the plus side is the money. Hate to be crass, but it is a business. Such a case generally means a sizable fee, which your friend can certainly afford to pay."

"Certainly," my dad agreed.

I acknowledged that such a case would be demanding on my time, but pointed out that I didn't have any major cases at present, so it shouldn't disrupt my schedule that much. Besides, I said, I'd probably bring on co-counsel to help. Whether my mother was satisfied with this explanation, or simply resisting the urge to counter it, I didn't know. But if either of my parents disagreed with this rationalization, they didn't voice it.

I offered some cons. A lot of exposure also meant a lot of scrutiny. If I messed up, everyone would know. Aligning myself with Goodwin, I could expect hostility from the law-and-order group, not to mention the victim's family and friends.

"True enough," my father said. "You are likely to be unpopular with certain groups."

"And I don't want any backlash or mudslinging sticking on you, Dad. I know you sort of have your eye on Justice Reagan's seat." The reference was to a Florida Supreme Court justice set to retire in a few months.

"She's got a point, Phil," my mother said.

After a brief silence, during which I could picture my father rolling his eyes, composing himself, he said, "Don't worry about me. I haven't decided if I will apply, but if I do, that should not be part of the equation."

"But dear . . ." my mother started to say, then abruptly fell silent."

"Finally," I said, breaking the silence, "my client is not only a lawyer but a judge, who will second guess me at every turn and want to be in control of everything."

"Also true," my dad said, sighing into the phone. "You would have to lay down some strict guidelines early on, establish your authority over strategy. But still, Renny is not a sideline sitter by nature."

A more intangible consideration, unspoken but understood by my father, if not my mother, was the anticipation of the challenge. Bill Lipton was a damn good trial lawyer. And he would try this case on every level, and in every forum he could, to get his win. My skills in turn would be tested.

There is a certain satisfaction, an emotional high that comes with victory at trial. Despite all the talk about truth and justice, it is as much a competition as any athletic contest. The adversary system on which the legal system is based encourages a gladiator approach to the resolution of disputes.

The theory is that two equally trained and skilled advocates zealously put forth their clients' view of the dispute to a neutral fact finder, usually a jury, and the truth emerges out of the competing versions. To a large extent, this works, but inevitably it produces a contest mentality in which both sides want to win. They want to win regardless of truth and regardless of justice. Truth and justice, if achieved, is the result, not the goal, of the opposing self-interests of the litigants and their advocates.

"Quote him a very large fee," my father suggested.

I knew what he was thinking. It was a variation of flipping a coin, picking petals from a flower, looking for a sign. If he accepted, you were meant to take the case. If he didn't, you weren't. I liked the idea, I said, for both practical and symbolic reasons.

We both knew, however, that despite this little game of pros and cons, I would take the case, because I wanted it. And money was only a small part of it. I would quote a large fee, though, because I knew Goodwin would pay. He would want to, as a confirmation that both he and I were worth it. Something the psychologists call the illusion of confidence.

"Listen," my dad said next, "I'm going to call Ron Swanson, see if I can get any additional information for you. The case may be assigned to an outside judge but he's still the chief judge in the circuit and will have a say in logistics. He's no fan of Renny, but he's very protective of his fellow judges. Let me see what I can find out and I'll call you back. Where are you headed now?" I told him, to the jail. "Okay, why don't you call me when you get through talking with Renny and I'll fill you in on what I can come up with."

"I don't want you losing sleep on this thing, Dad. I can call Judge Swanson."

"Yeah, but he's not going to talk with you without the other side being present. Besides, you don't want to call the chief judge at eleven thirty at night. Don't worry about it. He's a friend, and you're my daughter."

Enough said.

At the jail, I had quoted Goodwin a very large fee, half as a retainer due within ten days, the balance within sixty days, and an additional sum if and when the case went to trial. I couldn't tell whether it was disappointment or admiration that replaced the initial surprise on his face, but Goodwin gave a low whistle, repeated the figure, nodded and said, "Okay."

We talked about the particulars of the case. I purposely didn't share with him the contents of the probable cause affidavit until he told me everything he knew, answered all my questions. An early test of his promised honesty and candor. He surprised me, coming close to the picture painted by the affidavit in his answers.

He acknowledged going to Elena's condo on the night she was

killed, something he had denied to the detectives, and to me. He was responding to a message from her, he said. "She seemed very distraught, but didn't want to talk about it. I decided maybe if we were face to face, she would tell me what was troubling her. But when I got there, she didn't answer the door. Nor had she answered my calls. I didn't know if she had suddenly gone out, or simply was not responding."

"Why didn't you use your key to get in?"

"I didn't have it anymore. She insisted that I give it to her when I broke it off."

"Why didn't you call the police, or the security at the condo building, anonymously even?"

"I should have, I suppose. But I was concerned about divulging the affair, and I didn't really think she would commit suicide. Now I feel terrible that I didn't take it seriously." He looked up at me then, hesitating. We were only a couple of feet apart, but separated by the thick glass in the visiting area, talking by phone, both of which combined to put distance between us. "And no," he said, "there was no record of that conversation. It was a phone message that I deleted when I got it. Remember, I was trying to be careful."

"What about the e-mails that night? She was telling you she didn't want to see you, or talk with you."

"That was before she called me. Like I said, she was upset with me for breaking things off. I was trying to keep her from spinning out of control."

Translation: Keep her from making the affair public.

I didn't ask my client if he did it, if he murdered Elena Castillo. That's not to say it didn't matter to me. It did. On a personal level. But as a professional criminal defense attorney, it was the wrong question, for a number of reasons. My job was to achieve the best outcome for my client, or more precisely, what the client saw as the best achievable outcome. The relevant question was what could be proven?

My client was smart enough to know that, too. He knew that if he told me he killed her, I couldn't ethically put him on the stand to deny it. But if he insisted that he didn't kill her, and he was lying, he ran the risk of having me blindsided by contradictory evidence. But, although I did not ask him this question, and spoke in hypothetical terms, in generalities, he answered it anyway.

"Katie, I didn't kill her. I swear."

He said it looking directly into my eyes, his face solemn. Was he lying? People like to think they have a nose for the truth, that they can somehow sense when someone is lying to them. Who knows? I think my mother can. And I wanted to believe he was innocent, of murder at least. I wanted to believe my gut was right when it told me he was sincere.

But I also remembered a lawyer's observation at a seminar I attended years before. "Sincerity," he said, "is the most important thing you need in order to be a good trial lawyer. Once you learn how to fake that, everything else is easy."

As we settled into our seats in Dad's chambers, I observed the daughter, Robyn, looking around the room, and I followed her eyes, taking in anew the familiar surroundings myself. It was a mixture of professional and personal.

The furniture was wood and leather, old and comfortable. The many plaques on the wall displayed a history of professional achievement and distinction—chairmanships of Florida Bar and Judicial Conference committees, three judge-of-the-year awards, other recognitions by various local and state associations or groups. The floor to ceiling bookcases were filled with an assortment of books, accented by sports trophies, vases and other small sculptures. The paintings on each of the other walls were old fashioned, legal-themed pieces—British judges in wigs, that sort of thing—and one Norman Rockwell type caricature of a disbelieving jury listening to a lawyer's closing argument. On his desk and credenza were family photos.

I lingered on one of the family portraits, taken when I was about seven years old. Sarah would have been about nine, Rebecca eleven. I stared for a long time at the younger version of myself, trying to remember what I had been feeling and thinking behind the big smile. Was I really that happy? I thought perhaps I was. And, from the objective vantage point of almost thirty years later, kind of cute, too. Not beautiful, mind you, like my sisters and my mother, but then again, very few were. Beauty is not only subjective, it is relative as well, a painful lesson that has taken many years for me to appreciate.

In one corner was a free standing, abstract wood sculpture, a gift from Dad's sister several years ago. Paige Marston was a sometime artist and art lover whose taste was somewhat eclectic. My mother called her a free spirit. My father, who was not so diplomatic, called her a nut—and to her face. But a likeable nut, he always added. I agreed. I thought this particular piece very beautiful, though I had no clue what it was supposed to represent. And for some unfathomable reason, its startling contrast with the rest of the room seemed to perfectly reflect the hide in plain sight anti-conformity of its official occupant.

My father was a multi-layered person who did not fit neatly into anyone's box, despite the ardent, delusional attempts of others to do so. He was comfortable with the gray, able to see the subtleties of a situation, and was sincerely empathetic. And people tended to mistake empathy for shared beliefs.

He was dressed that day in dark grey slacks and a sweater vest, white shirt, a bit of the grey and burgundy tie visible at the collar. He was getting older now, and showing it, I noticed, but he still looked fit, younger than his years, and handsome in his own awkward way. He sat down in a chair at one end of the conference table, took a sip of coffee, then looked at Marci Goodwin.

"As I told Kate earlier, the judge who signed the warrant and who will handle the case is Eleanor Mitchell from Suwannee County. I know her from judicial education work. She's a fair minded, no-nonsense type judge, knows what she's doing, and her integrity is without question."

I nodded in approval, looking over at my client's wife. "This is good news for us," I assured her. "Our prosecutor has been known to engage in a little nonsense from time to time."

"This whole thing is nonsense," the wife assured us. "Renny has his weaknesses, and he may not always exercise good judgment in some things." Her hesitation hung in the room like a cloud, an oblique acknowledgment of her husband's infidelity. "But he is not a violent person. He is not a mean person, at least not intentionally." She looked down at the floor for that last part, then she looked up again at me and my dad, though it seemed that she was speaking just as much or more to her daughter. "He is not a murderer. He is simply not capable of it."

She said this with a firmness that struck me as just a little naïve. An historical and objective look at human nature suggested that almost everybody is capable of murder, given the right circumstances. Some people have a higher threshold than others, that's all. I didn't know where mine was, but I felt sure I had one. And I was sure Judge Warren Goodwin did as well. I did not voice this opinion, though, but rather said, "Anyway, I have a feeling Judge Mitchell will cut Lipton off at the knees if he gets out of line."

Looking at Marci again, my father said, "At Katie's request, I spoke with our chief judge, Ron Swanson, who has agreed that Renny can appear in street clothes for the First Appearance proceedings."

It was fairly common for defense attorneys to request at trial that a client be allowed to dress in street clothes rather than the jailhouse-issued jumpsuit. The reason was obvious. The image of the defendant as inmate was a powerful one. It suggested guilt, dangerousness. Kind of took the sails out of that presumption of innocence idea. And, when you thought about it, the same thing applied for the public at large, all those potential jurors out there. I nodded a thank you at my father and he continued.

"Didn't take much persuading for Ron. He didn't like the way this was handled, the arrest and execution of the search warrant, the media circus for the First Appearance. It's an administrative matter really too, so no need to consult with Lipton on it, or Mitchell for that matter."

"We've also arranged for him to be brought to the courtroom early," I said. "When the reporters and the public come in, he will already be seated at counsel table. No handcuffs. No leg irons." Marci and Robyn sat there, silent, their faces impassive. I guess they weren't all that impressed. "No perp walk" I said. "No show of him being led down the hallway or into the courtroom."

"Oh, I see," Marci Goodwin said, though it was obvious to me that she didn't. I changed subjects, reminding both wife and daughter of the need to look, and be, supportive. They both nodded, and I felt sure that when it came to the real thing, the public performance, Marci would play her part. As for Robyn, what you saw was what you got. She would look confused and distraught, as she was. I looked at my watch, then stood.

"It's time," I said.

Chapter Nine

My dad led us back down the hallway and into courtroom 3A through the back door, then left. It was better, he said, that he not have a more visible role in this. A couple of bailiffs greeted us somberly and assured me that my client was being brought up. The deputy clerks were there, but not the prosecutor. I sat at the table and directed Marci and Robyn to sit just behind me in the gallery. I opened my file and pretended to be taking notes.

Less than a minute later, Goodwin was escorted in through a side door. He saw his wife and daughter, whispered to the two bailiffs by his side, then when they nodded, he walked over to them. Normally, defendants were not allowed to have contact with family members, or others, in the courtroom—a precaution against the passing of weapons or other contraband. The bailiffs were willing to make an exception, however, for this defendant.

Despite the animosity he had aroused in their brethren, they worked with him every day, knew him as a person. And Goodwin was a jovial, gregarious sort. He had a politician's knack for remembering names. He asked about their families, seemed genuinely interested in their lives. Maybe he was guilty, maybe he wasn't, but either way, they were embarrassed for him. They were glad to be able to allow him at least this small measure of dignity.

Goodwin joined hands with his wife and daughter. As if in a huddle in a football game, the three of them leaned forward and the judge whispered something to them. Marci held her neutral look but Robyn sniffed a little, trying to hold back the tears. Goodwin whispered again and she straightened up, wiped her eyes and gave him a smile, a very small one. After about a minute, he came over, sat down next to me, leaned over and said, "Ready?" I nodded, and that was the extent of our communication before the double doors of the courtroom opened and some spectators, press and the State Attorney team—Lipton had two associates with him—came in.

I glanced in Lipton's direction, then refocused on the file in front of me, savoring for a moment the look on the prosecutor's face as he saw that my client was already present, and in street clothes. He and the others pulled out chairs at the prosecution table and put down their files. Then, as an afterthought it seemed, Lipton walked over to me. I stood to greet him, not wanting to have to look up to him. Standing, I was eye level with the man.

His face was pock marked, and his nose a bit too long for his angular face, but he was not an unattractive man. He kept himself fit and trim, had an engaging smile, and at fifty, still had a full head of dark brown hair which he kept a little longer than you might expect of someone in his position. He was a career prosecutor, having risen through the ranks quickly, becoming the head of the office ten years ago. Although politics had skewed his moral vision over the years, and the duties of administration had taken him more and more out of the courtroom, he had been, and still was, a very good trial lawyer. We shook hands and exchanged greetings. "Daddy helping you out on this one, huh?"

His smug smile was infuriating. I pondered an appropriate comeback, perhaps pointing out that he was the one with two assistants in tow, but instead, I said, "You want to just stipulate to a reasonable bond amount? You know my guy's not going anywhere."

He looked at me briefly, then at Goodwin, then back to me. There was that smug smile again. "I don't think so."

I didn't either. I nodded at my adversary and pretended to be interested in the papers in front of me as the prosecutor turned and headed back to his table.

Some of the reporters began to converge on us. The bailiffs were swift, however, in blocking their path. Back off, they were told, or they would be escorted from the courtroom. The reporters begrudgingly complied.

One of the bailiffs cocked his head toward his shoulder, listening, then said, "The judge is on her way." This prompted everyone to move over to their respective spots just as the door swung open, and another bailiff shouted, "All rise." The judge walked quickly toward the bench area. "The Circuit Court in and for Leon County, Florida is now in session." She climbed the four steps, then pulled back the large leather chair. "The Honorable Eleanor Mitchell presiding." She placed her paperwork on the bench, thanked the bailiff, then, as she eased herself into the chair, said to the audience, "Please be seated." Everyone did.

From her perch on the dais, barely visible above the desk top in front of her, Judge Mitchell surveyed the courtroom. She was not a judge in this circuit and all of us were probably strangers to her, but she looked at home. She glanced over at the deputy clerk and said, "Call the first case."

There was, of course, only one case on the docket, but the clerk dutifully rose and read the case number and the style.

"Counsel, state your appearances, please."

Lipton rose. "Bill Lipton for the State, along with Jamie Burns and Marsha Lynch." The other two lawyers stood and bowed slightly at the judge, who in turn nodded, then looked over at the defense table.

I stood. "I'm Kate Marston, Your Honor. I'll be representing Judge Goodwin."

If the judge made the connection to my father, her fellow judge with the same last name, she didn't show it. She looked out over the courtroom. One of the press photographers snapped a photo, the click of the camera seemingly like a cannon in the silence. She looked over at him and held the stare for at least ten seconds. The man dropped the camera down by his side and cast his eyes in that direction as well.

The judge finally looked down and began reading, saying, "Give me just a minute while I look over the paperwork." A hush fell over the room and the only sound heard was that of pages being turned. Of course, in a case of this nature, and of such high profile, I felt certain the judge had already read every scrap of paper having to do with the case, and had a pretty good idea of what she would do this morning. This reading of the papers in court was just for show. After a very long minute, Judge Mitchell looked up, surveyed the courtroom once more, then focused on Goodwin.

"Mr. Goodwin, I'm sure you are aware that the purposes of the proceedings this morning are to advise you of the charge against you, confirm that there is probable cause for the charge, appoint an attorney if you are unable to afford one, and to address the issue of bail."

Lipton rose quickly from his seat. "Your Honor. This man is charged with First Degree Murder." His tone of voice suggested incredulity as he added, "Surely, you are not going to consider bail in this case."

Mitchell, who had not taken her gaze from Goodwin while Lipton spoke, now turned her attention to the prosecutor and fixed upon him a glare that seemed capable of melting steel. She didn't speak for several seconds and the prosecutor began to shift on his feet, though he did not avert his eyes from those of the judge. Finally, she leaned forward slightly in her chair and spoke. "Mr. Lipton, I don't know how you folks usually do things around here, but where I come from, a lawyer does not interrupt a judge when she is speaking."

"Sorry, Judge but . . ."

Mitchell held up her hand to stop him. "There you go again, interrupting me." She waited several seconds, perhaps to let the message sink in, perhaps to keep herself under control. At any rate, Lipton remained mute, and she continued. "Not only is it unprofessional, it's just downright rude." Her tone of voice, tinged with a Southern accent, suggested a mother correcting a child. "Now, here's how this is supposed to work. When I want to hear from you on something, I'll let you know. If I don't indicate by word or act that I want to hear from you, that's your cue to be quiet, and wait your turn. Are we clear on that point, Mr. Lipton?" When the man did not immediately respond she said, "This is your time to speak, Mr. Lipton. Do you understand what I am saying?"

"Yes, Judge," came the terse reply.

"Good. Now, please sit down." As he did so, she turned her attention back to Goodwin. "Now, as I was saying, you are no doubt familiar with the process, but for the record, you have been charged with First Degree Murder. It has been made by Grand Jury Indictment so probable cause is not an issue. You also have retained private counsel to represent you, so there is no need to address that issue, either. We come, then, to the question of bail." She turned toward the prosecution table. "Does the State wish to be heard on this issue?"

Lipton rose and began to speak, choosing his words carefully. "Your Honor, the defendant is charged with the most serious crime we have—murder in the first degree. He faces death by lethal injection if he is found guilty. He has every reason to flee the jurisdiction of the court if he is freed, and he will have access to destroy or conceal evidence, tamper with witnesses and otherwise impede the investigation and prosecution of the case. The State of Florida demands that he be held without bail pending trial."

When the prosecutor sat down, Mitchell looked over toward me. "Ms. Marston?"

I slowly pushed back my chair and stood. "It is true that Judge Goodwin is not entitled to bail as a matter of right, but neither are you prohibited from granting bail." I paused. "And you should," I said. "This is not the ordinary murder case, nor is my client the typical defendant. He is a sitting judge, a respected member of the community."

"Not anymore," Lipton muttered under his breath.

I looked over at him and then to the judge, who, sensing some violation of protocol, but apparently having not heard what Lipton said, glowered in his direction. The prosecutor looked down, pretending to be writing something on the legal pad in front of him. I turned back to the judge.

"He has spent his professional career in this community. He has raised his family here. He and his wife of over thirty years own their home and other real estate in Tallahassee. They have two children. His roots in this community are broad and deep. The evidence against him is weak and completely circumstantial. We look forward to the opportunity to defend against this charge. Judge Goodwin is neither a flight risk nor a danger to the community."

I stepped over a couple of feet and put my hand on Goodwin's shoulder. "My client is paid a respectable salary as a judge, but he is not a rich man. The cost of his legal defense will be significant, and he is simply not in a position to be able to post a large bond. Nor is one necessary. I'm asking you to release him on his own recognizance."

Lipton appeared genuinely exasperated by my suggestion, almost gagging on it, though he wisely waited for a nod from Mitchell before responding.

"That's just preposterous, Judge. And it's insulting to the fine citizens who served selflessly on the grand jury. The fact that he is a sitting judge is an aggravating factor, not a mitigating one. For you to even consider such a request sends a message to the average citizen that the law is not equally applied if you are one of the chosen who wear the black robe."

Judge Mitchell hesitated several moments. When she spoke, she paid homage to the seriousness of the charge, but also pointed out, eloquently, that Goodwin was still presumed to be innocent at law and that we should not have a rush to judgment. She set a bond of $500,000, required the judge to turn in his passport, and prohibited any contact with the victim's family or any witness, except through his attorney. "Any other matters to be addressed this morning?"

Lipton seemed stunned. As he hesitated, I stood. "A couple of things, Your Honor, if you don't mind."

"Yes?"

"I need to have access to the alleged crime scene."

Judge Mitchell looked over at the prosecutor. "Mr. Lipton?"

"I'm not sure the forensics folks are done there yet, Judge. Besides, we can't run the risk of some destruction or alteration of possible evidence, then have the defense try to use it at trial against us. There are dozens of very detailed, thorough photographs of the residence. She can have those in the normal discovery procedure. There are also privacy concerns, Judge. The victim's parents don't want the defendant or his lawyer pawing through Ms. Castillo's personal items."

"The death occurred three weeks ago," I said. "It's hard to imagine there could be more processing of the residence. The residence is evidence just as much as anything else collected in this case. All I'm asking is to be able to view that evidence."

The judge looked at the prosecutor. "Find out if the forensics team is through with the place, which I suspect they are, or find out when they will be, and make arrangements for Ms. Marston to get in. And you can have an officer stand by if you'd like," she said, tilting her head down slightly and looking at him over her glasses, "to make sure no one messes with anything." She looked back to me. "What was the other matter, Ms. Marston?"

I cleared my throat. "The local judiciary has seen the obvious conflict of interest and has gotten Your Honor appointed specially to preside over this case. I suggest that there is a similar conflict of interest for the State Attorney. I assume that Mr. Lipton will be asking the Governor to appoint a special prosecutor for the case, in order to avoid the perception of bias. If I need to file a formal motion for disqualification, I can do that, but I thought I should go ahead and bring it up now."

Lipton had stood during my comments, anxious to respond, but wisely refraining from interrupting. He had apparently learned his lesson. Now, with a nod from Mitchell, he said, "Ms. Marston can file her motion, but I have no intention of shirking my duty to the citizens who elected me, and I am confident Your Honor will deny such a ridiculous motion. The citizens can rest assured that there will no favoritism toward this defendant."

"I didn't mean to imply that Mr. Lipton would be biased in favor of Judge Goodwin, Your Honor. My concern lies in the opposite direction, as just confirmed by Mr. Lipton's statement."

Mitchell looked at me for a few seconds. "You may file any motions you wish, and I will then consider them, but for the time being, let's both sides dial down the rhetoric. I will warn both of you that I expect you to focus on the case and not on personalities." She looked from lawyer to lawyer.

Both of us nodded dutifully in agreement, but neither of us meant it. Not for an instant.

Chapter Ten

The judge left the bench and the bailiffs cleared the courtroom. I spoke briefly with my client, and told him to call me when he had posted bond. Marci and Robyn were ushered out the side door, and I walked out the public entrance to speak with the press, as promised.

Bill Lipton was there, in the rotunda area, flanked by his assistants, preening for the cameras and clearly enjoying the attention. I stood there, just outside the courtroom entrance, watching for several seconds with grudging admiration as the prosecutor postured and blustered about the case. As the reporters noticed me, though, they began to abandon the prosecutor in favor of the untapped source, the reticent defense attorney. One by one they moved away from Lipton until he was left with only the one reporter who had asked the last question. With a frown that turned into a wry grin, he nodded in my direction. I nodded back.

My general philosophy in terms of speaking with the press is that less is more, but one had to be flexible, ready to adjust strategy when necessary. Unless and until the judge entered a gag order, I couldn't let Lipton's statements and innuendos go unchallenged. I needed to show him I could play this game too, and I would not be playing defense.

Looking out over the small group in front of me, I recognized a reporter who covered the courts for the *Tampa Bay Times*, but mostly it was local print and television reporters. The two cameras aimed in my direction bore the markings of the ABC and CBS affiliates. I held up my hand in response to the barrage of questions hurled at me and waited for the relative hush before proceeding. Then I cleared my throat and spoke into the two microphones held out in front of me.

"Judge Goodwin," I began, "looks forward to having his day in court.

We are anxious to have the opportunity to challenge the so-called evidence the State relies on. What we will find is that there has been a rush to judgment before all the facts were known, before all the evidence was carefully analyzed, and before all possible theories were considered."

"Ms. Marston, do you think the State Attorney's office is out to get Judge Goodwin because of his politics?"

I turned my attention to the questioner, James Whiting. He was the owner, publisher, editor and chief reporter for the *Capital City Beacon*, a small weekly that catered to the African-American community. He and Goodwin had been friends and political allies for many years, and he was no friend of Bill Lipton. His objectivity in reporting the news was never assumed. It was nice, however, to get such a set-up question.

I weighed my words carefully. "It is no secret that Mr. Lipton and my client have been on opposite sides of some controversial issues in the past, and that he strongly opposed the judge's appointment to the bench. One would hope that he would not let his virulent opposition to the judge's political views cloud his judgment in this case." I hesitated, waiting for the implication to set in. "But, and without wishing to impute malice to anybody, I think Mr. Lipton has looked at the evidence and seen what he wanted to see."

The other reporters attempted some follow-ups on the subject, but I deflected their questions. Less was more. There were the expected inquiries about the suggested sexual relationship between the victim and Goodwin, the e-mails and other specific items in the probable cause affidavit.

"I am going to withhold further comment on any specific allegations at this time, to avoid the sort of wild speculation that has gotten us to this point. We will answer these charges fully and completely, at the proper time and place. And I am confident that my client will be exonerated in a court of law, and in the court of public opinion."

"Ms. Marston?"

I looked over at the speaker, who was off to my right and back a couple of rows. Quentin Martin—everyone called him Marty—had been covering the courts for several years for the *Tallahassee Republican*. I didn't like him and didn't know anyone else who did, either. He was obnoxious and his reporting was biased, but he seemed to have a nose for scandal and he could write a good story. The kind that sold papers. I frowned inwardly but gave him a neutral face. "Yes?"

"Do you think you are up to the task of handling such a high-profile murder case?" Before I could answer, he continued. "I mean, you didn't handle murder cases when you were with the Public Defender's Office, and it's been several years now since you left there. I understand you are only working part time now, right?"

Hush and reporter are two words rarely paired, but a hush of sorts did fall over the other reporters then. Some, I suspected, couldn't believe the brashness, the rudeness displayed, while others were wishing they had asked the question first. All were anxious now to hear my answer.

"As usual, Marty, you don't have your facts straight." There were snickers from some of his colleagues. "I handled several murder cases when I was with the PD's office. I've been gone from there a little more than two years, not several, during which I have worked as a litigator at a private firm, and now in my own practice, handling criminal cases regularly."

It was an exaggeration, perhaps, but not too much. "It appears that Judge Goodwin has confidence in me, which should be all that matters." I hesitated, then added, "That being said, I do plan to bring on co-counsel in the case."

"Who will it be?" Marty again.

"That hasn't been finalized yet, so I won't say at this time. But that's not important anyway. What is important is that an innocent man has been charged with a very serious crime. Whether he will be convicted in the eyes of the public will depend in large part on how the press reports the story. It may be too much to ask that our prosecutor be objective under the circumstances, but I don't think it's too much to expect of you all. I hope you are willing to be skeptical of what those in authority tell you, look to see if there is indeed a fire underneath the smoke, before you allow the reputation of a fine jurist to be destroyed by baseless accusations."

I looked out over the faces before me, searching for some sign that my little speech on journalistic ethics might have had some effect, but I had the feeling that my words had fallen like raindrops on a group of people holding up umbrellas. They were aware it was raining but remained untouched by it, mistaking lack of analytical thought for objectivity.

"Now, if you will excuse me," I said, making my way past the group, "got to get back to work."

I took the stairs down to the first floor and out onto Monroe Street. The lack of sleep was beginning to catch up with me, but the air was cold and crisp, the mid-morning sun bright; it did much to refresh, and help clear my mind. I stopped into Goody's Deli, grabbed a coffee and bagel to go, then headed across the street to the Rose building.

Marty's questioning of my competence had stung, but it was a legitimate point. My response had been defensive, prideful, and not completely honest. In fact, although I was confident in my abilities, I was not so arrogant as to think it was a good idea to try a murder case by myself. There was just too much at stake. To paraphrase that great philosopher, Dirty Harry, a wise woman knows her limitations."

And I had, in fact, decided on co-counsel. My first call after leaving the Goodwin home the night before was to my parents. My second call was to the attorney I thought best fit the bill, Ted Stevens. After he gloated about correctly guessing who the client was early on, he gave me a tentative yes, subject to client approval, and we agreed to meet after First Appearance to discuss the details.

And Goodwin did approve, with conditions. He insisted that I be the public face of the defense, the lead attorney and spokesperson. "This is why I came to you, Katie. I think it would be to my advantage to have you alone in the courtroom against the might of the government. But if you want to bring on co-counsel, that's okay with me, so long as I have final approval of the person and it doesn't cost me any additional fee."

I thought his conditions reasonable, and said so. I understood the tactical advantage of the David versus Goliath approach. I also understood why he might want a woman as the defense attorney when the victim was a woman. I felt that I could accomplish both objectives with a co-counsel sufficiently skilled and experienced to be of real assistance, yet secure enough in himself not to pout about being second chair to me. Ted Stevens fit that description, I said.

Goodwin agreed.

So now, balancing my coffee, bagel and briefcase, I opened the etched glass door and entered the law offices of Morganstein and Stevens, which also housed my professional home.

Ted was standing, speaking on his phone, when I paused just outside his office. He smiled and motioned for me to come in as he continued talking, turning to face the window. I stepped inside but remained standing, trying not to eavesdrop on the conversation and instead taking an inventory of the man's office.

In the corner, next to the coat rack was the cane, rosewood, with a rubber tip and handle. A large bay window centered the north wall, allowing a view out onto College Avenue. Framed photos of his daughter were prominently displayed on shelves behind his desk, which also contained other family shots, including one of a teenaged Ted with his parents and his brother. On the walls, other photos captured sunrise on a beach, an eagle perched in a pine tree, a stark, black and white of an oysterman, upright in his boat, working the tongs. I walked over to study this one a little closer, noting the weathered clothes and skin, cigarette dangling from his mouth. A black and white poster of Marlon

Brando from *The Godfather* was propped up against a wall, its bottom resting on a table. Below it, on the table, was a framed black and white photo of Robert DeNiro as the younger Don Corleone in the sequel. I remembered the *Godfather* items from Ted's days with the State Attorney's Office, where I would meet with him to negotiate plea agreements for my clients. At one of those early meetings, when Ted first learned that I, too, was a fan of these classic films—I and II only we both agreed, not III—he had looked at me, a little surprised, then his eyes registered a new appreciation. "Lot of wisdom there, life-lesson-type stuff," he said.

"You mean, like if you can't persuade a person with logic and reason, you use violence and intimidation? Kill them if they really piss you off?" Ted shook his head slowly from side to side. "Katie, Katie. You're missing the big picture. It's about respect, family, and loyalty. It's about having principles, living by a code. Sure, the consequences of violating that code can be harsh, even brutal, but the underlying premise is as firm a moral base as you will find anywhere."

"So, when Michael has Fredo whacked, how does that fit into the family and loyalty thing?"

He shook his head again, looked at me sympathetically, like a teacher with a student who is having difficulty grasping a concept. "Sure, Fredo was his brother, but he betrayed the family. He broke the code. Plus, Michael waited until their mother was dead."

"Very considerate."

"Very respectful."

I raised my hands. "Okay, consigliore, I meant no disrespect."

He had frowned then, Brando style, but promptly accepted the plea deal I suggested. We have been fast friends ever since.

Now, as I looked around his office, I noted that the usual clutter was still as pronounced as ever. There were files, volumes of *Southern Reporter* and other law books, magazines, mail, and loose papers stacked on the desk. More were on the credenza, and the small library table against the wall to my left. Ted had once described his unique filing system to me as ordered chaos. I had agreed with half of that description.

A few seconds later, Ted finished his phone call and turned to face me. "Hey, Kate," he said, smiling, "sorry to keep you waiting." His dress shirt was tight against his chest, the sleeves rolled up on his forearms, his tie loosened around the neck. The way he stood, with his arms crossed, accentuated the muscles around his shoulders and biceps. On his left side, his eye drooped just a bit, and his mouth turned down slightly—the lingering effect of his injury—but disappeared completely when he smiled at me. "Have a seat," he said, as he plopped down in his chair.

I took the chair across the desk from him, then pointed to the photo of the old, weathered oysterman on the wall. "Just curious. This is you, right?"

He looked at the photo, then turned back to me. "In my earlier, more youthful days."

I smiled, then opened my briefcase, took out a file folder and handed it to Ted. "I made you a copy of the search warrant and other paperwork I have."

"Thanks," he said. "I followed the First Appearance on the Internet. They were streaming live coverage. You handled yourself well."

"You think so?"

"I do."

I didn't know if he was sincere or just trying to make me feel good, but either way, I appreciated it. I told him about the impromptu news conference, about Marty's jab, and my response.

Ted smiled. "That asshole. You handled it just right."

"At least I didn't hit him."

"That would have been more satisfying no doubt. But not so prudent." Ted had actually smacked the obnoxious reporter square in the face when they sparred in another case several years before. Ted had not been charged—there were no independent witnesses to the event—but he had apologized to avoid a civil suit. It will probably make Marty's day when he learns Ted is co-counsel.

I waited while Ted read the documents before him. When he was done, I repeated what I could remember of Goodwin's account. Ted took it all in, not interrupting. When I finished, I said, "What do you think? You still okay to work together on this?"

He nodded. "Of course."

"Great." I repeated the expectation of the client that I would be the lead attorney, the public face of the defense team. I also voiced my opinion that it ought to be the other way around, that he was the more experienced lawyer and should be the lead."

"Bullshit. You don't need anybody holding your hand, Katie, and I think it's good strategy to have you up front and center. I can be there to bounce ideas off of, offer a second opinion, do leg work and legal research, trial preparation. Whatever you want."

"We should discuss fee arrangements."

"The thrill of working with you would be payment enough for me."

"In that case, you're welcome."

"I wasn't finished."

"Oh, sorry."

"What I was going to say was that even though I would be content with the more intangible rewards, my partner has a different perspective."

"Man cannot live by thrill alone?"

"Exactly. Paul can be downright crass when it comes to making money from the practice of law—and he's very good at it, I might add."

I told him what Goodwin had agreed to pay me. He would pay additionally for costs, but not additional attorney fees. I suggested we split the fee fifty-fifty.

He shook his head. "You should get the lion's share because it's your case. The client came to you. That's the way it works around here anyway, and why Paul makes a lot more money than I do."

"All right," I said, and suggested an alternative percentage split.

He shrugged, frowned. "That's more than fair."

"Oh, don't worry, you'll earn it."

He smiled, hesitated. "And uh, Katie . . ."

"Yes?" I prompted.

"I was wondering if, uh, maybe you might want to go out sometime?"

I arched my eyebrows at him. "You mean like a date?"

"We don't have to call it a date," he said quickly, "if it makes you uncomfortable. Just two friends getting together for dinner or a movie. You know, something like that."

Sweat seemed to form instantly on my skin, and I could feel my cheeks begin to color. His proposition had taken me completely by surprise, my response an attempt to gain some time. Of course, it would be a date, regardless of what we called it. I did a quick mental check-off of the pros and cons.

On the plus side, I was flattered, and it awoke in me feelings for Ted that I had subconsciously suppressed—until now. The man was good looking, smart and funny, with an irreverence I could appreciate. And his shyness just now was endearing, made him even more attractive. He had some baggage, but who didn't. On the negative side, work-place romances rarely worked out, and complicated things even more when they fell apart. I was also aware of Ted's flirtatious manner, and his lack of fidelity to his previous wife. Been there, done that.

And then there was the booze, and at times other drugs. I didn't need that complication either. He had told me that was in the past, that he no longer had an abuse problem. Maybe. I hadn't seen outward signs of obvious impairment in some time, but that didn't necessarily mean anything. He could just be good at hiding it, as were a lot of functioning alcoholics. And there was always a risk of relapse anyway.

I began to rationalize. Get over yourself, already. He just wants to go out with you. It's not like the guy is asking you to marry him. He's single. You're single. What's the big deal? I wasn't sure how to add up the pros and cons, but after several long, awkward seconds, my head overruled my heart.

"I like you, Ted."

"But?" He had caught the hesitancy in my tone.

"I need to keep our relationship professional," I said, "especially while we're working together on this case."

"So, after the case is resolved?"

"Maybe."

"Is that like when I tell my kid maybe, and it really means no?"

"It means maybe."

He smiled. "Good." After a brief silence, he leaned forward slightly in his chair and said, "So, you think we can get a quick plea agreement, resolve this case quickly?"

I couldn't help but smile.

Chapter Eleven

I pulled off Riggins Road and into the Eastwood Office Plaza, found a spot in the shade of a magnolia tree, then headed into the building which housed the offices of my aunt and doctor, Mary Beth Winston. The waiting room was not crowded, a woman and child and an elderly couple the only others present. The girl stared at me as I walked over to the receptionist and signed in, then made my way to one of the chairs. I looked over in her direction and gave her a smile. She quickly looked away.

I picked up a magazine and started turning the pages aimlessly. A few minutes passed. The nurse stuck her head into the waiting room, called the elderly couple back. A short time later, the mom and daughter were called back as well, and I was alone in the waiting room. Suddenly feeling very tired, too tired to concentrate on reading anything, I put the magazine down, removed my glasses and slid down in the chair, extending my long legs out in front of me. I then leaned my head back, closed my eyes, and let my mind drift.

A lot had happened in the past several days. As I predicted, the news coverage of the Castillo case had quickly gone from local to state-wide to national. The news articles ran the gamut from straight factual reporting to the sensational, salacious, speculative pieces that seem so popular these days, complete with several provocative photos of the deceased.

I searched the Internet for any mention of the case or the players, telling myself it was because I might pick up information I didn't otherwise have. A snooping reporter might ferret out something, get someone to talk, give me some idea of what others were doing or thinking. To be honest, though, there was also a little vanity involved.

Okay, a lot of vanity.

The local paper ran a profile article on me, an embarrassingly nice fluff piece, mentioning my college basketball days, and my coincidental connection to the firm at which Elena had worked. The article tied in with my dad and his possible appointment to the Florida Supreme Court, with photos of us both and several complimentary quotes from lawyers about father and daughter.

The letters to the editor and comments to blogs had been evenly divided between those who were sure the prosecution was part of a vast right-wing conspiracy to bring down a judge they didn't like, and others who were ready to string him up. Michael Morton, the evangelical pastor of one of Tallahassee's largest fundamentalist churches, and an outspoken critic of Goodwin, had fanned the flames with a 'My View' column in the *Tallahassee Republican* two days before.

The angry pastor reminded readers of some of Goodwin's more unpopular clients and cases over the years, writing that the judge "and those of his ilk" were the primary reason the country had lost its moral compass, painting him as another degenerate politician in the mold of Bill Clinton. That Goodwin was still receiving a paycheck was an outrage, he declared.

The number of hate letters and e-mails I received in the two days thereafter increased considerably, but the private messages of support had been encouraging. That the latter numbered fewer than the former disappointed me, but did not surprise me. Hatred, mixed with zealotry, was almost always the more powerful motivator, more likely to have a public and vocal manifestation. Those who advocated respect and tolerance for differing views, who supported the rule of law and the notion of fair play, were, by the very nature of their beliefs, at a disadvantage against those who adhered to neither.

The editorial in the paper that same day, however, had been a big boost. Relatively balanced, it did not question the good faith of the State Attorney in bringing the charges, but cautioned the public not to assume anything. "We don't know if he is or is not guilty, but we abhor the rush to judgment that seems to have afflicted some in our community."

"Bingo!" I said aloud when I read this line. The seed of the defense theme had been planted in the public psyche.

"Katie."

"Yes," I said, vacantly, still inhabiting that nether world to which I had surrendered for a precious few minutes. The second call of my name brought me all the way back. "Hey, Nancy," I said, focusing on the nurse.

"You want to come on back?"

I put my glasses back on, stood and dutifully followed her to an examining room.

Nancy had been with my aunt for many years. She was efficient but not overly friendly. She had me stand on the scales, recorded my height and weight in her chart. She took my blood pressure. "One fifteen over seventy," Nancy said, with what seemed like grudging approval. She then left me to my thoughts.

They weren't much company.

Fortunately, my aunt presented herself shortly. She knocked lightly on the door, then entered before I could say anything.

Mary Beth Winston was a tall, sturdy woman, on the same eye level with me, and with a similar body type, though with more meat on her bones. She wore her hair shoulder length, pulled back from her face and kept in place with a barrette. She smiled, gave me a hug, then motioned for me to have a seat on the examining table. "So, how is my favorite niece?"

"I'm Kate, Aunt Mary Beth. You're thinking of my sister, Sarah. She's up at Dartmouth, remember?"

The woman looked at me then, pretending to be surprised, and confused. "Oh, so you are," she said, playing along. "Well, close enough. Still family." She gave me a smile. "So, how are you, Katie?"

"Fine."

She looked at me as if she wasn't so sure. "Well, I'm just glad to finally get you in for your physical. What's it been, almost two years?"

I gave her a sheepish grin. "I've been busy."

My aunt gave me a doubtful look. "Anyway, let's take a look, shall we?"

She was slow, methodical in her exam, all the while asking me questions, making conversation. She had a great bedside manner, always took her time, and made you feel as if you were the only patient she had. "So," she asked after a bit, "anything adding stress in your life these days?"

How about an emotionally draining divorce? How about the biggest case of my career? "Same old thing," I said.

"You exercising regularly?"

I nodded. "Still running pretty often, a little basketball."

"Uh huh. Eating healthy too?"

I shrugged. We both knew the answer. Aunt Mary Beth let it pass, and changed the subject. "Seeing anyone?"

An image of Ted Stevens popped into my head at her words. "Not really," I said. Friends had set me up a couple of times, but nothing came of it, I told her. My aunt frowned but didn't ask for details and I didn't volunteer any.

"I hear your Dad may get appointed to the Supreme Court."

"If they want the best person for the job."

"How's your mom?"

"Fine." When my aunt frowned, I said, "What?"

She shrugged. "She seems a little on edge these days. You haven't noticed anything?"

My mother was sometimes described by family members as temperamental, or excitable. We Marstons do like our euphemisms. In fact, undiagnosed bi-polar was more like it, most often manifested in manic behavior: going for days with little sleep, washing clothes or vacuuming in the middle of the night, that sort of thing. She could also fly off the handle on occasion, and with little warning that it was coming. Growing up around her, my sisters and I had learned how to gauge her moods, navigate around the land mines fairly well.

I shook my head. "Not really, but then again, I grew up with her. Normal is a relative term."

"Probably nothing," she said. "Just FYI." She paused, then changed gears. "Is she working on something for the Garden Club competition?" The woman busied herself with cleaning up, trying to appear only mildly interested in the subject, but I knew better. My mother and aunt were both avid gardeners and very competitive about it. One of them routinely took first or second place in the flower arranging competition each spring.

"Yeah, I said, "she's working on something real special this year. Top secret. She said to tell you she's going to kick your ass again this year."

My mother would never have been so crude in her choice of language, of course, but I felt I had more accurately articulated my mother's true feelings about the subject.

"Well, she's entitled to her opinion," my aunt responded neutrally, with a half-smile on her lips, then changed topics. "How's Maggie?"

"She's good."

"Is she handling the divorce okay?"

"Yeah, pretty much. I mean it's hard on everybody, but she's pretty resilient."

"The shared parenting working out?"

I said we were working together okay, but when my aunt probed, and once I started, the feelings of anger and frustration flowed from me like a river. The older woman listened patiently, nodding from time to time as I unburdened myself of the emotional baggage that had been weighing me down for months. My aunt had a talent for this, and I treasured the safe haven she had always provided. When all the built-up tension had been released, like air from a tire, my aunt changed gears again.

"Kind of surprised you would take Renny's case."

The look that passed between us then was a reminder that my confidant knew what I had never told my parents about Renny Goodwin. I did not respond immediately. When I did, I turned to face the woman directly, paused, and then in my best Al Pacino voice said, "It's not personal, Aunt Mary Beth. It's strictly business."

My aunt didn't seem to understand the *Godfather* reference, but she gave me a small smile. I asked her if she had seen the 'My View' column from Reverend Morton.

"That self-righteous, hypocritical clown."

"Not one of my favorites, either."

"Don't let that jerk get to you, Katie. Nobody takes him seriously."

I shook my head. "I've got a lot of hate mail that says otherwise."

"Let me re-phrase. Nobody with any sense takes him seriously."

"That may be, but—"

"Oh, he'll stir up the faithful for a while, but the boiling hatred and mean spiritedness will ease back to its usual simmering level soon. Just don't let him bait you into anything." She put her hand on my shoulder and seemed about to say something else on the subject when the vibrator on my phone went off.

I raised my hand in apology, pulled the phone from my pocket and checked the screen. My stomach twisted involuntarily. It was from Craig. It seemed that even on neutral subjects, my conversations with him these days were never pleasant. "Mind if I take this? It's from Craig. Might be important."

Aunt Mary Beth shook her head in mild disapproval but said, "Sure. We're pretty much finished here anyway. When you're dressed, come see me before you leave." As she made her way to the door, I put the phone to my ear.

"Hey, Craig." I tried to sound, if not cheerful, at least neutral.

There was a brief pause on the other end, then, "Listen, something's come up. I'm not going to be able to pick up Maggie after school." When I said nothing, he continued. "I've got to run over to Panama City for Pop. Pick up a car for a customer."

I could feel the blood rising to my face. "This is not fair, Craig, not for me and certainly not for Maggie. You know I have an afternoon class at the law school today. It's only one day a week I ask you to pick her up from school. Why can't you arrange your schedule to be able to do it?"

"I can't help it, Katie. I've got responsibilities around here."

Like I didn't. "You have responsibilities to your daughter too." There was silence on the other end. "Why don't you take her with you," I said. "She'd probably like that."

"That won't work, I'm afraid. I'm meeting a guy for dinner while I'm there. I probably won't be back till midnight."

"And who's going to look after her until I get off work?"

"I was hoping you could pick her up. She could sit in your class."

I sighed, loud enough for him to hear. "But she has basketball practice after school, and by the time she's finished, I'll be in the middle of my class."

"It wouldn't hurt her to miss one practice. I mean, it didn't seem to bother you a second ago when you wanted me to take her to Panama City with me." He paused. "But don't worry about it. I'll work out something."

My mind raced over the possible arrangements my ex-husband might contemplate. He'd probably get one of the office staff, who were always asked to do things well beyond their job descriptions. Maybe his mother, or one of the auto mechanics. Whatever was most convenient. Craig would not be too particular. Or worse, he'd have, that woman, playing mom to my child. The thought made me sick to my stomach. "Never mind. I'll take care of it."

"You sure?"

"Yeah."

"Great. Thanks Katie," he said much too quickly for me to conclude anything other than that he had been supremely confident in my response, and hating him a little more for it. "Tell Maggie I'll make it up to her." Then he hung up the phone without further comment.

"You tell her," I muttered, as if he was still on the line. If I was mad at my former husband, though, I wasn't exactly happy with myself, either. I'd let him manipulate me again. For about thirty seconds, I sat there, willing my blood pressure down, considering my alternatives. Finally, I cleared my phone and punched in the speed dial number. After the third ring, I heard the familiar voice on the other end.

"Hello?"

"Hey, Mom. It's Kate. I need a favor."

Chapter Twelve

My parents' house was located on Crestview Avenue, perched on a small hill overlooking Winthrop Park. They had made additions and renovations to it over the years, but the ranch style structure remained relatively modest for the area. It was the extensive and meticulously maintained landscaping that raised it above the ordinary, and gave it that charming, picture postcard look, the result of my mother's imagination, and the conscripted labor of her husband and children.

I parked in the shade of two heritage oaks, whose limbs spread out over the circular driveway. When I opened the car door, the cold air rushed in to devour the heated space in a matter of seconds. I made my way quickly to the front door, unlocked it and stepped inside.

"Hello. Anybody home?" No response. I stood there for several seconds, listening. "Mom? Maggie?" Still no response. I looked at my watch, frowned and called out again as I headed toward the kitchen, but it was obvious that I was alone.

My path took me through the formal living room which, like the yard, was carefully and tastefully ordered. It was rarely used for any normal activity by its occupants, but rather functioned as a museum or photo gallery, filled with family portraits and photos, various awards and memorabilia. I paused beside its centerpiece, a custom-made pecan cabinetry unit with sections of glass-enclosed shelving that covered most of the south wall.

There were numerous photographs of me and my two sisters, spanning our entire lives, chronologically arranged, the essence of our personalities crystallized there: Rebecca as homecoming queen; cheerleader; being crowned Miss Florida. Sarah, singing in the chorus; playing the lead in the high school production of *Taming of the Shrew*;

standing outside the entrance to Dartmouth College, where she now taught literature. Me, at about five years old, in an ill-fitting dance outfit; with the rest of the youth soccer team; at the free-throw line during the state championship game my senior year in high school.

Funny how some siblings have a marked resemblance to one parent or the other, while some are an obvious mix. My eldest sister, Rebecca, for example, was the spitting image of our mom, same naturally blonde hair, big pouting lips, blue eyes, voluptuous body. Sarah was a very pleasing combination of both parents. Hers was a wistful, understated beauty that seemed not only effortless but quite unintended. I, on the other hand, looked very much like my father, which wouldn't be so bad if I had been born a boy. My dad was not bad looking, maybe even handsome in a way, but the angular facial features, the tall, gangly body type didn't work so well on me. I was certainly not beauty pageant material, no matter how hard my mother tried. And she tried hard.

A reminder of those days beckoned to me from across the hall in the den, where the upright piano centered the far wall. I think it was the Springtime Tallahassee pageant, my sophomore year when my mother finally realized that you just can't fit a square peg in a round hole. I was about twenty pounds lighter then, and, as the boys liked to put it, flat as a board. Mom suggested, subtly, that the talent portion of the contest was my best bet, which in my case was playing the piano. I selected Beethoven's *Moonlight Sonata*, a piece I had practiced forever and could play well.

Just not that night. It wasn't awful, but it seemed that way to me. I left the stage on the verge of tears, humiliated. My mother never entered me in another beauty contest again. And I have played the piano maybe ten times in the past twenty years.

Still, that upright called to me, and I crossed the room slowly, stood in front of the instrument for a moment, then pulled out the bench and sat down. I lifted my hands and held them poised above the keys for a few seconds, then began playing, a Nat King Cole tune I retrieved from somewhere in my memory banks. Somehow, my fingers still knew where to go. I was just finishing when I heard the back door close.

"Hey, Mom!" Maggie ran over and wrapped her arms around me as I rose and stepped away from the piano.

"Hey, sport. What have you and Grandma been doing?"

"We've been shopping for dinner," my mother answered, putting two canvass bags on the kitchen counter and smiling in my direction. Mom was pushing sixty but you'd never know it to look at her. Although she was not athletic, she generally observed a healthy diet, watched her weight and worked out regularly at the gym—careful not to draw a sweat. As a consequence, she had the face, the skin and the figure of a much younger woman. "How are you, Mary Katherine?"

I was tempted to curtsey in response to her formality, but I just said, "I'm fine, Mom."

She looked at me as if she thought that was doubtful, then she began taking items out of one of the bags. "I knew you wouldn't have anything planned for dinner, what with the scheduling mix up."

Scheduling mix up was a nice, but inaccurate way to put it, but I kept the thought to myself.

"I was hoping you and Maggie would join us for dinner."

I couldn't resist a small smile. It had taken some doing to train my mother to use the name "Maggie" I preferred, rather than the more formal one that appears on her birth certificate.

"But it's such a beautiful name," she would insist when corrected. "I don't know why you would give such a beautiful name to a child if you weren't going to use it."

No surprise from the woman who still insisted on calling me and my sisters by our formal names: Rebecca Anne, Sarah Lynn and Mary Katherine. Of course, what she conveniently forgot was that it was she who lobbied so hard for Margaret Anne. "A good, respectable family name," she had said, When I expressed reservations, she said, "You can call her what you want, but she should have a proper name." And even though Mom eventually acceded to our wishes "to avoid confusing the child" she still seemed to hesitate ever so slightly when she said "Maggie," as if to acknowledge the involuntary nature of the breach of etiquette.

"We're going to have hamburgers and French fries!" Maggie said, holding both of my hands in hers.

"Sounds yummy." I looked over at my mother, the woman who was generally very picky about her diet, always getting on to me for not feeding my child, and myself, more healthy food. The woman gave me a shrug of the shoulders that suggested she was invoking the grandchild exception, which provides immunity for such hypocritical conduct. "You didn't have to make us dinner," I said.

"Nonsense. And I simply will not take no for an answer."

I knew it was fruitless to argue the point. Besides, we had to eat anyway. I started helping her remove the items from the bags. "Thanks, Mom. That would be nice." After a moment I added, "Will Dad be joining us?"

She looked at her watch. "He should be home any time now. We'll get him to cook the hamburgers on the grill."

"Good," I said, winking at Maggie, who adored her grandfather. Then I held my daughter out at arm's length a moment, noting the traces of mascara around the eyes and the blush on the cheeks. "Looks like somebody got into Grandma's makeup," I said, smiling at Maggie but striving for a slight tone of disapproval for the benefit of my mother.

Mom gave me a shrug. "She saw me putting mine on and wanted to see what she would look like. I didn't see the harm."

I sighed. I had told my mother on several occasions that Maggie was way too young to be wearing makeup. I suspected that, having failed to make me into a beauty queen, she was grooming my child for a possible run.

"Do I look pretty, Mom?" My daughter smiled up at me.

I looked at my daughter then, taking in the shoulder length auburn hair, the delicate facial features, the smattering of freckles over the white skin. She had the long limbs of both her parents, but seemed more comfortable with them, more graceful than I remembered myself at that age. "Of course, you do, sweetie. You look beautiful, despite the fact that you and Grandma have tried to cover it up."

My mother frowned but said nothing. After a long pause, she looked over toward the piano and said, "I didn't realize that you still played, dear."

"I don't."

"Well, it sounded beautiful," she said, trying hard to disguise the disappointment at my confession. She looked over at Maggie. "Perhaps she has your talent, Mary Katherine."

"Lord, let's hope she has more than that."

"With your permission," she said, "I can show her a few things, some fundamentals. Perhaps, if she shows interest, I could arrange for lessons." She looked over at Maggie, who had returned to stand beside me, stretching her arms over her head.

I looked over at my daughter. "What do you think, sport? Want Grandma to show you how to play the piano?"

She shrugged. "Okay."

"Just don't start her off with *Moonlight Sonata*," I said, and was surprised when my mother gave me a small smile and nod.

Maggie looked up at Mom. "Can I turn on the television?"

"**May** I turn on the television," my mother said.

"May I?"

"Yes, you may, but at six o'clock, you will have to turn it to the news."

Maggie shrugged, then made her way over to the den, turned on the TV and plopped down on the floor in front of it.

My mother and I began the food preparations. After a couple of minutes, she whispered, "How is Maggie handling the separation?"

"It's not a separation, Mom. We were divorced."

"Well, people get back together all the time after a divorce."

I sighed. "No," I said slowly and deliberately, "they don't."

"Craig is over his little fling, I'm sure, or soon will be. He will want you back."

I felt my blood pressure rise a couple of notches. "But I don't want him back, Mom." I stopped, counted silently to ten.

My mother shook her head, but was silent, concentrating on slicing the tomato in front of her. Her words carried the implied criticism that marriage was team work, and it was hard work. If it failed, it was a team failure. It was never just one person's fault. I was tempted to take her bait, to confront her about such comments, but I knew from past experience it was ill advised.

"Anyway," I said finally, "Maggie's doing okay." My tone of voice did not invite further inquiry.

My mother looked out toward the den and frowned slightly, but she said nothing more on the subject. Soon, we fell into a familiar, if not completely comfortable, silence. She expertly sliced the tomatoes and onions, carefully arranged them, along with the cheese, on a platter. She had me form the hamburger patties, insisting that they be uniform, perfectly sized for the buns. When she re-molded a couple, I didn't comment. After a few minutes, she checked her watch, wiped her hands on her apron, and called out to Maggie. "Time for the news."

The youngster did not turn around, but she dutifully lifted and pointed the remote at the TV. The picture changed to a commercial which was just finishing. Then the screen filled with the image of the two news anchors for the local CBS affiliate. They were chatting with each other as a voice-over announced that this was the Channel Six Eyewitness News, showing us images of reporters on the scene in different locations, then introducing the anchors. The music stopped and a serious looking man faced directly into the camera.

"Good evening," he said. "Mario Castillo makes it official. He will be a candidate for Governor of Florida next year."

The other anchor, a woman, took over. "The current Speaker of the House and son of former U. S. Senator, Raoul Castillo, made the dramatic announcement on the steps of the capitol before a crowd of supporters. Dennis Jackson has this report."

As the reporter spoke, the screen displayed a wide-angled view of the group gathered, then zoomed in for a close-up of Castillo, in front of a podium. A slight wind blew his short, jet black hair a little out of place. His parents could be seen in the background. The sound bite of the young Castillo's remarks included the expected tough-on-crime, pro-life, tax-cut mantra that had gotten him elected as one of the youngest representatives in Florida history, and propelled him to leadership in his party.

I didn't agree with much of the man's politics. I thought him hypocritical, and intuitively mistrusted him. I had to admit, though, that he was very bright, handsome and photogenic—not to mention politically savvy. He would be a formidable opponent for the incumbent.

The next image was of the reporter, standing on the sidewalk in front of the capitol, the crowd now gone. He summed up for the audience, including the inevitable reminder that, "Of course, it was only a short distance away from this spot, at the Jasmine Towers Condominium, that the candidate's sister was found dead—and a local judge has been charged with her murder."

The screen switched back to the anchors. "That's right," the woman anchor said, looking into the camera. "And I understand there has been a new development in that case, Dennis."

Back to the reporter. "Yes, Circuit Judge Warren Goodwin, charged in the death of Elena Castillo, now must answer a complaint filed with the Judicial Qualifications Commission, the body that investigates and prosecutes judges for misconduct. A spokesperson for the commission announced today that it will proceed against the judge for various violations."

The screen showed a view of the Florida Supreme Court Building as Dennis summarized the allegations in the complaint, which included favorable rulings for Elena's clients and charges of sexual harassment from two employees of the Clerk's Office. This was new, and troubling, if not completely unexpected. And it had Bill Lipton's hand print all over it. I felt sure that either he or someone in his office had initiated the complaint.

"So," my mother said, "looks like Renny's troubles are mounting."

I motioned with my head toward the television set. "Other than that, Mrs. Lincoln, how was the play?"

My mother and I shared a chuckle. So far, I'd seen nothing to corroborate the concern my aunt had expressed earlier in the day. After a few seconds, my mother pressed me for details on the case, and I gave her some alternative suspects and theories, the political complications.

She shook her head. "That's where Ruth Campbell lives, you know, Jasmine Towers." Ms. Campbell was an old friend and former neighbor of my parents. She and her husband had been professors at FSU. "She moved in after Jeremy died. I told her it wasn't a safe place to live. She should have stayed here in the neighborhood, where people could look after her. Bless her heart, she wouldn't listen."

When I didn't respond, she continued. "Ruth said she didn't want to have to worry about upkeep on the house, wanted something smaller, and liked the idea of being close to the university. And, she told me, they have all kinds of security there." She shook her head again. "Well, I'm not too impressed with their security."

Having aligned everything just so on the platter, she covered it in plastic wrap and set it aside. Then she turned to me. "It was probably one of those homeless people who hang around all over downtown."

"What do you mean?"

"One of them may have killed that poor woman. You should look into it."

I shook my head.

"Can't even go to the public library anymore without being accosted by one of them, looking for a handout. And we had our book club meeting that night. Ruth was all by herself. I gave her a ride home, watched to make sure she got in okay. That could just as easily have been her found dead that morning." She shook her head some more.

I looked at her, surprised. "You were there that night? At the condo?"

"What did I just say?"

"Why didn't you tell me this before. What time was this?"

"You didn't ask me," she said, seemingly indignant. "And it was about ten thirty or so."

She ignored my opened-mouthed stare and looked at her watch, then muttered, "I wonder where your father is."

When I regained my equilibrium, I questioned my mother further on the subject, pressing for details. There weren't many, and none of them were particularly enlightening. After that, we drifted back into an uneasy silence again for several seconds. Then my mother began a non-stop soliloquy of random commentary on a variety of subjects, from my sisters and other family members, to the details of her activities over the last week. It took the ringing of my cell phone to get her to pause.

I put the phone to my ear. "Hello?"

"Hi, Katie. It's Ted."

"Hi there. What's up?"

"We got the State Attorney's Response to Discovery today. Got the name of their eyewitness."

Somehow, I sensed what he was going to say next as I listened to the rustle of paper on the other end. "Yeah," he said finally. Here it is. It's a lady named Ruth Campbell."

"Ruth Campbell?" I repeated the name.

"That's what it says. Why? You know her?"

Chapter Thirteen

Renny Goodwin sat across the table from me, sipping his coffee, looking tanned and fit, flashing a relaxed smile from time to time. The navy-blue khakis, plaid sport shirt with no tie, and deck shoes matched his casual demeanor. The only hint of nerves was his constant manipulation of a rubber band he had picked up off the table, stretching it with his thumb and fingers.

To my right, Ted Stevens also had a casual look about him. Though he wore a tie and dress pants, he had loosened his tie and rolled up his shirt sleeves. His disheveled blond hair needed a trim, and it appeared that he had not shaven that morning. His eyes were bright and clear, though, a deep, sky blue which could be described as steely, but also as kind.

We were in the law firm's conference room, a large, pleasant space in the interior of the building, furnished with a long oval shaped, light walnut table and dark brown leather chairs with matching walnut trim. The walls were painted a soft, soothing green. A free-standing copper fountain in the corner and the soft, indirect lighting added to the soothing effect. The smell of fresh brewed coffee, with a hint of cinnamon wafted through the air.

"Okay," I said, leaning back in my chair, "the way I see it, the State must establish that the judge and the victim had a romantic relationship. That is crucial. It gives them motive, and consciousness of guilt in denying it."

Ted ran his fingers through his hair, took a slurp from the mug of coffee in front of him, and looked at Goodwin. "What about the e-mails?"

Before he could respond, I spoke up. "With neither of the parties to explain their meaning, or the context, they are subject to interpretation. They are ambiguous."

Ted looked doubtful. Goodwin nodded in agreement, but said nothing. Uncharacteristically, he had thus far been content to mostly listen to his two lawyers discuss strategy, snapping his rubber band.

I took a sip of Diet Coke. "We've not been told of any witness who saw them out together, or over at the Jasmine Towers, or acting in any way like they were lovers." I looked over at Ted.

"Not yet," he said, looking at Goodwin, "but we don't want to base our whole defense on the assumption that nothing will surface."

Goodwin asked, "What's the alternative?"

"You take the stand, acknowledge the relationship, admit that you lied to the police, not because you were guilty of murder, but of adultery only. You didn't want to lie about it, but you knew it had nothing to do with her death, and you didn't want to give them something to hurt you with personally and politically."

I tucked a small bit of hair behind my ear. "There's also Ruth Campbell, their eyewitness, who puts you at the scene around the time of death."

I addressed the comment to the client, but it was Ted who responded. "He was a mentor and friend. He became concerned when she seemed agitated, despondent over the phone. When she didn't answer her phone later, he decided to go over and check on her, and got no answer at the door. He assumed she was either mad at him and not answering the door, or simply not home. So, he left."

Goodwin studied the rubber band which was visible on two of his fingers. He flexed his hand and it shifted over to the other two fingers. "But then I will be seen not only as an adulterer but as a liar too."

The truth can be inconvenient at times, I thought, but what I said was, "On the other hand, people like contrition. And the fact that you admit the bad gives you some credibility when you deny the worse. It's a big jump from adulterer to murderer."

Ted nodded.

The judge looked up at the ceiling for a few seconds, as if considering a ruling on an issue of law before him. "Other than Ruth Campbell, they have no witnesses or evidence to place me at the condo that night, right? There should be nothing on the security cameras, or the key card code records. Right?" He looked at Ted, who had been charged with this part of the investigation.

"I spoke with the manager at the Towers. Every unit has its own regular key, but access to the garage and the garage elevator requires a key card. Same thing for the lobby elevators, but only after midnight. Entry is recorded and stored on the computer for thirty days. It will tell you which key card was used at what time and on what date to gain entry. It won't tell you who used the card, only the owner to whom the card was assigned."

"What about to the unit itself?" I asked.

"The unit belongs to the individual owner. They have a separate, regular key for their particular unit. They can give out as many keys as they want, or change the locks any time they want."

"Is there someone at the desk twenty-four seven?"

"There's someone there until midnight, though not necessarily at the desk, and there is a resident manager available by phone."

Goodwin placed the rubber band on the table and looked down at both his hands which he held out in front of him, as if admiring a new nail job. Now he looked up at us and folded his arms. "What about the security cameras? Have you seen the footage from that night?"

Ted nodded. "And for seven days on either side of that date."

"And?"

"They have cameras in the elevators in the main lobby, which are turned on after midnight, after the concierge goes off duty. There is a camera at the street entrance to the garage which catches the license plates of the cars as they come in, and a camera at the elevator there." He hesitated, looking at Goodwin for a reaction but got none. "You're not on any of the security camera footage."

"That's because I took the stairs."

Ted and I looked at each other, acknowledging the consciousness of guilt to be inferred from the act of walking up twelve flights of steps to avoid being seen, or videotaped. Was it guilt of adultery or murder, or both?

I asked, "How did you avoid being seen by the concierge?"

"He doesn't just stand there all night. Unless it's real busy, lot of foot traffic, he stays in the back room.

"And since you didn't have a key, that explains why you were knocking on the door, instead of just letting yourself in."

"Exactly," he said with emphasis. "If we were having an affair, why didn't I have a key to her place?"

"And why didn't they find the missing exterior hard drive or any of the other stolen items at your home or office?" I added.

Goodwin nodded and picked the rubber band back up, stretched it between his fingers. "The most reasonable hypothesis is that whoever took the hard drive, the flash drive and other items, also killed Elena. That has to be the State's theory." He snapped the rubber band lightly.

"What about your print on the sliding glass door?" I asked. "How do we explain that?"

Goodwin pushed his bottom lip out in a frown, then said, "Prints can remain on a surface for days, weeks, even months, depending on the conditions. All that print proves is that at some time in the past, I was in the place—which I have never denied."

He was, I had to admit, pretty convincing. But the best liars always are.

"I think for now," the judge continued, "we deny any romantic relationship, or that I was at her condo on that night." He looked directly at me, "That means you will have to discredit the testimony of Ruth Campbell. She's the only person the State has to put me anywhere near the place."

"But you **were** outside her door," I insisted.

"It is important, very important, that the jury not believe that, or at least have reasonable doubts about it. I know that Ruth is your former neighbor, and good friend of your family. Hell, she's a friend of mine, too, but we have to make a convincing case that she was mistaken. You can't afford to go easy on her. If you are not up to it, I'll understand. Stevens here can do it if that's better. I'd rather it be you, for obvious reasons, but I have to know you can go for the jugular if necessary."

I frowned, thinking about it. "If necessary, but let's see how it plays out. A lot will depend on if you testify. Nothing worse than beating up on a sympathetic witness, only to acknowledge later that they were telling the truth."

"Agreed," the judge said, "we stay flexible, keep our options open. Where do we go from here?"

Ted looked at me, then Goodwin. "In addition to key card records and the victim's work computer, Kate has consulted with an expert in pathology." He looked over at me again.

"Ethan Morrison," I said, "with Southern Pathology Group. He's the same guy who testified for the defense in the boot camp case, the one over in Panama City."

Goodwin nodded. "I know him."

"We want to see if we can challenge the ME's cause of death conclusion, at least muddy the waters," Ted said. "It would cost you some money but I think it's a good investment."

"It's critical," I said, "if we want to have accident or suicide as a viable alternative theory. Even if he doesn't testify, I need someone to consult, to advise about cross examination of the Medical Examiner. As I understand his report, he says that the fracture in the back of her skull occurred before the one in the front."

"Yeah," Ted said, "This is based on the position of the two fractures, and the location of the other injuries. He says she hit the ground in a frontal position, which is inconsistent with the fracture to the rear of the skull. There was also bleeding and resultant bruising found around this injury, but not the others. This suggests the blow to the back of the head came at least several minutes before the fall."

"Once you're dead," I said, "the heart quits pumping and you don't get the bruising. A fall like that, twelve stories up, you're going to be gone probably within seconds of hitting the ground. That's why there wasn't similar bruising or discoloration around the other injuries."

"Which is why we need our own expert," Ted said. "Maybe we have to concede it is murder and point the finger at someone else but, like I said, I'd rather keep suicide and accident on the table if we can."

"I agree," the judge said. "Morrison makes a good witness. I've had him in my court before. Just try to keep the cost down."

I then shifted gears and asked Goodwin about the charge that he had been giving Elena's clients more favorable treatment."

"Bullshit," he said.

"Eloquent, but would you care to elaborate?"

I could feel the air move as the judge waved his hands. "They've taken a few cases out of hundreds, and manipulated things to come out how they want. If you go through all my cases, I'm positive you won't find much of a variance. There was no quid pro quo going on, I can assure you of that. And people are forgetting, she was a damn good lawyer."

"The point is, you should never have been on her cases at all."

"I know that." He strived to control the irritation in his voice. "But I couldn't very well recuse myself without divulging the reason, or raising questions about the reason."

"Oh, what a tangled web we weave. . ."

"Yeah, yeah," he said. "We need to get someone to do our own comparison, put together a statistical profile that will dispel this myth. You know what they say about statistics."

Ted nodded. "Mitchell may not even let them get it in, and if she does, we'll have our own expert with a different conclusion."

"And I know just the guy for the job,' Goodwin said. "Rob Daltry. He's a statistics professor at FSU. I used him several times in civil rights cases to show a pattern of discrimination."

"Okay," I said. "I'll contact him." After a couple of seconds with no response, I said, "What about the complaints of sexual harassment?"

Goodwin smiled. "At least they're all female."

"I'm glad you can see the humor in this."

"Just looking on the bright side. Listen, this is also bullshit. Am I a big flirt? Sure. But I never abused my position to coerce any of those girls into any sexual act. And if they say otherwise, they are lying, probably prompted by threats or promises from Lipton's office."

I noticed he didn't deny the sex, only the abuse of position.

"Besides," Ted said, "None of that is admissible at trial. It's character evidence."

"Maybe,' I said, "but in the court of public opinion, there are no rules of evidence."

After several seconds of silence, Goodwin asked, "Any alternative suspects?"

Ted answered. "We're working on it."

Goodwin frowned, said to work harder at it, and suggested the possibility of another lover or a connection between her representation of Ricky Hobbs on gambling charges and the Castillo family's support for a constitutional amendment that would allow casino gambling in the state.

Ted liked the latter. "It's sexy. It mixes politics and organized crime. It suggests some secret conspiracy, a professional hit. People eat that stuff up."

"It also explains," the judge said, "why they wiped the place clean."

I nodded, though I felt this theory way too speculative at this point. "I'll be talking to Ruth Campbell after our meeting today, and viewing the crime scene. Ted will be running down other witnesses. We'll keep you posted."

"Maybe I should go with you to view the crime scene."

I shook my head. "The police are suspicious enough of defense attorneys. They would be positively paranoid about a defendant being at their crime scene—doing who knows what to possible evidence of his crime. Also, the witnesses will likely speak more freely if I don't have the man accused of the crime in tow. Worse, your presence might jog somebody's memory of having seen you there before, maybe even on the night of the murder. No, you need to keep a low profile in general, and especially avoid this kind of active involvement."

Goodwin reluctantly nodded his agreement.

Despite my core feelings about the man, and against my best instincts, I discovered a little sympathy for him. Sure, he was a sleaze bag, but I didn't think he was a killer, or at least I had my doubts. That's not supposed to matter, but it did. And this had to be very tough for him, facing what he was facing, and being asked to stand on the sidelines while someone else carried the ball. He was used to having the game on his shoulders. I could appreciate that.

"Remember," I said, minutes later as I escorted him to the front door, "The best profile is a low profile."

He nodded his acquiescence, but the smile he gave me did not fill me with confidence.

Chapter Fourteen

The Jasmine Towers building was located just behind City Hall, on Kleman Plaza, a short walk from the office. A cold, sharp wind blew across the open area, and I turned up the collar on my coat and walked a little quicker to reach my destination.

The hot dog vendor was stationed at his usual spot and the familiar aroma of steamed hot dogs wafted through the plaza courtyard, mixing with the competing smells of simmering jambalaya, steamed crawfish and other Cajun specialties emanating from the kitchen of Harry's Restaurant. My stomach growled involuntarily, telling me it was ready for lunch. It would have to wait, I told it.

I stopped momentarily before the entrance, my eyes tracing the rectangular contours of the building as it rose toward the steel grey winter sky. The architects had managed to give an otherwise box design some interesting lines with curved windows and balconies and other architectural details such as the brick accent and trim over the stucco base. All in all, not an unattractive place to call home, if you liked that sort of thing, which I didn't.

I remembered when plans had been announced, not only for Jasmine Towers, but for two or three more downtown high-rise residences about the same time, as if someone had put something in the punch at the last developer's convention or something. But they all seemed to be selling out and filling up with people who were apparently attracted by the relative maintenance-free living offered, and the convenience to the Capitol and downtown. No surprise that a lot of units had been bought by lobbyists and legislators who used them mostly during session.

Almost the entire front wall of the lobby area was made of a thick, tinted glass. So were the tall, double doors, which opened automatically as I neared the entrance. The lobby floor was a brown and tan marble, with small flecks of red here and there. Two matching marble columns framed the front desk. The area was trimmed in a light cherry wood.

The concierge behind the desk was short enough that only his upper torso and head were visible above the counter. He appeared to be in his mid-fifties, his thin mustache more gray than the little bit of hair on his head.

"May I help you?"

I read the name tag on his blazer—William (Bill) Avery. I introduced myself, and explained the purpose of my visit.

His smile tightened as he advised that a police officer was already there, waiting for me. He pointed to a clipboard on the desk and asked me to sign in. "New security protocol," he explained. "As is this," he added, holding up a key card, which he handed to me once I signed in. "For the elevators," he explained, "which are around the corner and down the hall just a bit. If I'm not at the desk, just drop the key card in the box on your way out." He pointed with his chin to a slotted box on the corner of the desk.

I looked in that direction and nodded, then turned to the man. "Is Roberto Gonzales on duty today?"

His eyes wandered around the room as if looking for a clue as to whether he should even be talking to me, balancing a fear of inviting trouble against his natural inclination to be of service. "No, I'm sorry. Roberto works in the evenings. Would you like to leave him a message?"

I thanked him, said I'd get up with his co-worker another day and headed for the elevator.

The name tag identified the officer standing at the entrance to Elena's unit as Brad Johnson. He greeted me politely, cut the yellow tape across the door with a pocket knife, opened the door, then stood back and waved his hand for me to enter.

Elena's place was a penthouse on the twelfth floor, its balcony facing west with a wrap-around to the south. It was pretty much as I remembered it from the open house party I attended—spacious, everything tastefully arranged and decorated. The professionally hung paintings were abstract in style. The white leather furniture, glass-accented table tops and shelving, the teak wood trim and matching floor combined to give it a contemporary look.

I turned around to face Officer Johnson, who was about three feet behind me, standing rather stiffly. "I might be awhile," I said. "You can go get a cup of coffee or something if you want."

"It's no trouble, Ms. Marston. Anyway, my orders are to remain here during your inspection."

"Make sure I don't run off with something, or plant evidence?"

"I wouldn't put it that way."

"Of course, you wouldn't. You are much too polite. But I suspect that's a paraphrase of how Bill Lipton put it."

"I wouldn't know about that."

"Okay, suit yourself."

I made a quick walk-through of the entire three-bedroom, three-bath residence, including the patio, before returning to the living room to begin a more methodical inspection, taking lots of photographs as I went. In the living room, there were no magazines on the end tables. The entertainment center was an expansive teak and glass piece with a large flat screen television in the center, and a stereo on the shelf just above it. The lower shelves of the unit had doors, behind which I found a modest collection of DVDs and music CDs. The other shelves contained photos, small sculptor pieces, vases, and a few hardcover books—mostly non-fiction titles, with a focus on politics and history.

One of the bedrooms had been converted into a den/office. The teak theme was continued there, with shelves covering two of the walls, a large window on another. The fourth wall contained a closet and the entrance to a bathroom. A small kidney-shaped desk with a black leather pad and matching leather chair were located against the windowed wall. I noted the power cord for the laptop, the empty CD carrier, the spot where the laptop would have been.

The master bedroom was on the southwest corner, where sliding glass doors led onto the wrap-around patio. The king-size bed was framed in teak, with a bookcase head-board which wrapped around in one piece to also provide the night tables on either side. Perched on top of the headboard was a ceramic Madonna, serenely surveying the room. I recalled Elena's response, at her party, when I commented on its size and placement. "Yeah, makes you a little self-conscious about having sex, what with her looking down on the whole scene." I had smiled with her then, but thought I detected a subtext in her comment that I couldn't discern.

The large walk-in closet was organized, orderly, and full of expensive, well-tailored clothes. In the master bath, I looked in the medicine cabinet. Nothing out of the ordinary. One of the cabinet drawers included a jewelry box, which I pulled out and slowly went through. In addition to jewelry, the box contained some silver dollars and other old coins, some random buttons, including a gold-plated one which looked like it had come from a blazer. I spread the contents out and dutifully recorded the contents with my camera.

I picked up the blazer button and examined it. Common enough. It could have been from one of Elena's suits, but it also could have been from the sleeve of a man's blazer. The police had apparently not found it significant—because it was still there. I made a mental note to see if Renny Goodwin had a blazer with a sleeve button missing.

Back in the bedroom, I pulled open the nightstand drawer, and rifled through it. I noted tissue, paperback books, crossword puzzles, pens and note paper with an elephant on it and her initials at the bottom. I again took photos of the contents, though nothing stood out as significant.

There were two sliding glass doors that led out onto the large balcony area. The wind had picked up a bit, making it quite chilly. I took in the view, from the south, moving west, the Supreme Court Building, the R. A. Gray Building, the Law School and the Leon County Civic Center, and over the trees, down Pensacola Street, a glimpse of Doak Campbell Stadium.

The balcony wall was about four feet in height. I tried to picture Elena Castillo, standing there, resolved to end her life. I put my hands on the ledge and lifted myself up. It would be a little awkward, but not too difficult for her to climb up on the ledge that way. But why? There was no evidence that she was depressed, or had mentioned suicide or anything like that. There was no suicide note, either.

I was considering these things when I heard the front door opening, and then the familiar voice of Bill Lipton. I shook my head. This was just like the bastard, to come over when he knew I would be here. I began to make my way inside, ready with a smart-ass remark for him. What I saw when I entered the living room, though, made me change my mind.

The prosecutor looked up as I entered the room, his face registering feigned surprise. "Oh, hello Kate," he said, "I didn't know you'd be here." To his right, the police officer looked uncomfortable, embarrassed. And there was no mistaking the genuine surprise on the faces of the couple behind Lipton.

I fought to remain composed, professional, to control the anger rising within me, but the flush in my cheeks betrayed me. "I specifically arranged the date and time with you, Bill."

"I'm sorry." He looked at his watch. "I thought surely you'd be through by now. But listen, we'll come back later."

Maybe, just maybe, it was an honest mistake, but I doubted it. "No, that's okay. I was just leaving." I closed the distance between us and, ignoring Lipton, addressed the couple behind him. "Senator and Mrs. Castillo, I'm Kate Marston. I'm very sorry for your loss."

The mother surprised me by taking my hand in both of hers.

"Thank you," she said.

The Senator was stiff, wooden. He didn't offer his hand. "Ms. Marston, if you are truly sorry for our loss, I have to ask you, why are you trying to protect the animal who murdered our daughter?"

An awkward silence fell over the room. Well, so much for the polite veneer. It was the kind of question that did not need, or deserve, an answer, but I felt compelled to say something, and figured the old lawyer answer—everyone's entitled to a defense—just wouldn't cut it. "He didn't do it," I said finally, breaking the silence. I wasn't sure my client was innocent, but this man couldn't be certain he was guilty, either.

The Senator didn't seem particularly impressed. He turned to the prosecutor. Lipton shrugged. "She's entitled to see the evidence, and the crime scene is evidence." He held his hands out, palms up, signifying it wasn't his fault.

No one spoke for a few seconds. Then Miranda Castillo stepped forward. "May I have a word with you, Ms. Marston?" She motioned toward the door and I nodded. Mrs. Castillo turned toward her husband. "I'm going to step outside a minute with Ms. Marston, dear. Be right back."

Lipton looked slightly alarmed but the husband nodded. In the hallway, we stopped and turned to face each other. The older woman took a deep breath, exhaled slowly, then said, "I must apologize for my husband. He has taken all this very hard."

"No need to apologize. I'd feel the same way. I can't imagine the pain you both must feel." I hesitated, then added, "I'm sorry about that in there." I pointed with my head toward the door. "If I had known you were coming . . ."

She waved me off. "That was your State Attorney's doing, I know. He's got his head so far up my husband's ass, he can't see where he's going. He's a little man with big political aspirations. Believe me, I've seen enough of them to know one when I see one."

I was a little surprised by her rather colorful language, but kind of liked what it said about the woman. I thought her assessment of Lipton rather accurate as well.

"My daughter spoke very highly of you, Ms. Marston."

"I didn't think she thought much about me one way or the other. We only overlapped a couple of months at the firm."

"She said you were smart and gutsy, and when she was scared to death starting with the firm, you made her feel welcome."

I didn't know if what she said was true or not. Elena had seemed aloof to me at the time, and supremely confident in herself. As if reading my mind, her mother said, "Despite outward appearances, my Elena was full of self-doubt. A mother knows. She was most frightened of failure." She paused, then said, "Which isn't such a bad thing, except that no matter how well she did, no matter what she accomplished, it was not enough."

I could relate to that.

"She was my only daughter, Ms. Marston. I will not ask you, as my husband did, how you can represent the man accused of her murder." I noted that she used the term accused. "That is your job, and I do not take it personally. After all, I understand that this man is a long-time friend of your family. I understand about family and about loyalty."

The woman hesitated a few moments, looking into my eyes. "All I ask is that you remember that she was my family, and that all I have left are memories. Ask yourself, as a mother, whether it is necessary to smear my daughter's reputation to do your job." I started to protest but she put a hand up to stop me. "What is necessary is necessary, but what is not, is not. I can understand and forgive a person who acts honorably and delicately." She hesitated a few moments more. "But if someone were to engage in unnecessary cruelty, try to bring shame to the memory of my daughter, then that would be like spitting on her grave. And that I could not forgive."

"Ms. Castillo, I liked and admired your daughter as well. And I assure you, although I have a duty to zealously represent and defend my client, I have no intention of doing anything to worsen your pain."

Not intentionally, I didn't, but I knew my words sounded as hollow as they felt. Of course, it didn't really matter what I did. The media dogs would be on this like it was a piece of fresh red meat. Still, no sense in reminding her of a reality she understood in her heart. Instead, I asked her about her daughter's mental health, if she had been upset about anything.

Miranda Castillo winced a bit, but then straightened up, frowned and said, "Elena could be moody, but she has never been suicidal, if that is what you are implying." The woman hesitated, then continued. "Elena told me everything, Ms. Castillo. We were very close. I would have known if she were depressed, if anything was bothering her."

"Yes ma'am."

"And you should know that when I say Elena told me everything, that includes the fact that she was having an affair with your client."

My stomach flew to the edge of my throat, then crashed back down with a thud. I did my best to give her a questioning look. "She told you she was seeing Judge Goodwin?"

"She wouldn't tell me his name, but said it was a judge, and by her description, there is no question it was your client." She paused, then continued. "It was something I counseled against, and finally convinced her to break it off." She looked off down the hallway for a couple of seconds, then back to me. "But he wouldn't take no for an answer. He was stalking her, and she was afraid of him, Ms. Marston, a fear that was apparently justified. She told me she was planning to change the lock on her door." She sighed. "I wished she had. Maybe she'd be alive now." I started to say something, but she waved me off. "You should know that if your client has denied this, he is lying to you. And also know that this is what I will testify to if required."

Chapter Fifteen

Well, I guess I should have seen that curve ball coming, especially when my client was so confident that the State had no evidence of their relationship. I thanked Miranda Castillo for her candor, excused myself, then turned and walked down the hallway, aware of her eyes on my back. Halfway down, I heard the door close behind me, and turned to confirm the empty hallway. I stood there for several seconds, trying to process her revelation.

It might not be as bad as it seemed. Miranda Castillo's testimony as to what her daughter told her was arguably inadmissible at trial. It was hearsay, and did not fit neatly within any exception. The closest was the state of mind exception, but generally, the mental state of the victim in a murder case was not relevant.

I set this issue aside for later, more thorough thought, and made my way down the corridor to unit 1224. I stopped to put some eye drops in as my contact lenses were bothering me. I blinked my eyes several times to work the solution around. Much better. Then I knocked on the door and heard the instantaneous barking begin on the other side. After a few seconds, I heard a "hush now," and the dog stopped. As I stood there, I imagined its occupant peering through the security peep-hole at me.

The door opened and Ruth Campbell stood before me. Just beside her, a Jack Russell Terrier peered up at me, his ears raised at full alert, his snub of a tail wagging furiously.

"Katie, so nice to see you. Come in. Come in." She stepped back, as did her dog, and I entered. We embraced—just the women, not the dog. The dog, figuring this was a signal for him to be friendlier as well, ran circles around us, stopping occasionally to sniff at the ankles of his visitor. As we separated, his mistress looked down at him.

"Pepper, behave now." She looked at me. "Please excuse him. He's just excited to see you."

"Yeah, I have that effect on the males." I bent down to pet him. "Do you remember me, Pepper? Or are you just smelling my cat?" Pepper backed away briefly, then approached, sniffed my outstretched hand, and submitted to a rub of his head and the back of his ears, smiling in agreement, his tongue hanging out.

"Ms. Ruthie, you're looking great," I said, rising and looking at my former neighbor. The petite woman was dressed fashionably casual, in black slacks, a burgundy knit shirt under a silk, multicolored blouse that tied the outfit together perfectly. Her hair, which was now completely silver, was thick, straight and short. Her eyeglasses had fairly thick lenses, thicker than I remembered. The frames were rectangular, and a pewter color that seemed just right for her face. She had a little stoop but not bad, and definitely looked a good bit younger than her seventy-eight years.

"You liar," she said.

"No, really."

"Well, not bad for an old biddy. And you, you've finally put a little meat in those bones."

"Thanks."

"I meant it as a good thing. You used to be skinny as a rail."

"Oh, so compared with how I used to look, I look better?"

She punched me in the arm lightly. "You know what I mean. Don't give me that lawyer stuff."

"Okay, thank you," I said, looking around the apartment. It was clean but somewhat untidy or cluttered. Some things never change. There were books all over the place, stuffed into the shelving along the walls, stacked on the floor and on end tables. The baby grand piano in the living room was stacked high with magazines, music books and sheet music. The place had a bit of the absent-minded professor feel about it.

The familiar photos and other mementoes of her life with her husband of fifty-plus years crowded the room, including photos and artwork from their many trips together. The couple had loved to travel. Jeremy Campbell, a music professor at F. S.U. had also been a world-renowned pianist who was often invited to play in exotic locations around the world, which the couple often accepted, usually adding extra time for personal travel and exploration. Even after her husband's death three years ago, Miss Ruthie had continued to travel solo, demonstrating an independence and self-reliance I admired.

There was also something else familiar, the smell of freshly baked scones. Cinnamon, I guessed.

"Would you like a cup of tea?" Ruth was not British, but her husband, Jeremy had been, and he had converted her from coffee early on in their relationship.

"That would be nice," I said.

"Oh good, I just brewed a fresh pot, and I have some cinnamon scones that came out of the oven just minutes before you arrived."

My olfactory senses had not betrayed me.

"You girls used to love my scones," she said, smiling.

"And your cookies, your pies and cakes, and everything else that came out of the kitchen of Chez Ruthie."

The woman beamed, then sighed. "With Jeremy gone, I don't have much occasion to bake anymore. It doesn't make a lot of sense to make something just for me."

There was wistfulness in her voice then, short of self-pity, which she swept aside quickly with, "Perhaps we can take our tea out on the terrace. It's a little nippy but all together pleasant with the sun out. And the wall provides fairly good protection against the wind."

"Let's," I said, then helped my hostess take the food and drink and servings outside. We first talked about family and friends, and did a little reminiscing, then I turned the conversation to the subject that had prompted my visit. "I appreciate your seeing me, Miss Ruthie. As you know, I'm representing Renny Goodwin concerning Elena Castillo's death. And you are listed as a witness." I hesitated for several seconds, searching for the right words.

Ruth helped me out. "It's a little awkward for you, and me too. I understand that my testimony is not very helpful to the defense."

An understatement, to say the least. "It is what it is. And you should know that you are under no obligation to speak to me about the case, except in a formal deposition—which is what a lot of witnesses require."

"And that is what the State Attorney's Office has strongly suggested," she said, frowning. "They say your job will be to discredit me, try to punch holes in my testimony."

I shrugged, held out my hands, palms up, but didn't say anything.

"I didn't much like their tone, though, and I don't like to be told what to do either." She slapped her hands lightly on her legs. "As you said, it is what it is. I'm going to tell the truth regardless of how it's done. If there are holes to be punched, then so be it. I feel bad that my testimony is not helpful. Renny's a friend of mine too. I wish I hadn't seen him that night."

I nodded. "I've read the police reports, but I was hoping you could tell me in your own words what you saw, what you remember about that night."

She took a sip of tea, held the cup in both hands. "I came home about ten forty-five."

"My Mom says this was your book club night."

"Yes, that's right."

The club had been in existence for about twenty-five years and Ruth, an English professor, was the chief founding member and book critic for the group. Although they had serious discussions, it was as much social as literary in its focus and the ladies had been known to consume large quantities of alcoholic beverages while discussing the relative merits of the month's selection.

"The meeting was at Masa's that night."

"Did you drive there?"

She shook her head. "No. I took a taxi. I don't like to drive at night too much, especially if I've been drinking."

I raised my eyebrows. "How much did you have to drink that night?"

"A couple of glasses of wine. Maybe three. Which is why I didn't drive. Plus, I just don't see as well driving at night. In fact, it was your mother who gave me a ride home. I was going to take a taxi but she insisted. And she didn't have anything to drink."

"Did she come up with you?"

"No, though she offered. Your mother is such a sweetheart. She's been really good to me since Jeremy died. Anytime I need something, she's there for me. When I go out of town, she comes over and feeds Pepper, takes him for walks, waters the plants. She's just a saint."

"I'm sure Mom remembers all you did for her when you lived next door and she was working. You looked after her obnoxious kids, and our house when we were gone. It's what neighbors do. It's what friends do. The fact that you have moved from the neighborhood doesn't change that for Mom."

"Is this where we tear up and hug again?"

"Could be, but let's wait for the string music," I said, smiling. "Anyway, so Mom brought you home. It was about ten forty-five. Then what?"

"I came in, took the elevator up to my floor."

"Did you come in the front or the garage entrance?"

"The front."

"So, the concierge would have seen you?"

She shook her head. "There was nobody there at the desk when I came in. Only when I came back out a few minutes later, Roberto was there."

"Roberto Gonzalez?"

129

"Yes, that's right. I went out to walk Pepper."

"About what time was this?"

"I'd say about eleven, eleven-fifteen."

"So, when you went up the first time, at ten forty-five, you go up the elevators, get out on your floor, is this when you saw the person?"

The woman gave me a sideways look. "The person?"

"Yes, the person you thought you recognized." I was not going to acknowledge the accuracy of her identification.

"Yes. That's right. I got off the elevator and I saw Renny at the end of the hallway. He was knocking on the door to the Castillo woman's residence."

"Are you sure? I mean, that's a pretty good distance, and the lighting is not all that good. And you would have been looking at his profile."

She crossed her arms. "It's not all that far, the lighting's good enough, and he turned in my direction when I got out of the elevator. And his hair. Even in profile, it's fairly distinctive." Then, to add further proof of her powers of observation, she offered additional detail. "I remember he was wearing a dark gray, three-piece suit, light blue shirt and a red tie." She shrugged. "Believe me, like I say, I wish I was mistaken, but it was Renny all right."

I rubbed my chin with my thumb and forefinger. "Did he recognize you? Did you speak to him, or he to you?"

"I don't know if he recognized me or not. He only looked my way briefly, then turned back to knock on the door. I was going to speak but I didn't want to shout."

"Had you ever seen him here before?"

She shook her head. "Nope. First time."

"How about other visitors?"

She thought about that for a few seconds. "Well, I know she's had a few parties. Nothing loud or anything but a lot of people. Other than that, I saw her with her brother a couple of times, and once with her parents. Actually, it's her half-brother, you know."

I didn't, I told her.

"Yes, that's what she told me Mario is Raoul Castillo's son by his first marriage."

"Couldn't tell by looking at them."

She nodded. "Anyway, I ran into them in the lobby and she introduced us, the parents and brother. I saw her with different men from time to time, nobody on a regular basis, and nobody I recognized. I didn't pay much attention really."

"How well did you know her?"

"Not very. We would speak in passing. That's all. She was not unfriendly, but not real friendly either."

I nodded, but said nothing.

"This tends to be a rather private place. People keep to themselves." Her tone betrayed a hint of sadness. "It's one of the things I miss most about the old neighborhood, I guess. I mean, there are several people my age I've become friends with but on the whole it's a different group, with a different lifestyle."

"You could always move back to Betton. My folks would love it."

"Oh no, I couldn't do that," she said, but without offering an explanation. When I got ready to leave a few minutes later, she insisted I take some scones with me. "For Maggie," she said.

On the elevator down, the smell of the scones filling the space, I was gripped by a sudden and somber sense of sadness. Unless something changed, I would have to find a way to discredit the testimony of this good and decent woman, make the jury think she was mistaken, perhaps in a way that robbed her of her dignity, made her seem foolish.

And I already had something I could use. She had just told me that when she came home that evening she entered through the lobby, not the garage elevator. But I had seen the footage from the security cameras which showed just the opposite. They showed Ms. Ruthie, in her large, bright yellow hat, going up in the garage elevator. I suspected that when we got the key card records, it would confirm what the video showed. It was a small thing, of course, but anything that threw a little doubt on the testimony of an eyewitness could be helpful. I tucked it way for future reference.

Many times, I am proud of my profession and of the work I do. This was not one of them.

Chapter Sixteen

Bradford, Horton and Waters, my former place of employment, was the oldest law firm in Tallahassee. Formed just after World War I by James Bradford and William Horton, its list of partners over the years was a whos who of local and state political, business and civic leaders, including a former governor and two state supreme court justices. Although a few of the larger statewide firms had eaten into some of its business, BH&W still wielded considerable clout.

Its offices took up the entire fifth floor of the First South Bank building, an unremarkable rectangular structure made of gray concrete and lots of glass. The bank and its building were owned by five of the senior partners. The reception area was very nicely appointed, but not overly opulent, a theme that continued in the inner offices.

It was largely a family business, with most of the partners and many of the associates related, if not by blood, then by marriage. I had been no exception, having joined the firm at the urging of my husband, a Waters, and the invitation of his cousin, Roger, also a Waters, amid promises to pay me significantly more than my salary at the Public Defender's Office.

I announced myself to the receptionist, who I didn't recognize, and was told, "Mr. Waters will be with you shortly, if you care to have a seat." I thanked her and plopped down in one of the leather chairs on the side wall. No one else was in the room.

Though he was Craig's cousin, Roger didn't particularly like my ex-husband. When I was going through the divorce, he had made it clear that he thought Craig was being a jerk. Although, objectively, this was an accurate observation, it violated the unwritten firm rule requiring unflinching family loyalty and solidarity. In the firm hierarchy, blood relations trumped relations by marriage. For this reason alone, Roger's stock had gone up several points with me.

He had also tried to mediate the intra-firm fissure over my disclosure of the proverbial smoking gun document to opposing counsel in a case after the lead counsel for the firm had intentionally concealed it. Roger had not been successful in mending the rift that resulted, and the incident led to my resignation from the firm, but I was appreciative of his efforts. And if I had an ally in the firm, one who might provide any useful information about Elena, it would be Roger.

The receptionist broke me from my momentary reverie, saying that "Mr. Waters is off the phone now." She led me back to his office, where he was standing, looking out through the glass wall toward College Avenue. He turned to face us and motioned me in.

Roger was a wisp of a man, at five seven and no more than a hundred forty pounds. His thin red hair and pale skin gave him a frail look, which was counter-balanced by bright green eyes full of energy that looked out at the world through small rectangular shaped glasses. He was an excellent trial lawyer, a workaholic, and at thirty-five, the youngest full partner at the firm.

"You're looking good." he said.

I self-consciously pushed a strand of hair away from my face. "You, too, Roger."

After a brief silence between us, he said, "You know, Katie, I'm hanging myself out there even talking with you about Elena."

"You have my word, Roger, nothing you tell me will come back to bite you on the butt."

Roger arched his eyebrows and looked at me for a long time, then said, "I don't imagine I know any more than you do, but go ahead, shoot. What do you want to know?"

I had several questions. Who were her close friends? How did she get along with the other lawyers in the firm? How about with the local bar in general? And with the judges? Any ideas about her emotional health? Was she a heavy drinker? Drug user? Had she made any enemies? Was she dating anyone? "And I don't care if it's fact or if you think it's true. I'll take gossip, rank speculation and hearsay."

"Perception being reality?"

"Perception being perception, and sometimes overshadowing reality."

Roger considered this for a few seconds. I could see the reluctance, the wariness in his eyes. "As you know, Elena's hiring was Jeb's doing all the way. Met her at some Florida Bar function, with her brother and father."

I nodded. "I remember the rumors, the speculation that his interest was more of a personal nature. Any truth to that?"

"I don't know."

I searched his eyes for signs of deception, and gave him a skeptical look.

"Really. I mean, maybe, but if so, it's been very discreet, which is hard to do in this place. No, I think the real attraction was the obvious one."

"Money?"

He raised an imaginary gun and pointed it at me. "Bingo." After a few moments, he continued. "She came from a family firm of sorts, too, which I think was part of the appeal for Jeb. Their firm included one of her uncles, who was the managing partner."

"And her brother, who was a state representative."

Roger nodded. "And our next Governor, according to Jeb. Their firm had real close ties with the present administration and with the leaders of the party. They were pulling in government contracts like crazy and attracting a lot of good lobbying clients. I think Jeb saw it as a way to get back some of the influence we had lost over the years."

"They also had close ties with organized crime down there, too, right? That's what I heard."

Roger got up from his chair, walked over and closed the door to his office, then returned to his seat. "All this is off the record, not to be repeated to anyone, including your client and co-counsel. Agreed?"

I raised my right hand, as if giving an oath. "On my honor."

He nodded, apparently satisfied.

"They **were** organized crime," he said. "That's where the family's money and political muscle came from—and why several of us argued against the association with them. Her father and two other uncles made it big in construction and real estate development, but there was also drug money in there—a lot of it in the beginning. The construction business, and later a PR firm and the law firm, gave them legitimacy, but their hands are still dirty, is my guess. Because of the *joint venture*," he said with sarcastic emphasis on the last two words, "we're now in bed with the folks who are trying very hard to get casino gambling legalized in Florida."

"Did she have anything to do with that ballot initiative?"

"No. That's being handled by Jim Bradford and Bill Horton. At least they are the front men on that from here, with a lot of behind-the-scenes consultation with the folks down in Miami. As a matter of fact, they have a summary judgment hearing before your dad coming up soon, a challenge to the ballot language."

"What's the connection to Ricky Hobbs?"

"What makes you think there's any connection?"

I gave him a frown. "Please. He couldn't pay her fee."

"Officially, she was representing him pro bono, but..."

I waited but when he didn't finish, I asked, "Was she being paid through those same gambling interests? Were they somehow connected with the scandal, with Hobbs?"

"You ever meet Hobbs?"

His words triggered a memory of our one and only meeting. It had been several months ago, before even a hint of scandal. He had been at a practice session for the F.S.U. women's basketball team. He had apparently been dating one of the players. I was a volunteer for the team and occasionally made it to a practice. Coach Sue had introduced us. He was taller than I had imagined, and had very large hands. He lingered with me, trying, it seemed, to place me. Finally, he snapped his fingers in my direction. "Yeah," he said, smiling, "you played ball for Duke a few years back."

"More than a few years back," I said.

"Good ball handler. You could have played in the pros."

I shook my head, but said nothing in response, embarrassed, but appreciative of the compliment.

"Yeah, once," I said to Roger, back to the present. "You didn't answer my question, though."

"My point is, Hobbs, he is an independent type of guy. He doesn't like anybody pulling his strings."

Still, I pointed out, he hadn't answered my question.

"I don't know. I'm out of the loop on that."

If so, I thought, it was by Roger's choosing. "Who's taking over for Elena with Hobbs?"

"That's Jim and Bill again, though, as I say, I'm not involved in that at all."

I remained skeptical, but decided not to push it. "So, how was she to work with? Good lawyer?"

He looked out the window briefly before responding. "I was Elena's supervising attorney, but she neither needed, nor wanted, much supervision." His tone seemed to have a hint of both admiration and resentment. "She was very skilled at getting people to do what she wanted."

"What was her secret?"

He looked at me as if I was very dense. "In case you hadn't noticed, Elena was a very attractive woman."

Ah, the popular male explanation for a woman's success in the business and professional world.

"Now, don't get me wrong. She had a sharp mind, and could be very logical, very persuasive in presenting her client's case." He hesitated, then said, "But let's face it, she was also beautiful."

"Stunningly," I agreed.

"And she also knew how to play hardball if needed. She would find your weakness, and exploit it."

"You speaking from personal experience, Roger?"

He looked up at me, alarmed. "Don't be silly. I'm a happily married man."

"Aren't you all," I said, with more bitterness than I intended.

"Besides," he said "I wasn't her type."

I didn't ask him what type that was.

After a few moments, he continued. "In answer to your questions, she got along okay with most of the other lawyers and staff, though there was legitimate resentment at the way she had been hired and the level of responsibility she had achieved in such a short time, meaning right away. I'm not aware of excessive alcohol use, nor of any illegal drugs. She was a workaholic, but no other mental disorders that I could tell."

I pressed him with a few more questions, which Roger dutifully answered, but when I stood to leave a few minutes later, I had the impression that Roger had not been as candid, or as forthcoming, as he pretended. We exchanged hugs and promised to keep in touch, and Roger escorted me to the lobby. Along the way, we passed by the conference room, a glassed-in interior space. I recognized Professor Charles Everhart. He was talking with Bob Gibson, Florida State's chief assistant football coach. I tried to get my former law professor's attention but they were very intent in their conversation and didn't notice as we walked by. It looked like a Ricky Hobbs meeting, without Ricky Hobbs, I thought, but didn't say.

Then, as if to confirm my observation, as Roger and I were saying goodbye in the lobby, Ricky Hobbs came walking in, flanked by two firm lawyers, Jim Bradford and Bill Horton. They, too, seemed intent in their conversation, but as they passed by, Hobbs gave me a glance, followed by a second look, just before they went through the door. His face registered uncertainty, as his mind searched its memory banks. Then there was recognition, a small smile and nod of the head before he disappeared down the hallway.

Chapter Seventeen

I had arranged to meet Natalie Olsen fifteen minutes before her scheduled hearing. Even without the physical description I had, she was easy to pick out. The petite blond standing near the entrance to the courthouse café had that uncertain, on-edge look common to domestic violence victims just before having to face their abuser in court for the first time. She was dressed in a dark blue pleated skirt and jacket, over a white blouse, with matching dark blue purse and low-heeled shoes, her jewelry elegant in its understatement. Her dress and manner suggested modesty and a fragile dignity.

Ten days earlier, she had sought and received a restraining order against her husband. Because such injunctions are entered based solely upon the sworn allegations in the petition, and without notice to the spouse, a hearing is scheduled quickly so that both sides can be heard.

Natalie had received assistance in filling out the necessary papers from representatives of Refuge House, a local advocacy organization that provided temporary housing, counseling, and other services for victims of domestic violence. One of those services was to help them obtain counsel where needed. I was on the organization's list of pro bono attorneys, and Emily Leifried, a board member, called me two days ago to ask me to take Natalie's case.

She first talked about Elena, who had, like me, been on Emily's list of volunteers. We both agreed it was awful, her death, but there was no mention of the fact that I was representing her accused killer, except indirectly. "I know you have plenty to keep you busy these days, Katie, and I hate to ask, but this lady needs a strong advocate, and you're one of our strongest."

"You think flattery will get you what you want?"

"I was hoping."

Emily gave me the essentials on the client and her situation: Married ten years to Jared Olsen, a local dentist. They had two children, nine and six years old. She had training and experience as a dental hygienist, but had not worked outside the home since her first child was born. No prior petitions or criminal charges, but the client related a history of escalating abuse.

I walked over to the woman, introduced myself and nodded toward the café entrance. "Let's go find us some coffee. We can sit and talk a few minutes."

We found a table in the corner, which allowed a modicum of privacy. Once we were seated, I reached over and put my hand on top of hers. "It's going to be all right," I said. "I'll be standing right next to you. He will be on the other side of the podium. You won't even have to look at him if you don't want to."

Her eyes registered gratitude but she said nothing in response.

I went over in detail what to expect at the hearing, discussed her options thereafter. She seemed to relax a bit as we talked. By the time we were ready to go, she had regained her composure, and a measure of confidence.

That composure and confidence, however, all but vanished when we walked into the courtroom minutes later and she saw her husband. "That's him," she said. "Second row, against the wall."

I followed her gaze to a man dressed in a dark gray suit. He sat upright, looking straight ahead. As we started down the aisle, he turned and looked our way. Natalie stiffened.

"Don't look at him," I said, but she couldn't help herself—nor could I. In his eyes I didn't see the hostility I had expected, though. Instead, he seemed sad more than anything else. I could sense my client's resolve weakening, the vacillation almost palpable in the short walk we took to the second row on the opposite side.

The judge looked out over her reading glasses at the crowded courtroom, sighed, then began calling the cases. Ours was the third one to be heard. "Ms. Marston, you are here on behalf of the Petitioner?"

"That's correct Your Honor."

She looked over at my client's husband. "You are Mr. Olsen?"

"Yes ma'am," he said, the soft, southern accent giving his voice a respectful tone.

"Do you have an attorney, Mr. Olsen?"

"No, I don't, Your Honor."

"Would you like to have time to hire a lawyer?"

He looked over at his wife, then back to the judge. "I don't think that will necessary."

The judge looked at him for a few seconds to assure herself he meant what he said. Apparently satisfied, she continued. "Very well. As you know, your wife has obtained a temporary injunction and is asking me to make it permanent. Do you have any objection to that? Do you wish to contest her petition?"

He looked over at his wife. "Do you have any idea what you are doing to this family? To our children?"

"Mr. Olsen." The judge's voice went up in volume a notch to get his attention. It worked. The man turned to the judge. "You need to address any comments you have to me. Do not speak directly to your wife, or her attorney. Do you understand?"

He nodded.

"My question to you is whether you wish to contest the issuance of the final injunction. If not, we don't need to have testimony. I'll just enter the order and y'all can be on your way. If you do, we will have a hearing, and I'll hear testimony in support of and in opposition to the petition."

The man looked down and shook his head. "No hearing is necessary, Your Honor. I'm just hoping she wants to sit on this awhile, give us a chance to work things out. I'm hoping she does still love me."

The guy was certainly persistent, and I could almost feel my client's resistance weakening as we stood there. "If the court pleases," I said, "I will certainly talk with my client about the possibility of reconciliation. I will be glad to act as an intermediary with him, or his counsel, if he hires one. But she wishes to have the injunction issued this morning."

The husband looked over at her. "Is that what you really want?"

"Mr. Olsen," the judge said, her voice raised again, "I told you not to address your wife directly."

"I'm sorry, Your Honor. Will you ask my wife if that's what she really wants?"

The judge rubbed her face with her hands.

The husband looked at me as he spoke to the judge. "I think maybe her lawyer is putting words in her mouth, trying to get her to do something she doesn't really want to do."

"That's why people hire lawyers in these situations, Mr. Olsen," the judge said, her tone suggesting that he should have done likewise, "to speak on their behalf. If Ms. Marston does not represent her interests the way she wants, your wife is free to fire her. But until that happens, I assume she speaks for her client."

"All right, then, if that's the way she wants it. But judge, she should be the one to leave the house. That's my house. I make the mortgage payment every month. She can go live with her mother. That makes the most sense. Plus, the kids should stay with me. My wife," he said, then hesitated a few seconds, as if he was reluctant to say what needed saying, "tends to be emotionally unstable. In the present circumstances, I think it best if the children stay with me in the house. Let her concentrate on herself, without the added responsibility of the children."

The man's words sounded almost reasonable, his tone suggesting care and concern rather than the self-interest I felt certain lay beneath them. The judge looked over at me.

"Completely unacceptable, Your Honor. Ms. Olsen has been the primary caretaker for the children since they were born—something

143

which seemed just fine with her husband until this morning. I am recommending that you award Ms. Olsen exclusive possession of the marital home and sole custody of the children. His visitation with the children should be supervised and he should be admonished not to talk to them about this case or the pending divorce case."

"Divorce?" He spat the word, as if it were some spoiled bit of food he had taken in his mouth. "Supervised visitation?" His glare was directed at me like a laser, hot with hate, the increase in tension palpable. The judge picked up on the change in tone as well. She quickly cut off his next round of protest, then entered the injunction, continued exclusive possession of the home and primary child custody with the wife, reasonable visitation to be arranged through a third party. She also addressed the husband, to make sure he understood what "no contact" meant, and the consequences of violating her order.

He nodded and said he did, the calm and reason having returned to his voice and demeanor. As we were walking out, though, he gave me that glare again. I stared right back at him, as if to say, "I know what you're trying to do. Maybe it worked on your wife in the past, but it won't work on me." The man gave me a sneer of a smile and looked away.

In the hallway, I had to reinforce my client against her second thoughts and fears. I walked with her to the south exit, putting some distance between her and her husband. I held onto both her hands and made her promise to keep her appointment with me for next week. She promised she would. I was not so sure, but I tried not to let it show on my face.

Outside, the early morning chill had given way to a pleasant mid-day warmth. The vivid blue sky was cloudless and the smell of blooming camellias drifted by, carried on a gentle breeze. All of it hinted at the spring to come, and just the sense of it made me feel better. I took my time on the short walk back to the office, letting the sunshine wash over me.

I was still lost in my thoughts when I stepped into the reception area and started toward the stairs, one hand up in greeting to Jennifer.

"Ms. Marston?"

I turned to face the receptionist. "Yes?"

"You have a visitor," she said, pointing with her chin in the direction of a young man seated against the side wall.

I recognized him instantly.

The man rose from his seat and walked toward me, extending his hand. "Ms. Marston. Nice to see you again."

"Likewise, Mr. Hobbs." I took his hand in mind, gave it one brief up and down in greeting, then let it go. "What can I do for you?"

His eyes looked straight into mine when he spoke, in a calm, soft voice. "I want you to take over my case."

Chapter Eighteen

I picked up Maggie from basketball practice, got her situated doing her homework, changed into my shorts and tee shirt, then took off on a run. I needed to clear my mind, and nothing did that better than a long run. It offered an opportunity for reflection, for sorting information, and at the same time, a great way to cleanse my mind of toxic thoughts and feelings I had stored up. And there had been a lot of that lately.

I felt the bite of the cold against my cheeks as I began to pick up the pace. My breath came in quick, rhythmic spurts of warm air in front of me, a kind of chant. Breath, two three, four. Breath, two, three, four.

Craig never understood this meditative quality of running. To him, it was always a means to a physical end. He'd make fun of the notion, mimic the priest on Kung Fu and call me Grasshopper: He liked Buddhist jokes, too, one of which came to me now:

What did the Buddhist monk say to the hot dog vendor?

Make me one with everything.

Yuk, yuk. The man was hilarious.

When I was in 10th grade, my Phys Ed teacher talked me into going out for track, suggesting I might make a good long-distance runner. I made the varsity that year, ran the 1600 and 3200. I wasn't the best runner on the team, but I was pretty good, and I loved it. I loved the solitude, the singularity of the competition. It also was a good complement to basketball, the sport for which I eventually received a scholarship.

My second year of college, I was diagnosed with clinical depression which, given the experience with my bi-polar mother, scared the shit out of me. I was afraid the old saying might be true, that the apple doesn't fall far from the tree. What really bothered me was that I couldn't just snap out of it, couldn't control how I felt. I was eager to do whatever was necessary to nip it in the bud, so to speak.

In hindsight, based on what I have since learned about the subject, I think mine was more situational depression than truly clinical, more post-traumatic stress syndrome. But that was no fault of the psychologist who made the diagnosis, as I had not told her about the traumatic event. Indeed, I didn't tell anyone except Aunt Mary Beth, and that was many years later. Nor do I care to discuss it here.

At any rate, I was put on medication, but I didn't like the way it made me feel. Running seemed to help, and so I did more of it. After a while, I was off the medication and free of symptoms. Then, I was scared to quit, afraid that I might slip back into that blackness of melancholy.

More than a habit, the running became a near obsession. Okay, there was nothing near about it. It was an obsession. I ran marathons for several years, after college and law school. When both my body and my doctor told me to slow down, I ignored them. And the resulting injuries that sidelined me would make me depressed, and more determined to get back to it, to run longer and harder. Which in turn, resulted in new and more severe injuries. A vicious cycle.

I don't exactly know when, or why, but I finally got the message and got off the merry-go-round, gradually began to put things in perspective, Now, I run for exercise and relaxation, for the calming and healing benefits, rather than competition. If it is still a drug of sorts, I am more a recreational user than a junkie now.

And the drug was working this day. When I made that final turn onto Hillcrest, I had achieved both physical exhaustion and mental clarity. As I slowed to a walk, I pushed the play-back button in my head and reviewed the meeting with Florida State's star quarterback.

Ricky Hobbs had a body that seemed to be built more for basketball than football. Tall, lean, wiry, he looked as if he was one tackle away from a season ending injury. But, as he himself had said, you don't have to have bulk to have strength or toughness, something he had demonstrated repeatedly on the field. In general, though, his was a more graceful, artistic form of the game. He was quick and slippery in the backfield, or when he tucked and ran.

He was shy in public, soft spoken and humble, always giving credit to the team when he was singled out for praise. His smile seemed to come easily for him, and he exuded charm. The young man had a poise and maturity beyond his years, and he did his best during our talk to appear confident, even a little cocky, but I sensed the insecurity underneath the façade, and could identify with it.

"So, Ricky, tell me again why you have come to me."

"Like I said, I heard you were a good lawyer, a fighter." When I didn't say anything in response, he added, "I saw you play once, remember? You give it all you got. And that's what I want."

I smiled. The description was flattering and, I hoped, accurate. "People say you were gambling big time, betting on games." It was both a question and an accusation. Best to get it out front from the get go.

Ricky hesitated a few seconds, as if trying to decide on truth or lie. "I've been playing cards, poker, betting on sports since I was in high school. I'm pretty good at it. But I never, I mean never, bet on a game I was involved in. Or any other FSU game for that matter. I would never do anything to affect a game either. Never thrown one. Never shaved points. Nothing. Even though there was a lot of pressure on me to do it. I know it looks bad. When you bet on games, it's easy to assume the worse. And it's hard to prove a negative."

"So, what's the story in this case? Who's this Jim Hunter guy?"

"He was one of the team managers. In charge of equipment, that sort of thing." He was looking down as he talked. Now he looked back up at me. "He used to run the bets for me. Worked for some guys out of Miami. I knew him from there. He got popped and tried to give me up as some leverage."

"He later recanted, though."

Ricky gave me a grin. "Yeah, our friends in Miami convinced him that it was in his best interest to keep his mouth shut—about me, and anybody else. Take the fall all by himself."

"And that's apparently what he has done. He entered a straight up plea and got county jail time."

"That's what they wanted me to do, plea it out."

"Who are these friends in Miami we're talking about?"

He waved his hand. "Better you not know at this point. But I can tell you, they are serious people." He hesitated a couple of seconds. "And the coaches, they knew about the gambling."

"Which coaches?"

He named two assistants. "I mean I was careful, but they knew. Every time they asked me about it, I denied it, but they knew. Gave me the lecture about it, how it could hurt the team, ruin my career."

"If you denied it, what makes you think they knew about it?"

"Cause they weren't talking to anybody else about it every other week. They just wanted to make sure I didn't get caught and, if I did, that they could say they didn't know."

"Plausible deniability, they call it."

"Yeah, that's right."

I didn't know whether to believe him or not. Problem for the university, though, was that many others would. And that was something the team, the coaches and the university had to factor in. As Hobbs said, it was very hard to prove a negative. There was nothing in writing. Nothing recorded. Just his word against theirs. And the NCAA would pounce on something like that. They would make the case that the coaches had known about the gambling, but had looked the other way. They looked the other way because they knew he could get them to a championship and that without him it wouldn't happen. Something like that could mean some pretty severe sanctions.

"Elena was working on a deal, a deal that would see the charges dropped, and a united front against the NCAA folks. I had denied everything to the NCAA investigators, and the State Attorney people, but I was keeping my options open." He hesitated a moment. "There were certain interests who were not pleased with that development."

"Who are these certain interests, as you put it? And why would they be adverse to a deal that swept everything under the rug?"

Again, he demurred as to whom, but offered as to the why, "Because the deal had me naming names, giving up some powerful and connected people, people who don't play nice. See, I was just supposed to keep my trap shut, take the fall if necessary. Best for everybody I was told. I was into them for some significant money then. I was told my debt would be forgiven. More important, I would get to keep on living."

"Why would Elena deviate from the script?"

"I don't know. Maybe she thought I was getting the shaft. Maybe she thought she could play both ends against the middle, put the squeeze on both the university and our Miami friends. Maybe it was something personal. She never really said. Just said there had been a change of strategy. I didn't think she had gotten the go-ahead from Miami, but I went along with it."

I didn't know quite what to think. It all seemed a little out there. On the other hand, people around here took their collegiate athletics, especially football, very seriously. You combine that with people who take their gambling seriously, and who make a lot of money doing it, and the stakes get raised considerably.

"And you think she was killed because she didn't follow directions?" I didn't hide the skepticism in my voice.

"Like I say, these people don't play nice."

"So, why aren't you dead? It would seem to make more sense to get rid of the source of the problem."

He shrugged again. "Yeah. Tell me about it. I'm taking precautions, that's for sure. And maybe I'm all wrong about this, but I thought you ought to know, in case it makes you a little nervous, and you don't want to take my case."

I gave him a long look, told him I could take care of myself, then abruptly changed the subject. "And the thing with Macy's?"

"That was a misunderstanding. The girl was coming on to me. She wanted to do me a favor. I didn't see anything wrong with that. She was giving me a discount. They do that sometimes at stores, hotels, restaurants. I bet you never seen a cop turn down a friendly discount. And if it wasn't quite right, then that was on her, not me."

I didn't say anything.

"So," he said, "are you in?"

I looked beyond him, at a large photograph on the far wall. It was a shot of the beach at St. George Island. Then I focused back on him. "You have come to me for legal advice and I agreed to talk with you. And as I said when we began, whatever you tell me is confidential. I can't say anything about it to anyone without your permission."

The quarterback nodded in approval and I continued.

"Now, whether you fire your current lawyers, as you say is your plan, is up to you, but whether I end up as your lawyer will depend on whether we can come to a meeting of the minds."

Ricky frowned. "We talking money?"

I couldn't hold back a smile. The man was certainly direct. I liked that. "Well, yes, there is the matter of my fee. That's part of it."

"How much we talking about?"

I told him.

Ricky frowned again. "There are plenty of lawyers who would take my case for free, just for the exposure."

"Then maybe you should go to one of them."

This time he gave me a small smile. Was he testing me? "I can't come up with that kind of money. I'm just a student. Don't even have a part-time job. And my mother, she's barely getting by. I'll pay your fee, but you'll have to wait till I get drafted and get my signing bonus."

I shook my head. "I appreciate your confidence, but I can't ethically accept a criminal case on a contingency fee basis." I didn't mention the very real possibility that not only would there not be a signing bonus for Mr. Hobbs, there may never be a signing at all. "I'll have to be paid straight, and with a retainer before I start. I can take payments, but it's all got to be on the up and up. You'll need to get your mother and other family members to help out. There can be no taint to any funds I receive as your lawyer. Are we clear?"

A grin flickered on his lips. "Yes."

"There's one other thing."

He looked at me expectantly, waiting.

"There is the ethical issue of a possible conflict of interest between my duty to my present client, Judge Goodwin, and you. If you are implicated in any way in Elena's death . . ."

"But I'm not."

I raised my hand. "Well, you've got a pretty damn good alibi, I have to say."

He nodded. "I was at a Heat's game, in Miami."

"And seen on national television, no less, with several alibi witnesses to boot."

"If I didn't, you know the police would be looking at me for it."

"Maybe." I had seen the clip that showed Hobbs at courtside, noted the time, done the calculations. No way he could have gotten back to Tallahassee in time. He was in the clear, as the actual killer. But he might have aided and abetted the killer in some way, or had information that would help Goodwin, but might point suspicion at him, if not for the murder, then something else. He had to understand where he stood.

"At this point, it appears that my representation of you would not conflict with my representation of Judge Goodwin, assuming you have been truthful with me." Ricky started to say something but I waved him off. "But you have to understand that if one arises, I couldn't represent you both. I would have to get off of your case."

The man frowned. "Why my case? Why not his? He paying you

more money?"

"In point of fact, you have not paid me any money, but that's not the reason. Judge Goodwin is my current client. He came to me first. If you become my client, it would have to be with that understanding." After a couple of seconds, I added, "So, you should seriously consider trying to make things work with your current lawyers, or alternatively, there are plenty of other lawyers I could recommend. Then there wouldn't be the potential conflict."

Ricky shrugged and nodded. Then he smiled. "Don't worry. There won't be no conflict." He stood. "And I'll be working on that fee."

Chapter Nineteen

Angelina Maria Perez lived on Wilson Street, in the Lafayette Park area. The house was a wood-frame bungalow on a small lot with mature landscaping throughout. The brick walkway that led from street to front porch was bordered by neatly pruned rows of boxwoods. I rang the doorbell, an old-fashioned push button which created a tinny buzz inside the residence, and waited, looking up and down the street. I had noted the older model Chevrolet Impala parked in the covered pull-through on the side and assumed the occupant was at home, so when no one answered after several seconds, I rang the bell again.

I could sense the eye behind the peep hole, checking me out. Just as I was about to ring the doorbell a third time, the door opened, but only about two inches, the safety door chain still attached. A short, rotund woman peered out at me from behind the door.

"Ms. Perez?" I smiled at the woman.

"Yes?" There was caution, maybe a little suspicion in her voice. And even in that one word, I could hear the accent.

"My name is Kate Marston," I said, offering her one of my business cards through the small opening. "I'd like to talk with you for a few minutes about Elena Castillo if I could."

Perez took the card, examined it briefly, then squinted at me. "You are the lawyer representing her murderer. Why should I talk to you?"

A common theme, it appeared. I gave a small sigh. "He didn't do it, Ms. Perez. I'm trying to find out what really happened. Elena's mother understands that, and I am here with her blessing." It was a bit of a stretch, I knew, actually more than a bit of a stretch. Nevertheless, it seemed to have the intended effect, as the woman relaxed just a bit.

"You talked to Ms. Castillo?"

I nodded. "We were at Elena's condo." No need to explain the circumstances, I thought. "I just want to learn as much as I can about Elena. I think it will help me find the real killer. I'd just as soon keep things informal, just speak with you a few minutes, but if you'd rather, I can set up a deposition down at the courthouse. Get everything on the record."

The woman thought about this for several seconds. I waited, patiently. "You can call Ms. Castillo, if you want," I said. "Check me out with her."

The bluff apparently did the trick. Perez unlatched the chain, opened the door wider and stepped back. "Please come in, Ms. Marston."

It was warm inside. It smelled of onions and garlic, lemon furniture polish and wood fire ashes. I was offered espresso but declined, politely. We sat in the living room and I took in the furniture and furnishings, old fashioned upholstered couch and chairs, fifties-style coffee and end tables. It was dark in the room, the lamp light dim. The oak floor was partially covered by a forest green carpet remnant. Photos, presumably of family, dominated both walls and tables. Some of them evidenced her close relationship to the Castillo family. There were also religious artifacts, evidence of her Catholic faith.

I took it slowly, complimenting her home, asking about some of the family photos. The housekeeper, initially reticent and reserved, began to warm up a bit, and when we worked around to the real subject of the conversation, she was remarkably forthcoming.

I learned that Angelina Perez's family was originally from Guatemala, coming to Miami in the mid-seventies. Her husband was befriended by the Castillo family and both ended up working for the family, he in their construction company and she as a housekeeper and nanny for many years, essentially raising both Elena and Mario. When I asked her about what Ruth Campbell had said about Mario being a half-brother, she agreed, but assured me that the parents had never made that distinction in the way the children were treated.

She had moved to Tallahassee at the family's request, to look after their daughter. This worked out fine for her, she explained, because her husband had died a couple of years back, and one of her daughters and her husband lived here in Tallahassee with their two children. "They asked me to live with them," she said, smiling, "but I told them I wanted my own place. Besides, a young couple with children, it's hard enough finding time to be alone. This way, I'm over there often and can help with the children whenever they need me, but everybody has their own space."

She showed me photos of a young Elena Castillo, told me a couple of anecdotes, tearing up on occasion. It was obvious that she had truly loved Elena.

"How often did you go over to Elena's?"

"I went over once or twice a week. Did light cleaning, laundry. She was not a slob, and she didn't do a lot of cooking. I would generally make a couple of casseroles each week for her. She ate out a lot too."

"Did she have any regular boyfriends? Anybody she introduced to you?"

The woman gave me a squint of the eyes, as if maybe I had crossed some imaginary line, but then she seemed to reconsider. "There were men in and out of her life. I didn't think anyone serious."

The woman could not, or would not, give me any names, but the good news was that she didn't know about Elena and Goodwin. "Doesn't mean she wasn't seeing him," she quickly added. "Elena tended to keep things to herself."

"Did Elena seem okay emotionally in the last couple of weeks? Did she seem to be having any problems, pressures?"

The woman frowned. "Elena did not kill herself, if that's what you are implying."

"I have to consider the possibility."

The woman shook her head. "She was very religious, Elena was. She would never do such a thing."

"Did she attend services here in Tallahassee. Did she have a priest she might have confided in?"

"Humph," the woman snorted. "She went to Saint Thomas Moore, near the university, but no priest would violate the sanctity of the confessional." There was indignation in her voice.

I could sense the rapport I had built up slipping away. "As I told Ms. Castillo, I don't want to pry into private matters, and I promise to be discreet. But if she was upset about something, it could possibly tie in with what happened to her. It might lead me to the real killer."

She gave me an appraising look. "You really believe your client is innocent?"

"I do." The lie had come easy. Too easy perhaps. But it seemed to please the woman.

"He was the judge in my nephew's case. Elena was his lawyer. Jorge, he's a good boy, just got in with the wrong crowd. Judge Goodwin, he listened to me. He understood young people make mistakes, and there should be consequences, but it shouldn't ruin their lives." After a short hesitation she added, "I didn't want to think he was the one who killed my Elena."

I nodded, glad to go with her on this theme. "That's why it's so important for me to know if there was anything going on with Elena that might suggest someone else. It is obvious to me that Elena was more than the daughter of your employer. You cared deeply for her."

The woman nodded, looking down.

"I'm sure Elena also trusted you, maybe told you things she might not have even told her mother."

Without looking up, she said, "Some things, especially, you don't want to tell your mother. Some things . . ."

I was silent, waiting. She looked down, fiddled with the button on her blouse, but said nothing. I prompted her again. "Ms. Perez, was there something bothering Elena in the weeks or days before her death?"

The housekeeper pulled a tissue from the container by her side and blotted her eyes. She sighed and looked up at me, hesitating for what seemed a long time. "No," she said finally, simply.

"Nothing?"

She blotted her eyes again with the tissue. "I'd like to help you Ms. Marston. I really would. But I can't."

My sense was that she knew something, but did not feel free to share it with me. I decided not to press it. Perhaps, in time, she would. I stood. "Ms. Perez. I want to thank you for your cooperation and your hospitality. My sincere condolences for your loss."

The woman stood then as well. "Thank you," she said, then walked me to the door. "Elena was not perfect, Ms. Marston, but she was a special person to me. I pray that you will, in your efforts on behalf of your client, respect her privacy."

Echoes of the mother's words. "I will do my best."

The woman looked me in the eyes and held it for a several seconds. "I believe you will," she said. She shook my hand lightly, then closed the door behind her as I stepped outside, squinting into the late afternoon sun.

* * *

I was sitting in my reading chair, my feet tucked underneath my legs, the cat on my lap. With one hand I held notes from the file. With the other, I rubbed Bandit's ears and head. The only light was from the table lamp on the round end table. First, I had tried to read a novel, then looked at the time, paced a little, then picked up the rapidly expanding Goodwin case file. I read my notes about my meeting with Angelina Perez, then I looked up at the clock again. I called Craig's cell phone. It went to voice mail. "Damn it," I said to myself.

At five forty-five, I had called him to make sure he was on his way over. I didn't really expect him to be on time, but I was livid when I found out they were still at the coast.

"Don't get your panties in a bunch, Katie. We've been out on the boat and it took us a little longer to get our stuff together. We're just pulling into Angelo's for a little bite to eat."

"Jesus Christ, Craig. I've got dinner on the stove for her. You know she's supposed to be back at six. And really, the panties in a bunch thing, a little over used, don't you think?" "Not in your case," was what I thought I heard him mumble. "What?" I said.

"Nothing. Anyway, everybody's hungry now, Katie. Don't worry. We'll get something to go. Shouldn't take long. We should be back by about seven, seven thirty at the latest."

I waited several seconds, struggling to keep my cool. "Okay," I said. "See you then." Then I hung up, afraid of what else I might have said otherwise.

Now, here it was eight o'clock and they still weren't back. I tried his cell for the fourth time, but it was obvious he had turned it off. Or had they been in an accident? So bad that nobody was able to call me? No, I knew intuitively that wasn't the case, and it made me madder. I cussed, and threw the phone down.

Bandit, alarmed, then perturbed, jumped from her comfortable perch on my lap to the floor and walked away, indignant. I went into the kitchen and got a brownie, put away the dinner I had made, and fumed.

Twenty minutes later, Craig's Suburban pulled up in front of the house. I stood at the open door, watching as Maggie scrambled out of the back seat, carrying her beach bag. Craig got out, took Maggie's bike from the rack on the back, then rolled it just inside the garage and leaned it against the wall. He bent and gave Maggie a hug. As he turned to walk back to his SUV, I called out. "Craig, you got a minute?" I thought I heard him sigh, but he turned to face me.

I examined my daughter as she approached. Maggie was sunburned and exhausted, and didn't look up as she walked up the steps. "You better hustle on up and get a shower, sport." Maggie nodded as she went through the doorway. I turned my attention back to my ex-husband, stepped down off the steps and drew to within a few feet of him, glaring, but not saying anything.

After several seconds, Craig broke the silence. "What is it, Katie?"

I could feel my heart pounding in my chest. Beads of sweat popped out on my forehead. I looked at my watch, then back at him. "You said you'd be here by seven o'clock—which, I might note, would have been an hour late. You know her bedtime is eight-thirty, and I'm sure you didn't have her do her homework this weekend. That's big bad mama's job, right? Now, here it is eight-thirty, and you come cruising in like it's no big deal. You don't call. You don't have your cell phone on. For all I knew, you'd all been killed in an accident, and I'm waiting for the Highway Patrol to show up at my front door."

Craig frowned, tilted his head at an angle and crossed his arms. "Why don't you cool it with the melodramatics, Katie. We decided to eat at the restaurant instead of taking it to go. So, it took a little longer, and it is no big deal. As you can see, we're all safe. But thank you for your concern."

"That's it? That's your response? You act irresponsibly, show me no respect, and when called on it, your answer is to just blow me off?"

He put his hands in his pockets. "I didn't want to hear you bitch about it, like you're doing now. You talk about disrespect? You treat me like I'm a moron. You want to micro-manage my time with her, dictate the terms of my relationship with Maggie. Well, you don't control me any more, Katie. That's why we're divorced. You need to give the drama queen act a rest."

My eyes became slightly unfocused from the anger that swept through me like a fire. Drama queen, indeed. I counted silently to ten, trying to calm down before I responded. "Well, you seemed to have proved my point tonight as to your irresponsibility. And you think it's okay to tell your child that you can't afford to eat because her mother takes all your money? You think that's being a responsible parent? All I can say is, you've got a lot of fucking nerve."

"Excuse me, but I thought it was more important that Maggie have some quality time with me than adhere to some strict schedule. You complain all the time that I don't spend enough time with her, and now you complain that I do. Make up your mind, Katie. And no, I didn't have her do her homework. The girl has an IQ of one forty. She gets straight As in school. She's not going to fall apart if she doesn't have all her homework done every time. And I haven't been saying things about you in front of Maggie, but she's not stupid, either. Fact is, things have been really tight, and you have been trying to break my balls. You are being completely unreasonable. I can show you the profit and loss statements from the business if you'd like."

"I know you can make the books say what you want. If thing's are so bad, how can you afford to keep the house on the bay and the boat, and the huge ring I saw on your girlfriend?"

"Oh, so that's what this is about?"

"No, this is about acting like a responsible adult and parent, about living up to your agreements. I'm asking for nothing more and nothing less. The fact is, Craig, you signed the Marital Settlement Agreement."

"That's because you made me feel guilty."

"You should have felt guilty. You worked hard at it. You earned it."

"Listen, Katie—"

"No, you listen. I'm telling you right now that it's going to stop. I'm tired of your bullshit and it's going to stop. You will get current on your child support by the end of this month and you will stay current. You will pick up and drop off Maggie pursuant to our agreement unless you and I agree in writing to the contrary. You will get your shit out of the garage by the end of the month or I'll call Goodwill and have them come get it. If I learn that you are continuing to bad mouth me in front of Maggie, or if you fail to abide by any of the terms of the marital settlement agreement, I will take your ass back to court so quick it'll make your head spin."

Craig opened his mouth to say something, then stopped, looking beyond me. I turned and saw Maggie, standing in the doorway.

"We'll talk about this later," Craig said as he walked away from me toward his SUV.

I watched as he got in his vehicle, slammed the door, started the engine and sped off. I stood there for a few more seconds, trying to formulate a plan as to how to handle the situation, what to ask or say to my daughter. I didn't know how long Maggie had been standing there, how much of the conversation she had heard. She was supposed to have been in the shower.

I wondered, though, if subconsciously, I had wanted her to hear it. I hoped at least now that Maggie had been there long enough to hear more than just my last tirade, that she at least had some context in which to judge my words. If not, I would just have to explain it to her. When I turned to face my daughter, however, she was no longer there.

Chapter Twenty

I found a space in the parking garage, grabbed my files and rushed toward the courthouse. I had been running a little behind from the time I woke up, having slept through the alarm. Then, trying to get Maggie awake, dressed, fed and to school on time was even more difficult than usual. No surprise, given the events of the night before. Neither of us, I'm sure, slept too well.

After Craig left in a huff last night, I went in search of my daughter, found her in the den, channel surfing through the television stations, sitting on the couch. I sat down beside her.

"Maggie?" When there was no response after a few seconds, I stood up, turned off the set and stood between Maggie and the television, forcing her to look at least in my general direction. "Can we talk?"

Maggie shrugged, put down the remote control.

I joined her again on the couch, and we both looked at the screen as if it were still on. After a few seconds, I said, "I'm sorry you had to hear that."

"No big deal," she said, eyes glued to the screen.

I could see the hurt and anger in her eyes that belied the cavalier words. My daughter was a genuinely good kid. She was generally obedient, good natured and not prone to melodrama. She was smart, scary smart really. She was diligent and conscientious in her school work, and well-liked by her friends. She had handled the break-up remarkably well, or so it seemed. I would like to think that I had done my part, trying not to expose her to her parent's problems, despite the lack of cooperation from Craig in this respect.

"You do understand why I was upset, don't you?"

"It doesn't matter."

"It does to me."

Maggie nodded her head slowly a couple of times, then turned and faced me. "Yeah, Mom, I get it. You and Dad don't get along. It's why you got divorced. It's why y'all fight all the time, why you can't seem to say anything nice to each other, or about each other, to me."

I stared at her. How could she say that? I wanted to correct her. The reason we divorced was because her father found himself a girlfriend, a younger, prettier model. And while Craig had no doubt bad-mouthed me to Maggie, I had been very careful not to do the same thing.

"When have I ever said anything bad about your father to you?"

"Oh please, Mother, you may be a little more subtle about it, but let me assure you, the message gets through."

I couldn't believe what I was hearing. "For example?'

Maggie frowned, held out her hands. "How about this?" She stood and faced me. "I'm sorry, honey, but your dad will not be picking you up as planned. Something came up." Then she rolled her eyes, conveying her disbelief.

I started to protest, but bit my tongue, recognizing in my daughter's mimicry, a sliver of truth. Even if it wasn't true, or was an unfair exaggeration, I had to accept that she saw it that way. And it stung.

"You think he is not a good parent, that he lets me do anything I want, that he doesn't pay his child support like he should."

All true, I thought, but didn't say.

Maggie sat down again next to me, put her hand on mine. "Yeah, Dad did something bad. I hated him for that. And his girlfriend. But, he's still my dad. And Brenda's not so bad once you get to know her. I don't want to have to feel mad, or sad, about it anymore."

I stared at my child, open mouthed. Finally, I said, "I should have been the one to say that." Maggie shrugged, and I continued. "I'm so sorry. I never realized. I certainly don't want to put you in the middle, and I'm sure your dad doesn't either. There are no sides when it comes to you. Both your father and I want what is best for you. We just don't always agree on what that is."

"No kidding," she said, then frowned at me. "You got to lighten up, Mom. Don't let him push your buttons."

I couldn't argue with another good point—so I didn't. I smiled at my daughter. "You are wise beyond your years, my child."

She shrugged. "That group at school, you know the one for kids of divorced parents? Ms. Lewis, the guidance counselor runs it. You hear things sometimes. Sometimes, they make sense."

I had encouraged Maggie to participate in the group, and had arranged things through the school, but I could never get Maggie to say anything other than "Fine" whenever I asked her how things were going. I looked over at my daughter. "I'll try to do better."

Maggie nodded her approval.

"I'm glad we could have this little chat."

She nodded again.

We hugged tightly for several seconds. When we separated, Maggie announced that she was going to do her homework.

"It won't hurt to miss it tonight," I said.

"Probably not, but it won't take me long. Besides, I'm not really sleepy."

I shrugged. "Okay, but I don't want to have to fight to get you out of bed in the morning."

"You won't."

"Uh huh," I said, knowing I would.

And I did, which of course, put me even further behind. I had hoped to meet with Ted and our client for at least a few minutes before the hearing, but that wouldn't be possible now, I thought, checking my watch again as I entered the courthouse entrance.

Courtroom 3A was packed, and a low volume buzz of conversation permeated the room. As usual, there were several representatives of the news media present, both print and television, local and statewide coverage. I finessed the reporters on the way in, giving a vague promise to talk with them later. Right behind the prosecution table, Jeb and Roger Waters sat stoically. Next to them were Raoul, Miranda and Mario Castillo. They turned to look at me as I walked to the defense table. I watched them out of my peripheral vision, but intentionally did not make eye contact.

I took my seat at the defense table, next to Goodwin. Ted was on the other side. We muttered greetings. If either was concerned that I had cut it close, they didn't show it. I barely had time to open my briefcase and take out my file before Judge Mitchell strode into the courtroom and took her seat.

"Ms. Marston, it is your motion, I believe?"

I rose. "Yes, Your Honor, we are here on our motion to compel discovery." I then told her we wanted three things. First, we needed access to the victim's work computer so our own expert could examine the hard drive. The State refused, saying that the investigators had returned it to the law firm, and were thus unable to comply with our discovery request. The law firm in turn had refused to hand over the computer.

I argued that we were entitled to view the same evidence the State had viewed, regardless of who had it now, to determine for ourselves what information may be relevant to the case.

The judge looked over at Bill Lipton and he stood.

"If she can convince the law firm to let her look at it, we have no objection, but we can't give her what we don't have." He then sat down, and I rose again.

"We are entitled to see just what the State had. The fact that they have given it to someone else does not relieve them of the responsibility to share that information with the defense. Alternatively," I said, looking over in the direction of Jeb and Roger, "I have copied the law firm of Bradford, Horton and Waters with my motion and see that two of the firm's lawyers are present in the courtroom, if the Court would care to hear from the law firm on its position, and rule on the matter."

The judge looked in their direction and nodded. Roger rose, came inside the railing, and stood beside the prosecution table. "Roger Waters, Your Honor, on behalf of the law firm of Bradford Horton and Waters." He then waited for the judge to speak.

"Do you wish to be heard on the defendant's motion, Mr. Waters?"

"Yes, Your Honor." Judge Mitchell nodded for him to continue. "Procedurally, I'd like to first point out that Ms. Marston's motion is improper as it relates to the law firm, as we are not a party to this criminal case. The proper procedure would be for her to file for relief in civil court."

I rose again from my seat. "Mr. Waters is correct. The firm is not a party in this criminal case. It thus has no standing to argue the motion at all. My motion is directed to the State. I gave notice to the law firm as a courtesy. I have no objection to the Court hearing from the firm as their interests are, in fact, affected, but I am not required to file a separate civil claim to obtain this material."

Judge Mitchell considered this for several moments, then turned to Roger. "I think, Mr. Waters, that procedural niceties aside, it is something that should be handled by me in this case. So, tell me why your firm has a problem with Ms. Marston's expert examining the hard drive in the same manner, and with the same protocol used by the State's expert."

"In a word, Judge, privacy." The firm agreed to allow the State's expert to examine the hard drive, but only in strict compliance with a confidentiality agreement, and the defense team already has everything that is not privileged client information."

Judge Mitchell was not convinced. "The problem with that, Mr. Waters, is that any privilege was waived the moment you agreed for the prosecution's expert to view the material. Once the State had access to it, it became evidence in this case, subject to discovery." She then promptly granted our motion. Roger nodded and bowed slightly, then retreated to his seat in the gallery. Mitchell looked at me. "What else you got for me, counselor?"

The second item was the key card records from the Jasmine Towers. Lipton waved his hand dismissively in my direction when I brought it up. "Your Honor, I believe we can short circuit this issue. Our office has obtained printout copies of these records for the dates they want. Ms. Marston is welcome to examine and to copy any and all of these records."

The judge looked at me. "Ms. Marston?"

"That's fine, Your Honor. I just wish Mr. Lipton had told me before today, so as not to waste the Court's time."

Mitchell frowned, indicating displeasure at the cheap shot, but didn't call me on it. "You said there were three items?"

"The last matter, Your Honor, concerns the request for the victim's medical records, and for our expert to perform a second autopsy. We want to confirm, or be able to refute, the medical examiner's determination of the cause of death. It is very important that our expert have the opportunity to examine the body and run some tests."

Bill Lipton was standing, shaking his head back and forth. "This is preposterous, Judge. After what this family has gone through, Ms. Marston has the nerve to come into court and ask you to let her dig up the body of their loved one, to pry and poke around on some fishing expedition, torturing the victim's family once again. They have the autopsy report and all the notes of the medical examiner. Their expert is free to review all this material. They can depose the medical examiner. But to put this family through this psychological torture is unpardonable. And we strongly object." At this, Lipton turned to look in the direction of the Castillos, and the patriarch of the family nodded slightly in approval.

I looked down for a few moments as Lipton finished, gathered my thoughts, then faced the judge directly. "I am very sympathetic to what the victim's family has gone through in this matter, as well as the toll it has taken on my client and his family." At this, I looked in the direction of Marci Goodwin, who sat with their daughters, just behind the defense table. "I do not request this lightly, but, Your Honor, my client's life is at stake here. We are truly sorry for any discomfort this may cause the family, but it is very important."

"What is it that you expect to find?"

"That's just it, Your Honor, we will not know until he examines the body."

Judge Mitchell shook her head. "Sorry, but you're going to have to give me more than that before I allow you to exhume the body of the victim. Your request to see her medical records is reasonable, say back three months, and I will order that, but absent some showing of a reasonable expectation that an independent examination will yield some helpful information, I will not allow the exhumation and additional autopsy."

Both Lipton and I thanked her and began packing up our files as the judge rose from her seat and exited the courtroom through a side door. On our way out of the courtroom, I stopped briefly to answer questions from the press, as did Lipton. Ted and Goodwin stood behind me. Ted had deferred early on to me in all matters relating to the press, and we had both admonished our client to make no comment and refer all questions to counsel.

A few minutes later, finished with questions, and as we made our way toward Goodwin's chambers, I noted Jeb standing against the wall. As we approached, he stepped in front of us.

"Hello, Katie. Ted. Your Honor." The southern patrician civility in the deep baritone voice masked the impatience, the animus I could sense beneath the surface.

The three of us nodded and muttered hellos.

Jeb looked at me and said, "Do you have a minute to discuss a private matter?" He then looked at Goodwin and Ted expectantly. They in turn looked at me.

"Y'all go ahead. I'll catch up." As they trailed off down the hallway, I turned back to Jeb.

He gave me a smile, but it was not a friendly one. "As a matter of courtesy, I thought it appropriate to speak to you before bringing your unethical conduct to the attention of The Florida Bar."

Chapter Twenty-One

Jeb's words caught me a little off guard, but I tried not to show it. "Excuse me?"

"Last time I checked, it was considered unethical to solicit another attorney's client."

"What are you talking about?" I asked, though I was pretty sure I knew.

"I'm talking about Ricky Hobbs. I understand you have contacted our client and encouraged him to discharge our firm as his counsel."

"You understand wrong. He called me for a second opinion. He was not happy with your representation. I encouraged him to explain his concerns to his lawyers and see if he could work things out. Based on your comments, it sounds like he's still not satisfied. Can't help you there."

"Oh, not to worry," he said, a sneer of a smile spreading across his face. "Mr. Hobbs decided to continue as a firm client."

"Then you're welcome."

"What?"

"For advising him to talk it out with you guys, instead of fanning the flames of his discontent."

"Humph," he snorted. "The point is, his disclosure of your unconscionable actions gave us grave concern. Not only is it a breach of ethics, but it lays you open to a cause of action for tortuous interference with a business relationship."

Jeb's comments were disturbing. Why would Ricky Hobbs say that I had contacted him, that I had solicited him as a client? In fact, I had been very careful, very circumspect in dealing with Hobbs, in part because I knew how Jeb would respond. Ricky had initiated contact, not me, and I had it documented in my notes of our meeting.

I sighed, looking off, then focused back on my former senior partner. "I'm not sure what Ricky told you, but the circumstances surrounding our contact are as I have outlined for you," I said, adopting a formal tone to match Jeb's."

"Well, let's just say there is a dispute of facts on the point and leave it at that, shall we. I just wanted to clear the air and hopefully give you a little guidance in the matter. I just don't want to see you do anything that might hurt your reputation." He paused, then added. "So long as you refrain from further contact with our client, that should resolve the matter. But...." He left the implication hanging.

I had this vision then, of wrapping my hands tightly around the man's throat. I was struggling to find a response I wouldn't regret later. John Edward Bradford was not someone you wanted to pick a fight with, and I didn't need the distraction. Not now. As it turned out, however, I couldn't help myself.

"While I appreciate your concern, Jeb, I don't think you should be lecturing me about ethics." The man started to say something but I cut him off. "You want to file a complaint with the Florida Bar? You want to try and sue me for tortuous interference? You go right ahead. But if you do, you better be prepared to lay everything on the table. I will make a full disclosure of the circumstances surrounding the discovery violation in the All American Insurance case, and I'll counter claim against the firm, and you personally, for sexual harassment."

There was a long silence then, and I could almost feel his anger, sense the force of will that now held the elder lawyer's tongue. Finally, he spoke. "As I said, my intent was, as a friend and former colleague, to warn you of the dangerous waters into which you have waded. I have done that, and though I am saddened that my advice has not been taken in the spirit in which it was offered, I still wish you all the best, Katie."

"You too, Jeb."

He turned abruptly and walked off down the hallway. I stood there for several seconds looking after him, at once both regretting and exulting in what I had just said to one of the most influential lawyers in the city. My departure from the firm had been unpleasant, but not a disaster. There had been at least a façade of goodwill and professionalism. I had just burned a bridge, perhaps unnecessarily.

But it sure felt good. And I could take some comfort in the knowledge that the fire had been smoldering for some time. Still, as I headed toward Goodwin's chambers, I flipped my phone open and dialed the number for Ricky Hobbs. I needed to get to the bottom of this. I got his voice mail.

Ted and Goodwin wanted to know about my conversation with Jeb, so I told them. When I finished, Ted smiled.

"I would love to have seen his face."

"Yeah," Goodwin agreed. "You think he was bluffing? About Hobbs deciding to stay with the firm?"

"Who knows? I've got a call into Ricky now, to try and clear things up. I'm not too concerned about it, either way, but if Hobbs is saying I contacted him, I need to find out why."

The two men nodded but said nothing further about it.

We then did a quick post-game analysis of the hearing, each of us agreeing that, in general, it had gone well. We had been fairly confident Mitchell would rule in our favor on the issue of the computer data, and we hadn't really expected her to allow the exhumation.

It might not be necessary," Ted said, "based on what your expert came up with."

I nodded. A week ago, I met with Ethan Morrison at his office. Although I knew of the pathologist and had talked to him on the phone, we'd never met face to face. He was a very short man, and thick. Not fat, just thick, with a neck that seemed to be simply an extension of his head. He had an unassuming manner, though it was obvious he knew what he was talking about. Better yet, he knew how to explain it in terms understandable to the average person without seeming to talk down. Sincerity seemed to ooze from his pores. I had liked him instantly and knew he would make a good witness.

He had offered two possible ways to counter the Medical Examiner's conclusion that Elena's death was a homicide. While he agreed that the fracture to the front of the skull occurred before that to the rear, he said that could be the result of Elena striking her head on a balcony rail or other protruding object on the way down. Another scenario, he said, was that she fell in her apartment, hit her head and was knocked unconscious. When she came to, she wobbled out onto the terrace and then either fell or jumped from the balcony ledge. It was not a real high percentage thing, he said, but was something that should have been explored, something I could argue with a straight face.

"Maybe he can come up with some specifics," Ted suggested, "things he would look for that weren't done by the official coroner. Maybe there are drugs they didn't test for. Maybe she had a terminal illness."

"Maybe she was pregnant," I said, and both men stared at me. I told them that among the numerous e-mails and letters I had received about the case was an anonymous note that asserted this as fact. "I take it with a large grain of salt, of course, but, just thinking, an unwanted pregnancy can be stressful, especially depending on who the father is. If you come from a Catholic family....."

"Abortion would not be an attractive option," Goodwin said.

I nodded, remembering the words of Angelina Perez—some things you especially didn't want to tell your mother. I turned to Ted. "What about the priest? He give you anything?"

He shook his head. "Father Miguel Barrista, invoking the sanctity of the confessional, said he could never reveal anything that may have been discussed."

"Technically," Goodwin said, "the privilege may no longer apply since she's dead, but I know the guy. He's not going to tell us anything regardless of any privilege, and regardless of whether you ask him sweetly or threaten legal action. He's the one who organized the protests over in Gadsden County for the migrant workers a few years back. Got himself arrested a couple of times. No, he's old school. You won't get anything out of him he doesn't want you to have."

"Okay," I said. "I'll put in the formal request for her medical records." The two men nodded, and I looked over at Ted. "Anything additional on the Castillo family and the Miami connection with gambling?"

Ted had grown up in Miami and still had family and friends there, so he had been the logical one to investigate this avenue. He pulled out a small notebook, flipped it open and began reading his notes. After a few moments, he looked up.

"Best I can tell, the Castillo family is behind the gambling amendment, despite the very public face they put on opposition to it. The little hypocritical shit, Mario, can't afford to be publicly in favor of gambling, else he'd lose his social conservative base. And apparently, those folks are so infatuated with the guy, they've put their blinders on when it comes to this subject. Officially, the party line from Mario's campaign is that it's a free country and everybody's entitled to voice their opinion. It's the other side of the family, they say, Jorge and his clan. What can they do? It's a fine line to walk, but they seem to be making it work."

"Any tie-in with Ricky Hobbs?"

"Oh yeah. His mother has worked for the Castillo family for many years in one capacity or another. Word is, it was in everybody's interest that he be properly represented in Tallahassee by someone who understood the priorities."

"Fall on his sword?"

"Exactly. They don't want anything to interfere with the gambling amendment getting on the ballot, and getting passed."

Something sharp pricked at the back of my brain then, a nauseating, sickening thought that made me feel a little disloyal for even thinking it, much less voicing it, but I did. "You do realize that Dad has that case, the challenge to the amendment."

Both men nodded but said nothing. After an uncomfortable silence, I said, "It's certainly another possible motive for murder, the push for the gambling amendment. We're talking big stakes here."

"A professional hit?" the judge asked.

Ted countered with what I had suggested to Ricky. "Why not get rid of the root of the problem—Hobbs?"

Goodwin frowned, looked at me. "Hobbs may be the necessary link."

I nodded. "I'll see what I can do."

As if on cue, my cell phone rang. I pick it up and saw that the incoming call was from Ricky Hobbs.

Chapter Twenty-Two

"There's a spot."

I looked where my dad was pointing, saw the empty parking space just ahead. "I must be living right," I said, flipping my signal and slowing to a stop just in front of the parking space. I eased the Yukon backward and between the lines in one deft maneuver.

"I'm impressed," my father said. "It's obvious which of your parents taught you how to parallel park."

"As I recall, my instruction on the subject came mostly from my high school driver's ed class."

He gave me a feigned look of hurt.

"Don't feel bad. It's hard to instruct when you have your eyes closed."

Dad smiled. "And you gave me good reason to close them."

"I wasn't that bad."

"Let's just say that you have improved quite a bit."

I looked at my watch. "We better get moving. Tip-off's in ten minutes."

Sometimes, as on this date, when it was a school night, I would catch a basketball game with Dad while Mom looked after Maggie. My mom, who cared little for the games themselves, and came mostly to be with Dad, liked the arrangement, and it was nice to have a little one-on-one time with my father.

It was still light out as we headed toward the Civic Center, but just barely, and the temperature was already dropping rapidly. I zipped up my parka and Dad buttoned up his blazer. I studied my father as we walked briskly along the sidewalk. He was showing his age a bit these days, but was still a handsome man. The tall, lean frame still moved with an athletic grace—even if he was a step or two slower than when he played college ball. His hair was more gray than dark brown now, and was thinning a bit but he still had most of it. And when he smiled, it ran deep and showed in his eyes, making him all the more attractive.

I asked him how it was going with the Supreme Court application.

We were walking briskly and he didn't break stride, but he turned his head in my direction. "They have the interviews set up with the nominating commission in two weeks."

"How's it looking?"

"A long shot."

"Everybody I talk to says you have a very good chance."

He gave me a bemused grin. "That's what they tell me, too. You get that a lot when you're a judge. People tell you what they think you want to hear. As the daughter of a judge, you're only one step removed."

"Maybe, but I hear this from people who don't know I'm your daughter. Most say they would hate to lose you on the trial bench, and don't know why you would want the headache of the Supreme Court."

"I wonder that too sometimes. I like what I do, and think I might feel a little claustrophobic in the cloistered world of the appellate court. On the other hand, I think it would be an interesting and different challenge. And, as your mother correctly points out, if I don't give it a try now, it might be too late later on. I'm pushing sixty, you know."

"Sixty's the new forty."

"Maybe, but have you noticed the last few appointments? They're all babies, in their early forties—which I guess is the new twenties."

"On the other hand," I said, "there is an advantage to appointing an older, more experienced person—besides the obvious one. If you get some loose cannon, who surprises you, who doesn't come down on the constitutional issues like you thought, or hoped, you're not stuck with them for twenty-five or thirty years."

"Good point," he said, smiling. "Well, maybe you're right. We'll see."

Inside, we made our way through the throng of people along the perimeter corridor, past the concession stands with their familiar smells of popcorn, hot dogs, beer and nachos. They mixed with the remembered smells of my days on a basketball court: the faint odor of old basketballs, freshly cleaned wood flooring, sweat and excitement, and institutional disinfectant.

That sense of anticipation that precedes the beginning of a game, a subdued, festive mood, moved through the crowd. We made our way to our seats just as the teams finished their warm-ups and gathered at their respective benches. The announcer began the opening introduction of the players, amid darkened lights, laser spotlights and rock music, and the roar of the crowd. As the players ran the gauntlet of high fives, I felt the excitement buzzing through the crowd, and wistfulness for something I had once shared with the players on the floor, but would never have again.

During the first half, FSU played terribly, turning the ball over ten times and shooting twenty eight percent. Their opponent, Maryland, didn't do a whole lot better on the shooting percentage, but they were protecting the ball better and getting more shots. Though my dad and I were not generally big talkers during a game, the conversation during down time inevitably led to the Goodwin case. He listened attentively to my summary, occasionally offering advice or opinion, but mostly just listening.

I told him about Ricky Hobbs.

When I reached the quarterback that day by phone, told him about my conversation with Jeb, and asked him where we stood, he was emphatic and to the point.

"That man is crazy. He wanted me to keep them as my lawyers, but I didn't like his attitude, told him I was going with you. He tried to talk me out of it, tried to suggest you had done something wrong, threatened me with lawsuits—and other things." I could almost sense his smile on the other end. "Guess they misjudged us both."

"And you didn't tell him that I called you and tried to solicit your business?"

"Hell no. 'Cause that's not the way it happened. That man was pulling your chain. You want me to do a statement? I'll do one for you. CYA."

I told him it probably wouldn't hurt, in case memories began to fade. Two days later, Ricky appeared at my office with a retainer check drawn on his mother's account. He signed a representation agreement, which obligated him for the rest, to be paid in installments. I told him I'd work up the CYA statement later. When I asked Hobbs again for names, specifics, he said it was better if I knew as little as possible. I pressed but he said, "Maybe later."

Right now, he said, I need only concern myself with the grand theft charge. He was working another angle on the rest of it. He would be back with me, and if necessary, he would tell me all. "Listen, I just fired a high-powered law firm whose fee was already paid in order to be able to pay you money I don't have to be my lawyer. I'm putting my faith in you, Katie. I need you to have a little faith in me."

I reluctantly agreed. The next day, I filed a motion for substitution of counsel in his case. And I had yet to hear anything further from Jeb.

"How did he pay for his fee?" my father asked. "Was it cash?"

"It was a check drawn on his mother's account."

"Hmmm."

"What?"

"You said his mother was a single parent, working as a hotel maid. That's a lot of money."

I nodded. It was both unethical and illegal for a lawyer to accept payment of a fee if she had reason to believe it came from illegal sources. "I asked Ricky about it. He said his mother had some money in savings and she had borrowed the rest from family and friends."

My dad frowned but said nothing more on the subject. Then he said, "So, what's with you and Jeb? Are you just trying to get under his skin?"

I held up my hands. "He's the one who escalated things. I just hope it doesn't have any effect on your application. Sins of the daughter and all that."

He shook his head. "Don't worry about it. If his support depends on what my daughter does, or doesn't do, then I don't want it."

I looked him in the eyes, knew it was the truth, and admired him for it. I looked back down at the court and up at the game clock. "It's almost half time. I'm going to beat the crowd, get some popcorn and go to the bathroom. You want anything?"

"No. I'm fine. Thanks."

Out in the corridor, I noticed Brian Reeves standing against the wall. He made eye contact and came forward, smiling as he approached. I saw no good alternative but to greet him.

Reeves was the president of the Seminole Boosters, and even without his official designation, he was one of the strongest and most vocal supporters of FSU athletics. He was also president of Sunshine Bank of Tallahassee, a local bank with branches in Tallahassee and the surrounding counties, with its parent bank in Miami. He was loud, aggressive and often obnoxious. I didn't particularly like the man, but he was part of that old Tallahassee family connection which included my mother's family, so I always tried to be polite.

He was a large man, had played offensive linesman—emphasis on offensive—in college and continued to work out and keep himself strong, though a good bit of it had gone to fat. He had no facial hair, and was pretty much bald. What little hair he had on top he shaved, which gave his head a shiny, large look. He reminded me of Jessie Ventura, in his looks as well as his directness. It was hard to imagine how that worked in the banking business, but apparently it did.

"Hey, Kate, my girl. How's it going?"

I started to point out that I was not his girl, far from it, but didn't. "Hey, Mr. Reeves. Nice to see you."

He had an un-lit cigar in his mouth, which he moved from one side of his mouth to the other by rolling it with his tongue. He took it out, gave me a huge smile. "What's this mister stuff. You make me feel old."

"Brian," I said, but without a lot of confidence.

"That's better."

"You enjoying the game?"

He frowned. "Who can enjoy this shit? They should be up by double digits."

I nodded.

"What they need is a Kate Marston."

I smiled, but said nothing in response."

"Shit. You can shoot better than ninety percent of the starters right now, make better passes and you got more heart."

"Quit, now. You're embarrassing me."

He grinned. "I hear your old man's up for the Supreme Court."

"That's right."

"Tell him to give me a call. I may be able to help him with the governor."

"Thanks. I'm sure he would appreciate any help you can give him."

He looked up and down the hallway, then leaned in closer. I could smell the saliva drenched cigar, the beer and nachos on his breath. "I also hear you have taken on the Hobbs case."

"Right again."

"I don't have to tell you how important this case is to the university, to the football program. Hell, to the whole athletics program, and this town."

I said nothing.

He tilted his head, moved his cigar in his mouth again, as if it might give him a better angle, enable him to see inside my head and determine if I really understood what he was saying. "Ricky's a good kid. Wants to make sure he makes the right decisions in this matter. I understand that." He waited a few seconds. "We have people who can help him, but he has to be loyal, if you know what I mean."

I thought I did. "I can't really talk about the case, Brian."

"Of course, of course. I understand. But just between us, you're going to look out for FSU too, aren't you? There is no conflict, right? I mean we can find a way to help out with his legal fees and all, if that helps."

"Brian. You're about as subtle as a sledgehammer."

He put up his hands. "Sorry, Kate, I just want you to understand how important this is, and what is in your long-term interest as a lawyer in this town. We have a real chance at another national championship next year. We can't afford some gambling scandal." The man tilted his head again, trying for the right angle perhaps.

I looked at him for several seconds before speaking. "I'm beginning to wonder if I have something tattooed on my forehead that says, 'This woman responds to threats and intimidation.' Do you really think that's going to work with me?"

There was the big smile again. "You misunderstand me, Katie. I'm not trying to intimidate you. Heaven forbid. But you're a smart gal, someone who can see the big picture. A person always has more than one way to play a hand. That's all I'm saying."

The man had been leaning in closer and closer as he spoke, his voice a hoarse whisper, so that he was now just inches from my face. I pushed the air in front of me with the back of my hand. "Do you mind? If I wanted the nachos, I would have ordered them."

He straightened up and stepped back a step.

"Thanks for the concern, and the counsel, Brian."

"Sure," he said, the smile fading.

"See you around," I said as I moved past him.

"Yeah," he said to my back. "Tell your folks I said hey."

I threw my hand up, but didn't turn back around or say anything. I got some popcorn and a drink and made it back to my seat just before the start of the second half. I told Dad about the encounter with Reeves.

"That asshole," he said, noticeably upset, looking around to see if he could spot the man. "I'm going to have a little chat with Mr. Reeves."

"That's really kind of sweet, Dad, but I'm too old for my daddy to fight my fights for me."

He smiled, a little calmer now. "I guess you can handle yourself, anyway."

I gave him a smile and a nod, and we settled back to watch the second half. F. S. U. did a little better but not well enough. They lost by twelve. As we were leaving, Dad collected his blazer from the seat next to him and put it on. Something caught my eye.

"Looks like you're missing a button," I said.

"Huh?"

"On your sleeve," I said, pointing at his left arm.

He twisted his arm and pulled it up, looking at the row of buttons. There were only three, as opposed to the four on the other sleeve. You could see the thread sticking out slightly. "Ah, so I am," he said. "Must have caught it on something."

I looked again at the empty spot and the three gold plated buttons still in place. Something clicked in the far reaches of my mind, but it didn't register consciously. It was only a vague sense of something familiar.

The walk back to the car was mostly silent, each of us perhaps lost in thought. I couldn't seem to shake a vague sense of unease, unsure of exactly why. I dropped Dad at the house and picked up Maggie. All the way home, I still couldn't shake the discomfort, and I began to understand or identify the source.

Once home, after I got Maggie to bed, I went to the den, and to the stack of files from the Goodwin case I had placed on the conference table against the wall. I thumbed through the manila file folders until I found the one labeled "Photos of Crime Scene." I pulled it from the stack, opened it and began searching for the ones taken in Elena's bedroom. I quickly found the one I was looking for and held it up to the light.

It was the close-up photo of the gold-plated blazer button I'd seen in Elena's jewelry box. Just like the one missing from my father's blazer.

Chapter Twenty-Three

Dick Wilson was not particularly athletic. He was slow and uncoordinated, and his vertical leap was practically non-existent. But he was sky scraper tall, with disproportionately long arms, and knew how to get good position under the basket. So, when the shot went up, and I could see that it would miss, I started drifting over to the side, positioning myself for the outlet pass. And sure enough, Dick came up with the rebound. He spotted me, zipped the ball over, and the fast break began.

A well-executed fast break is not only a work of art and a thing of beauty; it is wonderfully symbolic of a life in motion, fast, furious, but hopefully, under control. It requires a combination of finely tuned spatial skills, depth perception, speed, balance, and instinct; a mind's eye that lets you see even that which is not in your line of sight.

And I loved to be in the middle of it.

On the sides, two of my teammates were fanning out in two symmetrical arcs, the apex of which would converge on either side of the far basket Two opposing players were hustling back to prevent an easy basket, including the player assigned to me, Jimmy Cooksey. I took it directly to the basket, forcing Jimmy to cover me, then, trusting in the connectivity of cause and effect that lay just beneath the surface of the apparent chaos, I flipped a no-look pass to Bob on my right, who was a couple of steps beyond his man. Jimmy had to shift over to head him off.

Bob had the angle on Jimmy and should have just gone straight to the basket, but he tried a bounce pass to our teammate approaching on the other side. Jimmy anticipated it, scooped it up and headed back the other way. He flung it to one of his guys who had been slow getting back on defense—in other words, a slacker. The big man took the ball, bounced it the few steps to the basket and laid it in, no one within twenty feet of him. And that was the game.

As I said, a well-executed fast break is a work of art and a thing of beauty, the emphasis being on well executed.

"Sorry guys. My fault," Bob said, as we headed off the court. No one said anything for a several seconds, acknowledging and encouraging the taking of responsibility. Immediate contradiction would have seemed insincere, and somehow insulting.

"Don't worry about it," I said finally. "Jimmy made a good play."

"He is so quick," someone else said behind me.

I looked at the clock on the wall and announced, "That's it for me."

There were mock protests from some, gentle ribbing from others about getting my priorities straight, but everyone knew I wouldn't be leaving early if I didn't have to. Years before, there had been some resentment and skepticism when I joined the group. Who was this woman trying to play with the men? But I had gradually earned their acceptance with my ability, and my willingness to mix it up with them physically. Gender was not completely forgotten out on the court, but it was no longer a barrier to the natural competition we all brought with us.

With echoes of "see you later" in my ear, I headed for the locker room. Thirty minutes later, I was on my way to my appointment.

The sky had been overcast most of the day, and the mid-afternoon light was weak, pale, producing no real warmth, and entirely befitting my mood. The workout had been relatively short, but vigorous. It had gone a long way toward easing the tension that had been following me all day.

I had been anxious, nauseous, outside myself ever since I looked at that photograph the night of the ballgame. It may have been coincidental that my dad's blazer was missing a button that looked identical to the one depicted. After all, it was a common enough piece.

It was no doubt the same kind that was on hundreds, maybe thousands, of blazers worn by men in the city. Yes, it could simply be a coincidence.

On the other hand, I simply could not ignore it, either. I would not be my father's daughter, would I, if I didn't follow up on it. And it wasn't just the button. My father had been assigned to the gambling amendment case. What was it Elena had said, according to the friend Ted talked to? More important than the jury you pick is the judge you screw---and she hadn't said screw, Ted said. The thought sickened me. It scared me. But I couldn't ignore it.

Perhaps I should have just asked him right out, but I resisted this approach, for both good and bad reasons. So, I began a secretive investigation of my father. First, I rechecked Elena's cell phone records. There were a few calls to his office, but not more than to other judges, all of whom she had been recruiting for a Habitat for Humanity build. Nothing from her cell to my dad's cell or his home phone number. I was told by the phone company representative with whom I spoke that there were no accessible records to ascertain calls Elena may have made or received on her land line phone. Possibly Dad had called her there on his cell phone, but I had not been able to check my parents' cell phone records.

I next tried to establish whether he had an alibi, indirectly of course. I questioned my mother, ostensibly to nail down the timing of Ruth Campbell's supposed sighting of Goodwin outside Elena's door. I talked with her by phone, which was better, as there was less of a chance that I would give myself away as to my true purpose. My mother had always been eerily capable of discerning when one of her daughters was lying to her. Any handicap I could give her in this respect was prudent.

When I explained the purpose of my call there was silence on the other end for a few seconds, followed by a deep sigh. "So, you can try to make her appear to be a senile old woman who must have been confused, who doesn't know what she saw? I know it's your job, but she doesn't deserve that."

She was right on both counts, and I said so, but it was my job, and I had to do the best I could. "Even the smallest detail might give me something to use to show she was mistaken."

"She wasn't mistaken, though, was she?"

"I don't know." I hoped she didn't catch the lie.

She had reluctantly relented then told me when the book club meeting had broken up, when she had dropped off our former neighbor, and when she had gotten home, at about ten thirty, ten forty-five, and eleven o'clock, respectively.

"Was there anything that stands out in your mind? Did you watch the eleven o'clock news, for example? Was it already on when you turned on the set, or just starting? Or just about over? Was Dad home when you arrived? You think he could corroborate the time? If he wasn't there, do you remember when he arrived?"

"Am I a suspect, Mary Katherine? Is your father?"

Damn her sixth sense! "Of course not," I said, again hoping she could not hear the lie in my voice. "I just want to be very precise on the timing."

My mother sighed again, then said that no, she didn't watch the news when she got home. And no, my father was not home when she arrived. She reminded me this was his poker night. She had gone to bed around eleven thirty or so, and he had come in sometime around twelve thirty, maybe a little after.

Assuming my father was, in fact, at the poker game, he would have a good, and verifiable, alibi. It was what now brought me to the offices of Spiato Insurance Agency.

Anthony "Tony" Spiato had been my dad's casualty insurance agent for as long as I could remember, and a regular guest at Marston holiday parties. He was short, fat and jovial in that cliché way associated with fat people. It had been a natural transition for me to turn to Tony myself when I was old enough to need and pay for my own insurance. I had used the pretense of a review of my insurance coverage as a reason to make an appointment.

After the obligatory inquiries as to each other's families, we discussed my insurance coverage issues. As we were wrapping up, I broached the subject which was the real reason for my visit. "By the way, Tony, while I'm here, let me ask you something, unrelated to insurance."

"Uh huh?"

I reminded him that I was representing Renny Goodwin, and said I was trying to establish a timeline for things. "As it turns out, my mother gave their eyewitness a ride home that night and I'm trying to nail down the time. When I asked Mom what time she got home, she wasn't real sure, but she said my dad was already there, maybe a little after eleven o'clock." The lie had come amazingly easy. "I haven't had a chance to talk with Dad about it, but I'm pretty sure that was poker night for you guys, which would usually mean it would be more like twelve-thirty or one."

He looked at me, as if trying to figure out what I was asking.

"So, were y'all playing poker that night?"

He nodded. "Yeah. I remember because the next day is when they said the Castillo woman was found dead."

"Do you remember about what time the game broke up?"

"About twelve fifteen, twelve thirty. The usual."

I willed my face to remain passive. "So, it sounds like my mom must have been mistaken. Either she got home well before he did, or she was later getting home than she thought."

"Well, maybe not."

My heart, which had soared only moments before, now began knocking against my chest so loudly I felt that surely he could hear it. "What do you mean?"

"You asked me when the card game broke up, not when your dad left."

I started to say something but the words froze in my throat. I just stared at him expectantly.

"Actually, Phil left early that night. He got a call about ten thirty or so. He seemed distracted. After a few minutes he said he wasn't feeling too well and was going to go on home. This was around ten forty-five or so."

I closed my eyes then, trying with all my strength to remain composed, but I now felt the beating heart in my ears, felt the beads of sweat forming on my brow. "Are you sure?"

"Pretty sure." He paused, then said, "Hey, you're looking a little peaked. You okay?"

"I think I'm coming down with a touch of flu or something."

"Yeah, there's some of that going around." He stood, a signal that our visit was over. "Anyway, I hope that helps."

"It does. Thanks."

"Now, I could be wrong, or off a little bit. You might want to ask your dad, or some of the other guys."

"Not that big of a deal. And listen, I'll let you know what I decide on the umbrella policy."

"Sure thing, Katie. We appreciate your business. You take care, now."

I waved a goodbye as I headed out the door and maintained an air of nonchalance as I walked to my car. Once inside, though, a cold dread enveloped my entire body, and I began to shake uncontrollably. After about a minute, I managed to calm myself enough to start the Yukon, and put it in gear. Gripping the steering wheel so tightly I thought my knuckles would explode, I slowly drove out of the parking lot.

Chapter Twenty-Four

I removed my glasses, placed them on the desk, then rubbed my eyes. I felt paralyzed by fatigue, overwhelmed by the desire, the need, for sleep. I looked up at the clock on the wall. Fifteen minutes before my scheduled appointment with Natalie Olsen. Leaning back in the chair, I put my feet up on the desk, rested my head against the soft leather and closed my eyes. Within seconds, I was drifting into that nether world between the conscious and unconscious. My body surrendered immediately, but my mind was not willing to completely relinquish the thoughts which had held its attention moments before.

It was unlikely that Elena Castillo had been pregnant at the time of her death. This was the opinion of our pathologist expert, Ethan Morrison, with whom Ted and I spoke with yesterday. We met him for lunch at Famous Fred's, a barbeque restaurant near his office. The man had been rather emphatic on the subject. "You'd have to be an idiot, incredibly lazy, or corrupt to miss something like that."

My response, only slightly tongue-in-cheek, was that I wouldn't rule out any of those options.

Morrison chuckled at this observation, took a bite of pulled pork sandwich and said, "Neither would I, but I doubt the judge will allow a second autopsy on such an argument."

"Maybe it's best anyway," I said, "if we don't say anything about it until trial. If the coroner says he checked for pregnancy, we point out that he made no note about it. If he says he didn't, we put on Ethan to say it could and should have been done. Either way it suggests incompetence, which may translate into reasonable doubt."

Ted took a bite of rib. "The advantage is, the prosecution would have no opportunity to call our bluff, to refute the suggestion. And if you can somehow find a way to let the jury know that we wanted to exhume the body and the State resisted . . ."

"It looks like they're trying to hide something," I said.

"Exactly."

"What about an abortion?" I asked, turning to Ethan. "Would the M.E. have looked for, and could he have determined if Elena had an abortion?

Ethan shook his head. "He might not have specifically been looking for signs of an abortion, but even if he had, it would be unlikely there would be any evidence of it, unless it had been really recent, like within a week before her death."

We ate in silence for several long seconds then before Morrison suggested that suicide was still a viable argument, consistent with the physical findings.

"Still," I said, "it would be nice to come up with a motive, something the jury could accept as a reason she may have wanted to take her own life."

Both men nodded, but had no suggestions on this score, and we finished our meal with talk of things other than work.

The buzz of my phone brought me back to the present. I removed my feet from the top of the desk and sat back up in my chair. I glanced at the clock on the wall as I picked up the phone. "Yes, Jennifer?"

"Ms. Olsen is here for her appointment."

"I'll be right there."

I took my file, greeted Natalie in the lobby, then led her to the conference room. I sat at the head of the long, oval walnut table and had my client sit to my right, so as best to be able to look at her directly and also share documents.

My client, like her lawyer, looked tired, and more than a little anxious. I was not surprised. We were scheduled for a temporary relief hearing in her divorce case the next morning. Judge Carlson, who had handled the domestic violence injunction hearing had granted the injunction, but declined to award alimony or more than token child support. Natalie had been able to find a job with a local dentist, but it was only temporary and part time, and she was having a hard time getting by on her small salary.

My client seemed even more anxious, more haggard than I would have expected. There were large rings around her eyes, which had sunken further into the sockets since last we met. She had lost weight, and her dress hung loosely on an already thin frame. As soon as we were seated at the table, I learned the reason.

"He's been following me, watching me."

"Who? Your husband?"

She nodded. "He's been driving by the house at night. I've also seen him a couple of times, parked in the lot where I work, or down the street, watching me as I leave the office. He stays just long enough to catch my eye, then he leaves."

"That's a violation of the injunction. We can have him arrested."

The client shook her head. "That will just make matters worse. And I don't want the father of my children in jail. Besides, I don't have any proof; just his word against mine."

"Your testimony alone could be enough, but there are also ways to corroborate what you have observed. You can use a video camera, or your cell phone you know, to record it."

She frowned. "I didn't think of that."

"Did the children see him?"

"No. and I don't want to involve them in this. It's been hard enough as it is."

"Co-workers?"

My client shook her head.

I frowned. "At the very least, we need to bring it up at the hearing tomorrow. The judge can require him to be on electronic monitoring, which can pinpoint where he is at any given time. It can also be programmed to alert if he comes into specified hot zones—like your neighborhood or the strip mall where you work. You should call 911 on your cell phone anytime you see him. And call me too. Any time, day or night."

"I appreciate it, Kate. I really do. But you don't know him. I don't care what a judge tells him. I don't care what kind of monitoring is required. If I push too hard . . ." She didn't finish the sentence but her meaning was clear.

"It's going to be okay, Natalie." I reached over and put my hand on her shoulder. "Listen, I would not try to minimize the real danger to you. You are right that no piece of paper is going to stop someone who is willing to disobey a court order. I do know that if you let him intimidate you, it will only get worse. It's a scary time, for sure, but I will do everything I can to make sure you are safe, if you'll work with me."

"Okay," she said finally, letting out a sigh. "But you need to be alert too, Kate."

I smiled. "Don't worry. I'm used to it. I can take care of myself."

My client gave me a skeptical look, but didn't contradict me. Though she still seemed nervous, she began to relax noticeably as we discussed the issues and her expected testimony the next day. When I offered to walk her out to her car, she protested that it wasn't necessary, though she seemed relieved when I did anyway.

As I watched my client drive away, I had an eerie feeling that I too was being watched. I scanned the area in all directions, slowly, unobtrusively. A car, parked just on the other side of Adams Street, on College Avenue, caught my attention. It was a black BMW 740i. Something about it seemed strange, and familiar.

Could it be Natalie's husband? Or had my client planted the seed of paranoia in my mind. Natalie had obviously not thought anything of it, or perhaps she had not noticed it. I couldn't remember off the top of my head what kind of car he drove. I stared at the BMW for several seconds, then walked toward it. When I reached the intersection with Adams Street, the car's engine roared to life. As I waited for the light to change, I tried to see into the car, but the windows were tinted. After a couple of seconds, the BMW exited the parking space, turned right on Duval Street and soon was out of sight.

Back in my office, I looked through Natalie's file, finding what I was looking for rather quickly, in the financial affidavit which listed the income, assets and liabilities of the parties. Although the color wasn't noted, among the assets listed by the husband was a 2010 BMW 740i.

I called Natalie on her cell phone. "Hey, Natalie. This is Kate. Your husband drives a BMW 740i, right?"

There was just a hint of the alarm I wanted to avoid in my client's voice when she said, "Yes."

"What color?"

"Have you seen him?" The alarm in her voice was more than just a hint now. "Oh, my God. Did he follow me to your office?"

I thought then that maybe I should lie, tell her I just wanted to make sure I had it in my files. But I didn't think it fair to her. She deserved to know. "Maybe," I said, waiting through the tense silence on the other end for a couple of beats before repeating, "So, what color?"

"Black."

Chapter Twenty-Five

I was feeling a little jumpy when I left the office a short while later and began walking toward Kleman Plaza for my meeting with Professor Everhart. Sure, it could have been a coincidence, the car down the street, but I didn't think so.

And neither did Natalie.

Perhaps I had been wrong to even mention it to her. Would she be more alert, more likely to call the police if she saw her husband again? Or would she become even more scared, more reluctant to follow through with tomorrow's hearing? Her voice was weak, but not panicked, when she asked me, "What are you going to do?"

"There's nothing I really can do. I don't have an injunction against him. You do. And I can't really say it was him. All I saw was the car." I paused a moment. "And even if it was him, technically, he was more than five hundred feet away, as per the order." I could sense the combination of relief and anxiety on the other end. "If you see him again, anywhere, if you get a whiff of his scent, promise me you will call the police, and me. Day or night."

After a few moments, the voice on the other end said, "I promise."

I tried to sound confident and assuring to my client, but now, as I came to the corner of College and Duval, waiting to cross over to Kleman Plaza, I looked all around the area, up and down both streets. I saw no black BMW 740i.

Harry's was packed, and noisy. I quickly picked out the professor sitting at a small table in the bar area. I smiled in his direction and walked toward him. He stood and we exchanged hugs.

In addition to Torts and Evidence, the professor also taught Professional Responsibility on occasion, and he had a very pragmatic

197

approach to the subject, which I thought would be valuable to me at this point.

"I appreciate you meeting me on short notice."

"Beautiful woman wants to buy me a drink? That's an easy call."

"Yeah, right. Your diplomatic skills are great, but you might want to get your eyes checked."

He frowned. "No diplomacy about it. I know a beautiful woman when I see one."

"Okay. Okay. You're embarrassing me. I'm sorry I said anything." I moved my silverware absently, looked back up. "Anyway, thanks for coming."

This time he just nodded, looking at me closely, and then, as if sensing something underneath my cracked smile, something in my tone of voice, he said, "What's wrong?"

I ran my hand through my hair, smiled weakly." Just a little tired. Didn't sleep well last night."

The waiter came then and took our orders. When he left, Everhart leaned in closer. "You said you had an ethics issue you wanted to discuss?"

"Speaking hypothetically . . ."

Everhart nodded, understanding the convenient fiction that we were not talking about an actual case, or about me.

"Hypothetically, what if you were representing a client in a criminal case and you discovered information that led to another suspect, someone with whom you had a prior relationship?"

"A client?"

"Yes."

My father was not a client, but if I had said no, the obvious question would be, what is the nature of the relationship—and I didn't want to go there. Client was close enough.

"And this is a former client, not a current client?"

"Former."

The waiter came with our beers. When he left, Everhart leaned back slightly in his chair, made a tent of his fingers and rested his chin on it. "Speaking hypothetically, I'd say that if the information you have was obtained as a result of your representation of that former client, you can't divulge it, or use it in any way that is adverse to that client."

I nodded.

"If not, then your duty is to your current client. It may be a little awkward, depending on the nature and extent of the prior relationship, but you have a duty to the present client. You have to pursue that."

He paused a few moments, then said, "Now, you do have the option of withdrawing from your current representation. That doesn't eliminate the immediate problem, because you already have the information, and a duty to tell your client. But at least you wouldn't have to follow up on it. A new attorney would have that job."

"But I'd have to tell the client what I had so far?"

"Correct."

"Unless the information was obtained as a result of my prior representation?"

"Correct."

After several long seconds, and when it appeared he had nothing more to add, I said, "Thanks, Professor. That's pretty much what I thought. I just wanted confirm it with you."

He gave me a sideways glance. "This hypothetical case, is it a high-profile case involving a sitting judge?"

"Would it make a difference?"

"No," he said. "Just curious."

He didn't press it further, and I was glad. The undefined, vague tension between us relaxed then and we moved on to other topics. I could not, however, ignore the anxiety that seemed to have taken up permanent residency in my stomach. It gnawed at me, and the conversation with Everhart had made it worse. At the first available opportunity, I made my excuses and left the restaurant, afraid that he might see through the mask.

On the drive home, I replayed the conversation with the professor, but this time, imagining it the way it would have gone had I been more forthcoming.

"Okay, let's think this through. A conflict of interest has developed as to your continued representation of Warren Goodwin."

"Agreed."

"It's really pretty simple. You have two choices. You either disclose this new information to your client, and use it as best protects or promotes his interests, or you withdraw from representation."

"It's not that simple."

"Why not?"

"Because this is my father we're talking about, my flesh and blood."

"Exactly, which is why it makes it simple. You have to get off the case. Regardless of what he has done, you can't betray your father. You can convince yourself that what you have now is pure speculation, not enough to warrant disclosure. But if you go further . . . You have to get out now. It's that simple."

"But how do I handle it? What do I say to the client, to the judge, as my reason for withdrawing from representation?"

"Tell them you have developed a conflict that will not allow you to continue to vigorously represent your client. End of story. You don't have to tell them the nature of the conflict."

"What if they ask? What if the client wants to know to decide whether to waive the conflict? Or the judge wants to know in order to properly evaluate my motion—especially if the client objects? And I can't just be vague and say the conflict is with another client, and that to name the client would betray the attorney client privilege, because my father is not, in fact, a client."

"I see your point. If not a client, then it must be someone very close to you—a family member or close friend to whom your loyalty dictates that you abandon a client, and in the biggest, most visible case of your career."

"And if I say I need to withdraw but can't give a reason, that it's personal, the suspicion is really raised."

"So, make up a reason. You could say that the case is taking more time than you thought, that it has been physically and emotionally taxing, stressful. Say that you need to devote more time to your daughter."

"Yes, I could, but it would be a lie, and I am strangely old fashioned in this respect. I know, I know, you're going to say that I've already abandoned the honestly-is-the-best policy by concealing the conflict itself, and that is true, but I don't want to compound a lie of omission with an affirmative misrepresentation. The second problem with this approach is neither my client nor my co-counsel is likely to believe it. It would be way out of character for me to quit, saying it was too physically or emotionally draining. Nor would I want people to think that. Call it pride, ego, but there it is."

"There's also the problem that whoever took your place might come upon the same evidence, develop the same suspicions. And then no family loyalty could protect your dad."

"Yes."

A long silence, then, "You're right. It's not that simple."

Then something else occurred to me. Some people knew Charles Everhart as Judge. Could he be "the" judge? I managed to tuck this unsettling question away with a promise to come back to it later.

It was a little after eight o'clock when I pulled into my driveway. The house was dark and still. Before I got out of my Yukon, I noticed the car in my rear-view mirror, passing along rather slowly on Hillcrest Avenue. It was dark and I couldn't be sure, but it looked like a BMW 740i. A black one.

I jerked my head around quickly to try to get a better look, but my vision was blocked by the fence row hedge. I could see the tail lights, though, as the car moved down the street, and I watched until they disappeared beyond the hill that led down to Tennessee Street. When I got out of my car, I stood there for several seconds, listening and looking. Once inside I also looked out the window, careful to move the blinds only enough to see out, leaving the lights off so nobody could see in. A pick-up truck passed by in the minutes I stood there, and so did a Ford Mustang, but no BMW. I closed the blinds and scolded myself for letting my imagination get the better of me.

I had been so distracted I had forgotten to check my mail. When I went back outside to do so, I found no regular envelopes, but only a package, about the size of a DVD. In the light of the streetlamp and the flood lights I examined it. No return address and no postage.

Now, had I been thinking about it clearly, I might not have opened it, given recent events, but all I could think about was discovering what was inside. In my living room, I tore off the outer brown paper, opened one end of the cardboard container and retrieved what turned out to be, indeed, a DVD. It had no title or other markings. I looked inside the package and saw a slip of paper which I pulled out between two fingers. I unfolded it and read the typed message.

"A copy of this same DVD was delivered to the State Attorney's Office five days ago. Watch it. And ask yourself why it has not been disclosed to you."

Chapter Twenty-Six

So, as the note suggested, I watched the DVD.

It was divided into two separate segments. In each, a man was having sex with Elena Castillo. Though not of high quality, the images were clear enough for me to identify the participants—Lester Appleton, General Counsel to the Governor, and Brent Hargrove, President of the Senate. I also recognized the location of the scenes—Elena's bedroom—and the camera angle—from above the headboard. I remembered the Madonna statuette on the shelf there and Elena's comment about the Holy Mother watching. She must have hidden the camera in there somehow. I smiled at the irony.

After my second viewing, I read the accompanying note again, then I got Ted on the phone.

"You busy?"

"Watching the Lakers on T.V."

"We need to talk."

"What is it?"

Maybe my client's paranoia was beginning to rub off on me, but I didn't want to say more on the phone, in case it was bugged. "I'll tell you when you get here."

Silence for a couple of seconds, then, "I'll be there in ten minutes."

Fifteen minutes later, Ted was sitting next to me on the couch in my family room, the cup of coffee I had offered him in his hand, watching the DVD. It felt a little weird, like we were watching a porn film together, so I got up and walked into the kitchen, waited for the end of the recording, then went back in.

"So, what do you think?"

Ted looked as if he were about to make a joke, then thought better of it. "I'd say we have confirmation of the rumors."

"Doesn't look like the gentlemen involved knew they were being recorded."

"You think?"

"Which means Elena was setting them up, probably for a little blackmail, a little leverage to get what she wanted from them. This certainly gives us some alternative suspects. This DVD gives us concrete evidence of their sexual relationship with the victim, something the State does not have as to our client."

Ted nodded. "Which brings up the logical question, why isn't Goodwin on the video?" After a few seconds of silence, he asked, "You think it was Goodwin who left it for you? Edited himself out of it?"

"The thought occurred to me."

"I'm thinking our guy did it, Kate. He killed her. And he is manipulating the evidence, the prosecution, and his lawyers to get away with it."

"Maybe," I said, frowning. "How will we authenticate the DVD? When was it taken? Does it accurately depict the scene at that date and time?"

Ted smiled. "You call each of the studs shown on the video and ask them if it accurately depicts what was happening."

I smiled too. "With one of those warnings, like you see on car side mirrors—objects may be larger than they appear."

Ted snorted a short laugh. "Twist that dagger, woman."

"They deserve it."

Ted shrugged. "Maybe so, but on a sliding scale, I'd say Ms. Castillo's got them beat. Taping them without their knowledge? Then no doubt blackmailing them later? That's pretty low."

"You're suggesting maybe she got what she deserved?"

Ted shrugged again. "No, but when you engage in risky behavior, there may be consequences." He hesitated a beat. "Bottom line, as far as ethics go, they were all swimming in the shallow end of the ethics pool, but she was worse. That's all I'm saying."

After a brief pause, I said, "If it wasn't accident or suicide, if it was murder, I'm thinking that whoever left this video is probably Elena Castillo's killer."

Ted nodded. "And if not our client, who else? If it was someone else, why give you the DVD? Or the State Attorney for that matter? Why take the risk?"

"Maybe he, or she, felt guilty. Didn't want to see an innocent man convicted."

Ted gave me a skeptical look.

"You got a better idea?"

He didn't.

Nor did I like where my suspicions were taking me. I could think of one person who might fit that description. "You think there may be other tapes? Other men?"

"Could be. Better question is, do you think the author of the note is telling the truth, about having given a copy to the State Attorney?"

I thought about that for a moment. "I hope so. If Lipton got a copy of this days ago and he hasn't told us about it—"

"He's been withholding Brady material."

I nodded. Brady material referred to any information that might be exculpatory to the defendant, so named after the case which held that the prosecutor was under an affirmative duty to disclose such information, regardless of whether the defense specifically requested it. "Exactly. And Mitchell will not be pleased. Judges take this kind of thing very seriously. Grounds for dismissal."

"Maybe." I paused, took a sip of coffee. "So, how do we play this?"

"Well, we have to tell Goodwin."

I nodded.

"He will appear appropriately surprised."

"Indeed."

Ted took a sip of coffee, sat down the cup. "I say we give Lipton enough rope with which to hang himself, get that noose tight around his neck." He took another sip. "If he has it, the longer he waits to disclose, the worse it looks for him. If he doesn't have it, we gain nothing by telling him about it. We can spring it at trial."

I shook my head. "No, we can't. Since we requested discovery from the State, we are under a reciprocal duty to disclose any witness or exhibit we intend to use at trial."

Ted thought about it a few moments. "Well, we haven't decided yet if we intend to use it at trial."

"Nice try, but there's no question we reasonably can anticipate using this video at trial. We can hold off a bit, but we have to disclose it."

He shook his head. "It doesn't seem right."

"No, it doesn't." I coughed to clear my throat before continuing. "We wait a few more days. If we get nothing, I send a letter asking if there is any new evidence to disclose since our initial demand for discovery. If he doesn't cough it up then we file a motion. Right now, the arrogant bastard probably hasn't even considered the possibility that we have a copy. Either way, this video just might be the silver bullet we need."

"Yes, our anonymous friend has been very helpful," Ted said. "But why?"

The silence stretched between us as we both struggled unsuccessfully for an answer. Finally, I said, "We'll need to investigate our two new friends, discreetly, of course. I don't want them, or the State, to know what we know. Check out their alibis, see if we can pin them to the murder more convincingly. I can take their depositions when the time comes, but we don't want to show our cards too early." I looked at Ted and arched my eyebrows.

"I'll get on it," he said.

At nine forty-five the next morning, I walked out of the State Attorney's Office into the atrium area on the fourth floor of the courthouse, took my cell phone out of my purse, and punched in the number for Ricky Hobbs. As I listened to the phone ringing, I moved over to the large fixed glass window and looked out at the Capitol building across the way.

The moral dilemma concerning my father that I had wrestled with the night before had not resolved itself overnight, but I had managed to push it back into a deeper chamber of my brain. The pressing requirements of my other cases had helped to divert my attention. So had the DVD. The all-consuming obsession had become, for the time being, simply a nagging, pestering companion who announced its presence from time to time with a dull, throbbing pain in my temples, and a tightening in my stomach. I had showed up at the State Attorney's Office feeling tired, running a low-grade fever, and not on my game, which is not the way I like to go into plea negotiations. But I didn't have much choice.

Charlotte Blanchard was one of the more experienced prosecutors in the office, and one of the most reasonable when it came to working out a plea agreement. When she called and suggested we meet, I saw it as a good sign. I told Ricky I'd call him right after with the results.

Just when I thought I was going to get Ricky's voice mail, he picked up.

"Hello."

He sounded sleepy.

"Hey, Ricky. It's Kate Marston. You able to talk?"

"Sure. How'd it go?"

I told him. "Here's the deal. You plea no contest to petit theft on the Macy's thing. You get a withhold of adjudication, six months probation with conditions: you stay away from Macy's and do 100 hours of community service. You can get an early termination of probation upon completion of the hours. Standard court costs and fines."

I waited a few seconds for him to digest what I had said. "On the gambling charge, they are willing to drop the charge if you cooperate in their statewide grand jury investigation. You'd have to give them names, details, testify before the grand jury, and at trial if necessary. You do that, not only will they drop the charges, but you get immunity from prosecution based on anything you tell them."

The silence on the other end lasted for several seconds before I added, "This is about as good as it gets, Ricky. No felony record. No criminal record at all."

"What about the NCAA?"

"The State Attorney has no control over what they do, but it sure can't hurt if the prosecutor decides not to pursue criminal charges." More silence on the other end. What had I expected? Joy? Relief? Gratitude maybe?

"If I do a tell-all to the State, and the NCAA gets a hold of it, don't matter what they do on the criminal charges, I'm toast as far as playing football goes." He was probably right, I said, but reminded him that the Grand Jury proceedings were secret, and it was a crime to disclose testimony given before the Grand Jury. "Maybe it won't go to trial and you wouldn't have to testify."

"Can they convict me on either one of the charges? They ain't got a case, do they?"

"The gambling charge is weak, what with the main witness against you having recanted, and being less than credible anyway. But, if you'll excuse the pun, it's not something I'd want to gamble on, not with the stakes so high. The grand theft charge, well, you accepted almost five hundred dollars' worth of free clothing. We'll have a hard time trying to explain that away. And this is a package deal. They are willing to give on that to get what they want on the gambling. Apparently, they have much bigger fish they want to fry."

After a pause he said, "I'll give them names, and details, but I can't testify. It needs to be anonymous. If it gets out I'm cooperating, I'm a dead man."

I hesitated. His observation had the ring of truth, at least from his perspective. "I'll see what I can do, but I have to tell you, the prosecutor seemed pretty firm on this part. It is the biggest part of the equation."

"Can't do it," he said. "That wasn't even supposed to be part of the deal."

"What do you mean?"

"Nothing. Never mind. Just see what you can do, and I'll work on it from this side."

"That's just what I'm afraid of. Listen Ricky, this is serious stuff. I think your best bet is to come clean. If you have information that people don't want divulged, you're in danger. If other people know it, it lessens the danger to you. Besides, I'm going to need to give the prosecutor a proffer, something specific so she can evaluate whether they can use it without the necessity of you testifying." I waited through the silence for several seconds until my client responded.

"Let me try something first on this end. If you can't get them to go along with what we want by the end of the week, I'll give them names and details."

"Ricky?"

"Yeah?"

"Be careful."

I could feel his smile, sense his confidence returning on the other end. "Don't you worry. I know how to scramble."

I was tempted to extend the football metaphor and remind him I'd seen him get sacked on occasion, too, but I let it pass. Didn't want to jinx him. When we disconnected with promises to talk again within forty-eight hours, I stood there for several seconds, wondering whether I should go back right then, and approach Charlotte with the alternative. I decided not. No sense getting her annoyed by looking the proverbial gift horse in the mouth. Better to wait and see if my client came around. Besides, I thought, looking at my watch, I had only five minutes before my scheduled hearing in Natalie Olsen's case.

When I got off the elevator, I saw my client and her husband standing close together, talking. I rushed over and put myself between the two. "Mr. Olsen, do you want to go to jail? You are under a court order to have no contact with your wife."

The man tensed up noticeably and for an instant, seeing the rage behind his eyes, I thought he might hit me. But he seemed to will himself under control, held his hands up, backed up a couple of feet, smiling at me. "We were just talking about the case, seeing if we could come to an understanding," he said, looking at his wife, who refused to meet either his or my eyes, preferring instead to look at her shoes. "Uh huh."

"It's all right, Kate," my client said, tiredness, surrender in her voice. "We were just talking about the children."

"No, it is not all right. Neither of you has the right to ignore a court order." I turned and faced the husband. "Now, if you don't walk right over to the other side of the hallway, and do it quickly, I will call a bailiff over and show him a copy of the injunction."

Ah, if looks could kill, I would have been dead on the floor. The husband drilled into me with those eyes as if trying to physically enter me. I could almost feel the hatred emanating from the man. He put up his hands again and said, "I'll let you ladies talk in private." He looked at his wife. "Think about what's best for our children, and for us, Natalie."

My client would not meet his eyes, continuing to look at the top of her shoes. I watched her husband turn and walk slowly across the rotunda area and lean against the far wall. Satisfied that he was no longer a threat, I turned back to my client. "What's going on, Natalie?"

The woman looked even more stressed than she had the day before. She ventured a small smile, brushed her hair to the side with her fingers. "I want you to dismiss the case, get the injunction lifted so Jared and I can try and work things out."

"You what?" I strove for incredulity, but I'm sure the anger came through as well. I tried to tell myself that it was fear, and intellectually, I knew this to be true. Honestly, I wanted to slap the woman to her senses, but the irony would have been too much, so I silently counted to ten as I looked across the rotunda at the husband once, then turned back to my client.

"Not going to let you do that, Natalie." I moved a little closer and used my superior height to crowd my client, who looked up at me with eyes wide, questioning.

"Listen, it's clear to me that your husband has been violating the injunction, and he's got you real scared. Now, I know you don't want to confront him. You don't have to. That's why you have me. I just need you to be strong for a little while. For yourself, and for your children."

I waited several seconds for Natalie to take in what I was saying. "Now, I'm going to put you on the stand in there and you are going to tell the truth. I am going to get the restraining order continued and have it clarified to your husband. We will get you a reasonable amount of temporary child support and alimony. Then, after a few weeks, when you are not under the stress of his stalking and harassment, we can talk about it. But if you don't tell the judge the situation, I will withdraw and tell him what has been going on."

After several long seconds, Natalie looked up at me, nodded and said, "Okay."

I nodded too, satisfied. "Wait here. I'll be right back."

I turned and walked across the rotunda area, where her husband was still leaning against the wall. The man gave me a victor's smile as I approached, no doubt anticipating the formal capitulation from his wife's attorney. I smiled back at him, stopped about two feet away. Though he outweighed me considerably, we were approximately the same height, so I was looking directly into his eyes.

"Mr. Olsen, if you ever speak to my client, call her, send her a letter, an e-mail, a card, flowers, drive by her house or her work, make any attempt at communication, except through me, I will do everything in my power to see that you are not only held in contempt, but are charged criminally and prosecuted to the fullest extent of the law."

"To the fullest extent of the law? Did you really just say that?"

I spun around and headed back toward Natalie, pretending not to hear the "bitch" which was said to my back. I entered the courtroom without looking back.

Chapter Twenty-Seven

The Tallahassee Garden Club was founded in 1926. Beginning with my great grandmother, Betty Anne Winston, who was a charter member, the Winston family has been well represented in the organization, often serving as officers. Both my mother and my Aunt Mary Beth, for example, have been president. This tradition may very well end with their generation, however, as I am the only female offspring still living in Tallahassee, and much to my mother's chagrin, I have inherited neither her passion for, nor skill at, gardening.

The club was headquartered in an old, large wood frame house that sat on half a city block. Built in 1840, the house's doors and woodwork were heart pine, most of the lumber hand-hewn from native trees, and its bricks from a local kiln. It was a popular venue for weddings and special events. Craig and I were married there, as was my older sister and two of my cousins.

Its annual Spring Flower Show, which included a floral design competition, held at the center, was one of its most popular and well attended events. So, it was no surprise when I found the small parking lot on the property full, as well as the over-flow makeshift parking area on the lawn. I drove slowly past the line of cars, searching for an open space.

"There's one." Maggie tapped her finger on the window glass, pointing in the direction of a small sliver of grass between a Honda Odyssey and a telephone pole.

I studied the space, taking into account the size of the Yukon, and shook my head. "No way."

Maggie's friend and neighbor, Penny Hunt, was also shaking her head, looking doubtful.

"I'm going to have to park on the street," I said as I gave one last look around, then headed toward the exit. I circled the block until I found a space on one of the side streets, then we made our way to the building.

The flower arranging competition was held in the exhibition hall, which was an extension of an already large dining area in the original house. The large rectangular room, with its two crystal chandeliers, gleaming hardwood floors and mock columns was perfect for receptions and small dances. Today, there were tables along the walls and several arranged in the middle of the floor, all of which displayed the many entries.

At the end of the room, across from where we entered, two doors led into a kitchen. Off to the side of that entrance were tables with urns of coffee, tea and hot chocolate, a tub with iced soft drinks and trays of fruit and various pastries. Maggie and Penny, as if guided by radar, made a beeline for this area.

As luck would have it, my mom and aunt were among the folks gathered there, chatting and drinking their coffee. By the time I got there, Maggie and Penny had a cup of hot chocolate in one hand and donut in the other, having tolerated a quick hug from Mom and Aunt Mary Beth.

"Mary Katherine, so glad you could make it," my mother said as she gave me a quick hug and peck on the cheek. "And I'm delighted you brought Margaret Anne, Maggie," she corrected herself, "and her friend." She looked over at the pair, then back to me. "Penelope is it?"

"Penny, but give her a donut and you can call her anything you want." I smiled at the youngster who, as if on cue, took a large bite out of the donut in her hand. I nodded toward Maggie. "She's been looking forward to this." Perhaps, I said, the gardening gene had just skipped a generation.

My mother smiled and nodded approvingly. I turned to face my aunt. She gave me something slightly less than a bear hug.

"How's my favorite niece?"

"I'm fine, Aunt Mary Beth."

"I'm happy to hear it, sweetie, but I was talking about your sister Sarah. You hear from her recently?"

My mother gave us a look just a little short of horror, until she picked up on the inside joke. "I always thought Rebecca Anne was your favorite," she said, referring to my other sister, "and Sarah Lynn your second favorite." The two women looked at me and cackled. There was something about being around my aunt that brought out the teasing, free flowing humor that my mother generally suppressed.

I clutched at my chest. "Knife to the heart."

Aunt Mary Beth draped her arm over my shoulder and gave it a squeeze. She looked toward my mother and said, "Come on, Martha Anne, let's show them around."

The two women gave us a tour of the exhibits, lingering on theirs, which were displayed on opposite sides of the room. Aunt Mary Beth had done a rather traditional arrangement of light and dark tulips and daffodils, elegant in its simplicity. My mom had gone for the unusual, an underwater arrangement. Three glass cylinders of varying heights, with colored glass stones in the bottom, were filled with water and perched on a small mirror. Each contained two roses, under the water, the stems of each held in the mouth of florist frog.

"Cool," Maggie said, and I agreed.

Many of the other entries were quite good, very original. Some were just original, the lack of comment by our guides thereon reminding me of the old admonition of my mother that if you couldn't say something nice, you shouldn't say anything at all.

While Aunt Mary Beth showed the kids around the rest of the center, my mom and I worked our way outside to the patio area. We found an empty wrought iron table underneath a Dogwood tree, pulled up a couple of chairs and sat down. It was a beautiful, early spring day. Perfect temperature, low humidity, not a cloud in the sky.

Mom asked me about Maggie, her school, basketball team, remarked on her progress on the piano. She told me she had met Craig's new girlfriend somewhere, a charity function or something. "I was not impressed," she said, her tone of voice and facial expression suggesting this was an understatement. I noted that the topic of possible reconciliation with my ex-husband did not follow. She looked away for a few seconds then turned back to me.

"How are things going, Mary Katherine?"

"Good."

She looked unconvinced. "You don't look good."

"Thanks, Mom."

She waved her hand in dismissal. "You look tired, sweetie."

"I am tired. I do have a ten-year old kid, you know."

"It's Renny's case, isn't it? I knew this was a mistake."

"Most lawyers would love to have this case. It's a good thing, Mom."

She nodded, still unconvinced it seemed. "How can they possibly think Renny killed that young woman? Do you have any alternative suspects?"

I looked at her closely. Did she know something? Suspect it? "I can't really talk about the case, Mom. Attorney-client privilege."

She frowned, acted hurt, but then shrugged. "Well, the reason I bring it up is you asked me the other week about the timing, when I dropped Ruth off, when I got home, that sort of thing."

"Yes?"

"Well, I ran into Tony Spiato the other day. He mentioned that you asked him about your father and when he left the poker game that night."

I could feel my cheeks begin to redden, but was powerless to stop it. "Yeah, just trying to nail down the timing, like I said." I avoided making eye contact with my mother, choosing instead to study the coffee in my cup, but I could sense her eyes boring into me. If Tony reported our conversation accurately to my mother, then she knew I lied to him about what she told me.

And she had to wonder why.

"Anyway, talking to him caused me to re-think the matter."

This time, I stole a quick glance her way. "Yes?"

"I told you, I think, that your father came home at his usual time, about twelve or twelve thirty, but now that I think about it, he did come home early that night, just a little after I got home. About eleven fifteen, eleven thirty, I'd say. I remember because the news was on." She shook her head and tapped it lightly on the side. "Don't know how I could have forgotten that."

A low buzzing had begun in my ears as I listened to my mother's rather strange recantation. It seemed that I was more reading her lips than hearing her words by the end. I put down my coffee lest I drop it. Was she covering for my dad? Did she have her suspicions? I didn't know for sure, but suddenly, that magical power my mother had always possessed, to detect when one of her children was not being truthful with her, shifted to me.

As I dared a longer, deeper look into my mother's eyes, I knew she was lying.

Chapter Twenty-Eight

I pulled into the circular driveway of my parent's home and saw that the garage door was open but no cars were there. Good. I had taken my mother up on her offer at the Garden Club to keep the kids for a while and take them to a late lunch at the club with Dad. I stopped by my office briefly, but I had business here now, best done alone.

I parked and walked toward the open garage. Bolted to the roof line at its entrance, the old basketball goal and fiberglass backboard looked down on me. There were traces of rust on the rim and the net was frayed. The sight of it instantly pricked my memory, drawing a trickle of images: my dad and me playing HORSE, the one-on-one games when I was older. He never let me beat him, never patronized me, though he liked to make it close. He had made it fun.

Dad, who was a natural athlete himself, thought sports and general physical fitness was an important part of being well-rounded, a concept to which my mother gave only lip service. Dad didn't push it with Rebecca, who became a beauty queen molded in my mother's image, with her same disdain for any activity that might produce perspiration in public. Sarah, though independent minded from an early age, and not enamored with my mother's ordered world of femininity, was also hopelessly uncoordinated.

Then I popped out, another girl. I think he began to see the narrowing of the canvas, so to speak. And so, in the battle for the essence of what I was to be, my father fought with a greater urgency than he had with my siblings.

My mother was no passive bystander, of course. She pursued her vision of me as the proper young lady with the same determination and intensity she had shown with both of my sisters. But, for whatever reason, the sports thing took. The beauty pageant thing just never did.

Now, seeing that basketball goal again brought pangs of guilt and anxiety mixed with nostalgia. The idea that my father could be a cold-blooded killer seemed preposterous to me. He was one of the calmest, gentlest persons I knew.

Not that he didn't lose his temper from time to time. He did. And according to his brothers, Dad had resorted to physical violence on more than one occasion in his youth. I recalled one illustrative story they told. My parents had been married only a short while, and were visiting his family in the Tennessee rural farmland where he was raised. A man at the local dance, drunk, had made inappropriate remarks to my mother. Phil Marston asked him politely to watch his language, to which the drunk had replied, "Fuck you—and your whore wife too."

My father was reputed to have suddenly and savagely attacked the man, hitting him repeatedly in the face until his brothers pulled him off, afraid that he might kill the man. My dad always insisted that the story, if not completely untrue, was much exaggerated. His brothers, he said, were famous for their tall tales. Besides, I thought, even if true, that was long ago, a different time and place, and certainly different circumstances.

Had he wanted me to take Renny's case? Had he manipulated me? With his daughter as the accused's attorney, he could get close to the case, receive inside information without raising suspicion, couldn't he? How much had I unwittingly told him? And what about that DVD left at my house, an item that arguably only the killer possessed? If not Renny, who else would have a motive to help the defense in such a fashion? Perhaps my father couldn't bring himself to confess, but he didn't want his buddy to take the fall either.

I shook my head vigorously, as if I could shake the thoughts from my head. Walking through the garage, I noted the golf clubs next to the door, leaning against the wall, the golf shoes next to the bag, bits of dirt and dead grass clinging to them. The garage, like everything at the

Marston house, was ordered and organized. There were shelves along each wall, an enclosed cabinet, tools on hooks and in boxes. Bikes leaned against the far wall, next to an extra refrigerator. A wood working bench and shelving formed an L in one of the back corners.

I opened the back door and stepped inside and could hear the sound of the television. "Anyone home?" I called out as I made my way through the laundry room and into the kitchen. "Mom? Dad?" I listened closely as I moved from room to room and confirmed what I had assumed. The house was empty.

I went then directly to the den, which my father used as an office. This was where he kept bills and receipts, documentation for taxes, expenses related to the home and family. My dad was a little OC in keeping all his receipts and records of everything, perhaps a habit formed when he was in private practice and sought to count everything he could as a business expense.

I opened the file drawer on the left side of the desk. The folders inside were alphabetically arranged and I found what I was looking for quickly—the one that contained my parents' cell phone account. I pulled it out and opened the folder up on the desk. I located the bills for January, and the two months before.

I looked for any calls to and from Elena Castillo, especially on the night Elena was killed. Tony Spiato said that my father received a call on his cell phone about ten thirty that night and left soon thereafter. The medical examiner had estimated that Elena Castillo died somewhere between 11:00 p.m. and 12:30 a.m.

I had memorized Elena's numbers, both her cell and land line, but I had also written them down on one of my business cards just in case. I ran my finger quickly down the in-coming and out-going calls for either number. There was nothing in November, and nothing in December either, and I felt relieved.

It was short lived.

On January 6th, two days before Elena's death, there it was, a call from my father's cell phone to Castillo's home phone number. The call lasted approximately five minutes. I held my breath as I ran my finger down the column of numbers for the eighth of January. My finger flinched when it came to rest on the in-coming call at 10:31 p.m. It was from Elena's home phone number. Then an outgoing call to Elena's land line. Neither call lasted more than a minute.

I knew from the phone company that calls to and from a cell phone are reported on one's bill, but not so for calls to and from land line phones. Goodwin called Elena on her cell. Dad had called her land line number. This explained how the detectives knew of Goodwin's calls but not of my father's. Unless the police looked at Dad's cell phone records, as I was doing, they would not know of these two phone calls the night of Elena's death.

If my father left the poker game, which was in Southwood, around ten forty-five as his friend had said, he would not have had time to make it to Elena's condo, kill her, then make it home by eleven fifteen or eleven thirty, which is when my mother now says he came in. But, was she telling the truth? I thought that she was not, that he had arrived home, as she initially said, around twelve or twelve thirty. If so, where had he gone and what had he done in that ninety or so minutes from when he left the poker game, until his arrival at home?

"Katie?"

My mother's voice pierced the silence like cannon fire, making my entire body twitch. I heard the front door close and my mother's steps across the hardwood floor, only a few feet from where I sat. I had not heard the car pull up, nor her footsteps up the walkway, either. I had been transfixed on the awful truth laid out in front of me. Now, I hurried to hide it, shoving the bills back in the file folder. I quickly jammed the folder back in the desk drawer, and was closing it when my mother appeared at the entrance to the room.

She looked at me, eyes wide in surprise. She glanced in the general direction of the file drawer, then back to me. Had she glimpsed my movement to close it? I needed an answer to the unasked question evident on my mother's face. What was I doing there? Not just at the house but in the home office, sitting in my father's chair, rifling through drawers.

I rose from the chair. "I came by to pick up Maggie and Penny."

My mother looked at her watch.

"I'm a little early," I said. Then, looking around, I asked, "Where are they?"

She moved her jacket from one arm to the other. "Your dad has them. Should be along shortly. I wasn't feeling too good, so I left early." After a brief silence, she pointed with her chin toward the desk. "Looking for something?"

"When I realized no one was home, I was looking for something to leave a note, saying I was going to get a sandwich and come back." Not bad, I thought. Plausible, though I doubt it would stand up to close scrutiny. There were notepads and pens next to the telephone in the kitchen, which was where members of the family would normally leave a note for each other.

My mother glanced again at the desk where the drawer had been open, looked back at me and said, "I'm glad I caught you then." As I pondered whether her statement was some sort of code, a twisted pun, she turned and walked out of the room, speaking over her shoulder, "I'm going to put on something more comfortable. Be right back."

I listened to my mother's footfalls on the hallway floor, looked at the file drawer again and saw that, in my rush, I had not shoved the folder down completely in the drawer. It had caught on the top when I closed it, as if I was earmarking the place for future reference. I opened the drawer, lifted the file, straightened out the crease in it, placed it back in its proper place, then closed the drawer again.

Chapter Twenty-Nine

Clarissa Barnhill, the chief correspondent for the local ABC affiliate was just a little over five feet tall and maybe a hundred pounds. She craned her neck upward to look at me, holding the microphone up to my face.

"Ms. Marston, we understand that the motion to be heard today concerns a certain sex video featuring the victim, Ms. Elena Castillo, and several powerful politicians. Can you tell us the names of the men on the video? And does it include your client, Judge Goodwin?"

I looked at my questioner. I had been very circumspect in the language I used in my motion, not naming names, nor alluding to their position or occupations, nor giving other identifying information as to the men depicted in the video. I suspected Barnhill was just guessing, trying to get me to confirm. I had also been mindful of Miranda Castillo's admonition, and my promise not to attack the character of her daughter if possible. Well, it hadn't been possible, had it?

As expected, the news media slurped it up, and the story of the "sex tapes" had gone national in a matter of minutes. It was no surprise that the rotunda area was busy with news media types, both television and print, as well as the new age journalists, which included any fool with a website or a blog who would hold forth on any event they wanted, spouting opinion and rumor as fact, and call themselves journalists.

They had rushed toward me when I got off the elevator, like children to an ice cream truck, though more urgent, insistent, shouting out questions to me, sticking microphones in my face. I had recognized Barnhill and figured she deserved first chance at whatever information I was willing to share. Plus, I thought I had a better chance of objectivity, even favorable treatment, from Barnhill than the non-locals.

"Mr. Lipton has the DVD," I said finally in answer to Clarissa's question. "Perhaps he can tell you what's on it, or better yet, show it to you."

This last statement produced a lascivious smile or two from some of the reporters, mostly men, but it did not deter Clarissa, who refused to relinquish her position of advantage to the others who were shouting questions at me. "But you filed the motion, so you must have some information, some factual basis for your allegations. How did you find out about it?"

"You understand, I'm sure, better than most, the reluctance to name my sources." There were a few smiles and chuckles in the crowd, including from Barnhill. "Besides, my source was anonymous."

"Then how do you know it is reliable?" Barnhill asked, again ignoring the shouted questions behind her.

I smiled. "You ever consider becoming a lawyer? You're pretty good already at cross examination."

Someone shouted out, "She's concerned with her reputation." More chuckles.

I nodded in appreciation of the point made and held up my hand. "I think the person best able to answer if the information is reliable is the State Attorney."

Then, as if on cue, the elevator doors opened and out stepped Bill Lipton and his entourage. "Speak of the devil," an anonymous voice in the back mumbled, then the swarm of reporters turned, almost as one, and descended upon the prosecution team. Amid the barrage of shouted questions, Lipton looked over at me, gave me a small, tense smile and nod of the head. I gave him a mock salute in return, then turned and walked into the courtroom.

With the agreement of client and co-counsel, I was going to go this motion alone, present a David and Goliath image. As the doors closed behind me, closing out as well the din of reporters' shouted questions and the popping of camera flashes, I looked around the room. The clerk was at her station, chatting with the bailiff. Both looked up and nodded at me. The pool camera for the news media was set up on the side wall, angled to get a view of both attorneys' tables as well as the judge's bench area.

I set my briefcase on the floor next to the defense table and took out my file, placed it on the table. I checked my watch. Still a few minutes before the scheduled hearing. I tucked my blouse in and straightened my skirt, pulled down on the sleeves of my jacket. My shoes, low high heels, were a little too small and not broken in yet. I had never been comfortable in the more formal attire required in my job, but it was an occupational necessity, so I adjusted.

I remained standing, opening my file and reviewing my notes as the courtroom began to fill up behind me. I turned and looked out over the gallery. Raoul and Mario Castillo were seated in their usual spot behind the prosecution's table. Noticeably absent today was Miranda Castillo. I couldn't blame her, and frankly, I was glad not to have to meet her eyes. Sitting on the back row, Reverend Michael Morton was surrounded by about a dozen of his flock. He and fellow church members had been regulars at court proceedings in the case, but today their ranks seemed to have swelled. I suspected they had been drawn by the prurient nature of the subject matter. Bunch of hypocrites.

Lipton and his assistants filed in wordlessly, setting up at the other counsel table. In contrast to my single file folder, they had brought apparently the entire file, or close to it, hauled in on a buggy. Lipton came over. "I wish you had come to me informally on this. No need to get the court involved."

"I tried, Bill. I sent you a letter."

"You were pretty vague, though. You weren't specific about videos. Besides," he said, leaning in closer, "what makes you think we have what you're looking for?"

I shook my head. "Still trying to play the angles I see. I know you have it. You can try to deny it to the judge if you want. If you want to take that chance, you go right ahead."

The prosecutor studied me carefully, probably trying to determine if I had something to back up my allegations. He seemed about to say something when the bailiff rapped his knuckles on the side door to the courtroom and shouted out, "All rise."

Judge Mitchell walked briskly to the bench area and took her seat. She opened the file, looked over at me and said, "Ms. Marston, I have read your motion. Then, without inviting me to elaborate, she turned to the prosecutor and said, "Mr. Lipton, I didn't see any written response to the motion from your office. Do you, in fact, have in your possession such a video?"

The moment of truth.

Lipton rose slowly from his seat and cleared his throat. "May it please the Court." He looked over briefly in my direction and nodded slightly. "Counsel." I gave him a nod of my own and Lipton turned back to face the judge. "Your Honor, first let me say that I am sorry that the level of professionalism in the local bar has deteriorated to the extent that counsel files a motion before discussing the matter with opposing counsel. If Ms. Marston had given me the courtesy of bringing it to my attention, I'm sure I could have allayed her concerns. You see . . . "

"Mr. Lipton," the judge said, interrupting, "can you answer my question, please? Do you, or have you had in your possession, the video referred to in the motion?"

The prosecutor cleared his throat again. "Well, Judge, let me put it this way. Our office received a package several days ago. The package contained a DVD, with no accompanying note. We played it. The video indeed appeared to have images of sexual activity between unknown persons. The location depicted resembled the bedroom of the victim in this case so we took it seriously and went on the assumption that the woman was Ms. Castillo."

"Duh," I said under my breath.

Lipton gave me a quick sideways glance then turned his attention back to the judge. "Of course, as Your Honor is well aware, with modern technology, an individual can piece together unrelated images into one video to make it look like just about anything they want to. Think Tom Hanks, as Forest Gump, speaking with President Kennedy."

"I've seen Forest Gump, Mr. Lipton. Are you suggesting that the video was altered, a visual illusion, so to speak?"

"We had to be sure, Judge. If the video was a hoax, and we put it out there in the public, the persons depicted on it would have been unnecessarily embarrassed, not to mention the family of the victim. It would have been irresponsible to do so without making sure it was legitimate."

Judge Mitchell frowned, waiting for him to continue. When he didn't speak again, she prompted him. "And? Did you have it tested?"

"Yes, Your Honor."

The judge sighed, frowned. The phrase, "pulling teeth" came to mind. "And?"

Lipton looked around the room then, as if understanding for the first time that they were not alone. He lowered his voice a notch, as if that might make some difference. "We hired an expert in this field, Dr. Richard Reynolds, from FSU, who examined the video for us." Lipton looked then into the courtroom audience. I followed his gaze to the front row where a smallish man with glasses and an ill-fitting plaid jacket gave a barely perceptible nod. Lipton turned back to the judge. "I have him here if the Court wishes to question him, but I can represent that what he has told us is that this is a copy, not the original video. It does not appear to have been altered in the sense I spoke of earlier. The people in the video are there at the same time and at the location depicted. It has, however, been edited to eliminate some indeterminate amount of footage."

He waited for a few seconds to let the implication of his last words permeate the room. Of course, he was not content with just the implied. "We think," he said, "that this video was taken off of the victim's laptop or one of the DVDs stolen from her residence by the defendant, edited by him to remove the part that depicts him and the victim, and that he is the person who sent it to us."

A low buzz quickly swept through the courtroom, and just as quickly fell silent as Judge Mitchell glared out over the crowd.

"That's the most logical conclusion" the prosecutor said. "Who else would send such a video to us? Why would they? Who has the most to gain by making it public? The defendant has been out on bond. He has the freedom of movement necessary to have done it." I sensed an implied criticism in his voice directed to the judge who had been the one to let him out, but if the judge picked up on it, she ignored it. She continued to stare attentively, and neutrally, in his direction.

The prosecutor continued. "This is further supported by the defense's motion which has brought us here today. How would they know about it? It just doesn't make sense otherwise."

The judge turned to me. "Ms. Marston?"

I stood quickly, took a moment to compose myself, then began. "While I appreciate Mr. Lipton's concern for the reliability of what was presented to him, in all due respect, that was not his call. And he knows it. If a witness came forward and said he had seen the victim with another man right around the time of the alleged murder, would he delay disclosing the existence of this witness until they had checked out his story to determine if it was reliable?

I answered my rhetorical questions. "Of course not. The State does not get to decide what evidence is reliable enough to disclose to the defense. One has to wonder if we had not brought it to the court's attention when, if at all, it would have been disclosed."

I paused a few seconds to let the point seep in, and to organize my thoughts. Something in my peripheral vision caught my attention then and I glanced in the direction of the Castillos. A man was leaning over, whispering in the former senator's ear. His back was to me but the stocky build and large bald head were familiar. When the man turned and gave me a profile, I recognized Brian Reeves, president of the Seminole Boosters, and of Sunshine Bank.

I momentarily lost my train of thought and had to look down at my notes before continuing. "At any rate, as I've said, that's not the point. The point is, the prosecution has intentionally and deliberately withheld exculpatory evidence from the defense, contrary to the requirements of *Brady v. Maryland.* This is prosecutorial misconduct on the highest level, taken with a cynical and arrogant disregard for the rights of the defendant, and the integrity of these proceedings. Under the case law I have cited in my motion, the proper remedy for such misconduct is a dismissal of the charge, and I ask that the Court do so."

Bill Lipton somehow managed to insert righteous indignation into his response. How dare I attack his integrity or that of members of his office. A dismissal, under the circumstances would be a miscarriage of justice. Even assuming there was found to be a violation of *Brady,* where was the prejudice to the defense? "After all, Ms. Marston will now have the evidence, if she didn't before, in plenty of time to use it in preparation for trial."

I responded that the actions of the prosecution had so tainted the process that confidence in its integrity has been irreparably damaged. What else had been hidden from the defense? Public confidence in the system required a dismissal of the case.

Both of us looked then to the judge expectantly.

Mitchell gave Lipton a hard stare for a few seconds. "I would be inclined to grant the motion if I thought it had truly prejudiced the defense in the preparation of the case. Dismissal is a very harsh remedy, though, and under the circumstances unwarranted."

There was an audible sigh of relief from the prosecution table.

"That being said, Mr. Lipton, please do not interpret my ruling as an endorsement of your handing of the matter. It is not. You will not get another bye if something like this happens again."

"Yes, ma'am."

"I am also ordering the State Attorney's Office to pay defense counsel the reasonable fees incurred in bringing this motion to my attention." She looked at Lipton. "And I don't expect you to quibble with Ms. Marston as to the amount." She looked over at me. "If you would, please prepare a proposed order for my signature."

I nodded as the judge began to rise from her chair. Lipton rose to object but the judge had already stepped down from the bench and was headed to the side door. "Your Honor," he called out, raising his hand like a student asking to go to the restroom, but Mitchell neither stopped nor turned around. When the side door closed behind her, Lipton let his arm drop to his side.

Chapter Thirty

The White Cat was a small Italian restaurant, located in a converted residence just off of Thomasville Road, on Glenview. It had opened a little over a year ago and had gotten good reviews, but I hadn't tried it out yet. So, when Ted suggested it, I readily agreed. Interestingly, the place was owned and run by Ted's ex-wife and her new husband.

The restaurant was crowded, and noisy. We were at one of the booths in the bar area, glad to have been seated without a reservation. The small television above the bar was set on a sports channel, muted. Ted was studying his menu intently, his brow furrowed.

"What's to think about?" I asked.

He looked up. "Pizza?"

I nodded, and we both put down our menus. A waitress appeared next to our table and took our orders. When she left, Ted smiled at me. I pulled a strand of hair behind my ear, gave him a small smile in return. I looked around the room. An uncomfortable silence fell over the table. This was going to be harder than I thought.

Earlier in the evening, Maggie had watched me getting dressed, putting on my make-up. "Where are you going on your date?"

"It's not a date. Mr. Stevens and I are working on a case together, so we're just getting together to discuss things and get a bite to eat at the same time. Strictly work."

Maggie gave me a smug smile, as if she thought she had uncovered some secret code, some hidden meaning in my words. "Uh huh."

"It's not a date," I insisted.

My daughter looked unconvinced. She shook her head, but didn't say anything for a few seconds. "So, the nice dress, the make up?"

I gave my daughter a sideways glance, but didn't have a good

231

response.

"Anyway, if it was a date, I'm just saying, I think that would be a good thing."

"You would, huh?"

Maggie put her arm around my shoulder, like an older, more worldly sister. "Sure." She hesitated. "Mr. Stevens is cool. A little goofy at times, but I kind of like that. And Annie is fun, too," she said, referring to Ted's daughter. "We could make it work."

"Hold on. Hold on. Let's not get carried away. We're just going out to dinner. You've got us walking down the aisle."

In fact, it was about as close to a date as I wanted to get—for now. I meant what I had told Ted about not mixing professional and personal relationships. Besides, I was a little gun shy in general about starting up any relationship with another man. I was afraid to get close to someone else, to trust them, to get hurt. Yes, I know, that's a real cliché, but it was how I felt.

When Ted showed up at my door that evening, though, I felt a distant but familiar nervousness that was not altogether unpleasant. And it hadn't left me. I couldn't deny the attraction, the allure, which had only grown stronger. I was determined to keep things professional between us, but it hadn't been easy.

"So," Ted said, breaking the silence, "You want to hear what I've found out on our two studs?"

"Yes, indeed. Do we have a winner? A solid alternative to Goodwin?"

"If by winner, you mean of the stupid award, then yes, both get the gold. As to solid alternative suspects, it doesn't look like it." He shook his head slowly. "They've been caught in a very embarrassing situation, and we can argue that they had a good motive to keep Elena from going public, but unlike our client, it looks like they both have airtight alibis. Both Hargrove and Appleton were out of town on that night. All kinds of corroborating witnesses and documentation."

"Very convenient."

He shrugged.

The waitress arrived with our drinks, a beer for me and Coke for Ted. I was pleased to see that he seemed to be sticking to his vow of sobriety because I knew the problems booze had caused him in the past. I felt a little guilty at times to have a drink in front of him, but he took pains to disabuse me of this notion.

It was good for him, he said. "Like weight training. No pain, no gain."

Maybe so, but still, it had to be hard. I waited until the waitress left, took a small sip of beer, then said, "What about the connection to the gambling amendment? That got any legs?"

Ted frowned. "Lester Appleton is the point man for the governor on it and Brent Hargrove is steering it through the legislature. So yeah, I think there may be a connection. My thought is that Elena was a secret weapon in a rather intense lobbying effort, which included bribery, coercion and blackmail. Whatever worked. Now, whether that has anything to do with her death, as your Mr. Hobbs suggests, is another story, but I got a feeling this goes way deeper than anything we have proof of. And the Castillo family is right in the middle of it."

"What about Brian Reeves? How does he fit in?"

"Still working on it. It looks like, though, his bank is a subsidiary of a bank in Miami that is majority-owned by the Castillo family. There are several different companies, all with different configurations of officers and stockholders, so it's hard to get a clear picture, but that's what it's looking like right now."

I gave him a long "Hmm" then took a swallow of beer. "I need to talk with Ricky. He's been holding back with some key information that we need. It's time to put it all out on the table."

Ted nodded. "Speaking of which, I can't believe Jeb actually filed the complaint with the Bar."

"Me either."

The official document had come in the mail three days ago, setting forth the accusations of improper solicitation, interference with an established attorney client relationship, and giving me twenty days to file my response.

"I think he must have gotten a lot of pressure from the Castillo firm in Miami. I told you about the little visit I received from two of their lawyers?"

Ted nodded, and with a rather poor impression of Marlon Brando as Don Corleone, said, "I'm gonna make you an offer you can't refuse."

The men, dressed in their expensive looking suits and their arrogance, had come by the office the same day as the Brady hearing. No appointment, no phone call ahead of time. They told Jennifer they were in town on business and asked if Ms. Marston could spare a few minutes. Ms. Marston said she could.

I ushered them into my office, we made introductions, and they got right to the point. They had been disappointed to lose Ricky Hobbs as a client, but after doing some research on me, and watching me in action, they understood why he had sought my counsel. They wanted me to come work for them, set up and operate a Tallahassee office. They promised me a lot of money, important clients and a flexible schedule. I thanked them and politely declined.

They expressed their disappointment, and their certainty that I was making a big mistake. They urged me to take my time, think about it some more, and to take their cards just in case I changed my mind. I wouldn't, I assured them, but took the cards none-the-less. All in all, very creepy.

I gave Ted a weak smile. "And, I thought I had done a pretty good job of CYA too, but there was Ricky's signed statement attached as an exhibit."

The statement had set forth just what Jeb said it would—that I had contacted Ricky and suggested he leave his attorneys and retain me, offering a fee discount and making promises of a more favorable outcome than he could get with his current counsel—all kinds of nasty, and untrue, stuff. I immediately regretted not getting that affidavit from Ricky, setting out the true facts and circumstances. But he had been so adamant on the phone when I told him of Jeb's threat, I had been sure there was nothing to it. And I had heard nothing from Jeb after I called his bluff. Until now.

"You think they forged his signature?"

I shook my head slowly from side to side. "Don't know, but it sure looks like Ricky's signature. I wouldn't put forgery past them, but it's rather risky for such a small return."

"They may have misrepresented to him what he was signing. They shove something in front of him, suggesting it releases them from liability and further responsibility, some bullshit that makes sense. He doesn't look at it. Just signs it."

"Maybe."

"You still haven't gotten up with the elusive quarterback?"

I shook my head. "He's avoiding me like I was a rushing defensive end. He hasn't returned my calls. His mother said she would get him to call, but nothing."

"Not a good sign."

I nodded, took a sip of beer and watched as Ted ran his fingers through his hair, then gave me a grin that shone in his eyes. "Well, that's something I'll have to deal with," I said.

Ted took a large swallow of Coke, put down the glass. He looked past me then and I turned to see what had gotten his attention. "Hello, Beth," he said, standing. "You remember Kate Marston."

By this time, the woman had made it to our side and I looked up at Ted's ex-wife. She had put on a little weight since I last saw her, but was still quite pretty, with long, straight, dark hair that framed a symmetrical face.

"Of course, I do," she said, smiling at me. "How you doing, Kate?"

"Can't complain," I said. "I really like your place here. And I hear the pizza is great."

"Everything's great. But the pizza is really outstanding. They taking care of you okay?"

"Oh yeah," Ted said. And then, as if on cue, the waitress arrived with our pizza. Beth backed away a bit.

"Well, it was good to see you, Kate. Y'all enjoy yourselves, and please come back."

Ted put a slice of pizza on a plate and passed it to me, then did the same for himself. We ate in silence for some time until I remarked that he and his ex-wife seemed to be getting along remarkably well. I remembered that his divorce and custody battle had not been pleasant. Indeed, I had, in fact, testified on behalf of Ted, which made Beth's friendliness now even more surprising.

He shrugged. "Who Knew?" Ted took a bite of pizza, held it out in front of him. "This really is outstanding."

I nodded my agreement.

"After the dust settled, Beth decided she wanted to open up her own restaurant. So did Mike. That's her new husband. He used to work for Beth's father in his restaurant in Panama City. They wanted to get out from under his shadow, do it on their own, so to speak. So, they came here. I think Daddy staked them, but they know what they're doing."

He took another bite of pizza. "Somehow, it just slowly got better between us. We get along great now, and I come here all the time."

It gave me hope, I said, and he just nodded. The silence fell on us again until Ted broke it with, "Uh, speaking of the connection to the gambling amendment..." He seemed uncomfortable. "I read where your dad denied the challenge to it."

"Yeah," I said.

Ted was looking down at his pizza, not saying anything.

"You got something to say, Stevens, go ahead. You think my dad ought to be a suspect?"

He looked up at me now. "Shit, Kate. I hate even bringing it up. Phil Marston is the straightest of arrows. I know that."

"But," I said, prompting.

"You got to wonder, what with the full court press this thing has, that they wouldn't at least approach him in some way, see if there was some way to influence his ruling." When I didn't respond right away, he said, "There is also the mystery of the DVD someone dropped in our lap. We have assumed that whoever killed Elena took her lap top, flash drive and DVDs, right?"

"Right."

"So, assuming for the moment it was not our client—"

"Big assumption."

"Yes, but assuming it was not him, you have to ask why the killer would want to help us out, would take the risk of exposing him or herself to capture?"

I had been naïve to think that Ted would not follow this thread to its logical destination. Maybe, somewhere down deep, I wanted him to. "Perhaps," I said, voicing what I was sure he was thinking, "it was someone whose conscience was bothering them, someone who doesn't want to see an innocent man punished for something they did."

"Yeah," he said, giving me a sideways glance, "the conscience can be a powerful force sometimes." Ted hesitated a couple of beats, then added, "Maybe we're looking for someone who is a friend of our client, or at least knows him."

"Makes sense. Both the victim and the defendant are in the legal profession. If the killer is not our client, it could very well be someone who knew them both." I hesitated a few moments, then stated the obvious. "Like my father."

"Ah shit. I really feel terrible now."

I put my hand up. "No need to apologize." I did my best to appear neutral, even reassuring. I took a bite of pizza to give me time to think. What I did and said now might make a big difference on what happened next. If his logical train of thought had led him down the same tracks I had followed, had he also done an independent investigation of this theory? Had our client?

"It's a legitimate point," I said. "You should follow up. Ask Dad outright about it. Ask him if he had an intimate relationship with Elena, whether he is aware of any sex tapes featuring him. See if he has an alibi for the night of the murder. See if it can be corroborated." I waited a bit before adding, "For obvious reasons, it shouldn't be me."

Ted rolled his head in a wide arc, folded his arms in front of him and looked at me closely. I strived for just the right combination of tone and words to send conflicting messages, but had no idea if I was successful. I could feel the perspiration forming on my forehead and I didn't dare meet his gaze.

"Look," I said, finally. "I appreciate that it's a delicate subject, and your reluctance to bring it up and your obvious discomfort with the whole subject is, well, endearing." I smiled. "I think it's a preposterous notion, but then again, I'm not exactly neutral."

Ted smiled. "I'm not either, but it is still ridiculous. We don't have the time to waste on it."

"Wouldn't take much just to ask him about it, diplomatically of course."

"I don't know a diplomatic way to ask a sitting judge if he violated his oath of office and the judicial canons of ethics, much less whether he is a murderer."

"Didn't say it would be easy."

He waved his hand. "Already too much time wasted on it. Let's move on."

I looked at him then, trying to gauge whether he meant what he said, or simply wanted to drop the subject for now. Had I thrown him off the scent?

The nagging, unsettling question about Charles Everhart that I had earlier tucked away, inexplicably popped up to the surface now, and I brought it up to Ted. He gave me a surprised look. "Preposterous, I know, but he does have a connection to the victim, and possibly to Ricky Hobbs and the gambling allegations." I told him about seeing him at the law firm. "And he is known to many people as Judge."

"Might be another a waste of time," Ted said, "but I can check on his alibi for the time of the murder, discreetly, of course."

I nodded my agreement. "I'm pretty sure you will find that he was in North Carlina for the holidays and didn't return until just before classes started, but still...."

"At any rate," Ted said, shifting focus, "whether you go after the sex or the gambling angle, I'm pretty sure you won't be too popular in the Castillo household."

I shrugged, remembering Miranda Castillo's veiled threat. "No, I don't think so."

After a few moments, Ted said, "Anything on the pregnancy angle? You think she may have had an abortion?"

"If she was pregnant, it doesn't show up either in the autopsy report or her medical records. Nor is there any record of an abortion. Of course, the last time she saw her regular physician in Miami was six months before her death."

"You think she may have gone to somebody up here?"

I frowned. "If so, there is no record of any payment for medical care in her bank or credit card records, except a $25 charge to a walk-in center in November for a flu shot."

"So, dead end?"

"Looks like it. It was just a hunch, anyway, based on that anonymous letter and what the housekeeper said. The Perez woman was pretty vague, though. I'm thinking we need to put her under oath in a formal deposition."

"Okay," he said.

"In the meantime, I think I'll give it another try with the priest."

Ted took a huge bite of pizza and with his mouth full said, "What, you think you're going to bat those big brown eyes at him and he's going to change his mind?"

I shook my head. "I don't know, but it's worth a try, especially if we have corroborating evidence, if he only has to confirm what is established."

We didn't have any corroborating evidence, but Ted had the courtesy not to point that out. Instead, he said, "Assuming Elena was pregnant, you think Goodwin knew? You think he could have been the father?"

I shrugged. "If so, he's a damn good actor." I let that thought hang in the air for a few moments.

"If our client is the killer, though, if he was the one who sent you the DVD, where did he hide it? And what about the hard drive, the jump drive and the key to the apartment? The police searched his house and his office thoroughly, and found zip."

"He may just be very clever," I said.

Ted started to say something, then stopped, seemingly distracted by whatever was on the T.V. behind me. I turned to see on the screen a woman with a microphone, facing the camera. In the background was what appeared to be a South Florida scene with a two-lane black top road, and behind it, a canal. A photograph of a smiling Ricky Hobbs appeared simultaneously in the right upper corner.

A quiet fell over the place as other customers took notice of what was on the television. The sound was muted but the words appeared at the bottom of the screen as the woman spoke, and I tried to read them quickly. The bartender pointed a remote in the direction of the T.V. and increased the volume. I had by then determined the gist of the breaking news, but, as with everyone else, watched and listened intently as the woman with the microphone gave us whatever details she had.

"Again, it appears that Hobbs was the driver of the automobile and that no one else was with him. There were no other vehicles involved. Authorities say it appears that Hobbs lost control of the car as he tried to maneuver the corner and plunged into the canal behind me." The reporter glanced over her shoulder briefly. "A passerby noticed the car partially submerged and called police, who discovered the star quarterback, still behind the wheel, with his seat belt still buckled. He was pronounced dead at the scene."

A collective moan passed through the crowd at the restaurant. I don't know if I was a part of it, but I do know that those last words, though by then fully expected, buzzed through my mind like a chainsaw, noisy and ripping apart the carefully organized thoughts I had been prepared to articulate. I remained speechless as the woman gave a quick summary of Ricky Hobbs' football career, including a note of the gambling scandal. She looked appropriately somber as she signed off.

"And so, Ricky Hobbs, Florida State star quarterback, promising NFL recruit, dead at age twenty-one. This is Marilyn Aliento in Miami."

It took several seconds before the din of conversation resumed, and it seemed more subdued. Both Ted and I stared at the television long after the story had ended. Finally, we turned to face each other. Ted took a swig of Coke and set it down.

"Damn," he said.

Chapter Thirty-One

I walked the short distance to Hillcrest Avenue, where I turned left and began jogging slowly toward Tennessee Street. The extensive cloud cover blocked the sun and kept in the early morning heat and humidity. The air was still, heavy and smothering, as if a blanket had been draped over the city.

The sweat beaded up quickly as I began my run, and before I had gone a block, it was flowing freely from my forehead, forming stains under my arms, down my back and inside my running shorts. The good news was that, in very short order, I had no tight muscles. The steam room quality of the outdoor air loosened everything including the jumble of thoughts and ideas that bounced around inside my head.

One of those thoughts was that my father might be a murderer. It was a persistent, nagging reality that haunted me, stalked me, drained me emotionally, and made it extremely difficult to focus on other aspects of the case. I found myself avoiding both my father and my mother, afraid that my body language, my tone of voice, or a slip of tongue might expose the festering sore.

At some point, I would need to confront my father with the evidence I had. I probably should have already. I told myself that I needed more evidence, to know one way or the other. But I knew deep down that was a lie. Were he not my father, I would not hesitate, indeed would be eager, to point the finger at him. Instead, I put it off. I tried to re-direct my energy, focus on my other alternatives, my other theories of defense.

With the mysterious death of Ricky Hobbs, the theory that Elena's death was somehow tied to the push for casino gambling in the state moved to the top of my list. It could be that Ricky's death was, as the authorities were saying, an accident, but I didn't think so.

Neither did Ricky's mother. I called her a couple of days after the news broke, to express my sympathy. She seemed distraught, upset, but in control of herself. She thanked me for calling, then said, "Ms. Marston, I scraped together a lot of money for your fee, for you to help my son. Now that he's dead, I figure he didn't use up all that fee." I thought she was suggesting that I refund part of the fee, which seemed rather crass under the circumstances, but she had something different in mind. "I want you to clear his name, Ms. Marston, to find his killers."

"What do you mean? The police say it was a single car accident. No one else was involved." This came not only from what had been reported in the news, but from a copy of the incident report that Ted had obtained from one of his contacts in Miami. The theory was that Ricky had a lot of stuff on his mind, that he was feeling depressed. Decided he didn't want to be around a lot of people. So, he buys some booze and just starts driving. He wants to get away from things that remind him of his troubles. By the time he gets to Opa Locka, he's pretty drunk. So drunk that he doesn't even notice he has missed the turn until he plunges into the canal, where he hits his head on the roof or something and is knocked unconscious, and drowns.

When I repeated this to his mother, she snorted. "That's a lie. They set it up to look like an accident."

"Who is they?"

She ignored my question. "They say Ricky was depressed. First of all, my boy don't get depressed. Don't nothing get him down. He ain't never had it easy, not one day of his life, but he was always a ray of sunshine. He was always sure things were going to work out. Just like he was when he gave me a kiss and left the house that night. And that's what I told the police when they come around."

She stopped for a few moments, sniffling into the phone, then regained her composure and continued. "They say he was drunk, but

243

everyone who knew Ricky, knew he didn't drink—or do drugs either. My boy may have had some problems, but no way did he drink all what they say. Not unless someone had a gun to his head or something. And if he was drinking, why was there no beer cans or liquor bottle in the car?"

She was on a roll now, the emotion-filled words spilling out of her, her anger and frustration evident in her voice. "What was he doing fifty miles away from his house, practically to the Everglades, driving around by himself? He don't know nobody over there." And if it was an accident, then why wasn't there no skid marks? A person don't drive right into a canal like that without at least trying to stop."

All good questions. Whether rhetorical or real, I had no answers for her, but I repeated the one that she had ignored earlier. If it wasn't an accident, if it was murder, who was behind it? She said she didn't know. She knew he was gambling, that he was being pressured by some people, but he would never give her details and assured her everything was going to be okay. I wasn't sure I believed she was telling me the complete truth, but I didn't know why she would share all of her suspicions about Ricky's death, ask me to investigate it, and then hold back. Apparently, he kept both his mother and his lawyer in the dark.

"Oh, they say they're still investigating, but they not going to do nothing 'cept cover the whole thing up. I need you to get to the bottom of it."

I didn't appreciate the tone of entitlement, but also couldn't ignore the grief, the helplessness in her voice, either, so I told her I would look into it. In fact, I had already asked Ted to follow up, as it seemed rather suspicious to me, too.

And if one potentially key witness was dead, another had disappeared. I had gone back to Angelina Perez's house, hoping to get more detailed and complete information. Her car was not in the driveway but I knocked on the door anyway. A neighbor, walking by with her cocker spaniel, told me that the woman had moved back to

Miami. Ted tracked her down, served her with a subpoena for deposition. Angelina had called me then.

"You lied to me, Ms. Marston. You said Elena's mother wanted me to talk with you."

I could have tried to rationalize, to spin it with semantics, but she was right. I had intentionally misled her. "I knew she wanted to avoid publicity, to keep things private if possible."

"And now? A deposition?"

"That depends on you, Ms. Perez. A deposition may not be necessary if you will answer some more questions, privately, but honestly and completely. If not, I'll need to ask you some questions under oath, get it on the record. I hope you understand that . . ."

The woman disconnected at this point. She also was a no-show for her deposition. Ted followed up and reported that she had flown to Guatemala. We had no address for her there, and there was no indication that she would be coming back to the States any time soon. Ted checked with the son and daughter-in-law who lived in Tallahassee, but they refused to speak with him.

I was turning all this over in my head as I made my way past Leon High, turned on Miccosukee and headed toward Hillcrest again. I was coming up to the intersection with Terrace when I noticed the man up ahead. He was stapling something to a wooden utility pole. When he finished, he looked my way for a few seconds, then started jogging in my direction.

Something didn't seem quite right. He could have been putting up fliers asking about a lost pet or something. People did that on occasion in the neighborhood. But he didn't have any additional fliers in his hands, and I didn't see a vehicle nearby. He was dressed in running clothes and appeared to be out for a jog. But if so, it seemed strange that he would carry a staple gun with him.

The man passed to the other side of the street as we got closer to each other. He waved to me as we passed, and I waved back, though I didn't recognize him. Then the man turned down Terrace, going north. Curious, I angled a little closer to the side of the road so I could read what was on the flier he had stapled to the pole. The lettering was large enough for me to read it without stopping in front of it—but I did. The message made my heart skip a beat.

"IS YOUR CHILD SAFE?"

I looked back over my shoulder. The man was still jogging down Terrace. He would soon be out of sight. I figured that with my speed I could probably catch up to him if I tried. Even if he was running to a waiting car just out of sight, I might get a tag number which could lead me to the man later. I turned and took a couple of steps in his direction then stopped, looked back in the direction of my house, and child. I turned again toward the jogger, who was just passing from view, hesitated only a moment more, then started running toward my house at full speed, wondering then why I had even hesitated at all in my choice.

As I raced up the street, I tried not to think of anything except getting there as quickly as I could. It took me less than sixty seconds to make it to my garage door. I pulled out the key from my pocket and hurriedly put it in the lock, but the deadbolt lock offered no resistance when I turned it, and the door opened with just a turn of the knob. Had I forgotten to lock it? I saw no sign of forced entry as I rushed through the door, my heart in my throat.

"Maggie. Maggie." I ran down the hall toward my daughter's bedroom. The door was open. Had it been closed when I left? I was pretty sure I had closed it myself, to keep from waking her as I prepared for my morning run. With trepidation, I stopped at the doorway and peered in at the empty bed.

Panic now gripped me as I staggered backward against the wall. I did a useless, unfruitful search of the small room, pulling back the covers fully, as if Maggie could be hiding in the small quarter of space there. I looked under the bed, opened the closet. "Maggie? Maggie? Where are you?"

I then rushed down the hallway, calling her name and looking frantically in every room, nook and cranny. If she was here, if she was alive, my daughter would have answered me by now. It wasn't that big of a house. I stopped and listened for the sound of the shower. Nothing. I headed to the master bedroom and bath, a favorite of Maggie's because she liked to use my hair products, but I heard no sound of water running from that direction, either.

I crossed my sleeping quarters quickly, noting the pulled back covers of my own bed, and no sign of Maggie. I noticed the light from the bathroom slipping out from underneath the door. Had I left the light on? I couldn't remember. I flung open the door.

The scream that escaped from my lips then was completely involuntary, born of surprise, and delighted relief. My child was standing in front of the mirror, bath towel wrapped around her, brushing her hair. Maggie, startled at the sudden, unexpected image of me in the mirror, wide-eyed and screaming, screamed herself. Long and loud. Then she stopped, held her hand up to her heart and, noticeably shaking, turned to face me. "You scared me," she said, tears forming in the corners of her eyes.

I grabbed her and held her close and tight in both arms, which did little to calm my daughter as intended, the child not understanding the palpable tension and relief evident in my actions. Finally, I held Maggie at arm's length. "Didn't you hear me calling you?"

Maggie pulled out the ear plugs and I could hear the music pouring through the speakers. "I guess I had the volume up a little too loud," she said.

I smiled my relief, wiping a tear from the corner of my eye. "I guess you did."

"But Mom, why the panic? You scared me to death."

How much did Maggie need to know? "Did you see or hear anything unusual when you got up?"

She looked at me then, a bit of alarm in the eyes. "What do you mean, unusual? What's going on?"

I hesitated a moment. No reason to unnecessarily alarm her, but she needed, deserved some explanation. "Maybe I'm just being a little paranoid," I said. "I saw this creepy looking guy on my run. Then when I got back, the door was unlocked. You weren't in your room and you didn't respond when I called your name."

My daughter reached over and gave me a big hug. "I'm all right, Mom."

When the hug ended, I asked her, "Did you go outside for any reason?"

Maggie shook her head.

I tried my best to calm my own heart, to not unnecessarily frighten her. On the other hand, I needed her to be alert. "Probably nothing," I said. "The creepy guy I told you about, he put up a sign on the telephone pole. When I passed it, I read it, and it said, 'Is your child safe?'" When Maggie's eyes grew wide, I added, "Probably just a generic message, you know like those public service ads that say, 'It's eleven o'clock. Do you know where your children are?' Some creepy busybody with nothing better to do."

But even as I said it, I didn't believe it. "Just a good idea to be careful, be on the lookout for anyone or anything suspicious." I always carried my cell phone with me when I ran, in case Maggie needed to get in touch with me, but I was re-thinking leaving her alone at all.

The ring tones from my cell phone—the William Tell Overture—interrupted my thoughts. I fished it from my pocket, flipped it open and looked at the number. It was one I did not recognize. "Hello."

"You shouldn't be so careless, Ms. Marston, leaving your door unlocked like that. Next time you might not be so lucky." The voice was a deep baritone, one I didn't recognize. It was calm, almost reassuring, and all the more menacing for it.

"You son of a bitch. Who is this?" I waited a couple of seconds but the caller did not answer me. "Who are you? What do you want?"

I waited again for several seconds, angry and scared at the same time. I could hear his breathing, but still no spoken response. Then the line went dead.

Chapter Thirty-Two

The Co-cathedral of St. Thomas More was located on the corner of Tennessee and Woodward, right across the street from the F. S.U. campus. As a result, many of its members or attendees were students. But its congregation also included a good number of working-class families and immigrants, the latter most likely because of its activist priest. The parking lot had only a few cars. I found a spot close to the building, parked and then sat in my car, collecting myself.

My meeting with Craig had been an hour ago, but I could still feel the tension in my neck and shoulders, the twitch in my fingers. I had been dreading it, but knew I had to tell him. He needed to know. So, I called him and asked to meet. "It's about Maggie," I said when he began to make excuses. "It's important."

"Okay," he said after a few beats.

We met at the Uptown Café. He was late by ten minutes. He slid into the booth opposite me, and without any word of greeting, said, "Okay, Kate, I'm here. What's so important you couldn't tell me over the phone?"

I told him.

"My God, Kate," he said when I finished, "what were you thinking? Leaving a ten-year-old alone, and with the door unlocked?"

I wanted to remind him of the many times he had done the same, when she was even younger, but what I said was, "I didn't leave the door unlocked."

"Uh huh."

"Don't you see? Whoever left that note, whoever called, they wanted to let me know they can get inside my house."

Craig frowned. "You need to get off the case."

"What?"

"Goodwin's case. That's what this is all about, right?"

I nodded. "They weren't specific, but that's the most logical conclusion."

"And Ricky Hobbs. You think he was killed by these same people, right? So, no question. Just drop the case."

"It's not that easy."

He looked at me in what appeared to be genuine disbelief, followed closely by anger. "What do you mean, it's not that easy? Of course, it's that easy. We're talking about our daughter here. Is she worth another headline for you?"

I wanted to reach across the table and smack him for the cheap shot, but the fact was, I understood the sentiment. "First, I don't know for sure that would make a difference. If they threatened me, they would do the same to Ted."

"Not your problem."

I shook my head slowly. "You don't understand. I just couldn't do that. It's not who I am. It's not the lesson I want Maggie to learn."

He took a long, deep breath and exhaled. "Yes, I do understand. You can't admit any weakness. You don't want to be vulnerable. Well, that's all right, for you, but not when you're putting my daughter in danger. I don't want to teach her a lesson. I want to keep her alive."

"And that's why I'm telling you this. I want you to know exactly what's going on, so you can be alert to possible threats or danger." I waited a couple of beats, then added, "Maybe Maggie should stay primarily at your place at night for the time being, until this is over."

It was obvious that I had surprised him with this suggestion. He looked at me, his eyes wide, assessing. When he finally spoke, his tone was softer. "Listen, Katie, I'm sorry. This is not your fault. It's just, you know . . ."

"I know."

He reached over and put his hand on mine. I looked into his eyes and just for a brief moment caught a glimpse of something I'd thought existed only in my memory. Then just as quickly, it was gone and I wondered if I had imagined it.

"Of course, I'll take Maggie," he said. "She'll be safe with me. You do what you need to do." After another beat, he said, "You called the police, I suppose?"

I nodded. "They took down the information, said they'd file a report."

"But they're not going to do anything about it."

"Well, in fairness, not a lot they can do. They suggested taking extra precautions, let them know of anything suspicious, that sort of thing, but there's not much to go on at this point."

Craig shook his head. "That son of a bitch better hope I don't find out who he is."

"Or me."

We talked then about the logistics, a modified parenting schedule, specific security precautions, and about what we should tell Maggie. It was agreed that I would pick her up from school today and explain the situation to her, careful to impress upon her the potential for danger, the importance of being alert, but without making her paranoid. It would be enough that her parents were. In the back of my mind were thoughts that Craig might try to exploit the situation as a reason to lower his child support or as grounds to change custody arrangements more permanently, but I couldn't worry about that now.

I brushed these thoughts aside, got out of my car and headed for the church. I inquired of a young woman as to where I might find Father Barista and was directed to the rectory. He was seated behind a mission style oak desk and greeted me with a questioning smile as I entered the small office. The priest looked older and taller than I expected, with a big bushy mustache. His skin was the color of pewter, and worn looking, as if he had been working the fields with some of his parishioners. Perhaps he had.

I introduced myself.

"Yes, I recognize you from the pictures in the papers, though I must say, they do not do you justice. But then, true beauty cannot be captured so well by a mere camera. No?"

Central casting had clearly blown it here. The guy seemed more Latin lover than priest. I felt the involuntary blush at my cheeks, tried to think of a quick, self-deprecating comeback, but couldn't. "Thank you," I said finally, feeling it was somehow the only appropriate reply.

"You wish me to hear your confession?"

Again, his words and manner put me off balance. "I'm not Catholic," I stammered, then kicked myself mentally for such a lame response.

He arched an eyebrow at me, tilted his head. "You are a child of God, Kate. That is all that matters. Anything you tell me in confession will remain a secret." He put his hand over his heart.

I was both pleased, but a little disconcerted with the use of my first name. "I appreciate it, Father, but that's not why I'm here."

He arched his eyebrow again at me, then frowned. "It's just that you seem troubled, as if you are carrying a great emotional weight upon your shoulders."

Was he able to look inside me so easily? Or was he just guessing? I mean, after all, who wasn't carrying around emotional baggage to some degree? "I'm afraid it's nothing more than bad posture," I said, standing up a little straighter.

He smiled. "Well then, if it is not to be a confession, we may speak here." He waved his hand in the direction of the only other chair in the room and I sat down in it. He sat back in his chair and said, "What did you wish to speak with me about?"

"I wanted to ask you about Elena Castillo. I understand you knew her."

He nodded. "Yes," he said slowly, stringing out the word, making it two syllables. "But as I told your colleague, what was his name?"

"Ted Stevens?"

He smiled. "Yes. A lapsed Catholic, that one, but he has a good heart." He shook his head. "Anyway, as I told him, I cannot repeat what was said in the confessional." There was a trace of scold in his voice.

I gave him my best shocked look of horror. "Of course not, and I would never, in a thousand years, ask you to do so." This time it was I who placed a hand over the heart.

"I was hoping that maybe you might be willing to share with me anything you observed, or sensed that would help me find out what exactly happened to Elena and who might be responsible." I looked at the man for some reaction, but his face remained passive.

He looked at me for a long time, put his hands on his knees and nodded gently to himself. "I sense that whatever is troubling you, Kate, it is not the fear that an innocent man has been charged, is it?"

This was insane. It was a cheap parlor trick, I was sure. Or was it? "What do you mean?"

"Sometimes the light of the truth can be too bright."

Talk about indirection. This guy was a master at it. Part of me wanted to scream at him to get to the point, but part of me was afraid of what it might be. I looked at the priest now. "I'm still not sure what you mean."

His frown was one of mild disappointment, mitigated by an understanding of human frailties essential to his role. "There are some secrets so dark, so sinister, that we feel we can not reveal them to anybody. They gnaw at you, eat at you from inside until you become a hollow shell, morally, mentally and physically."

"Are you saying that Elena had a secret, something she couldn't talk about?"

He shrugged. "I wasn't necessarily talking about Elena."

Creepy. Very creepy. I shook it off. "What was Elena's dark secret, Father? What was it she could only reveal to her priest?" I realized the volume and pitch of my voice had risen. "Please," I said, more softly.

The priest reached across the desk and placed his hand on mine and looked deep into my eyes. I thought for a second he might in fact answer my question, but instead, he said, "I've given you all I can. It is up to you now." Then he rose from his seat, signaling the end of our conversation. I left unsatisfied and unsettled, but I shook it off.

After I left the church, I went by Bruster's Ice Cream, bought a couple of chocolate milkshakes, then headed for Maggie's school. I parked and did a quick surveillance of the surroundings, searching for anyone or anything that seemed out of place or even remotely suspicious. Of course, a hit man could look like any other parent, his car like any other car, so I wasn't sure what I was looking for. At any rate, nothing made my danger detector tingle.

The final bell rang a couple of minutes later and students began to file out the doors. Maggie was easy to spot. The tall, lanky child stopped and stood just outside the doors, adjusted her backpack, and scanned the area for my car, shading her eyes with a hand and frowning. Her auburn hair fell loosely around her face. My heart swelled at the sight of her.

As she brushed a loose strand of hair with her fingers, she saw the Yukon and her frown turned to a smile. She waved and began walking quickly toward me, covering the distance in seconds. She put her gear in the back seat, then climbed in the front and fastened her seatbelt.

"Hi, Mom."

"Hey, sport." I handed her the milkshake.

She knew at once what it was, took it eagerly and sucked on the straw for a couple of seconds. Then she looked at me suspiciously. "What's going on?"

"What do you mean?"

"The milkshake. What's the special occasion?" She put her lips to the straw and took more of it in.

"No special occasion. Just felt like a milkshake—and it would have been rude not bring one for you." I pulled out onto the street.

"Yes, it would," she said with certainty. Still, her suspicions remained. She gave me a sideways glance and repeated, "But really, what's going on?"

I looked over at my daughter, then turned my attention back to the traffic. When I didn't respond right away, she said, "It's about the creepy guy you saw this morning, right? The guy who called the house?"

Damn, but this kid was perceptive. After a couple of seconds, I nodded, still looking straight ahead. "Well, yes, we do need to talk about the situation." I turned briefly to face her, but now she was looking straight ahead. As I navigated the busy traffic on Tharpe Street, I told her of my concerns, of the conversation with her dad, doing my best to walk that fine line between adequately preparing her but without unduly alarming her.

She took in the information, nodding occasionally, swallowing hard and saying "Okay" several times. I could tell that she was upset, but she tried not to show it. In fact, she took it better than I thought she would, asking questions about what she should be on the lookout for, what she should do in certain situations. When I finished, she shrugged and said, "Makes sense to me." I felt both proud and guilty.

We rode the rest of the way to the office in relative silence, punctuated by questions or comments about more routine matters. It was a bit awkward, but by the time we parked and walked in the building, a certain equilibrium had returned. While I sifted through my mail and e-mails, and returned phone calls, she sat on the couch in my office and read her homework assignment.

One of my phone messages was from a former client from my days at the Public Defender's Office. Brandi Peters was a drug addict and a thief, and not necessarily in that order. She had an extensive juvenile and adult record, even though she was only in her late twenties. The last time I saw her was three years ago, when she was sentenced to a year in the county jail for possession of drug paraphernalia, shoplifting and resisting arrest.

I didn't really want to return her call. My assumption was that she had gotten arrested on some new charge and wanted me to represent her. Two problems: She would lie to me about her case, changing her story to suit whatever new evidence surfaced. And she would never pay my fee. She would try to persuade me to take her case pro bono, for old time's sake, or would promise me from here to tomorrow that she would pay whatever I wanted, if I would just let her pay in installments. But bottom line, I'd never see a cent in fees. In short, she was a high maintenance, non-paying client I did not need at this time.

That being said, I felt it a professional obligation, not to mention just good manners, to return your phone calls promptly. So, stealing myself to the anticipated conversation, I dialed the number. Maybe I could just quickly steer her to the Public Defender's Office. She would qualify, and I would feel guilty referring her to one of my colleagues when I knew she wouldn't pay. One the other hand, maybe I could refer her to one I didn't like.

Brandi picked up on the third ring.

Chapter Thirty-Three

The headlights of my Yukon barely cut through the fog as I navigated the narrow dirt road that twisted through the woods. The trees on each side seemed to close in on me, their branches occasionally scraping the side of the SUV, their canopy blocking out any additional illumination offered by the sliver of moon that hung in the night sky. The road widened on occasion sufficient for two vehicles to pass in relative comfort and safety, but in most places, both vehicles would have to veer off into the woods a little, with the risk of getting stuck in the soft sand.

Not that I was likely to meet another vehicle out here, which seemed to be just a little past the middle of nowhere. Brandi's directions had been detailed and so far, accurate: "Go 10.2 miles past the truck route on Highway 20, turn right onto Tom Thumb Road. Go about three miles till you see an old barn on your right. Just past that barn, on the left, you'll see a dirt road. There should be a little wooden sign, but sometimes it comes off the post there. Anyway, that will be Pine Tip Trail. Follow that exactly 1.4 miles and you dead end at our place. You can't miss it."

I checked my odometer. According to her directions, it should be just ahead another tenth of a mile. Sure enough, around the next bend in the road, my headlights illuminated a double wide trailer that sat in a small clearing. Lights were on inside and when I pulled up close, next to an older model Buick Regal, the porch light came on, the door opened, and the petite silhouette of Brandi Peters framed the doorway. Two large dogs—they looked like a mix of yellow lab and hound—rushed from around the side of the trailer and toward my car, barking furiously, their hackles raised.

Brandi shouted at them, "Tom, Jerry, hush, now. Hush."

And they did, almost immediately, but still circled my car excitedly.

Brandi called from the porch. "It's all right." They won't bother you."

Looking out at the dogs, it seemed that their initial aggressiveness had been replaced by tail-wagging and friendly curiosity, so I opened the door and slid out, talking to them and offering the back of my hand in friendship. Both of them sniffed a few seconds then apparently satisfied, turned and trotted toward Brandi. I followed, though not at a trot.

It was too dark to make out much, but I noted the rusted out pick-up truck off to the side and a small wooden shed toward the rear of the property. Several old appliances huddled underneath an awning on the left side of the trailer. A few discarded tires dotted the area. The trailer had vinyl skirting around the bottom, but little else in the way of adornment. The cleared area—you couldn't call it a yard—had no grass, no shrubs, and no plantings.

When I stepped onto the small metal porch, Brandi smiled. "Hey, Katie. Good to see you."

"You too," hoping my voice didn't give away my lie.

She looked from side to side quickly, then opened the door and motioned for me to enter.

"You're looking good," she said once we were inside.

"So are you." I lied again. Even in the dull yellow glow of the porch light, I could tell that the years and the drugs had not been particularly kind to Brandi Peters. It was even more apparent in the full light of the living room. I remembered the cute girl I met that first time at the juvenile detention center. She had long, blond hair, a well-toned and proportioned body, and large blue eyes that looked innocent and seductive at the same time. Effective tools for a con artist. Her hair was shorter now, dull and limp. She was way too thin, and her skin pale, pasty. The large blue eyes that looked up at me were twitchy, unfocussed.

"You want a beer?" She picked up a can of Bud Light from the side table next to a recliner, held it aloft.

I shook my head. "Look, Brandi, I don't want to be rude, but this isn't a social call. You said you had information about Elena Castillo. Valuable information, you said, and the proof to back it up. I came out here in the middle of nowhere, in the middle of the night, so you can show me what you've got. I'd rather just get down to business and get on my way."

She frowned, took a swig of beer. "Yeah, it's a long way to come, I know, but like I said, Jimmy likes me to stay close to home. He would have asked questions."

Jimmy was Jimmy Black, she said on the phone. The trailer was his, on family land. He was her boyfriend, she said. And an abusive boyfriend, I suspected, based upon Brandi's comment and his criminal history. Yeah, that's right, I checked him out. Only prudent. Brandi said he would not be there when I came, but I couldn't be sure. I needed to know who and what I might come up against.

I knew Brandi. She was a druggie and a thief, but she had never been violent. I wasn't too concerned about her, as far as my safety was concerned. Her boyfriend, on the other hand, had been in and out of jail over the years for numerous crimes, including a couple of aggravated domestic batteries, and most recently for cooking meth. Not a good combination, and judging by Brandi's appearance, I also suspected Jimmy was back in business, and she was using—despite what she had told me on the phone.

I looked around the small space, which contained both kitchen and living room. It was cleaner and tidier than I had anticipated. "Where is Jimmy?"

Her eyes grew wide for a moment, and she stared at me. "What's that matter? I told you he wouldn't be here."

I shrugged, and she did the same. "He's out with his brothers," she said. "On business. He won't be back till late."

I pushed my lips out, nodded my head. "So, what do you have for me?"

"Did you bring the money?"

"Let's see what you have first."

"I told you to bring the money with you."

"And I told you, I'm not agreeing to anything until I know what you have and I can verify it."

"But I already told you, on the phone."

She had, in fact, done just that. And her revelation had been so unexpected, so excitingly ripe with possibilities, that I had agreed to meet her, alone, and at the time and place she had insisted upon. When she called me at the office, I thought it was to ask me to represent her in another criminal case. After the preliminaries, I asked her, "What can I do for you, Brandi?"

"It's not what you can do for me, but what I can do for you."

"Ask not what your country can do for you, ask what you can do for your country."

"What?"

"JFK's inauguration?"

Silence on the other end.

"Never mind. Just talking to myself. Anyway, you say you called to offer me some help?" I was pretty sure Brandi Peters never did anything for anybody unless she was working some angle for herself, but I didn't voice my skepticism. "I'm listening," I said.

"I have information, valuable information about Elena Castillo which you will want to have all to yourself."

She had my attention. "What do you want to tell me?"

There was a bit of hesitation on the other end, then she said, "It's something you won't get from anybody else. And I got proof of what I tell you."

I knew where this was heading. "Like I said, I'm all ears."

"Well, first, if I tell you, and you agree it's valuable, I was thinking

261

you and me could agree on some compensation for what I have."

Bingo.

"Brandi, I'm not in the practice of buying information from people."

"You'd pay a private detective for information, wouldn't you?"

"You're not a private detective."

"Same difference. I'm just coming to you instead of the other way around."

She actually had a point. "Okay, if you have information on my case, and it is of value, then we can talk about how much it might be worth."

"This is dynamite stuff."

"Brandi, quit treating me like a mark. Either tell me what you have, or say goodbye, cause I'm not going to negotiate with you, especially in the dark."

"How do I know you won't just take what I tell you and say it isn't worth anything?"

"You wouldn't have called me if you thought that."

"You're right. I know I can trust you. That's why I called you first."

I wondered about that, too, but didn't say it. Instead, I remained silent until she decided to speak again.

"Okay, what I have is this. Elena Castillo was pregnant."

I was intrigued, but not convinced. "The medical examiner says different."

"That's cause he wouldn't know from the autopsy. She got an abortion three weeks before she was killed."

Now she certainly had my attention. My heart and my mind raced and I struggled to keep a matter-of-fact tone in my voice. "What makes you think she had an abortion?"

"I don't think she had an abortion. I know it."

"How do you know it?"

"Because I was there."

Startled, I had no ready response. The best I could manage after a few seconds was, "What?"

She then laid it all out for me. For the past year, she had been working as a nurse's aide at the Big Bend Women's Health Center. She reminded me that, before she had been interrupted by a series of criminal convictions, she had been enrolled at Tallahassee Community College, on track to become a nurse. After her last stint in jail, she said, she had gotten clean and sober, re-enrolled at the college, and managed to land a job at the center. One of the procedures with which she assisted was abortions.

Things had gotten complicated recently in her personal life, she said, and she'd been forced to drop out of school and quit her job at the center—one of the reasons she needed money—but she had been part of the team that performed Elena Castillo's abortion last December.

I didn't know if any of what she was saying was true, but I knew that the subpoena I'd served on the center for any medical records it might have on Elena had drawn a response from the organization that it had no such records. When I pointed this out to Brandi, she had an answer.

"That's because she didn't use her real name. I knew who she was, though. Recognized her first time she came in, from pictures I'd seen of her in the news. She dressed down, no make-up and all, but that kind of beauty you can't hide. I checked in her purse when she wasn't looking, just to be sure. And it was her."

"But if the records are in a different name, how could I prove they were really hers?"

"You have me."

That didn't exactly instill the necessary confidence, I told her.

"I got the records. You can check them and see that the information will match her, including blood type, all that stuff."

"Still . . ."

"I got something else, too. I got something that will not only prove she was there and had her abortion. You will be able to prove who the father was."

This literally left me speechless. And when I didn't respond after several seconds, Brandi prompted me. "You still there, Katie?"

"Yes," I managed. "What do you have? Blood test results on the fetus and mother?"

I could almost feel her smile of satisfaction over the line, like a fisherman reeling in a big one. She had me, and she knew it. "So," she said, "interested?"

I was, but Brandi refused to tell me more. She would show me what she had, answer any more questions I might have. But I would have to come to her.

And I had.

Now she wanted to press her advantage, or try. She frowned. "Maybe I should contact her family. They got lots of money, and I have a feeling they'd pay to keep what I have secret." She got up from the recliner and walked into the kitchen, took another beer from the refrigerator and popped the top. She looked at me, nodded, then took a large swallow. She began to pace then, stopping at intervals to rearrange something in the room, straighten the magazines on the coffee table. She stopped momentarily and faced me, waiting for my response.

"Listen, Brandi, you don't want to mess with the Castillo family. Blackmail is neither legal nor healthy."

She seemed to be considering this as she took another swallow from her beer and set it down. I wondered if she already had contacted the Castillo family, but then thought not. She was not the sharpest knife in the drawer, but she had enough sense to know when a con was too risky.

"I'd rather deal with you, Katie, but like I said, I need the money. Things ain't working out so good with Jimmy." She began to fiddle with a thread on her pullover knit blouse. "I need to make other arrangements, if you know what I mean?"

I thought I did. "Why don't you come with me tonight, Brandi. I can take you to Refuge House, or if you want, put you up in a motel for a couple of nights." She started shaking her head. "I'll help you get a restraining order against Jimmy."

Still shaking her head, she gave me a crooked smile. "I do that, he'd kill me."

"If he even looks at you crossways, I'll put his ass in jail."

She crossed the room then, adjusted some knick knacks on a shelf. With her back to me, she said, "Jimmy's okay. I can handle him for the time being." She turned back to me. "But I can see what's coming and I need to put some distance between us, and soon. That's why I need some money."

"Well," I said after several seconds of silence, "why don't you just show me what you've got, and we can take it from there."

Suddenly, her eyes opened wide and she tilted her head, as if listening for something. She walked over to the window, parted the blinds and looked out into the darkness.

"What is it?"

She pushed at me with her hand as she continued to look out the window. After a few seconds she straightened up and turned to me. "Thought I heard something, but nothing out there. She gave a short nervous laugh. "Tom and Jerry would let us know if someone came up, anyway." She looked back toward the window one more time, then turned back to me. "Okay, let me go get my file."

I watched as she disappeared down the narrow hallway and I was suddenly very anxious to get out of there. Why had I agreed to come way out here, alone, with no back-up, and no back-up plan? I certainly didn't want to be there when Jimmy came home.

I had considered telling Ted about Brandi's call, and my arrangement to meet with her, but I didn't for a couple of reasons. First, he would have insisted on coming along, despite Brandi's explicit direction that I come alone. I didn't want to have to debate the issue with him or worry that he would find some way to follow me, and risk

Brandi getting skittish, more so than she had sounded on the phone. In addition, I didn't know if Brandi was trying to scam me, or if the information she claimed to have would pan out, but if it did, if there was some way to determine the paternity of Elena's unborn child, I wanted to make sure it wasn't my father. I needed to keep this to myself.

Brandi returned with a large brown envelope. She motioned for me to join her at the small dinette table between the kitchen and living area. I sat down next to her as she slid the envelope over toward me. I opened it up and removed the contents. There wasn't much there: Admission sheet, nurse's notes or chart of the procedure, and discharge summary. The patient's name was listed as Priscilla Quiones. Her height, weight and age were all consistent with that of Elena, but they weren't exactly unique. They would have matched hundreds of women in Tallahassee. There were notations of blood pressure, blood type. There was a sheet in which the patient checked off boxes, answered questions about her medical history. Some of this information might be helpful in narrowing it down a bit more, but none of this would hold up in a court of law as proof of any connection to Elena Castillo. And this is what I told Brandi.

She pointed to the admitting form, at the signature at the bottom. "You get a handwriting expert. He should be able to compare the signature there, plus the other writing on the form, and see if it don't match up."

I pursed my lips, nodded slowly. "Possibly," I said. "but you said you have evidence by which I could determine the father of the fetus."

"Oh yeah." She got up from her seat and moved the few feet across the kitchen to the refrigerator. She opened the door and bent over. She moved some things around on the bottom shelf then pull out a plastic container the size of a small loaf of bread. It was opaque, but you could see that there was some kind of liquid inside—and something else. Brandi placed it on the table in front of me.

Instinctively, I sat back in my chair, but I couldn't take my eyes off the container. "Tell me that's not what I think it is."

"What do you think it is?"

"Is it the fetus?"

She nodded.

"Oh, my God!" My poker face deserted me then, scrunching up to display my shock and disgust. "How did you... more importantly, why did you..." I let the unspoken words drift in the stale air of the trailer, along with the smoke from Brandi's cigarette.

She shrugged. "Normally, they discard the fetus. They contract with a company that incinerates it, like they would a severed arm, for example." That she could be so cold, so cavalier about it gave me a chill, but I kept my thoughts to myself. "When the Castillo woman came in, though, I was thinking, she's gone to the trouble of hiding her identity, so it must be something she wants kept secret."

"Duh."

She frowned. "Her being the daughter of a big politician and all, famous kind of, I was thinking it may prove valuable somewhere down the road. I wasn't quite sure when or how I would be able to use it, but I thought sure an opportunity would come along."

"Quick thinking," I said, meaning to be sarcastic, but Brandi literally beamed with pride at the perceived compliment.

She then told me how she had altered the paperwork so the company's numbers matched the clinic's, secreted the fetus and placed it in a jar of formaldehyde solution to preserve it, and brought it home, biding her time for an opportunity. "This," she said, "can confirm that Castillo was the mother, but it can also confirm who the father was. Specifically, it would tell you whether it was your client." She hesitated a beat, searching my eyes for something. "I would think that would be something you'd want to know before you decided to go public."

She was absolutely right. And she knew that I knew she was right. But I persisted in trying to play it cool. I told her that I would take the records, the specimen, do the necessary tests, and if everything could be verified, I would get with her and we'd talk about some reasonable compensation. We haggled for several minutes. I ended up giving her five hundred dollars cash as a good faith deposit, and taking with me a copy of the records and a small portion of the specimen which Brandi sliced off for me in the kitchen and put in a small plastic container. Gross, for sure, but I took it.

I couldn't wait to get out of there. And I drove faster than I should have. Faster than was safe. I was almost to where the narrow trail met up with Tom Thumb Road when I met another vehicle coming my way. The headlights were on high beam and the vehicle was, like mine, barreling down the road. Nearly blinded, I barely had time to veer off to the right, into the small brush along the side, and the soft sand underneath.

The truck slowed to a near stop as it passed and I got a look at the driver. Long, dark hair and beard. I recognized him from the photo on his criminal history print-out. It was Jimmy Black. He stopped just a little past me, engine idling. I pressed down on the accelerator and my tires spun in the loose sand.

The door of the pick-up truck opened and I could see Jimmy slide out. I gunned the engine but the wheels spun uselessly. He started walking toward me. I put the Yukon in reverse, straighten my wheels best I could, and pressed down again on the accelerator, more gently this time. The back tires got a little bit of traction and moved me a couple of feet. I then put it in drive, and eased down on the accelerator. Gradually, it caught purchase in the sand and moved forward. I waved my hand up as acknowledgement to Jimmy and then drove away.

Chapter Thirty-Four

I drove fast down the narrow dirt road, looking in my rear-view mirror to make sure Jimmy hadn't turned around to follow me. He hadn't. I stopped when I made it to the paved road, clouds of dust settling around the SUV as it idled. I let out a long deep breath, took another, then held it, waiting, watching in my rear-view mirror for headlights. Nothing. I turned right and headed toward Highway 20 and had gone about a hundred yards when I stopped again. For a long minute, I sat there, forearms resting on the steering wheel, staring straight ahead, thinking. Then I made a three-point turn and headed back the way I had come.

As I got close to the trailer, I cut my headlights and crept the rest of the way, guided by the lights inside the distant double wide and the pale glow of the obscured moon. Barely above an idle, I eased the SUV into position so that it was pointing away from the trailer. Might need to make a quick exit. I eased out, closing the door gently, and looked toward the trailer, listening. I could hear raised voices, but couldn't make out what was being said. It seemed that I had been quiet enough not to draw the attention of the occupants.

But apparently not quiet enough to pass unnoticed by the dogs. They came barreling around the side of the trailer again, barking furiously. They stopped though, and quieted, when they got close, perhaps realizing a familiar recent scent, remembering that I had been an invited guest only minutes before. The dogs wagged their tails and gladly accepted the rubs on the head, then parted for me to make my way up to the trailer.

The dogs' barking had apparently not been noticed inside as the voices were louder now, mostly Jimmy's. And more than voices, I heard the sound of flesh on flesh. Slap! A scream of protest, anger and fear from Brandi. Slap! Another scream, this one more a resignation than anything else. I knocked on the door, loudly. Silence inside. I could picture Jimmy and Brandi inside, looking toward the door, not quite believing they had heard what they'd heard. I knocked again. This time, I heard the footsteps across the living room, stepped back as the aluminum door swung open and Jimmy Black framed the doorway.

He was tall and skinny, maybe six three, 160 pounds, with arms that seemed much longer than necessary. His face was just as it appeared in his booking photo—large, hooked nose, raw boned and ruddy cheeks, somewhat hidden beneath a scraggly beard. Picture Abraham Lincoln with long, greasy hair. One hand held onto the door, the other rested against the frame.

"Who the hell are you?" His face reflected anger and puzzlement. Then a flicker of recognition. He looked behind me toward the Yukon. "You the bitch I passed on the road." He looked over his shoulder toward Brandi, then back to me. "So, my girlfriend here, she sold you some grass?"

"She what?"

"That's what I thought." He turned back again toward Brandi. "Since my sweetheart seems unable to tell me the truth," he said, then turned back to me, a fake smile on his face, "maybe you can tell me who the hell you are and what you're doing here." The smile was gone now.

I could see around him to where Brandi sat in the recliner. More curled than sitting really, peering out at me, the fear and surprise obvious in her face. "I'm Brandi's lawyer, Jimmy," I said, forcing myself to look directly into his dark, angry eyes, "and I've come to take her away from here." I looked past him again at the cowering woman in the recliner, who seemed truly bewildered. "Go get your stuff, Brandi. You're leaving."

Jimmy turned to look at his girlfriend, who hadn't moved, then back to me. "You crazy, bitch? You come to my home, trespass on my land, and tell me what's gonna happen?" His tone managed to reflect genuine surprise mixed with contempt and anger. "No," he said, shaking his finger at me. "What's gonna happen is, you're gonna get your scrawny ass back in your fancy SUV and get the hell off my property. Then me and Brandi are going to finish our discussion."

I started to point out that he was a fine one to be talking about scrawny asses, as it looked as if he had no ass at all, but recognized immediately that levity might not be the best approach with the man just now. When I made no move to turn my "scrawny ass" around, he made his case more strongly.

"I could shoot you dead, right here, right now, and wouldn't nothing happen to me. I got a right to defend my property. You ought to know that if you're a lawyer. Stand your ground." He spoke with an uninformed conviction that would be amusing if it wasn't so dangerous under the circumstances.

"That's only if your life is in danger, Jimmy, not your property. You really think anybody's going to believe that you had to use self-defense against me, that you were afraid I was going to do serious bodily harm to you?"

He thought about this for a bit, pulling on his beard with his thumb and forefinger. I could almost see the little wheels turning inside his skull, considering his options, playing out the scenario, evaluating his made-up version of the events for a self-defense claim.

"Listen to me, Jimmy. You're not going to do that."

"No? And why not?"

"Because you're not stupid—and neither am I." I pulled my cell phone from behind my back. "Before I came back here, I called my partner. He knows exactly where I am and why. I told him if I didn't call him back in fifteen minutes, to call the law. I told him a former client wanted my help with an abusive boyfriend so I came here to see and counsel her, since her boyfriend wouldn't let her leave their trailer.

I told him about the marijuana plants I saw at the rear of the property, the scales, baggies and loose marijuana in the kitchen, the ingredients for making meth, and the telltale curl of smoke from the shed out back."

I held up my cell phone so he could see the large 911 numerals on the face, "All I have to do is press send and be connected in seconds. And if I do, I can tell them all that, plus what I have heard and seen since I arrived."

I was lying, of course, about having called Ted, or anyone else, before coming back here, but now, in hindsight, it seemed like an excellent idea. I had to hope the spur of the moment bluff was believable. It seemed to have the desired effect, because although Jimmy bore into me with eyes that seemed to glow with anger and hatred, he made no move toward me, nor did he say anything right away in response.

"Now, I don't give a shit about the drugs, and I won't report the domestic battery I witnessed tonight. But I am taking her with me. I'm going to file for an injunction tomorrow—which you will not oppose—and you will stay the hell away from her. If you try to stop her now, or make any aggressive move toward me, I press the send button and report everything."

I paused a few moments to let him consider this, then, anticipating his thoughts, the weighing of his options, I closed the deal. "Even if you could somehow beat the criminal charges—beyond a reasonable doubt is a very high burden of proof after all—you are on probation. And you know how easy it is for them to prove a violation of probation. The burden of proof is only by a preponderance of the evidence."

Jimmy stood there for a long time without saying anything. Finally, he turned toward Brandi again and said, "This what you want, babe?"

But before she could reply I chipped in. "I'm her lawyer, Jimmy, and I'm speaking for her now. It doesn't matter what she says, she's coming with me." When Jimmy turned back to look at me, I told

Brandi once again to get her stuff. I told Jimmy that if she didn't start moving in the next five seconds, I would push the send button on my phone.

He didn't look back at Brandi, but he turned his head to one side and lifted his chin, an apparent signal that she should do as I instructed, because she hustled out of the chair and toward the bedroom. "Whatever," he said, sneering in my direction. "I don't really give a shit anyway. But you know she'll be back. She's in love."

The way he said love it had two syllables. "Maybe," I said, "but she won't be back tonight. And I'm serious when I say you can't have contact with her. Violation of an injunction is not okay even if she says it is."

"She'll drop it within a week."

Again, he was probably right, but I didn't reply this time. I just shrugged and looked out over the surrounding property, then back to him. Jimmy and I stood facing each other in silence for an eternity as Brandi gathered her belongings together. As I stood there, I was second guessing the instruction to have her pack. The longer we stood there, the more the opportunity Jimmy had to consider his options, to evaluate the situation. And that was not a good thing.

My concern was that his emotions would begin to take over any logic he was utilizing. He might start thinking about how he was being disrespected, humiliated even. As long as I could keep him thinking rationally, I had a chance of getting Brandi and myself out of there in one piece. But I wasn't sure how long that would last.

Thankfully, Brandi came from around the side of the trailer just then, carrying a large suitcase and wearing a backpack, apparently having wisely chosen to exit from the back rather than the front door. The dogs gave her an escort. She didn't even look in Jimmy's direction, but went directly to my SUV, placed her stuff in the back, then climbed in the passenger side.

I followed after her, turning occasionally to make sure Jimmy was still standing in the doorway. He was. I watched him in my rear-view mirror wave to us as we headed down the narrow dirt road. Then he turned, went inside the trailer and closed the door. From his cavalier manner, I didn't think he would get in his truck and follow us, but I didn't want to take any chances. I drove fast on the way out, my speed born of both the circumstances and my now familiarity with the road. I looked in the rear-view mirror regularly but I saw no headlights behind me. I felt reasonably sure that he had not followed us, but I kept a pretty good pace all the way back to Highway 20.

Brandi was also visibly nervous, turning to look behind us several times, wringing her hands in front of her. She didn't speak until we made it to the paved road, where she seemed to grow less anxious, more solemn. She looked over at me, managed a small smile. "You got some balls on you, lady. I thought he was going to pull out his gun and shoot you."

"His gun?"

"He had it in his waistband, in the back, underneath his shirt."

My stomach cramped a little and a thin film of perspiration formed on my skin at the thought. I knew that he probably had a gun, but I hadn't thought he had it on him all the time we were talking. I looked over at Brandi and shrugged. "Like I said, Jimmy may be mean. He may be a real asshole, but I was hoping he wasn't completely stupid, or so high on something he couldn't think straight."

"Well, I appreciate what you did, but you didn't have to do that. I could have handled him. I always have."

I looked over at her. "That big bruise around your eye says different." I waited a couple of moments, then added, "I knew he'd want to know who I was and why I'd been out to see you. I didn't want to read about you in next morning's paper."

Brandi shrugged but didn't say anything in response, which was probably as close to a thank you as I was going to get.

"You told him I was there to buy pot?"

"I couldn't tell him the truth. Then he'd want in on it. He'd insist on running everything and get most, if not all, of the money."

"Did you get the . . ."

"Yeah," she said, pointing with her head toward the back seat.

We then discussed what to do next. Brandi wanted me to take her to the bus station. She had family in Alabama, she said, who would probably take her in. Jimmy, she reasoned, didn't care enough about her to try and find her, or travel to Alabama if he found out. She just needed to put some distance between them for a while. Contrary to Jimmy's cocky assurances, she had no intention of going back to him any time soon, she said.

I was doubtful, but I didn't contradict her. I did, however, strongly discourage her leaving town, partly for her and partly for me. Wherever she was, she needed an injunction, and that would take a little time. And why should she let him control where she lived? She had a right to stay right here, and I would make sure she had the full protection of the law so he didn't bother her. And, I reminded her, we had a deal working on the Castillo case, or did she not care to get any additional money if things panned out as she represented? Or maybe it was a scam all along and she wanted to get out of town before I discovered it was all bogus?

"No, no. It's no scam. I swear. You can send the money to me in Alabama. I'll call you with the address when I get settled in."

I shook my head. "But if it does turn out to be as you said, I may need you as a witness, to verify or authenticate the records and the fetus."

"I can't do that. What I did, taking those records, the specimen, like you said, that's a crime. I'd get in trouble."

"Maybe not. You might be protected as a whistleblower if the clinic was a party to falsifying medical records." I paused a moment as she considered this. "And if I can't use what you have given me, then it's not going to be worth anything to me." This, I could see from the expression on her face, made sense to Brandi. "Now, maybe I won't need you to testify, depending on what I find out, I may be able to leverage things. But I'm going to need you to be handy just in case."

Brandi understood leverage, too. She nodded. "I'm not going to testify, but I'll stick around for a little while. I guess it would be a good idea to get that injunction. Couldn't hurt. I got a couple of lines on jobs, temporary gigs. But I need a place to stay, at least for a few days."

"I got just the place for you," I said as I located the speed dial number on my phone and pressed send. It was a confidential number for a confidential location.

Someone picked up on the second ring. "Hello. Refuge House. May I help you?"

Chapter Thirty-Five

I pulled into my parents' driveway a little before five thirty. I had finally bitten the bullet and called my father yesterday, asked him if we could meet and talk.

"What's it about?" he asked.

"Renny's case."

After a short pause, he said he would be tied up with hearings the rest of the afternoon, and suggested I come by the house after work. "Maybe bring Maggie, have dinner."

"I need to speak privately."

Another pause, this one longer. "Why don't you come by about five thirty. Martha Anne has her yoga class on Wednesday afternoons. She won't be home till after six. That should give us some time to ourselves."

As I parked my Yukon, I was shoring up my nerve, and trying to figure out how my most recent client, Brandi Peters, fit into things. I got her settled in last night at Refuge House, assuring her that I would help her transition into her own place soon. I filed a petition for a domestic violence injunction first thing this morning, got the temporary restraining order entered, and I expected a sheriff's deputy would serve it on Jimmy Black sometime today.

What to do with the information she'd given me the night before was still a puzzle, but I hadn't had much time to sort it out. It could very well be some scam on her part, and I was naturally suspicious, given my past experience with Brandi. But if it panned out, it could be the most significant development yet in this case. If Goodwin turned out to be the father, it would be crucial that the State never know. If it turned out to be someone else, it would blow the State's case right out of the water.

Either way, Brandi would want to be compensated, and very well, especially in the former situation, more for her silence than anything else.

She was unpredictable, and I would have to keep some distance from her. Despite what I had said last night about whistleblower protection, I had little doubt that what Brandi had done in taking the records and the fetus specimen was illegal. I had to be careful not to be seen as an accessory after the fact.

With these thoughts pressing down on me, and doing my best to set them aside for the time being, I got out and approached the house. Dad met me at the front door and I followed him into his den.

"How's it working out, Maggie staying with Craig?"

"Okay," I said. "Craig and I have our issues, but when I laid out the situation, I have to say, he stepped up to the plate."

"You know she can stay with us anytime."

"Yeah, I know."

"Have there been any more threats?"

I shook my head, looking down at the floor.

"So, you think it's related to Renny's case?"

"Maybe."

"Is that you wanted to talk with me about?"

"Sort of."

My father frowned. "Rather cryptic this afternoon, aren't we?" He didn't wait for an answer to his rhetorical question. "So, what did you want to talk about privately?"

"Well, it's no secret that we've been investigating a possible connection between Elena's death and the push to legalize casino gambling. I think the threat was meant as a message for me to back off." I then laid out the evidence of how the various people and events were interconnected, with gambling the common thread.

"Makes sense," he said when I finished.

"That's not to say, however, that it was a professional hit. It's a possibility, but there are a couple of problems with that theory. First, it assumes that Elena was killed because she had somehow double crossed her uncle and his friends who were behind the gambling push. But that doesn't make sense, that she would suddenly change her allegiance because of a sense of fairness toward some football player who got caught gambling."

My dad pushed out his lips in a frown of sorts and motioned with his hand for me to continue.

"It's hard to imagine that such a drastic measure would be taken against a family member, or that Raoul Castillo would sit by and let it happen." I paused a moment. "Makes more sense that they would deal with the more direct threat, Ricky Hobbs."

"Looks like they might have done just that."

"Yeah, but why not go after him first? Why go after his lawyer, a Castillo family member who had shown a great deal of loyalty? From a strict business perspective, it makes no sense."

After a long silence, my father said, "Can't argue with your logic. So, what do you think happened? What's your theory? You think Elena's death is unconnected then to the gambling thing?"

"I think there may be a connection, but only in the sense that the killer was somebody who Elena had used to advance that goal. I think the State's theory of a jilted, blackmailed lover is a pretty sound one."

He arched his eyebrows and tilted his head at an angle, the question obvious.

"That could be Renny, of course, as the State theorizes, but not necessarily. That sex video was edited, perhaps by someone else who was on it, but now isn't."

He said nothing. I searched his face for an acknowledgment of where I was going, but I couldn't read him. "Assuming Renny was having an affair with Elena, he was not in a position to help with Hobbs' case as it wasn't in his division, nor could he do anything to help directly on the gambling amendment."

My dad arched his eyebrows at me. "But I could."

I nodded.

"And that would make me a target of Elena Castillo's blackmail efforts."

I nodded again.

"So, you want to know if I was having an affair with Elena Castillo? Is that why you're here? You think I may have killed her?"

There was not the righteous indignation in his voice that I had half-way expected. Even the guilty resort to such when cornered. Instead, his voice had a resignation about it.

"I want to know the truth," I said. Then I laid out much, if not all, of the evidence I had against him, including the lack of an alibi and the blazer. I held back on the phone records for the time being. A test.

There was a long silence as my father looked down at the floor. Finally, he brought his eyes to my level. He sighed, and I thought he had aged ten years in the last ten seconds. "You really think I am capable of murder?"

I noticed that he was not denying it. "I don't know what to think, Dad. I'm just following the evidence."

"How long have you had these suspicions?"

Still, he had not directly answered the implied accusation. Was he stalling for time to think of a plausible story? "Does it matter?"

"It does to me."

"When I saw you had a missing button on your blazer, at the basketball game."

He nodded, picked a piece of lint from the front of his shirt. "I wish you had come to me sooner. You didn't have to snoop around behind my back." When I didn't respond after a few seconds, he continued. "First, let me assure you that I did not kill Elena Castillo. Nor did I have an affair with her." He hesitated again, looking down. "I realize, however, that you have evidence that points to me, and I appreciate that you have been placed in an awkward position."

"Awkward position?" My voice went up in pitch and volume, incredulity in its tone. "Awkward?" Suddenly, I felt like the parent and he the child. "My stomach has been tied in knots for weeks. And the worse thing, I couldn't tell anybody. How could you do this to me? You knew, when I asked you if I should take the case, that there was a real possibility that my investigation might lead me to you."

The man shook his head. "You want answers. I understand."

"Like I said, Dad, I want the truth."

I had a silly thought for a moment that he would give me a Jack Nicholson impersonation and declare that I couldn't handle the truth. But he didn't. He leaned back in his chair and took a deep breath. He looked at the ceiling as he spoke. "Elena Castillo was a beautiful woman, and I was flattered by her attention. We were in Inns of Court together and I saw her at Bar meetings. One night, we were at Harry's restaurant for a subcommittee meeting. She invited me up to her place, to take a tour."

My father brought his gaze to my eyes briefly then focused on his hands as he continued. "We ended up in her bedroom. She kissed me and began undressing me. She was very aggressive. She practically ripped my jacket off. Maybe that's where the button fell off. I didn't even notice it. Anyway, I was, as I've said, flattered by the attention. I was drunk, got caught up in the moment. I know that's not an excuse." He looked at me briefly again, then back to his hands which were clasped in front of him. "But it went no further than that. I pushed her away, buttoned my shirt, and left. We did not have sex."

The image of Bill Clinton, looking directly into the camera and saying, "I did not have sexual relations with that woman," came to me then, and I wanted to ask him his definition of sex. But though I was angry, incredibly angry, I couldn't bring myself to cross examine him more sharply on this point. "She get you on tape?"

He nodded. "She told me later she did, but I never saw it."

"She was blackmailing you with it, to get you to rule in favor of the

281

gambling amendment."

My father looked up at me. "She tried. A couple of days after this, she asked to speak with me privately. I thought maybe she wanted to clear the air, perhaps even apologize for coming on so strong. She apologized all right, but it was for having to tell me that what happened in her place had been recorded on DVD. She said it needn't ever see the light of day if I ruled correctly on the case."

"What did you do?"

"I asked to see the DVD. She refused. She said if I ruled the way I should, then I would get the original and all copies. If I didn't, I could watch the video on the six o'clock news. I thought maybe she was bluffing, but couldn't be sure. I told your mother about it, and we discussed it. I told her I couldn't submit to blackmail. I figured it was a bluff, but either way I had to call her on it. Your mother agreed."

After a few seconds of silence, I prompted him. "And?"

"I wanted to go to the police, get her arrested for attempting to blackmail a public official, but your mother didn't want that. She didn't want the publicity that would follow. And I couldn't very well go against her wishes, under the circumstances. So, I called Elena and told her I would not be influenced by such threats. My ruling would be on the merits. If she gave me the original, and any copies, I would not come forward and expose the attempt to blackmail a public official. I gave her a bluff of my own."

I prompted him again. "And."

"She acted like she didn't know what I was talking about. She asked if I had been drinking. I suspect she was thinking I might be recording the conversation or perhaps had involved law enforcement."

"So, did you ever get the video?"

"No."

In the silence that followed, I pondered the plausibility that he would not have fought very hard to get that footage.

"Martha Anne was right. Going public would not have done

anybody any good. I guess I should have notified the authorities, but would they believe me? Whatever happened, it was not going to affect my decision."

"Not to mention the fact that it would have been extremely embarrassing to you, ruined your chances at getting appointed to the Supreme Court."

He seemed genuinely hurt by this, but I didn't feel sorry. "True enough. I'm not proud of it, but it was certainly a consideration, mostly for your mother's sake. I left the ball in Elena's court. I waited to see if she would make it public but she never did, and she died before I ever rendered an opinion."

"So, you didn't talk to her by phone that evening? You didn't go to her condo?"

"No."

"How do you explain the fact that you left the poker game before eleven and didn't make it home till after midnight? How do you explain the phone call you received from Elena just before you left the game, and your call back to her?"

He seemed surprised at the depth of my information, which surely, he realized, had been obtained behind his back. Again, I felt no remorse.

"The only call I got that night was from your mother, telling me she was leaving her book club meeting, and saying she'd see me when I got home. If there was a call from Elena, I never got it. She must have called, then hung up. And the reason it took so long is, first, we were at Jack's house, which is in Southwood, a pretty good distance for me to travel. I stopped at the Gate station on Magnolia to get gas, and at the Sun Trust ATM to get some cash. Then I went across the street to the Walgreens to get some Prilosec. I left the card game early, as you said. That's because I wasn't feeling too good, had some bad acid reflux. Anyway, that's why it took me a little longer than you might expect to get home."

I gave him a doubtful look.

He leaned over and opened the desk file drawer I had rifled through before when looking for their phone bill. "I think I may have the receipts."

He thumbed through the file folders, pulled one out, placed it on the desk and opened it. He sorted through the papers. "Here's the receipt for the gas." He thumbed some more, pulled out a second document. "This is the ATM receipt." He handed both to me. "The Prilosec is in the medical insurance file," he said, pulling another folder from the drawer, opening it and finding what he was looking for quickly. He then handed this document to me.

I studied the three receipts. A mix of relief and anger washed over me as I verified the date and the time of the computer-generated documents. But there was still another matter not explained. "What about the phone call from and to Elena that night?"

"Like I said, I didn't call her. And if she called me, it didn't go through and she never left a message."

I waited a couple of sad moments, then met his eyes. "Dad, I saw your phone records. You got a call from Elena's home phone to your cell phone at approximately ten thirty that night. Then you called her about ten forty."

"What? You must be mistaken," he said, as he opened the file drawer again, thumbed through the files and pulled out the folder. He found the pertinent phone bill quickly and began to read through it. The room was silent as he read through the entire document. When he found the entry for that date and time, he eyes seem to register genuine surprise, puzzlement. Why the big act? I didn't know unless it was to buy some time, time to think of some explanation. Finally, he looked up at me.

"Ah yes, now I remember. I did get a call from Elena. She left a voice mail to call her back, so I did. I missed her and left her a message. The phone bill shows that both the incoming and outgoing calls were for less than a minute in duration. There was never a conversation. That's why I didn't remember it to start with. But as you say, there is a record of the calls."

He gave me a small, weak smile. I didn't know what to think. I suppose that could explain the calls, and the receipts he had shown me supported his alibi. Mostly. It still would have been possible for him to have done all those things and also made it to Elena's place within the estimated time range of her death, but just barely. On the other hand, how did I know the receipts were legit, not doctored in some way?

"Listen, Kate, you don't have any choice here. I should have told you this from the start, but I was embarrassed. We're past that now. You have to use this information to your client's benefit."

"Don't think I won't," I said, unable to keep the anger from my voice.

"You should."

Was he bluffing? Was he gambling that he knew me well enough to know what I would do? Hard to tell, but looking at him now, my heart was ready to explode. He looked like a little boy sitting in the principal's office awaiting his punishment for some school infraction.

"If I call you to the stand at trial, you will testify to what we have discussed?"

He nodded.

"And you will cooperate in providing any additional information I ask for?"

He nodded again.

"If I spring it at trial, the prosecution will have no way to effectively respond. Who knows, maybe it won't be necessary, but you should be prepared."

He nodded one final time. "I'm sorry," he said, standing.

I walked over to him and the two of us embraced.

Chapter Thirty-Six

I handed the smiling teenager at the drive-through window a ten, took the bag from her and put it on the passenger seat, the drink in the holder in the center console. Waiting for her to return, I opened the bag, retrieved a French fry and bit off half of it. I instantly opened my mouth and drew in air between my teeth in an effort to cool it down a bit.

The young girl returned with my change, another smile and a "Thank you for choosing McDonald's."

"You're welcome," I said as I put up my window and slowly began to pull out of the parking lot, simultaneously setting up my moveable feast. I wedged the cardboard container of fries between the console and my seat, unwrapped the burger enough to get at it and took a huge bite. I placed the empty bag on my lap as a place mat. When the traffic moved forward, I maneuvered onto the six-lane speedway known as Capital Circle.

Just after I turned onto Capital Medical Boulevard, my cell phone rang.

"Hello," I managed through a mouthful of hamburger.

"It's Brandi. I got the message you called."

"Yeah, girl. How you doing?"

"Going stir crazy. I need to get out of this place."

"That's why I called. I got something lined up for you."

"What's that?"

I took a swallow of the Coke Zero through the plastic straw and returned it to the holder. "I've got a cousin who owns a RV park down on the bay in Panacea. He's got an empty trailer you can stay in. It's not big, but should be plenty of room for your needs. And, no rent for the time being."

No response on the other end.

"Are you overwhelmed with gratitude? Is that why you are speechless?"

"Sorry. No, I appreciate it. Any where's better than here. But I still got to eat, pay for other stuff. I can't afford to spend all my savings just waiting around here."

"The other good news is I've also arranged for you to work at Angelo's, as a waitress. You've done that before, right?"

"Yeah, but . . ."

"I know you have other plans, Brandi, but this is only temporary. The owners are aware of your situation, and they need some extra help just now."

"Listen, Katie, it's not that I don't appreciate you doing all this, but I was thinking by now, you would have verified the information I gave you and we could close our deal, me and your client. I need to get on down the road. Haven't you heard back from your handwriting guy?"

"Actually, I have, and he says he thinks it may very well be Elena Castillo who filled out the medical history form and her signature on it, but he wasn't real sure. Whoever filled it out, he said, was trying to disguise her handwriting." I hesitated a moment, then said, "Promising, though."

"What about the DNA test?"

"I'm heading right now to see my expert witness."

I could almost feel the frown on the other end. "You're just now doing that?"

"Hey, give me a break. It's only been three days, and I got lots of stuff to attend to." When she didn't say anything for a few seconds, I said, "Listen, I know you're anxious to get out of town, but you're going to have to be patient. Your hearing on the injunction is a week from tomorrow. You definitely need to hang around for that."

Silence on the other end.

"That's part of the deal," I continued. "If you want to get paid, I have to verify the information first. And then, as I said, I may need you as a witness to lay a foundation to get it in."

"Wait a minute. That wasn't part of the deal. I never agreed to be a witness."

By this time, I had pulled into the parking lot for Southern Pathologists Group. I found a spot partially shaded by a small, white oak tree, parked and left the engine running, and the air conditioning blowing. "It might not be necessary. Let's not get ahead of ourselves. We'll cross that bridge if we have to."

"I'm willing to give you first crack at this, Katie, but I'm not going to wait forever. Your client, the judge, needs to come up with something reasonable, and soon. If not, I'll be forced to go elsewhere."

I could sense the frustration, the impatience in her voice, but I knew she was bluffing. "Like I said, Brandi, first things first. The DNA test is going to take a bit of time. This isn't like CSI where they get it in a matter of hours."

"So, how much we talking about, money wise? The judge got a figure in mind?"

"We didn't talk specifics."

Actually, we hadn't talked generally either, but she didn't need to know that. I hated my father for lying to me, for putting me in an untenable position, but my loyalty to him overrode my duty to my client. I'd had to choose, and I did. I'd tried to convince myself that it would be different if I really thought my dad had killed Elena. If so, I would not cover for him. But deep down, I knew it wouldn't matter. My dad had concealed his relationship with the victim and he had lied to me about the phone calls between them that night. Of that I was sure. Had he also lied to me about the extent of his relationship with Elena? When Elena told her mother she was having an affair with a judge, was it he, and not Goodwin, to whom she referred?

"It wouldn't really do any good to speculate until we know exactly what we have," I told her.

"And when's that gonna be?"

"Like I said, I'm in the parking lot of our pathologist right now. I should have a good idea of the time frame after I talk with him. As soon as I have something more definite, I'll let you know."

I was walking a fine line here. I couldn't let Brandi dictate things. On the other hand, I needed to keep her happy, or at least somewhat satisfied. I didn't want her to bolt, to try and work some deal with the Castillo family, or heaven forbid, with the State Attorney. I couldn't afford to have this go public, at least not yet. Maybe never, depending on what the testing revealed.

"Okay," Brandi said, but she didn't seem real happy about it.

I shut off the engine, grabbed my briefcase from the floorboard, slid out of the Yukon, and was immediately assaulted by the hot, humid air, an unwelcomed first taste of the summer to come. In the short time it took me to walk across the lot to the entrance, I was already beginning to sweat. Mopping my brow with the sleeve of my blouse, I entered the cool, air-conditioned reception area and sighed audibly.

The woman behind the glass sliding window smiled and said, "You must be Kate Marston."

I nodded.

"You can go on back," the woman said. "Last door on your left."

I followed her direction and stopped just outside the room. The door was open and Dr. Ethan Morrison looked up.

"Hey, Katie, come on in." He had been reading a journal when I came to the door, which he now put aside and motioned for me to have a seat in one of the chairs across the desk from him.

The office was small, tidy and sparsely decorated. The walls were painted a beige which would probably be called something like Desert Sand by an interior decorator. On the wall behind the desk hung several plaques, diplomas and awards or framed letters of appreciation. Three of the awards, I noted, were for his work with the Innocence

Project, an organization which used DNA testing to exonerate prisoners.

Morrison was dressed in khakis and a denim shirt, sleeves rolled up on the forearms, and no tie. He flashed me a smile. "What's up, Katie?"

I pulled the packet from my briefcase and slid it across the desk. "I'd like you to do a DNA comparison. I have information that the sample inside is from the fetus carried by Elena Castillo, aborted three weeks before her death."

He looked up and his eyes widened. "Where'd you get this?"

"Someone who worked in the clinic where the abortion was supposedly performed. Best you don't know the details."

He looked back down at the packet in front of him, opened it and began to examine its contents. "Curious. Sounds vaguely illegal."

I shook my head. "A person approached me, said they had information relevant to the case. Literally dropped this in my lap. What was I going to do, give it back?" Morrison didn't respond to my rhetorical question. "I have an order authorizing me to obtain the victim's medical records. I figure this fits."

"Humph," he said, which I took to be disagreement, but he said nothing further.

"So, can you do it? Can you tell if it is, in fact, from a fetus and if so, whether Elena Castillo was the mother?" I hesitated a moment and asked the real question. "Will you?"

He seemed to consider not only the logistics of my questions, but the ethical and legal ramifications as well. After a long several seconds, he came to a conclusion.

"Sure," he said. "And I assume you want this yesterday?"

"Today will be soon enough."

"Seriously."

"Seriously, how soon can you do it?"

"This is not CSI," he said, mirroring what I had told Brandi minutes before, "but I'll put a rush on it. Should have something for you in a few days."

"That would be much appreciated. And, Ethan, if it is a match, I'd also like you to compare with Renny Goodwin's DNA sample."

He nodded. "How about the two guys on the video?"

I nodded. "Them too. And Ethan, I need to keep this close to the vest for the time being."

"Understood."

I hesitated a couple of beats, then said, "And I'd also appreciate it if you didn't mention this to Renny or Ted."

The eyes widened again, the eyebrows arched, but he said, "Okay."

"I'm dealing with someone on this who wishes to keep it just between us, at least for the time being. If we get positive results, well... " The lie came easy for me. Too easy.

"You don't have to explain yourself to me. You're the one who contracted for my services. I work for you. It's your business what you want me to disclose, and to whom. This will be just between us, until you tell me different."

You'd think his vow of loyalty would have made me feel better, brought me some measure of relief from the tension that was chasing me. But it didn't. As I walked out of his office that day, crossing the scorching hot pavement of the parking lot, the lead ball that seemed to have taken up permanent residency in my stomach was just as large, and just as heavy.

Chapter Thirty-Seven

I put down my pen, took off my glasses and rubbed my eyes. The only sound in the office was the tick of the wall clock. I looked up at it, then checked my wrist watch to confirm the time, just after nine o'clock. I really needed to stop, go home and get some rest, but I also needed to finish the brief that was due the next day in the District Court of Appeal.

It had been a long day, having started around five o'clock, when I awoke from a bad dream. In the dream, I had been driving on a mountain road, somewhere out west, with grand vistas. I was in a sports car, a convertible. As I came to a bend in the road, neither the steering wheel nor the brakes would respond, and I watched helplessly as the car plunged off a cliff. As it did, I seemed to be temporarily suspended in the air and I could see for miles into the distance, and also to the ground far below, the scene weirdly beautiful and terrifying at the same time. I realized I was about to die. Then I woke up.

All morning, I felt on edge, pressed for time as I worked to get the brief done and filed by tomorrow. Like everything else, I had been putting it off, the Goodwin case having pretty much consumed all my time recently. I put Renny and his problems completely aside today, however, to concentrate on the brief.

Well not completely. I did have a brief conversation with Ted about Everhart. He told me that, as I expected, his alibi checked out. He had not returned to Tallahassee from North Carolina until the day after Elena's death. Perhaps I should have been disappointed at the elimination of another alternative suspect, but in fact, I was relieved.

A little basketball at lunch time had been a good release of tension, but it also made me realize how physically tired I was. Now, seven hours later, I was running out of energy. I got up and went into the kitchenette, rummaged through the small refrigerator, looking for something to eat, something to fuel the body for a little more work.

There wasn't much there; a half-eaten sandwich from a couple of days ago, some yogurt, a couple of apples, and several soft drinks. I retrieved the sandwich, removed the protective paper, peeled back the bread and examined it. Nope, I thought, not that hungry. I grabbed a Diet Mountain Dew, and from the freezer, a packaged frozen egg and sausage biscuit. While I cooked the biscuit in the microwave, I opened the cabinet drawer which contained popcorn and other munchies and grabbed a bag of chips.

Back at my desk, while I ate, I put a call in to Craig's and got Brenda. I mustered up some civility and asked her politely to put Maggie on the line. Instead, she handed the phone to Craig.

"It's awful late," he said. "Past her bedtime."

He no doubt enjoyed turning the tables now, throwing my words back at me. "Yes, it is, and if she's already in bed, don't wake her."

I figured she wasn't, though, and sure enough, after a sigh and slight hesitation, Craig handed the phone to my daughter.

"Hey, Mom."

"Hey, sweetie. How's it going?"

The sound of footsteps and a door closing, then she responded. "Okay."

With further prompting, she became a Chatty Cathy, giving me a blow by blow of her day at school, soccer practice, the little gossip in her circle of friends, which she normally didn't talk to me about. It was as if, since she wasn't living with me all the time, I was more of a confidant. Strange, but there it was.

When she came up for air finally, she seemed to realize how one-sided the conversation had been, and asked me what I was doing. Very polite, I thought, pleased. She chastised me gently for working so late and for eating junk for dinner. Then she asked me when the Goodwin case would be over and we could "get back to normal."

"I miss you, Mom."

"I miss you, too."

"I mean, Brenda's okay, but I hardly see Dad. He works all the time."

Her words both broke my heart and lifted it at the same time. "It will be over soon," I said, and vowed to make more time for her in the meantime.

"You coming to my soccer game Friday?"

"Of course."

"Okay, good." I could hear Craig's voice in the background, muffled through the door. "Well," Maggie said, "I guess I better go. Love you, Mom."

"Love you too."

I finished editing the brief around nine forty-five and packed up to go home, checking the lock on the back door and turning off the lights as I made my way to the front entrance. There, I slung my handbag over my shoulder, turned on the alarm and stepped out into the night.

It had been one of those perfect late spring days that started off cool and warmed up with the sun during the day, the temperature hovering around eighty degrees, with low humidity. Now, the sky was overcast, blocking out the moon, the air thick, damp and unsettled, as if the night itself had become anxious.

I crossed the street and walked, head down, along the sidewalk to the firm's parking lot. Somewhere in my subconscious, the implicit warning registered, I'm sure, but not on the surface. When I was about twenty feet away from the Yukon, and just about to unlock it with the remote, I sensed movement to the side and behind me. A figure coming quickly toward me. Male, dark clothing, ski mask. Before I could react, he was next to me. Something in his hand. A knife. Long blade. I tried to turn fully to face him, but he pushed me from behind, toward the SUV. The man quickly forced me face down on the hood and held the knife to the side of my face. My arms dangled uselessly by my side. My handbag fell off my shoulder and to the pavement.

"You say a word, bitch, you do anything stupid, I'll cut you."

The voice was low, guttural. I didn't know if it was disguised or not. It didn't seem quite natural. I tried to place it but could not.

"You understand, bitch?"

I nodded, said nothing. My breath became short. I willed myself to stay calm. In one easy movement, he flipped me over so that I was bent backwards over the hood, his body leaning in close, pressing against me, his knees pushing against my thighs, spreading my legs. I felt his hand at my throat.

"What do you want?" I asked."

I sensed the movement a fraction of a second before the blow landed to the side of my face with such force that my head whipped to the side and my cheek felt the cool of the hood. The pain was intense and instantaneous, but I didn't feel or hear anything break. I tried to concentrate, to focus on every little detail so that I could accurately report the event later and hopefully identify my attacker. That's what they did in the movies, right? That's the tough gal image I had of myself.

But it wasn't that easy. Try as I might, something in my mind wanted to deny it, to ignore it, to watch it through a fog of illusion. I kept thinking of Maggie and what she would do without her mother. Would he rape me and be gone? Or did he plan to rape me, then kill me? The man was wearing a mask, had taken some pains to disguise himself. That suggested that he did not intend to kill me. He was certainly capable of violence, though. That had been established early and emphatically.

"You need to learn what happens to bitches who sniff around where they shouldn't."

I could feel my skirt being pushed up further, over my waist. I felt his hand on my thigh and heard the rip of my panties, then felt my bare buttocks against the metal of the hood. The man had backed up just a little then. It was just enough for me to obtain some leverage with my left hand on the hood, underneath my body.

First, I activated the Yukon's alarm with the key fob to distract him. Then I pushed up with my left hand and simultaneously began to move my right hand, which still held the key fob, toward his face. With as much strength and force as I could muster, holding the fob like a small knife, I aimed it at the opening in the ski mask around his left eye. I felt it connect with soft flesh, penetrate into the socket.

The man howled and stepped back, holding his hand to his eye. I used the break in his grip to jump off the hood.

"You bitch! You bitch!" He was rocking now, trying to gain control over the pain. "You fucking put my eye out!"

"Good," I said, and without really thinking, and though he was still holding the knife, I moved toward the man as if I were a field goal kicker. Just as he turned back to face me, I aimed for the sweet spot between his legs and kicked up with all my might. The man howled again and this time he bent over, his knees together and slowly lowered himself to the ground.

I quickly considered my options, and went for the SUV, got in and locked the doors. With the alarm no longer sounding, I laid on the horn. The man stirred, looked up at me. I couldn't see his face but could feel the hatred underneath his mask. He stood there for several seconds, raised his knife in my direction, then took off down College Avenue.

I kept the horn blaring until I felt sure he was gone. But taking no chances, I got out, quickly retrieved my handbag, and returned to the Yukon. I pulled out my cell phone and punched in 911.

It seemed like a long time, but within three minutes a police cruiser pulled up, blocking the entrance to the parking garage, blue lights flashing. I slid out of my vehicle as the officer slid out of his. "Oh great," I muttered to myself when I saw that the officer was Ken

Gautier. Of all the cops patrolling the city tonight, I draw the one I had recently ripped into at a suppression hearing.

Kenny G stood by his patrol car, speaking into the small radio fastened to his shoulder strap. He approached me cautiously, alert, taking in his surroundings—just what I hadn't done.

His face registered neither surprise, nor the smugness I half-way expected. "Ms. Marston," he said as he approached, "you called in to report an assault? A sexual assault?"

"Attempted sexual battery, to be precise," I said.

"He looked around quickly. "He's gone?"

I nodded. "He ran off in that direction," I said, pointing. "Hobbled would be more accurate," I added."

Kenny G gave me a raised eyebrow.

"I kicked the son of a bitch in the balls."

The officer couldn't suppress a small smile but he said nothing, just looked off in the direction I had pointed. He shone his flashlight on the garment that lay on the ground about five feet in front of my vehicle. "Yours?"

I nodded.

He didn't move immediately to retrieve my underpants. "Why don't you tell me what happened," he said, his tone soft.

I gave him a quick summary. He didn't interrupt me. When I finished, he said "Excuse me," then stepped back a couple of feet and spoke into the radio clipped to his shoulder strap. He asked for back up, needing someone to process the scene. He gave a description of the assailant for the issuance of a BOLO, gave our location, then turned back to face me.

"Are you all right, physically? Were you injured?"

I shook my head. "Nothing major. He twisted my arm a bit, hit me in the face with the back of his hand. I put my hand to my cheek and winced at the touch. "It hurts a little but not bad."

He looked a little closer now at my face. "You mind?" he said, raising his flashlight. "I'd like to get a closer look in the light."

"Sure," I said, turning my face, pointing with my finger. "It was on this side."

Gautier shined his light on the side my face. "Yeah," he said, turning his head a bit to get a better view, "I can see the bruising beginning there. Looks like you also got a bit of a busted lip." He put his finger at the corner of his mouth.

I ran my tongue to the place indicated and tasted my blood. I had not noticed it before.

"Any other injuries that you know of?"

"No."

"Should I call the paramedics?"

"No. I'm all right."

The officer nodded, hesitated a moment, then began to ask me follow up questions, panning for more details. It was a welcomed distraction for us both. It wasn't long before back-up arrived. The area was cordoned off, CSI folks began to collect evidence, take photos. Soon thereafter, a woman detective I didn't recognize arrived and asked me more of the same questions. I felt like telling her I'd already told Gautier everything I knew but I knew the drill, so I repeated myself.

Eventually, she came to the inevitable request that I go to the emergency room for an examination, a rape kit preparation, in the hopes it might provide physical evidence helpful in identifying my attacker and assisting in his prosecution. I was sure they would find nothing useful. I was also all too familiar with such exams. Even where there is no allegation of penetration, they assume there has been. They are embarrassing, humiliating even, despite the best bedside manner of the nurses who perform them. The detective sensed my hesitation, tried to reassure me, and confirmed that she could not require it, and that she would respect my decision either way. Then I thought about what I would advise a client in the same situation. After a long pause, I nodded in agreement.

Chapter Thirty-Eight

We sat in the reception area for the circuit judges' chambers, all of us silent, uneasy, waiting for Judge Mitchell to call us back. Ted, Goodwin and I sat on one side of the room, Lipton on the other. In a break from the usual, he was not accompanied by associates. The discomfort in the room was probably due to the fact that part of what we were here to discuss with the judge was the recent sexual assault on me and its connection, or lack thereof, to the case.

It was stupid, really, this embarrassment. I think it makes it worse for a victim, implies there's something to be ashamed about, increasing the trauma for her. Sort of like when your kid falls off his bike. He doesn't realize he's supposed to be so upset until everyone starts making such a fuss about it. My philosophy is that you acknowledge the hurt, sympathize with the child, then help them get back on and start peddling again.

That's what I had done for myself. And I was peddling hard. As I expected, the forensic exam at the hospital had not been a pleasant experience, nor had it turned up anything useful, but it wasn't so horrible, either, and it was over. Dwelling on what had happened seemed unhealthy to me, and unproductive.

After discussing it with my client and co-counsel, I amended our witness list to include my name. Our theory was that the attack, and the threat to Maggie before, were attempts to get me to back off my investigation into organized gambling and its connection to Elena Castillo. Lipton filed his objection, as well as a motion in limine to prevent me from being a witness. Both sides had agreed to hear the matter in chambers—in the interests of my privacy—a gesture I appreciated.

No one in the room made eye contact, but I stole occasional glances at the others. Bill Lipton's hair seemed to be a little thinner these days, the skin a little looser around the neck, but he sat erect in the chair and looked sharp, professional in his dark blue suit. So did Ted, in a scruffy sort of way. His hair needed a comb, a trim, or perhaps both, and he had a five o'clock shadow at nine in the morning. But the subtle gray plaid suit fit him well and coordinated nicely with the light blue shirt and the paisley tie underneath. I thought him especially handsome these days.

Ted's reaction when I told him of the attack had been just what I needed. He was sympathetic, supportive and protective in a big brother sort of way, but he did not treat me as a victim. He never suggested that I should withdraw from the case. He had, in essence, encouraged me to dust myself off, get back on the bike and start peddling again. He had become in that instant even more attractive to me, and it made me second guess my request that we keep our relationship strictly professional during the case. And to his credit, he had scrupulously adhered to that request, never pressing the issue. In short, he had been a perfect gentleman. Damn it.

My client seemed to have aged a good bit in the few months since we met at the Black Dog Café that morning. He looked a little haggard, despite his best efforts to appear unaffected by his circumstances. Surprisingly, he had, as I counseled, kept a low profile. I didn't know what he was doing with his time, but he had not meddled as I had feared. At least not openly.

He wore gray slacks this morning, and a navy-blue blazer. I had checked out his sleeves first thing. All buttons present. I found myself doing that a lot lately. Anytime I saw a man wearing a blazer, I looked to see if he had a sleeve button missing.

Judge Mitchell opened the door that led back to the chambers and poked her head out. "If everyone is here, you can come on back."

As was typical for visiting judges, Mitchell was housed in the vacant office of Judge Lonnie Weaver, who was currently assigned to one of the outlying counties. Much like its usual occupant, the room had a generic, non-descript look about it. Except for a couple of family photos on the credenza, this could have been anyone's office.

Mitchell motioned us to seats on each side of the conference table. "Ms. Marston," the judge said, looking at me, "let me first say that I am sorry to hear about your recent, ah, experience."

"Thank you, Your Honor."

She turned to Lipton. "The State has objected to the amended witness list filed by the defense and has also filed a motion in limine seeking to prevent Ms. Marston from being a witness at trial. I will hear your argument."

Lipton sat up a little straighter in his chair. "It's quite simple, Judge. Either Ms. Marston remains as counsel or she becomes a witness. She can't do both. It's prohibited by the Code. Now, I don't really care if Ms. Marston wants to get off the case, so long as it doesn't result in a continuance. We're three weeks away. I've already sent out my subpoenas, lined up my expert witnesses."

"You have no objection to her testifying, so long as she is not counsel of record?"

"Depends on what she plans to testify to. I do object if she plans to testify that she has been threatened and attacked by some unknown person or persons. It's irrelevant. There is absolutely no basis to connect those incidents to this case. To put this wild speculation in front of the jury would be confusing, misleading and highly prejudicial to the State." He paused just a moment, then said, "Nor is the death of Ricky Hobbs of any relevance to this case. His death was a tragedy, but it has been officially ruled an accident. They are just trying to muddy the waters in hopes the jury will look past the evidence against the defendant."

Mitchell looked over at me. "What specifically is the connection?"

"Mr. Stevens will be handling the motions this morning," I said.

The judge looked a little surprised, but nodded and turned to my co-counsel.

Ted leaned forward, resting his forearms on the table. "It's simple, Judge. We think that the death of Elena Castillo and Ricky Hobbs, and the threats to Ms. Marston are related to the push to legalize casino gambling in Florida."

"This is preposterous," Lipton said, then quickly put up his hand in apology before Mitchell could admonish him.

Ted ignored the interruption. "The attacks on Ms. Marston are logically connected to this case." He turned to me. "Although her assailants did not mention this case specifically, she is not working on any other case, or involved in any other situation in which someone might be prone to threaten or physically attack her."

That was not completely accurate. The names of Jared Olsen and Jimmy Black came to mind. And I had given those names to the detective when she asked me if I'd pissed off anybody recently. But, I added, I had seen the eyes, if not the face, of the jogger and he was neither of these men. The guy in the garage had been shorter than Black, taller than Olsen, and more muscular than either. I didn't discount the possibility that they could have hired someone to do the job, but it didn't seem likely.

Ted looked at me briefly as if he were reading my mind, then turned back to Judge Mitchell. "Now, maybe it is not connected. Maybe the attacks are unrelated to her investigation in this case, but it is certainly a reasonable inference which we should be able to argue to the jury."

The judge frowned. "And what about the prohibition against being both lawyer and witness in the case?"

"Technically, that's not completely accurate. The rules provide that an attorney can't provide harmful testimony and remain as counsel. There is no conflict of interest if the testimony is helpful, which this would be."

The judge looked over in Lipton's direction. He frowned. "You would think, that if the intent was to warn Ms. Marston away from something, there would be some reference to exactly what they wanted. Or that Mr. Stevens, who is also counsel on the case, would receive similar threats."

I had to admit, he had a point, but not good enough to keep the testimony out. The case law was pretty strong that a defendant should be given every latitude in presenting his theory of defense, so long as there was at least some evidence to support it. And we had it here.

The judge apparently thought so, too. "It's a good argument, Mr. Lipton, to be made to the jury, but I'm going to allow this evidence." She waited a beat then looked in my direction. "I understand that you've been through a lot recently, Ms. Marston, things that might take a pretty heavy emotional toll. Do you wish to withdraw for this reason?"

I answered without hesitation, "No ma'am. I have no intention of withdrawing." I looked over at my client who seemed pleased, but not surprised by my response.

Mitchell frowned. "Very well. Is there anything else this morning?"

"Yes," Ted said. "We also have a motion in limine, Judge, concerning alleged hearsay statements of the victim." Both sides in a case often sought a pre-trial ruling from the judge as to whether certain evidence or argument would be allowed, as it greatly aided in determining strategy.

"Oh yes," Mitchell said, "I read the motion. She then looked over her glasses at Lipton. "Does the State intend to offer these statements?"

"We most certainly do, Your Honor."

"How do you plan to get around the hearsay rule?"

"The 'state of mind exception' applies here, Judge. The statements to her mother show that she was in fear of the defendant because she had broken off their affair and he was harassing her."

Mitchell looked over at Ted. "Mr. Stevens?"

"First of all, according to the mother, the victim never named Judge Goodwin. She only referred to a relationship with a judge. There are two dozen judges in this circuit. The State can't connect it to our client. More importantly, the 'state of mind exception' does not apply because the existence of a relationship is not a state of mind."

Lipton, who had been champing at the bit to respond, looked in the judge's direction for her approval. When she nodded her head, he said, "First, according to what the mother told me, her daughter did indeed specifically name the defendant as the judge to whom she referred, and person she was afraid of."

I strained to keep my mouth from dropping to the table, to keep a neutral face, but inside, my stomach was churning. It appeared that Miranda Castillo had decided to take off the gloves, and she was not above lying to make her point.

Lipton continued, "The statements aren't offered to prove the existence of the relationship, except to show how she was feeling about the defendant. Certainly, Your Honor, the jury should know that the victim was afraid of this man." Here, he glanced over at Goodwin, then returned his focus toward Mitchell. "It explains why our eyewitness saw him pounding on the victim's door. She didn't want to let him in. It goes to motive and opportunity."

Ted started to respond but Mitchell held her hand up and looked at the prosecutor. "It may be relevant, but it's still hearsay, Mr. Lipton, and I agree with the defense that there does not appear to be any exception that applies. The state of mind exception would not cover statements about the relationship and the break up. I'll withhold final ruling until trial, but you are not to make any reference in opening statement to these conversations and you are to approach the bench and make a proffer before offering them into evidence."

The frustration and displeasure were evident on Lipton's face, but he nodded at the judge and said, "Yes, Your Honor."

When we stepped out into the hallway minutes later, it was hard not to high-five in victory with the members of the defense team, given the favorable rulings from Judge Mitchell. Although she could change her mind at trial, I thought it unlikely. And it also made my next play easier. Telling Goodwin and Ted I'd meet up with them later, I came up alongside Lipton and asked if he had a minute to talk as he walked back to his office.

"Sure," he said. "You want to gloat a little?"

"No, not at all. I thought maybe it might be fruitful for you and me, and the victim's family, to meet before the trial starts. Maybe there is some resolution that is acceptable to everyone."

He stopped walking and looked over at me, squinted his eyes. "What you got in mind?"

"I'm not sure, but I think it's worth a good faith effort."

He shrugged. "Okay. I'll set it up." Then he looked up and down the hallway briefly before returning his gaze to me. "Listen, Katie, I didn't say anything in there, and you may be too much under his spell to accept it, but have you considered the possibility that your client may be behind the threat and the attack on you?"

"What?"

He switched his briefcase from his right to his left hand. "The man grew up playing dirty tricks politics behind the scenes, manipulating people and events to get what he wanted. He is the ultimate Machiavellian. The ends justify the means. And he may be corrupt, but he's clever, too. He killed her, and ever since, he has been maneuvering to get off, planting false clues and red herrings all over the place."

The thought had, in fact, occurred to me, but I wasn't about to admit it. I shook my head. "He's not that clever," I said. Not exactly a ringing endorsement, I realized, so I added, "Have you ever considered the possibility that he might in fact be innocent?"

Lipton shook his head and smiled. "No." And with that he walked off down the hallway.

Chapter Thirty-Nine

Lipton, Elena's parents and I filed into the large conference room at the State Attorney's Office, somber and wordless, a leftover from the silent elevator trip we all shared. Our meeting, suggested by me last week, had the blessing of Judge Mitchell, who, at our pre-trial conference two days ago, had requested—politely insisted would be more accurate—that the attorneys make one more effort to negotiate a plea agreement. "Even if you can't reach a plea agreement," she said, "perhaps you can stipulate to certain facts, the authenticity of records or other documents, qualifications of experts, anything that might streamline the presentation."

On the same day of the pre-trial conference, I got the call I'd been waiting for from Ethan Morrison. "Sorry to be so late in getting back with you, but I have the results of the DNA tests."

I had tried not to pester him, as Brandi pestered me, even though the few days' turn-around he had promised turned into more than a week. "And?"

He began an explanation of his methods and the parameters of testing. I interrupted him after a few seconds. "Ethan, please. Bottom line?"

"Oh yes, sorry. Bottom line, the sample you provided was indeed from a fetus. I can say definitively that Elena Castillo was the mother, and that Warren Goodwin was not the father." He hesitated, then added, "Nor the guys on the sex tapes, either." He hesitated again. "That's good news for you, right?"

"Yes, it is," I said after a brief hesitation. "It means there is a yet-unknown person out there who was the father of Elena's unborn child, someone who may have had a motive to kill her. It also suggests a reason she may have contemplated suicide."

It also meant, however, that I could no longer justify withholding the information from my client. I could perhaps explain my reluctance to mention it before, saying that I didn't really trust Brandi, that I didn't want to get his hopes up until I had verification. It was a little lame, a little squirrelly, but plausible. There was no explanation, however, for why I would not tell him now. Not a good one anyway.

The problem was, once this information was divulged, no one would be satisfied with simply knowing that Goodwin was not the father. Not the State, not my client, not the news media. Right now, only Ethan Morrison and I knew the truth, and I needed to keep it that way for a little while longer, at least until I could get Ethan to run a couple of more tests. One of those tests would be on the DNA sample my dad had given me, at my request. No questions asked, no explanations given.

But what to do about Brandi Peters? Not wanting to handle it on the phone, I'd traveled down to the coast yesterday and talked to her as we sat outside at a picnic table in the RV park. I didn't want her knowing the results of the tests, but I didn't want to lie to her, either. Not that she would believe me if I said the results were negative as to Elena. She knew better. So, I said that Elena was the mother. Then I'd had to choose between two unattractive options.

If I told her Goodwin was not the father, she would wonder why I didn't make it public, might prompt her to try another angle. On the other hand, if I told her, or let her presume, he was the father, she would be more demanding as to the amount of money she wanted. Blackmail would not be too harsh a description. Actually, either way, she was going to ask for more money than I would want to pay out of my own pocket. It seemed almost inevitable that I'd have to involve Goodwin in the negotiations.

So, I had chosen to be vague, simply telling her the information would be useful to the defense and I was authorized to negotiate a payment to her. She hadn't pressed it. "So," I said, "what do you think is fair compensation for the information?"

She took a drag on her cigarette and exhaled. "I was thinking twenty-five thousand would be reasonable."

I pretended to almost fall off the bench. "That's more than I'll get as his attorney." It wasn't true, but still, she needed to keep things in perspective. "He's a state employee, Brandi. The man makes a pretty good salary, but he's tapped out."

She seemed skeptical, but said, "Well, what did you have in mind?"

"I was thinking somewhere around five thousand would be more than fair."

And so, the bazaar was opened and the haggling began. We ended up at ten thousand, which I thought really was more than fair. I said I'd have to clear it with my client, and that it would take a few days to get that much money together. She still seemed skeptical, but acquiesced. I had bought myself a little time, but I'd have to either go to Goodwin, or empty my own savings. Otherwise, Brandi would begin to suspect something wasn't right. She might try to contact Goodwin directly. That would not be good.

On the drive back to town, I wondered if the unwanted pregnancy might have moved Elena to take her life. But that didn't make sense, as she had aborted the pregnancy. Maybe it was guilt over the abortion. That didn't really make sense either, but I couldn't help but think it was an important piece of the puzzle. And there was one more possibility I wanted to explore, one more piece I wanted to try to fit.

It was why I had suggested this meeting. "You got any coffee, Bill?" I asked, breaking the silence.

"Of course. He went to the door, poked his head outside. "Stacy?"

A few moments later, his secretary appeared at the door. Lipton turned back to the group. "Everyone want coffee?"

After a slight hesitation, Miranda Castillo said, "Thank you."

Her husband waved his hand and shook his head. "Thank you, no."

"They also have Cuban coffee, Senator," I said.

Castillo's eyebrows arched in surprise.

"Yeah," Lipton confirmed, "one of our assistants brings it in. Got some of the others hooked now. They say it's real good."

I could see that the Senator was torn between not wanting to appear sociable with the defender of his daughter's killer, and the lure of a good cup of espresso. "Thank you. That would be nice," he said finally.

The young woman made a mental note of each of our specifications, then withdrew to fill our orders. We all took seats around the conference table.

We started off with stipulations, procedural concessions that streamlined the trial. These generally benefited the prosecution, whose burden it was to go forward with the evidence, but I agreed to much of what the prosecutor requested, gaining in return, similar concessions from him. The secretary returned with the coffee.

Then we moved on to the subject of what disposition might be possible in the case, what could each side live with? I started it off, trying to set a particular tone.

"My client says he is innocent of the charges. And I believe him." I was looking at the Castillos, who I knew were my real audience, but could see in my peripheral vision Lipton rolling his eyes. "Moreover," I said, turning my attention to the prosecutor, I think the State's case is extremely weak and our chances at trial are very good."

Lipton started to protest but I held my hand up to stop him, then turned to face Elena's parents again. "I would not be properly representing my client, however, if I did not weigh the risks of a conviction and counsel him in this regard. He is not inclined to plea to something he didn't do, but if there is a chance of resolving this case without further emotional pain to the family, I am willing to take it to my client and objectively review it with him. If we go to trial, we all know that things will come out that will be an embarrassment to both the Castillo family and to Judge Goodwin and his family."

I let that sink in for a few seconds before I turned again. "That's about the best you can hope for with a jury. And if you stick with the 'I did nothing defense' and the jury hears that she was alive when he dumped her body over the balcony wall, well . . ."

He looked again to the Castillos, then back to me. "So, in the spirit of compromise and, as you say, to spare the family any more grief, we can put this thing to bed with a plea tomorrow, before the jury is picked. After that, it will have to be a plea straight up as charged."

I nodded slowly, as if considering the offer carefully. Goodwin would never go for that, and we both knew it. He wouldn't plea even to a misdemeanor. "I'll discuss it with my client and get back with you before the end of the day."

There was little left to say after this. There were a few awkward, unnecessary observations and lamentations about the publicity surrounding the case, an optimistic prediction that we would find something that would be acceptable to both sides, but we had reached a dead end and we all knew it. I was the first to stand, signaling the end of the meeting. The others followed suit, grabbing suit coats, purses, and shuffling toward the door. I lagged behind, bringing up the rear. As the others moved toward the door, I stopped for a moment at the place where Raoul Castillo had been sitting. With my body blocking the view, I retrieved his discarded coffee cup, put it in the plastic bag I had brought and stashed it in my purse.

Outside the building, on the sidewalk, I took in a big gulp of air, as if I'd been underwater and had just come to the surface. I paused a moment, calmed myself, then started the walk to my office. The morning sun felt warm on my face, soothing. After about fifty feet, I took my phone out and punched in the number for Ethan Morrison.

On my drive back from meeting with Brandi the other day, I had tried to reason out answers to some pretty big questions. Who was the father of Elena's unborn child? What had caused her to seek an abortion? Had she confided in her mother, sought her advice? By all accounts, mother and daughter had been very close. She went home frequently, called her almost every day. Yet, my gut told me that Miranda Castillo didn't know about the pregnancy or the abortion. And if not, why not?

I remembered what Angelina Perez had said. Some things, especially, you don't want to tell your mother. And the priest, obtuse though he may have been, had hinted at it. What secret might be so deep and dark that Elena couldn't share it with her mother, but might confess it to her priest?

Maybe, like me, her secret involved a family member. Certainly, if Elena was pregnant by her own father, she wouldn't want to tell her mother. It was a viable theory, I thought. Of course, I was already on the Castillo family shit list. Accusing the former United States senator of incest would undoubtedly make it markedly worse.

Which is why I didn't plan to, unless and until I had the proof.

Ethan Morrison picked up on the fourth ring. "Hello?"

"Hi, Ethan, It's Kate Marston."

"Hi, Kate. What's up?"

"I'm going to need you to do another DNA comparison."

Chapter Forty

The courtroom crowd was quiet, expectant, as the prosecutor rose from his seat at counsel table. Lipton walked slowly, deliberately to the podium in front of the jury box and placed his file there, then stood off to the side. His hands were clasped in front of his chest, his head bowed slightly, as if he were praying. Perhaps he was.

As he stood there, I recalled our phone conversation two days before when I called with my client's response to his plea offer, which was "Not only no, but hell no."

"What's he looking for?"

"He needs a dismissal."

"Would he like an apology as well?"

"That would be nice, but not required. Look, he wants to keep his job and his reputation. A plea to anything would mean he would lose both."

"That ship's sailed," he said, his tone suggesting disbelief at what he had heard. "If he thinks he comes out of this with his job and reputation intact, he's crazy. The JQC is after him big time and even if he somehow manages to beat this rap, everyone will always wonder."

"You made a reasonable offer, Bill," I said, striving for a conciliatory tone. "He knows the risks, but he says he's not going to plea to something he didn't do."

I could feel his shrug on the other end of the line. "Well, I guess I better go polish up my opening statement."

And now, I watched as Lipton set the mood with the jury for one of the biggest cases he would ever try. This was serious business, he was saying, and he would treat it as such. After a few seconds, He looked up at the jurors, his hands still clasped, and began his opening statement.

"Elena Castillo was a bright, beautiful woman with a promising legal career. On the night of January 8th of this year, her life was tragically cut short." Here, he turned toward Goodwin. "It was cut short by this man," he said, pointing an accusing finger at my client, holding for a few seconds, then turning back to face the jury.

"On the night of her death, the defendant called Elena from his office at the courthouse at around ten fifteen, then again at ten thirty. We know this because the victim's cell phone records show incoming calls from the number assigned to his office at those times. The first call lasted approximately three minutes. The one at ten thirty lasted less than a minute."

The prosecutor started to pace slowly in front of the jury box as he continued, looking down at the floor. "Shortly after that, he went over to her apartment. We know this because, one," he said, holding up one finger, "the courthouse security system, which records where and when an employee's key card is used to go in or out of the building, shows that the defendant's key was used to exit the garage at ten thirty-five."

He stopped pacing then, looked at the jurors and held up a second finger. "Two, Mrs. Ruth Campbell, a neighbor of Elena's, who also happens to be an acquaintance of the defendant, was returning to her unit at around ten forty-five that night. As she was about to enter her residence, she saw the defendant in front of Elena's unit, pounding on the door."

He paused, allowing the weight of this key fact to settle over the room. "Now, Mrs. Campbell didn't see him actually enter the victim's residence, but we know he did go in. How do we know that? Because, despite his efforts to cover his tracks, he left his fingerprint on the sliding glass door." He paused again briefly. Jurors love scientific evidence—prints, DNA, etc. So, he let them absorb this piece of the puzzle. "Exactly what happened in that apartment," he said, "we may never know. There are only two people who know for sure, and one of them cannot tell you because she is dead, silenced forever."

I was on my feet in a half second. "Objection. Request to approach."

The judge waved for us to come forward. Once we were gathered at the bench, I said, "Judge, I'm going to have to move for a mistrial. Mr. Lipton has started right off by commenting on my client's right to remain silent."

Lipton was quick with a response. "I was just pointing out the obvious," he said. "I'm acknowledging the fact that we will not be able to answer all their questions about the details."

The judge looked at me. "I'm going to deny the motion for mistrial." Then to Lipton she said, "But you be careful."

He nodded and we stepped back to our respective positions in the courtroom. Lipton continued to lay out his case, ticking off the evidence which would lead them to the conclusion that Elena's death was a homicide, and that Goodwin was the murderer. He outlined the evidence that suggested the defendant had tried to cover up his crime, that he had vacuumed the place, wiped down all the surfaces, locked the front door, engaging the deadbolt, and lied to the detectives. But, Lipton said, as is often the case, the killer had made mistakes.

He walked over to the prosecution table and retrieved the water bottle there, took a sip and placed it on the table. He began speaking as he made his way back to the front of the jury box. "So, what were those mistakes? Well, first, he missed one fingerprint, the one on the sliding glass door to the terrace."

Lipton gave the jurors a disgusted frown. "And though he tried to destroy any evidence of his relationship with the victim by deleting e-mails and other computer records, removing portable devices, he was careless. We were able to retrieve some of those deleted e-mails. We also have the cell phone records of both the defendant and the victim, corroborating their frequent communication."

Lipton paused, and three of the jurors look over in Goodwin's direction. "I expect that the defense will try very hard to point the finger elsewhere. They will try to tear down the victim, attack her character."

"Your Honor," I said, standing, "I have to object as being argumentative. I hate to interrupt counsel, but it sounds more like a closing argument than opening statement."

"Overruled," the judge said before Lipton could even respond. I shrugged and sat back down. It was sort of like a basketball game. You had to feel out the ref early. Was she going to call the fouls closely, or let you play?

"As I was saying," Lipton said, "I expect the defense will attack the victim's character in a desperate attempt to divert your attention from the real evidence in this case. They will try to focus on an eccentricity of hers that may seem not only odd but distasteful to some of you." He hesitated a beat, then said, "She filmed herself having sex with men."

Even though this salacious little tidbit was well known now, some in the audience, though none on the jury, let out a small, quiet gasp. Lipton ignored it, his body language and tone suggesting that the whole matter was inconsequential. As did his words. "The defendant will try to suggest that these other men, who are also prominent, high profile public officials, had a motive to kill the victim, that they were being blackmailed by these videos. The fact is, there will be no evidence of blackmail. And these men, unlike the defendant, have air tight alibis for the night of the murder."

The man gripped the sides of the podium now with both hands and leaned forward slightly. "They will also try to insinuate that there is some vast conspiracy of government officials and organized crime to legalize casino gambling in Florida, that some mysterious, unknown hit man murdered Elena Castillo. But there will be no evidence of this other than in the imagination of the defense."

The prosecutor stepped away from the podium. His hands were clasped again. "When you weigh all the evidence, you will conclude that Elena Castillo's death was not an accident. It was not a suicide. It was cold blooded, premeditated murder." He turned once again to point a finger at Goodwin. "And this is the man who killed her."

As Lipton made his way back to the prosecution table, the butterflies began swirling again in my stomach, the slight nausea returned. No matter how many times I did this, no matter how much I prepared, the first time I addressed the jury in a trial was the most stressful part. It always took a while to untangle my nerves.

Judge Mitchell looked up at the clock on the back wall. "Let's take a brief recess," she said, thus prolonging my misery for a few more minutes.

During the break, I checked the voice mail on my cell phone. I was hoping for something from Ethan Morrison, but the sterile, computerized voice told me, "You have no new messages."

Last Thursday, the pathologist had promised me a rush job on the two additional DNA samples I gave him. "I should have something in a few days," he said.

I pointed out, politely, that the last time he said it would take a few days, it turned into more than a week. "Jury selection for the Goodwin trial begins on Monday," I said, trying to impress upon him the urgency of the situation.

"I'll try. That's all I can promise. There are other people involved in the process, you know. There is a procedure, a protocol, which must be followed."

I thanked him and promised not to pester him about it, something we both knew was a lie. He didn't ask me from whom the samples had been taken, either, which saved me another lie. His discretion was just as valuable as his scientific expertise.

As of this morning, Ethan still had not contacted me. I broke my promise and called him, leaving a message when I got his voice mail, just before heading into court. I needed the results, I said, and I needed them before the State rested its case. "Hope you got something for me. Leave me a message on my voice mail. I'll get back with you during a break."

I considered calling again, but that really would be pestering. I spent the rest of the break time thinking about what I was going to say to the jury when I went back in.

* * *

I could feel the eyes of the jurors on me as I approached the podium. They had just heard a pretty convincing story from my opponent. I would need to meet Lipton head on, address his main points effectively, or I would lose this jury before the first witness. Although they are instructed by the judge not to form any fixed opinion about the case until they have heard all the evidence, studies have shown that about eighty per cent of jurors have pretty much made up their minds after the opening statements.

I stood away from the podium, directly in front of the jury. "There used to be a radio program of news and commentary by a man named Paul Harvey." Three of the older jurors nodded, already seeing where I was going. "He would tell a story which in itself was interesting and seemed to lead to a natural conclusion. Then after a commercial break, he would tell you what he hadn't told you before, which led to a different, more accurate conclusion to the story. He would always end with . . ." I paused to let the jury finish the sentence in their heads, if not out loud, then I said, "and now you know the rest of the story."

I sensed openness in the faces of the jurors that had not been there minutes before, so I decided to get right to it while they were receptive. "So, what is the rest of the story here? What did Mr. Lipton not tell you during his opening statement? And perhaps more to the point, what will he not be able to show you during the trial?" Always good to couch it in terms that suggested the State was somehow trying to hide something from them.

I pushed a strand of hair behind my ear and adjusted my glasses. "Let's first look at his contention that Elena Castillo's death was a homicide." I kept this part vague as I didn't want the State, or the medical examiner, to know where I planned to go on cross of this

317

witness, then I moved on to where I thought we would have the best chance with the jury. "But let's assume for the time being, that it was murder. What is missing from the State's case to show that my client is the one who did it?"

I first attacked the only physical evidence they had to tie Goodwin to the scene, the fingerprint. I pointed out that my client never denied being in the victim's residence, but it was months before her death. "And you will hear, from the State's own expert witness, that there is no way of knowing when that print was left there, and that it could in fact have been there for months. Indeed, there is absolutely no objective, scientific evidence to show he was there that night. No DNA, no hair, no fibers, no blood, no video from the condo security cameras that record the comings and goings of residents and visitors. Nothing."

I next addressed the eyewitness. "What the prosecutor did not tell you is that this is an elderly witness whose vision is not very good, who had consumed several drinks that evening. She observed the person from a distance of more than 200 feet, in a dimly lit hallway, and for only a few seconds. You will also learn that her memory of a significant fact of that evening is faulty, all of which will lead you to conclude that while well meaning, she is just flat wrong."

I began to pace in front of the jury box as I continued. "And the motive? This supposed intimate relationship that went bad? They have no concrete, reliable evidence of such a relationship. Talk about innuendos and speculation! Not a single person will take that witness stand and say they saw them check into a hotel, saw her sneak into his chambers after hours, saw him even go into her apartment. No one ever saw them kissing, holding hands, touching each other as lovers might or in any way acting toward each other in a way that suggested a romantic relationship."

I paused for a few seconds, then continued. "And that is because their relationship was just as my client told the detectives, strictly professional. He was a mentor to this young lawyer. The e-mail messages between the two should be so interpreted. A little playful banter, joking between friends. After all, they worked on committees together. She was heading up the effort for a Habitat for Humanity project. It was quite natural for her to have several phone conversations with the judge about this—as she did with other lawyers and judges. And so they deleted e-mails. Doesn't everybody from time to time? What is so sinister about that?"

I searched the jurors' faces for some acknowledgment of the truth of this last observation, an acceptance of the premise, but they were a pretty stoic bunch. I pushed ahead. "We don't intend to attack the victim's character, as Mr. Lipton suggests. But you should be allowed to consider what the State, in its rush to judgment, apparently did not. The truth is, the victim did have sexual relations with other men. And this is not based on speculation, gossip or innuendo. It is based on a video which the State withheld from the defense."

Lipton almost shot out of his chair. "Objection. Request to come side bar."

Mitchell waved her hand. "Overruled."

Good for the goose, good for the gander. The judge was going to be consistent in giving both lawyers a good bit of leeway in opening statement.

"Why Ms. Castillo would secretly record her sex acts with these men may never be known for sure, but you have to wonder why the State concealed the existence of the video from me until confronted with the issue in front of the judge. You will learn, though, that each of these men, as well as the victim and her client, Ricky Hobbs, had some connection with the people who were behind the effort to legalize casino gambling in the State of Florida."

As much as Lipton tried to dismiss this theory, I knew the jury would be receptive, and I could see it now in the way some of them leaned forward in their seats. "More importantly, you will wonder why the State chose not to investigate this possible connection."

I looked over at the prosecutor, and thought maybe he actually squirmed a little in his seat. I turned back to the jury. "So, when all the evidence is in, not only will you have a reasonable doubt as to my client's guilt, you will be convinced that an innocent man has been persecuted for political purposes by Mr. Lipton's office."

And with that, the battles lines had been drawn. I stepped back to counsel table and the judge looked over at Lipton. "Call your first witness," she said.

Chapter Forty-One

"I could tell right away she was dead."

The witness sat erect in the chair, his hands together on his lap, his thumbs knocking together at a rate of about 120 beats a minute. He was one of the students who had discovered Elena's body. "She wasn't moving at all and she was like all twisted up, real unnatural like, you know, laying there in the shrubbery. I knew she wasn't just passed out drunk or something."

I suspected the young man would know passed out drunk when he saw it. I also knew that the student had himself consumed vast quantities of alcoholic beverages in the hours before his discovery. I could have cross examined him on this point, but to what end? His testimony helped establish the timeline, that's all. "No questions," I said when Mitchell asked if I wished to inquire of the witness.

Similarly, there wasn't a lot to do with the first officers on the scene who cordoned off and secured the area in which the body was found, or the doorman who made a tentative identification of the body and arranged for entry into the victim's unit.

Both Oscar Manning and Debra Brown testified but Oscar provided the principal narrative, giving the jury an overall view of the investigation and providing some basic facts. There was little to challenge or on which to cross examine extensively. I did successfully object when Lipton tried to get in hearsay information through the detectives, such as the matching of the print found on the sliding glass to Goodwin, which e-mails had been deleted on Elena's laptop and recovered by the computer experts, the fact that the victim had an exterior hard drive, a flash drive, CDs and DVDs which she kept next to her computer at home, all of which were missing. On this latter point, as well as the existence and location of extra house keys, the State's principal witness would be the housekeeper, Angelina Perez. Unless the State had better luck in finding her than we did, I had told the judge in a pre-trial hearing, she would not be available to testify to this.

Lipton assured the judge that Angelina Perez was not, in fact, missing, that his office was flying her in from Guatemala, where her location was not a mystery. "The defense chose not to depose her. That's their problem."

"Not so, Your Honor," I said. "We tried very hard to locate this witness, and serve her at the address Mr. Lipton provided in discovery, to no avail. If he has somehow managed to get her back here from Guatemala, we will need to depose her before she testifies."

The judge said she'd wait for the witness to arrive and then sort it all out, but indicated that the defense would, at a minimum be allowed to talk with the witness before her testimony.

I also didn't object to introduction of the condo records showing the times Elena's key card was used to come and go, and the receipt from Harry's, on the plaza, for a take-out order the night of her death. They tended to show that Elena used her key to enter through the garage at 8: 30 p.m. and had paid for dinner from Harry's at 8:50 p.m. Lipton could establish the authenticity of the records fairly easily, and besides, I wanted those records in evidence for my own purposes.

My first significant cross was of the medical examiner, Larry Williams. He was about sixty years old, slight of frame, and with a hunched over posture that made him look ten years older. He had very fine, thin hair and a scraggly mustache that seemed hardly worth the effort. But he was a practiced witness and his feeble appearance was belied by a strong baritone voice which gave him a certain air of authority when he spoke. His conclusions seemed reasonable, too, consistent with the physical evidence. My cross examination focused on two small, but significant points.

"Dr. Williams, if I understand your testimony, you concluded that the victim's death was not accident or suicide because she had fractures to both the front and back of her skull. Is that correct?"

"That was one of the reasons."

"Because it wouldn't make sense that she could get both of those injuries when she hit the ground, right?"

"Yes."

I nodded my approval of his reasoning. "And based on the other injuries, you concluded that the fracture to the back of the skull occurred first."

"That's correct. The other injuries make it clear that she struck the ground face first. It is simply impossible that the fracture to the back of her skull was the result of impact with the ground. It had to have occurred before."

"Let me ask you this. Is it possible that the victim hit her head on another balcony ledge or railing or some other protruding object as she was falling?"

The man cocked his head and squinted at me, a little surprised it seemed at my question. "Actually, I did consider this possibility, briefly."

I was disappointed. I had not asked him about this in his deposition, hoping to catch him off guard at trial. A fundamental rule of cross examination is that you never ask a question you don't know the answer to, unless you don't care what the answer is. And the fact was, I didn't know why he had rejected this theory. But I didn't have much of a choice now. Either I asked him to explain, or look like I was hiding something. So, I asked him.

He told the jury there were two main reasons. One was the degree of bruising and discoloration around the first fracture, suggesting that death had not occurred for at least several minutes after the first injury. The blood must be pumping through the body for there to be bruising, and the lack of any significant bruising around the other injuries suggested that death had occurred within a very short time after she hit the ground. The second reason was that he had done a visual examination at the scene and had not seen any object or part of the building which would have been in the path of the victim's fall.

I tried to divert attention from the first reason by concentrating on the second one. "A visual inspection?"

"That's right."

"Isn't that just a fancy way of saying you eyeballed it?"

"Objection. Argumentative."

"Sustained."

"Did you do any measurements, Dr. Williams, or ask an engineer to measure the distance of other balcony ledges, to account for thrust from her balcony, initial direction of the fall, projected arc, adjustments for wind, or any other factors?"

"It wasn't necessary. You could see that there was nothing in between the balcony and the ground upon which she could have struck her head."

"So, the answer would be no? You performed no scientific measurements or tests in order to reject this theory?"

The witness appeared to be a little frustrated. Good. "No, other than the visual inspection, I did no tests or measurements."

I let that sink in for a few moments before addressing my second point. "One final thing. Let's assume that the blow to the back of the head occurred, as you opine, several minutes before her fall from the balcony. That is consistent, as you say, with the bruising and discoloration, right?"

"Yes."

"So, let's say the victim falls and hits her head on, I don't know, maybe the edge of the coffee table, or maybe just the wood floor. But not as the result of a struggle. She just loses her balance and falls. Maybe she is knocked unconscious for a while, maybe several minutes. Then she comes to."

Williams started shaking his head.

"I'm not through yet. Hear me out. She is still very woozy. She's not thinking clearly. She goes out onto the terrace for some fresh air. Then, she either climbs up on the ledge and jumps off, or she falls."

He was shaking his head again.

"Wouldn't that be consistent with the physical evidence? Wouldn't it explain the two skull fractures, the difference in bruising and discoloration?"

"Well, yes, in that limited aspect, but it would be highly unlikely that the victim, after suffering such a blow to the head, would, number one, regain consciousness, and two, vacuum the floor, wipe down all the surfaces, somehow dispose of the vacuum cleaner bag, the CDs and DVDs, the exterior hard drive and flash drive, delete files and e-mails from her laptop, and then, for some unknown reason, climb up on her balcony ledge."

The bastard sat there, smug. Unfortunately, he made a good point, and I needed to defuse it. "Just to be clear, you have no personal knowledge that the floor was vacuumed and the surfaces wiped down after the victim received that skull fracture, rather than before?"

"I am relying on the police reports."

"So, your answer would be no?"

He frowned. "As with all investigations into the cause of death, we have to rely on the facts as established by the investigation, in addition to our physical findings. You can't look at things in a vacuum."

"I appreciate that, Dr. Williams. I just want to separate what facts," I said, making quote marks in the air with my fingers, "are based on your personal knowledge, and which are based on what you may have read or been told." I waited a few beats, then asked, "So, do you or do you not have personal knowledge of when the surfaces were cleaned, the floor vacuumed?"

"I do not."

"Same thing for the supposed missing items, then? No personal knowledge?"

He frowned again, clearly frustrated. "No personal knowledge," he said.

If Angelina Perez testified, the jury would have that factual basis, but I'd cross that bridge when I came to it. "So, aside from these findings, for which you have no personal knowledge, let me go back to the question I asked you earlier. That scenario I gave you, about the victim having struck her head, recovered, then later fell or jumped from her balcony ledge, which is consistent with your physical findings as to her injuries, isn't it?"

After a long silence, the witness gave me a terse, "Yes."

* * *

During the break, I checked my phone messages. There was one from Ethan Morrison. He still didn't have the results, but said he should have something for me by tomorrow afternoon.

I had not told either Goodwin or Ted about this new possibility, of course, nor could I now. I would not be able to call Brandi as a witness, either, regardless of what Morrison might come up with. For to do so would be to admit that I had purposely withheld important information from my client, which in turn would lead to the inevitable question of why. Just as well, perhaps, since Brandi had made it clear she did not want to testify. She had also made it clear that she was not going to wait much longer to get paid.

* * *

After the break, Lipton announced that Angelina Perez would be arriving later in the day and he expected to call her the following afternoon. He would make her available to me for questioning, under oath, if I desired. I did so desire, I said, so we arranged a time to do so.

The witnesses the rest of that day included the computer forensics expert who explained to the jury how files that were deleted on a computer remained in the hard drive nonetheless, until recorded over. Using a special software program, he had been able to retrieve some of the e-mails between Goodwin and Castillo. My cross was very limited. I had him admit that he had no way of determining how many files or e-mails had been deleted, who had deleted them and why. He also acknowledged that it was not unusual for people to periodically empty their system of old e-mails and files.

The courthouse security head explained how the computerized system recorded whose card was used to enter and exit from secured areas, and how all calls made from any phone in the court system was logged as to number called, and time. She provided the foundation for introduction of the appropriate records showing the two calls from Goodwin to Elena, and his exit from the garage at 10:35 p.m. on the night of Elena's death. The last witness before lunch was arguably the State's most important.

Chapter Forty-Two

Ruth Campbell walked slowly, but steadily to the stand, her short, gray hair freshly cut and styled. She wore middle height heels, a dark green jacket and skirt, over an olive silk blouse. She looked, well, dignified is the best I can come up with. She was sworn by the clerk then took her seat. She placed her hands in her lap and looked pleasantly at Lipton, who stood at the far corner of the jury box.

The prosecutor led her slowly, carefully, through the basic introductory questions, establishing a rapport with the jury, allowing them to get a feel for this crucial witness. And Miss Ruthie did well, projecting neutrality and competence, an intelligent, educated woman who was confident but not arrogant.

She gave her occupation as retired, a former professor of English at FSU for 34 years. She had lived at Jasmine Towers for a little over three years now, having moved in shortly after she lost her dear husband of almost forty-five years. This, of course, was all irrelevant, but any fool could see the risk of objecting. Mercifully, Lipton moved on fairly quickly to what was relevant.

"So, Mrs. Campbell, Did you know the deceased, Elena Castillo?"

She shrugged slightly. "Only in passing, really. We would literally pass in the hall, or ride the elevator together, but just casual conversation."

"But you knew, from personal experience which unit was hers?"

"Yes. It was just down the hall. Her number was 1202 and mine was 1224. Hers was a penthouse."

"Mrs. Campbell, do you know the defendant in this case, Mr. Warren Goodwin?"

"Oh yes. I've known Renny for many years."

"And how do you know him?"

"We have mutual friends." She looked over in my direction. "If I am not mistaken, my husband and I were first introduced to him by Ms. Marston's parents." She turned her attention to the jury then. "We were neighbors, the Marstons and us for many years and Renny was at one point a law partner of Phillip Marston, as well as a close friend. So, we went to each other's parties and other events in common."

"I see," Lipton said, nodding his head as if this was the first time he had heard this bit of information. "Let me direct your attention to the evening of January 8ᵗʰ of this year," the prosecutor said, not only to focus the witness, but to signal to the jury that the main course was about to be served. And there was a noticeable shift in the jury box as jurors straightened in the seats, looking up from their note taking. Several leaned forward slightly.

"Did you see your friend, Mr. Goodwin, that evening?"

"Yes, I did."

"Could you tell the jury the circumstances, the place and time?"

Ruth Campbell's testimony was completely consistent with what she had told me in her home, and just as damning to my client. After Lipton had her describe in detail what she had seen that night, he asked, "Is the man you saw that evening, knocking on the door of the victim's apartment at approximately ten forty-five, in the courtroom today?"

She didn't look over at Goodwin but said, "Yes, he is."

"Could you point him out and describe what he is wearing?"

"He's right there," she said, pointing an extended arm in the direction of Goodwin. "He's sitting in the middle, wearing a dark gray suit and a white shirt."

My client smiled at the witness and tipped an imaginary hat in her direction. She returned the smile. A two-edged moment for us. Lipton then turned toward the defense table, looking at Goodwin. "Let the record reflect that the witness has identified the defendant, Warren

Goodwin."

"The record will so reflect," Mitchell said without looking up from her notes.

The prosecutor frowned. "Now you were how far away when you saw the defendant?"

"Oh, I'd say about two hundred feet."

"What sort of lighting do they have in the hallway there?"

"There are ceiling fixtures all along the hallway."

"Fairly well lit, then?"

"Fairly. They're not glaringly bright, but the entire hallway is illuminated, if that's what you're asking."

"But still, you saw him mostly in profile, only a few seconds face to face, and at a distance of some two hundred feet. How can you be so sure of your identification?"

My former neighbor looked at Lipton as if he were a student who had not been listening. She repeated some of the things he had just pointed out—the opportunity she had to see him, good lighting, reasonable distance, her good eyesight for distances. "Also," she said, "Renny, Judge Godwin, has some distinctive features. He still has a full head of curly hair, which he wears on the long side. Something you don't see that often in men his age. And the suit he was wearing that night. It was a gray three-piece suit that I have seen him in many times."

"And you are sure it was him you saw?"

The woman nodded her head. "Yes."

"Thank you, Mrs. Campbell." He turned to me. "Your witness."

I stood and began speaking as I approached the podium.

"Mrs. Campbell, nice to see you again."

"You too, dear."

"Now, this man you saw in the hallway, you say he was knocking on the door?"

"Yes."

"Then he wasn't using a key to unlock the door?"

330

"No."

I looked up at her, as if surprised by her answer, pausing to let its significance resonate with the jury. "So, he didn't have a key?"

"Objection," Lipton said, rising. "Speculation."

I raised my hand. "I'll withdraw the question." The point had been made anyway.

"And Mrs. Campbell, you can't testify that this man ever entered the residence, can you?"

"No, I can't."

"Nor can you testify for sure whether anybody was even in the residence at that time to let him in."

"No."

"You went back out a few minutes later to take your dog for a walk, didn't you?"

"Yes."

"Did you see this man, or anyone else near the vicinity of the apartment?"

"No."

"Now, let me back up in time a little bit. You said that you were coming back from your book club meeting, and that my mother dropped you off at some time between ten thirty and ten forty-five. Is that correct?"

"Yes."

"Now, if I understand the layout of Jasmine Towers, you can enter through the main entrance, where there is the concierge desk?"

"Yes."

"Or you can enter through the garage entrance and go up the elevators there?"

"Yes."

"When you came home that evening, did you enter through the lobby or through the garage?"

"I came in through the lobby."

"Are you sure?"

She thought a moment. "Yes, I'm certain."

As sure as you are that you saw Renny Goodwin that night?"

She hesitated then, perhaps sensing a trap, but she had already committed herself. "Yes."

I walked back to defense table and picked up the document Ted handed me. "As I understand it, to enter the garage or the elevators at the Towers, you need a plastic key card that reads the bar code?"

"That's right."

"Are you aware that the management keeps a record of every time one of those key cards is used. A computer records the card number, the time, and the entry used. This was testified to by an earlier witness, the person in charge of security for the condos."

"Yes, I am aware that such records are kept."

"Let me show you what has been marked as Defense exhibit 6. This is a print out of computer records of those entries. If you will go to the second page, for the date of January 8th, there is one entry for portal two, the elevator in the garage, at 10:42 p.m., with a key card assigned to your unit, 1224."

She looked at the document for a long time, then shook her head. When she looked up she seemed genuinely confused, unsure. "I don't understand. There must be some mistake."

"I want you to assume further that the concierge on duty that night has already testified that he does not remember you coming in through the lobby that evening, but does remember you going out at approximately eleven o'clock, with your dog. In fact the two of you spoke he says, and he remembers you coming back about twenty minutes later. But he does not remember seeing you come in before that."

She shook her head again. "He wasn't there the first time I came in."

I went back to the defense table and retrieved another folder. "Let me show you what has been marked as Defense exhibit 7, a still photograph taken from the video tape of the garage elevator. From its angle, you can't see the face of the occupant, but do you recognize the hat, Mrs. Campbell?"

I had recognized it when I first saw the film footage from that night. Ms. Ruthie had a thing for exotic hats, and this was one I had seen her in often. A large broad brimmed thing with feathers, canary yellow in color. Hard to miss, or forget. It was obvious that the witness recognized it as well, and was truly confused. She stared at the photo for several seconds. I prompted her. "Mrs. Campbell?"

Her voice was quiet, the tone tentative as she said, still looking at the photo, "I do have a hat just like that, but that's not me. Couldn't be. Not that night." She looked up at me.

"You would agree that it's a fairly unusual hat, wouldn't you?"

"Yes."

"Know anybody else in Jasmine Towers with one like that?"

"I don't know of anyone in Tallahassee with one like that. I bought it in Paris five years ago."

I waited a few moments, then in a soft tone said, "Is it possible, Mrs. Campbell, that you were mistaken as to which entrance you came through that night when you came back from your book club meeting?"

"I suppose so," she stammered, "but I felt sure I came in the lobby entrance. I mean, it's closer to where I was let off. There'd be no reason to go through the garage."

"Isn't it also possible, Mrs. Campbell, that you saw a man in profile two hundred feet away, who was dressed similarly, and had a similar hair style as Warren Goodwin, and you made an assumption that's who it was?"

She shook her head again, looking small and drawn. When she looked back up at me, there was a twinge of sadness in her eyes. She straightened herself in the seat, though, and mustered some authority for her voice. "I remain convinced that the man I saw that evening was your client and my friend, Judge Warren Goodwin." She looked over at the computer print-out and the photo. "I can't explain this. Either it is wrong or I am, but regardless, I made no assumption when I saw him. I recognized him, even before he turned to face me."

I stood there for several seconds, both proud and ashamed of the job I had done on cross. I thanked the witness, told the judge I had no further questions, and returned to my seat. It was obvious that this little inconsistency had been missed by the prosecution as Lipton was whispering angrily at the associate next to him. He found his composure quickly though. He asked all the right questions on redirect to repair the damage but I suspect that he could not completely. The lasting image was of a confused, perhaps senile old woman whose certainty was now in question. Whether I had managed to walk that fine line and get out without the jury hating me, well, I couldn't be sure, but I had done the best I could.

We recessed for lunch after that. Ted, Goodwin and I walked to the office, reviewing and critiquing the day's testimony so far and our plans for the afternoon and the next day. The discussion continued once back at the office, centering around whether Goodwin would testify. After an exhaustive analysis of the pros and cons we left it undecided, allowing our client to think about it for a while longer.

I excused myself and, back in my office, placed a call to Ethan Morrison. "Hey, Ethan," I said when he picked up. "This is Kate. You got something for me?"

"Well, I have the test results back."

"And?"

"Bottom line or nuance?"

"Bottom line first, then nuance if you will."

Silence for a couple of seconds on the other end, then, "Neither of the DNA samples you gave me is a match with the known sample of the fetus. Neither is the father."

I was both relieved and disappointed. I started thinking about how this affected my strategy, and what I needed to do next. There was something in Ethan's voice, though, that suggested he was not through, so I asked, "Nuance?"

"That is not to say, however, that the results were not very interesting."

Chapter Forty-Three

With Miranda Castillo, Lipton quickly proffered her testimony concerning Elena's hearsay statements that Mitchell had ruled inadmissible. "For appellate purposes," he said.

I didn't like it but couldn't really object. He had a right to put on the record what the testimony would have been so the appellate court could determine if it was error to keep it out. For Lipton, if the jury wasn't going to get to hear it, the prosecutor wanted everyone else to. So, with the jury absent, Miranda Castillo calmly and blatantly lied on the stand, claiming that her daughter had specifically named Goodwin as her lover and that she was afraid of him.

Even though it was simply a proffer, a record of what would have been testified to if the judge had not sustained our objection, I felt compelled to cross examine the witness, to make sure the record was complete on the subject. I asked her point blank about our conversation in which she specifically said that Elena had not mentioned the name of her lover.

She gave me a cold stare. "That's not how I remember it, Ms. Marston."

Well, that went well, I thought, as I sat back down. Had to give it a try, though.

The prosecutor recalled Oscar to the stand as his last witness for the day. The detective told of their meeting with the judge and his adamant denial that he had anything other than a professional relationship with Elena, and that he had not seen or talked to her in a week or more.

On my cross of Oscar, I had him acknowledge that he had found no witness who saw Elena and Goodwin engaging in any conduct that suggested there was some romantic relationship between the two. He also admitted that he had no documentary evidence, other than the e-mails and the phone records, to suggest they were having an affair.

"They were apparently very careful," he said.

I looked at the jury a moment, sighed, then looked back to Oscar. "Detective, I didn't ask you if they were careful. But since you put it that way, your conclusion that they were apparently very careful is based, is it not, on the fact that you could find no corroborating evidence of this alleged romantic relationship."

"That's part of it, I guess."

"Didn't come across any sex tapes with my client and the victim, either, did you?"

Oscar frowned. "No, we didn't uncover such a tape."

"But you did for other men, right?"

"Yes, that's right."

"To be clear, you have no records of where they checked into a hotel room together, went on weekend trips together?

"No."

"No receipts, no witnesses who placed them dining together in some remote restaurant, even out to a movie together?"

"I guess not," he said after a little too long of a hesitation. "But there were the e-mails and the phone records," he repeated.

I gave him a long look to suggest my incredulity, looked briefly to the jury, then to the judge. "Nothing else," I said.

When we recessed for the day, I made arrangements to speak with the housekeeper early in the morning before court reconvened, told Ted and Goodwin I would meet them later at the office, then headed for the reception area for the judges' chambers on the third floor. I had asked the bailiff to deliver to Miranda Castillo a hand written note during the last break, but I wasn't sure she would meet me as requested. When I entered the room, though, she was waiting for me. The only other person in the room was the receptionist.

"Mrs. Castillo, thanks for coming." I turned to the receptionist. "Hi,

Marry Ann. My dad said we could use the conference room for a few minutes, if you would be so kind as to buzz us back." I pointed with my chin to the double doors leading back to the judicial chambers. When Marry Ann hesitated, I said, "You want to call him and get the okay?"

She smiled, reaching with her key card toward the remote opener attached to her desk. "That won't be necessary."

I heard the familiar click of the lock being released, opened the door and motioned for Elena's mother to follow me down the hall. Once in the room, I offered her a chair but she said she would prefer to stand.

"What's this all about?

"You really may want to sit for this," I said, motioning with my head toward a chair.

Reluctantly, perhaps out of pure curiosity, she did so. I joined her, placing my briefcase on the table and opening it, pulling out a file folder.

"You gave some interesting testimony today, with the proffer."
She said nothing.

"Of course, we both know it was a lie. She never told you the name of the judge, or that she was afraid of him."

The woman rose from her seat. "If you asked me here simply to call me names, this meeting is over."

I put up my hand. "No, not at all. Just making an observation. And to tell you I understand where it is coming from. Maybe I'd do the same thing if it were my daughter. But that's not why I asked to meet with you. I wanted to tell you about an astonishing new development that could have a profound effect on the case, and on your family."

I had said the magic words. The woman sat back down and looked at me expectantly.

"I told you when we first met that if I could do my job without unnecessary embarrassment to your family and the memory of your daughter, I would."

She frowned. "Didn't do too good with that promise, did you?"

"I understand your bitterness, and that you think I betrayed that promise, but you must understand I really didn't have much of a choice. That DVD fell in my lap and I couldn't ignore it."

"Humph."

"I don't expect you to accept my explanation, or my sincere apology for having to do so. Your motherly instinct to protect is understandable and admirable. I don't blame you for trying to make sure your daughter's killer does not get off. I didn't, however, appreciate the threats to me and my family and the physical attempt at intimidation. That was a mistake. Only made me more determined."

"Ms. Marston, no one in my family had anything to do with those alleged attacks or threats to you or your family. I would never countenance such activity—regardless of what you may have done."

I couldn't tell if she was telling the truth, or whether she would even know what her husband or other family members might have done, but my whole plan depended on my assessment that Miranda Castillo was the power behind the throne. I waved her off and said, "But that's neither here nor there. What I have to tell you now is something you may be able to control, in the interest of your family, and allow me to effectively do my job without further embarrassment to your family."

She turned down her lips. "You've already done the damage. The fact that you parade your witnesses into court tomorrow is not going to make it any worse, really."

"As I said, this is something new."

"Well, then get on with it if you please,' she said, impatience growing in her voice.

I nodded. "I think, Ms. Castillo, that your daughter kept a secret from you. She had an abortion three weeks before her death."

The shock and anger on the woman's face confirmed what I had suspected. She didn't know. Before she could leave in a huff, I opened the file and took out Morrison's first report, the one in which he concluded the fetus was Elena's, and passed it over to her.

She started to read, then looked up. "This could be a forgery, or the lies of someone you have paid."

"Could be, but you can have your own experts check it out." She didn't respond so I continued. "You and Elena were so close. Why did she not tell you this? What could there be about it that she would not confide in her mother?"

Miranda Castillo kept her face passive, but I detected a small twitch at the corner of her mouth, a small recognition of the implication, perhaps.

"So, I have to admit that I surreptitiously collected a sample of your husband's DNA at our meeting at the State Attorney's Office and had it compared with that of the unborn child."

Her stoic, poker face disintegrated, replaced by a mix of shock, disgust, and fear. "This is an outrage! She started to stand but stopped, and looked at me expectantly.

"He wasn't a match."

"I could have told you that," she said, but I could sense the relief in her voice. Any relief, however, would be short lived.

"It wasn't a match, Mrs. Castillo, but it was very close."

"So?" she demanded.

I opened the file folder in front of me and took out Morrison's most recent report and pushed it over toward her. "This is from the same expert. He's very good, very reliable, and very discreet." As she picked it up and began to read, I continued. "He says that based on his analysis, the father of Elena's unborn child will share markers with your husband. He will be either a sibling or a son, most likely a direct descendent. They're that close. My sources tell me that Elena's uncle is incapable of fathering a child."

The woman lifted her head and gave me a look of pure horror as she realized what I was saying. Then she returned to her reading. I waited for her to get to the conclusion section, then continued. "As of now, the only people who know the contents of that report are you, me and my expert. And he doesn't know that the sample I gave him was from your husband."

She arched her eyes at me. "Your client doesn't know?"

I shook my head.

"What do you want?"

"Tomorrow morning, if the State doesn't dismiss the case or Judge Mitchell does not grant my motion for judgment of acquittal, my first witness will be my expert. My second witness will be your son, Mario."

The woman was either a great actress or had been genuinely surprised by this information. She held her hand to her heart. I imagined a hundred thoughts were running through her head, options instantly evaluated and rejected, set aside for further review.

"How do I know this is not just a fabrication?"

"I guess you can't be sure, but regardless, if I have to put on a defense, then you can evaluate my expert's testimony tomorrow, just like everyone else in the courtroom. You can have your own test done, but there isn't enough time before trial starts back up tomorrow. You can ask the prosecutor to seek a continuance, but he'll want to know why."

I paused a beat or two for her to consider this, then continued. "Mario may have an alibi for the time of death. Supposedly, he wasn't in Tallahassee that day, at least from what we have learned. Of course, that doesn't mean he couldn't have gotten someone else to do it for him." I hesitated again to let the weight of this awful possibility sink in. "Regardless, it doesn't really matter in terms of his political future. It is now dead."

The woman nodded in agreement and understanding. I didn't know how she would handle the apparent conflict of loyalties, but I was counting on her continued desire to protect what was left of her family. "Right now," I said, "this can stay between you and me."

She was silent for a long time, and I didn't press her. Finally, she rose from her seat, file in hand. "I appreciate the courtesy," she said, extending her hand to me. "I'll see if something mutually beneficial can be arranged. We will both know tomorrow morning."

* * *

The next morning, Bill Lipton asked to meet with the judge in chambers before trial resumed. There, he told the judge of his intention to announce a dismissal of the case in open court. Mitchell arched her eyebrows in a silent question.

"It's a combination of factors, Your Honor. First, Ms. Marston's cross examination of the medical examiner raised some issues that, quite frankly, I hadn't considered before. Second, one of my key witnesses, the housekeeper, Ms. Angelina Perez, cannot be located."

Lipton gave me an accusatory looked, then turned back to the judge. "She flew in yesterday, met with our investigator, and checked into a hotel. She apparently checked out in the middle of the night. We can't find her anywhere. She was to be my last witness this morning. I didn't have her under subpoena, so I doubt you'd grant a continuance under the circumstances."

The judge pursed her lips, suggesting but not confirming his conclusion.

"And another of my key witnesses, Ms. Castillo, has indicated her intention to recant a portion of her testimony. Specifically, she says that after thinking about it, maybe Ms. Marston was correct, that her daughter never really named the defendant as the person with whom she was having an affair. She says she's not sure anymore."

The room was silent for several seconds.

"Anyway," Lipton said, "just thought I should give you a heads up."

I looked over to him. "I appreciate the courtesy, Bill, and more importantly, I admire your integrity and courage in doing the right thing."

I'm sure the statement sounded insincere, but it wasn't. It was the right thing to do. Lipton was no doubt reading the handwriting on the wall as to his chances of a conviction, and it was also obvious that, through the missing housekeeper and the recantation of testimony, Miranda and Raoul Castillo were exerting a good bit of pressure on the man. Still, it would have been much more politically expedient, and less embarrassing, to continue the prosecution and get a not guilty verdict, than to give up in the middle of the fight, so to speak, to essentially admit you shouldn't have started it in the first place. The guy was showing some class here, and it didn't hurt to mend a few fences by acknowledging it.

My co-counsel nodded his approval of my observation and said, "I agree." My client, whether prone to be more cynical and less forgiving, or afraid that anything he said or did might cause Lipton to reconsider, remained silent, his face betraying no emotion.

"Very well," Judge Mitchell said, rising from her chair. "Let's go let everyone else know."

Chapter Forty-Four

After the prosecutor's surprise announcement that morning, I neither saw nor spoke with Renny Goodwin for a month, not until he came to my parents' home to celebrate my father's appointment to the Florida Supreme Court. The official investiture ceremony and reception was held earlier in the day, but my mom wanted to have family and close friends over for a more informal gathering. He and Marci still fit in that group.

My sisters were there. Rebecca, her husband and three children had come a couple of days early, as had Sarah, accompanied by her live-in boyfriend of two years, a fellow professor named Dan. Ted was with me. Yeah, we started dating after the trial. Things were going pretty well, but neither of us was rushing into anything. Ted was a hit with my sisters and their families. Even my mother, who had been skeptical at first, had warmed up to him.

Dad and I had reached an accord of sorts. I believe both of us have rationalized the choices we made, though we both will have to deal with the guilty knowledge resulting from those choices. I don't know if my mother knows the full extent of the evidence that pointed to him as a suspect. If she asks, I will tell her, but that seems unlikely. My mother does not believe in airing family dirty linen.

Neither does Miranda Castillo. She called me about a week after my meeting with her, to thank me for "bringing this matter to my attention, and for your discretion." She told me that she believed she and her husband had gotten to the truth of the matter. "While Mario has shamed himself and his family, we are convinced that he did not kill his sister, nor have it done." I could imagine what methods had been employed to get to the truth of the matter. Her voice had conviction.

"Be assured, however, that his political career has been put on hold."

She allowed that her daughter's death may very well have been the result of accident or suicide, as Bill Lipton had hinted and as some in the press had speculated. I thought perhaps she was right, and said so. It wasn't very satisfactory, but life isn't like a T.V. show, where everything gets neatly wrapped up at the end and justice descends upon the land. I didn't share this last thought with her, though. No sense adding to her distress.

Mario made his announcement two days later at a press conference. "Because of personal family matters, I have decided to end my candidacy for the office of governor. He thanked his supporters, vowed to continue his service to the people as their representative, and asked that both his privacy and his decision be respected.

Neither was, of course. There were speculations galore as to why he had dropped out. Some suspected a medical crisis, either his or someone in his family. One theory, which came closest to the truth, was that one of his opponents had some dirt on him and had forced him out of the race on the threat of making it public. Maybe he fathered a child out of wedlock, one of his campaign staffers perhaps. Maybe he was gay. Maybe he was under investigation by the FBI, related to the gambling amendment—which, incidentally, would be on the ballot in the fall, the Supreme Court having affirmed my father's ruling.

But since there was nothing to find, nothing had been found in the three weeks since his announcement and the furor had already begun to die down. I doubted anyone would discover the real reason behind his decision. I planned to live up to my promise. As far as Brandi Peters knew, the father of Elena's unborn child was Warren Goodwin. Since double jeopardy had attached, Goodwin couldn't be tried again, and thus she had lost her leverage on him.

She still could have tried to extort money from the Castillo family to keep Elena's pregnancy and abortion a secret, or try to sell her story to the tabloids or some scandal television show. So, with the cooperation, and financial backing of Miranda Castillo, I paid Brandi what she wanted, plus a little extra, but conditioned on her turning over the clinic records and the rest of the fetus specimen to me, which I handed over to Miranda Castillo.

Brandi had resisted, had tried to bargain for more money, but in the end, she agreed. She was, after all, a con, but not a fool. She appreciated the wisdom of not crossing the Castillo family, and realized that she could be prosecuted criminally for what she had done. Any money she might realize from further sale of the information would be subject to forfeiture. Now, with the physical evidence gone, she had a strong disincentive to go public, plus a lack of credibility to go with it.

Her decision might have just saved her life, I told her, alluding to the popular speculation, which I had pressed as part of our defense, that organized crime figures, intent on bringing legalized gambling to Florida, had been responsible for the deaths of Elena Castillo and Ricky Hobbs. She had bought it.

In fact, whether it was true or not, I didn't know and perhaps never would. It was an intriguing theory, and popular with conspiracy theorists, but still had the logical holes I had observed earlier, at least as to Elena's death. Ricky Hobbs' "accident" still seemed suspicious to me, and from Ted's last report, there was some movement in official circles to take another look at it. The FBI had become involved. What, if anything would come of it, I didn't know, but at least Ricky's mother had some new hope, and was appreciative of our efforts.

As for the jogger, with his threatening poster and phone call, and the attack on me that night in the garage, Elena's mother had been right about that. I now knew they had nothing to do with the Castillo case or the move to legalize gambling.

After the attack in the garage, when the detective asked me if I knew anyone that might be upset with me, Jared Olsen had been one of the names I gave her. But he didn't fit the physical description, nor had I recognized his voice. The detective had followed up anyway. She saw no sign of an eye injury, and he had an airtight alibi. Then, shortly after the Goodwin case ended, I got a call from Natalie Olsen.

"I read about the attack on you in the paper. They said you gouged the guy in his eye?"

"That's right."

She was silent for a few seconds, then, "One of my kids, Alicia, she came home from visitation with Jared. It was about the time you got attacked. She said her uncle, Jared's brother, had been there part of the time, and that he had a bandage over his eye. He told her he got it playing racquet ball without his goggles. I didn't think much of it at the time."

I asked, and she gave me a physical description of the brother. It fit. She then gave me his name and address. "He's not a nice guy, Katie."

As soon as I hung up, I called the detective on my case and relayed the information. Within twenty-four hours, I had identified the man from a line-up as the jogger with the poster. I hadn't seen the face of my attacker, and I couldn't positively identify his voice, but his physical size and shape were consistent.

The man broke under interrogation in a matter of minutes. He confessed his involvement and pointed the finger at his brother as the person who put him up to it, and paid him for it. So much for family loyalty.

Speaking of which, I used to be embarrassed by the wives of politicians who, in the glare of some scandal involving their unfaithful husbands, stood by their men, professing allegiance to a higher duty. I thought it was just so much bullshit. They obviously had no self-esteem, no pride, having traded it for a meal ticket, or some illusion of prestige they imagined came with their association with the man.

No doubt, this was true for many such women, but having now seen it, up front and personal, I was less tempted to be judgmental. Perhaps such women showed not cowardice or low self-esteem, but a courage and strength that others could not muster.

Watching Marci Goodwin today, from across the crowded room, I thought she looked as happy as I'd ever seen her. For that matter, so did Renny. I was glad that he had taken my advice not to make any public attacks on Lipton or law enforcement in the wake of the dismissal. He had been, in fact, very magnanimous in his brief statement the morning the case was dismissed.

"As I said all along, I was innocent of the charges. This was a rush to judgment that should never have occurred. That being said, I hold no grudge against Mr. Lipton and his office. When push came to shove, he showed that he is a man of integrity and courage."

Goodwin's conciliatory tone probably influenced reciprocal restraint on the part of Lipton, who could have subtly insinuated that he still believed the man was guilty, but instead stuck by his initial public announcement, staying neutral when those in the press inquired further, or when the blogosphere was abuzz with speculation. It also couldn't hurt Goodwin with the JQC, either. When we spoke earlier this afternoon, he told me he thought he was close to working out a deal.

"I admit to inappropriate comments and behavior with the clerks. In return, they recommend a public reprimand. I imagine the Supreme Court would go along with it."

"I imagine so," I said, though the idea seemed ludicrous to me, considering what I knew, and that I still had my suspicions that the man may have gotten away with murder. Then again, the JQC didn't know what I did. They had some of the same proof problems Lipton had come up against. The man didn't deserve to wear the judicial robe, but maybe the JQC was thinking he would not run for another term, and if he did, the voters would turn him out of office.

If so, they may be underestimating Renny Goodwin. Despite all that had happened, perhaps because of it, his political base remained strong, and there was no question he would run again. While it was certain he would draw opposition, it wasn't at all certain he would lose.

One thing was certain, though. He wouldn't get my vote.

Two hours into it, the party was going well. Consistent with my assigned junior hostess duties, I went around collecting discarded items for the trash can, bottles and cans for the recycling bin, asking after guests. Through the open doorway, I made eye contact with Ted, who was playing some Wii game with Maggie and a couple of Rebecca's kids in the den. I smiled at him and he smiled back. He put his finger on his chest, mouthing "Need me?" I shook my head and waved him off, then slipped out onto the back terrace to place another bag in the trash can.

Even in the shade, it was bloody hot. As a result, there were only a few people willing to venture out of the air-conditioned space. One of them was Ruth Campbell, who had come out to let her dog run around a little, do his business. She took him with her just about everywhere she went these days and Mom had assured her he was welcome in their home.

Ms. Ruthie had arrived today well before any of the guests, in order to help get things set up. It was a little awkward at first between us. I had not seen or talked with her since the trial, as I probably should have, to apologize, which made me feel even more guilty. So, I apologized profusely when she approached me, dog at her side, leash in her hand.

She waved me off dismissively. "You have nothing to apologize for. You were doing your job, and very well." She smiled and patted me on the arm. "I told you before, I can take it." She hesitated a moment, then said, "Just like Renny told me right after the trial, no hard feelings."

She seemed sincere and, I must admit, it took a load off my shoulders. "You're a special person, Ms. Ruthie."

"So are you, dear," she said, smiling. Then she added, "But, for the record, I'm still sure there must have been some mistake with those key card records and that film footage. I swear I came in through the lobby that night. And the photo of me with that hat must have been from another evening."

I nodded, not wishing to make an issue of it. "Maybe so."

Now, as I approached her in the back yard of my parents' home, she smiled at me briefly, then turned her attention back to Pepper.

"He sure misses having a yard to run around in," she said, looking straight ahead. "I think he enjoys my visits here with your mom as much as I do." Still looking forward, she said, "You ought to have a dog, Katie."

"I've got a cat."

She shook her head. "Not the same."

"My boyfriend has a dog." I realized with surprise that I had, for the first time, referred to Ted as my boyfriend. I kind of liked the way it sounded, and felt. "You met him, didn't you? Ted?"

She looked over at me. "Yes. He seems quite nice."

"He is."

"And handsome."

"I agree."

Ms. Ruthie smiled at me, then looked back over the yard. "Now what is he getting into," she said, starting to walk quickly to where Pepper was digging furiously in one of my mom's flower beds. Bits of dirt were flying. "Pepper, stop that this instant."

The dog looked up, as if to say, "What'd I do?" Then, realizing that he must have done something wrong, he skulked away, his little short tail held low. He stopped after a few feet and turned toward his mistress.

"You get on back to the terrace," she said. The dog obediently scampered up toward the house where he sat down next to his water bowl and looked in our direction.

I surveyed the scene of the crime, for that is what my mother would consider such a desecration of her plantings—and identified the mutilated plants as the gardenias Mom had me pick up a few days ago at Tallahassee Nurseries. She would not be happy, but I pretended to Ms. Ruthie that it wasn't horrible, either. "No big deal," I said, bending down to try to salvage a bit of my mother's handiwork. "You know Mom. She changes these plantings regularly anyway."

Ms. Ruthie was not fooled. "I feel really badly about this." She looked toward her pet. "Bad dog!"

Pepper responded by lying down and putting his paws over his eyes.

I chuckled lightly, standing some remnants up and pushing soil around them to prop them up. "You teach him that?"

She shook her head. "He's just a natural ham. Plays on your sympathies quite well."

"I'll say. How can you stay mad at something like that?"

"I can't."

"There," I said, patting down the soil, "all better. Nobody will be able to tell the difference." On the last sweeping of dirt, though, to smooth out the surface, I had felt something. Something metal. I removed it from the bed, brushed some of the soil away and saw it was a key. I recognized the peculiar shape and size of it right away.

Ms. Ruthie stepped a little closer. "Find something?"

My back was to her. "No," I said, discreetly slipping the key into my pocket and standing. "See," I said, pointing. "Good as new."

Ms. Ruthie frowned, but said nothing. Then we both walked back to the house, where I excused myself to go wash my hands.

At the kitchen sink, as I washed the dirt from my hands, I did the same for the key, and confirmed what I had suspected. "Jasmine Towers," was inscribed on the head of the key, and I knew in my marrow that it would fit Elena Castillo's door. My head was spinning and my heart raced, pounding inside my chest. I dared a glance at my father who was in conversation with Jim Bushnell, one of our neighbors, in the dining room. A cell phone rang. It was on the kitchen counter. My mother's.

"Will you get that for me, honey?" My mother called out from the dining room where she had just appeared next to my father.

I nodded, numb, picked it up and took the call. It was from one of her book club members, expressing her regrets that she and her husband were not going to be able to drop by. I promised to relay the message, which I did in abbreviated fashioned, across the noisy room, mouthing the name to my mother, shaking my head. She nodded in acknowledgment. When I started to put the phone back on the counter, something clicked in my mind, like a piece of a puzzle fitting into place.

As I made my way to the den/office, I retrieved my cell phone from my back pocket and started scrolling down the numbers of family and friends stored there. You know, when you use speed dial, you sometimes can forget what the underlying number is. Mom and Dad were next to each other on the list. I stared at one then the other for a long several seconds.

At the desk, I opened the file drawer and pulled out the folder containing the phone bill statements, and quickly found the one I was looking for. I ran my finger once again down the recorded incoming and outgoing calls for each number, and confirmed my mistake. I now knew why my father had seemed surprised when he saw the same entry, and the reason for his contrived explanation to me.

The knock on the door startled me, but before I could respond, it opened and my mother stepped into the room and closed the door behind her. She looked over at the open file on the desk. "You seem to be overly interested in our cell phone records," she said as she took a seat opposite me.

I reached in my pocket, pulled out the key and placed it on the desk. My mother looked at it for a few moments, then back to me, her face neutral. I said, "I found this out in one of your flower beds."

"I'll resist the temptation to ask what you were doing digging in my flower bed."

"You and Dad discussed Elena's threat to go public with her supposed sex tape. Dad said he should call her bluff. You told him yes, but you really didn't want to take that chance. Even if he could explain things, there would always be questions, people would wonder.

Mom said nothing.

"Let me tell you what I think happened," I said. "You arranged to meet with Elena, to discuss the situation, to reason with her, threaten her, pay her, whatever was necessary to get that DVD from her, and her promise of silence. You had one of Ms. Ruthie's key cards, which she had given you so you could look after her plants and Pepper when she was out of town. You used it to enter the building through the garage elevator, wearing one of Ms. Ruthie's hats, taken during one of your trips to water her plants. You knew if the camera picked you up, everyone would think you were her. You also figured you'd returned it before she knew it was missing.

"Elena let you in. You talked, but she didn't want money. She wanted a favorable ruling from Dad on the gambling amendment case, something you couldn't deliver. You argued, somehow you got into in a physical struggle. She hit her head on the edge of the table or something. She wasn't dead, but you thought she was and you panicked.

"You didn't have time to find and erase the incriminating files on her computer. Besides, you couldn't take the chance that forensics could retrieve anything you deleted. So, you decided to take the laptop with you, and the CDs, DVDs and other accessories, figuring you'd destroy them later. Then you went about erasing any evidence that you had been there. And you determined to make it look like an accident or a suicide. You pulled her out onto the terrace, then managed to lift her up and over the balcony ledge. When you left, you took this key off the hook in the kitchen and locked the deadbolt."

Both of us stared at the key on the desk between us. Finally, my mother looked up at me and said, "My, but you do have a wild imagination, Mary Katherine. Sometimes a little too wild, I'm afraid." She looked down at the desk, hesitated, then said, "I tried to tell you not to take the case. I knew nothing good would come of it. I felt bad that Renny was charged, but it was his own actions that made him a suspect."

"But you didn't want his conviction on your conscience, so it was you who sent me the DVD, hoping to help the defense. If I hadn't been successful, what would you have done? Let an innocent man be convicted for something he didn't do?"

She shook her head again. "Yes, indeed, a wild imagination. At any rate, it never came to that, did it? And Renny Goodwin may not be a murderer, but he is not innocent, either, not by a long shot. He has sailed close to the wind throughout his legal career. He has abused his judicial power, and treated Marci shabbily for years." She hesitated a couple of beats, then said, "And I know what happened that night at the party between the two of you, when I came in the room, and you left in such a hurry. I didn't tell your father because they were such good friends, and because I was afraid of what Phil might do. I let it go." She hesitated again for a couple of seconds. "On the grand scale of things, I don't consider that Renny Goodwin has suffered an injustice."

"I always thought that justice on the grand scale was for God to decide. All we can hope for is some form of earthly justice."

She frowned. "Good point, Mary Katherine, especially under the present circumstances. She stood. "I'll leave you to ponder it for a minute, try to decide what earthly justice might be? If you can set aside your wild speculations for a bit, when you're done in here, please put away the file and come on out. I'd like to get some good family photos while the light is still good."

I took her advice and stayed there for some time, reflecting on this notion of justice, earthly and otherwise, evaluating the situation, considering my options, mostly just trying to recover my emotional equilibrium. When I left the room, I made my way to the terrace, where my mother had corralled the rest of the family.

"There she is," she said, smiling at me, as if what had just transpired between us was forgotten, or had never happened. She directed me and my sisters to our places in front of a bed of azaleas. I remembered a similar shot taken some thirty years before, one of the many framed photos on the shelves in the living room.

Once she had us all lined up like she wanted, she handed the camera to Ted to take the shot, then she joined the group. Though not very symmetrical, she placed herself, not next to Dad, but to me, so that I was between both parents. She and he locked their arms around my waist.

Ted looked through the lens, looked up at us, then through the lens again. "Okay, on three, big smiles. One, two..."

..”

CPSIA information can be obtained
at www.ICGtesting.com
Printed in the USA
JSHW052308050622
26714JS00005B/15